I0681745

INCEPTION

PAUL HEINGARTEN

This book is a work of fiction. Names, places, characters, events and situations in this book are purely fictitious. Any similarity to actual persons living or dead is entirely coincidental.

Copyright ©2023 Paul Heingarten

All Rights Reserved

No part of this book may be reproduced, or stored in a retrieval system, or transmitted in any form or by any means, electronic, mechanical, photocopying, recording, or otherwise, without the express written permission of the publisher.

Published by Decatur Media

New Orleans, Louisiana

www.decaturmedia.com

Cover design by Christian Bentulan

ACKNOWLEDGMENTS

To Andrea, my beautiful bride. Thank you for loving me, supporting me, and putting up with me and all my loony ideas, mood swings, and for keeping me from stopping writing all those times I felt like it.

To my family, for their continuing love and support.

To Lisa Herrington, my sister in crime. Bayou Writers brought us together, and I'm ever thankful you remain in my circle as a wonderful, supportive, guiding spirit.

To Jenny Bodle, thank you for all the conversations, advice, support, and for being way more than just a PA... a great friend.

To Carissa Andrews, I'm very thankful to have you as a mentor, and you continue to impress me with all you do as an Indie Author and for Indie Authors!

To Sonya and Tony Strong. Thanks for all the advice and suggestions in the indie publishing / marketing world!

To Kayla Richey. I'm thankful we've been able to meet, and I'm very grateful for your help with feedback on my writing.

To the Bayou Writers Club. I'm grateful for your support as well, and for giving me the encouragement to carry on my publishing journey even when the tides aren't cooperative.

Special thanks to my street team, the "Krewe of Paul" for helping me become the best writer I can. Find out about the Krewe of Paul and get free books at my site www.paulheingarten.com

For Andrea, with all my love

PLACES AND RACES OF LING GALAXY

PLANETS

Agmon

The Far Reach planet of Agmon once shared a similar state to Zormad. Trading markets on this desert planet offer a modest economy for some, but starvation and fear of disease are much more familiar to her residents than survival. Malone Stanton used his limited but growing control of Essence to transform Agmon into a lush paradise, gaining many new followers. Omegana has followed by establishing a post for their Horde on this planet.

Bertold

Sister planet of Delfina, Bertold offers a mostly water covered environment with several islands scattered about. The Omegans have considered this planet in their ever-expanding operations, which involve spreading their military might about for coordinated attacks by what they refer to as their "Horde".

Bimlok Major

While the planet of Bimlok Major itself is largely unremarkable, mostly rocky soil with sparse foliage, the moon of Bimlok Major has been useful to none other than Malone Stanton and his ever-growing collection of devotees. But let's not get too far ahead of ourselves.

Cerulia

Cerulia, home to the Cerulak Race, was another former bustling center of industry in Ling Galaxy in the past. When the Dark Times hit this planet, as it did all of Ling, the rugged determination of Cerulaks to forage and persist gave them a second shot at prosperity, through the repurposing of the spent and discarded items found throughout Ling Galaxy.

Delfina

A mining planet, Delfina also offers a rather arid and bleak environment. Industry on the planet required tremendous indoor facilities for a sustainable quality of life. It is on Delfina that the Railen were relocated by the Universal Alliance (The governing body over Ling Galaxy, also referred to as the "UA") and placed in a former analysis facility as their temporary home, a move that proved to be permanent rather than temporary.

Grondia

This is one of the Central planets of Ling Galaxy and key to the existence of Ling Galaxy and her inhabitants. Lush and tropical in climate, Grondia is home to the Nara and the Spring, where Essence originates from. Essence is the life-giving substance that is harvest by the Nara and delivered to all of Ling Galaxy. Grondia is hidden from most in Ling Galaxy by a dimensional barrier. Only pure Nara citizens are able to travel to and from Grondia.

Omegana

Home to the Omegan race, Omegana is cold and industrial. Metallic structures and cities cover this planet's surface, where the Omegans have developed their abilities and technological capabilities in the cycles since their service to the Nara ended.

Tausian

Arid and desert climate, Tausian is another of the forgotten planets of Ling Galaxy. Former site of a Replication Center, the planet has wandered in recent years into a derelict state. Its native population of Tillians have managed to survive in the lean years, but only barely.

Wenzo

No stranger to the workings of the nefarious, Wenzo's location midway to the center of Ling Galaxy gives it and her residents a key location for illicit trade. Syndicates, organized crime, friendly organizations, thrive and prosper on this dank place.

Zormad

One of the Far Reach planets, Zormad, has a dry, arid climate. Many cycles past, the planet was a bustling center of industry and production. However, changing times mixed with consolidation of industries has left this former metropolis on the far side from prosperity. One of the planet's more prominent native races is the Mardaks.

RACES

Ling Galaxy is vast, with a large collection of races. Here's some of the more common ones.

Celestiak (Lookers)

Celestiak are an offshoot of the Railen race begun by Malone Stanton not long after his escape from prison in Ling Galaxy. In his quest to claim the throne of Ling Galaxy by way of merging himself with

Essence itself, Malone has discovered the ability to travel inter-dimensionally. This gives him the ability to travel across Ling Galaxy in an instant. Through time and careful research, he's been able to pinpoint this ability and has recruited his own team of followers. While he calls himself and his own "children" Celestiaks, the term "Lookers" has been given to them by many others in Ling Galaxy. The Lookers schemes have brought them into the attention of several Lawkeeper groups throughout Ling Galaxy, such as the UA Military and even the Mardak Sentries and Regulation, a force that developed among the Xeno on NewEarth. Finding a Nara is a very important goal to those who want to travel to Grondia, as it is believed the very physical makeup that allows a Nara pure to return to Grondia can be harvested and replicated. Capturing Lookers has been shown to be the only way to effectively eliminate their real threat to the societal and physical order of Ling Galaxy.

Cerulak

A race of scavengers by necessity. Former miners during the period of extensive mining and production in Ling Galaxy, consolidation by the UA left the Cerulaks out in the cold and forced to fend for themselves finding, repurposing, and trading scrap throughout the galaxy. Like the Mardaks, the Cerulaks are fierce survivors, but have been faced with threats from more powerful races than theirs, like the Railen and Omegans. Still, the Cerulaks persist and include in their treks out into Ling Galaxy a search for Railen Trackers. The Cerulaks are more pragmatic about the Railen Trackers, though. They aren't interested in pulling in an actual Looker or a Nara; they just want the quick payoff a Tracker has been known to bring on the black markets of Ling Galaxy.

Mardak

A hardy race, the Mardak claim Zormad as their original home. Their kind are stout in build, with apelike features. Their trades often include those of the trading and scrap business, which they adopted out of a need to replace the economy lost when their home planet, Zormad, fell from its place on the economic boom period of Ling Galaxy. They reside in several cities on Zormad, most notably Tas Ralong, where the seat of their government is.

Nara

Slender, a bit taller than the average human, with a glowing bluish smooth skin, the Nara race has been stewards of the Essence since the beginning of Ling Galaxy. Their life purpose is to develop, process, and deliver Essence to Ling Galaxy. While Essence delivery is essential, it's very common for Essence delivery missions to run into trouble from those trying to capture Essence for their own purposes, while killing any Nara found in Ling Galaxy on their Essence delivery runs. The dangers involved in traveling around Ling Galaxy have required the Nara use various forms of protection, like the Omegans for a time. A force of Nara Security has also handled the chore of protection of the Nara and Essence, as well as a collection of beings known as Scions.

Omegan

Reptilian in appearance and cold hearted in nature, the Omegan race were once servants to the Nara. In their Nara service, the Omegans provided protection for the Nara tasked with sending Essence to all planets of Ling Galaxy. Once the Nara determined the overall danger to their Essence delivery was manageable by their own Nara Security, the Omegans were released. In their freedom from Nara service, the Omegans have grown restless. Through aggressive leaders like Emperor Zakmar, the Omegan Empire is on the move to assert themselves as the dominant race in Ling Galaxy.

Railen

The Railen were originally Nara citizens. Over time, a group of Nara became unsatisfied and even frustrated over how much suffering was taking place in Ling Galaxy, while the Nara only seemed interested in providing the Essence necessary to sustain life. The unrest of these Nara eventually led to an attempted coup and hijacking of the Nara Essence production with the intention of giving Essence out freely to those who needed it in Ling Galaxy, trying to help the famines and general poverty around the galaxy. The Nara guilty of the attempted sabotage were subjected to Disconnection, the Nara process that physically alters law breakers ("Violators") so they are unable to physically travel to Grondia ever again. The Railen were then sent into Ling Galaxy to live out their existence as refugees, unwanted by their birth planet. Their time spent in exile in Ling Galaxy has fostered a spirit of vengeance among the Railen, and their long-term sights are set on reclaiming what was taken from them: access to their home of Grondia and Essence. The Railen are hellbent on finishing what they started many cycles ago and staking claim to all that was once theirs.

Tillian

Diminutive in size, but ever the crafty ones, the Tillian race in Ling Galaxy offers technical abilities in their heritage. Among the scrapping and repurposing races, the Tillians have shown themselves to be very versatile in this work. They don't boast a physical threat, but have been able to make themselves useful, often through trading services on any of the various markets throughout Ling Galaxy, or even in the UA proper - under careful watch by the UA faithful, of course!

Xeno

You know them as humans. Members of an exodus from an Earth on the verge of destruction, the Xeno traveled away from their Milky Way Galaxy and ended up in Ling Galaxy, residing on Zormad. There, they set up a colony called NewEarth and are working at establishing themselves in a new home.

Governments

Amid the chaos of the Essence Wars, these groups are struggling for control, whether that is maintaining the existing order or establishing a new one.

Universal Alliance (UA)

The central governing body of Ling Galaxy, the UA presides over the vast reaches of Ling Galaxy. It's control is of course limited and their authority has come under fire from other groups like the Omegans who want to take over.

Nara Empire

The Nara preside behind a dimensional barrier in Ling Galaxy. Led by Ellene Ballo, they provide the Essence to the entirety of Ling Galaxy to ensure it's survival. They advise and council the UA.

Malone Stanton / Omegan Alliance

Malone's quest for power in Ling Galaxy brought him into the line of the Omegans. Their mutual lust for control and power gave them a good reason to team up. Their alliance is fragile, but has proven to lift their respective chases further along (for now!)

Syndicates

The assorted collectives of smugglers and other nefarious groups in Ling Galaxy could care less about the victor of any battle between the UA and anyone, as long as the paydays keep coming in. They have made deals with many in Ling Galaxy who have a need and the means to pay for it.

CLARION KISMET

ONE

SELINA RAVENCRAFT CROUCHED BEHIND the wheel of a transport vehicle and tried to be invisible. The early evening's fading light helped that a bit, but the Depot she was at wasn't dormant, and time wasn't on her side. The facility belonged to the NewEarth colony and was a central point to handle any supplies needed.

In over twenty years, the settlement of humans went from a fledgling band landing on the planet Zormad to an established community. The human inhabitants of NewEarth strived for a life that was theirs, filled with fewer worries of survival and more hopes for the future.

It was a balancing act, anyway, as all bets for them were off when they landed in Ling Galaxy. They'd already been visited by several bands of others - some curious, but far more were just interested in whatever humans had that was worth stealing.

A series of short bird-like whistles gave Selina a signal. Glancing toward the building, she spotted Warrah Malek, her friend and partner in crime. Warrah's job on this particular heist was the lookout, and the signal meant the crew moving the transport around were inside the Depot building for the moment. Selina had minutes, if she was lucky – seconds, if she was realistic. She slithered through the truck's undercarriage, looking for anything and everything good. Finally, she reached the rear hold and spotted a collection of heating units. The portable devices proved very useful in the desert climate of Zormad, where evening temperatures neared freezing. The citizens of NewEarth had sparse supplies, but through a mixture of dogged determination and shrewd bargaining with their local neighbors, a crude but established supply chain began.

In addition to their practical use, rotating them around the NewEarth housing units, the heating units had value in another arena - the Trading Markets in the nearby town of Tas Ralong, which got Selina and Warrah concerned about them at all.

Selina eased the rear gate of the truck down. The hinge gave a tattletale whine that Selina tried to quiet by slowing down the opening of the entrance. A glance over to Warrah, she saw a thumbs-up signal. Like a cat, Selina hopped onto the floor of the truck's rear, nearby their prize. The devices were two-foot square and nearly three feet tall. Way too big to carry more than one, but that was going to be all they needed. Selina crouched down by one unit and gingerly rolled it to the end of the truck. She was nearly hopping down to the ground when she heard Warrah whistle again - this time, a sharp shrill. *Trouble!* Peering back over one side of the truck, Selina saw the worst - the driver of the transport and an assistant walking toward the vehicle. A hot rush of panic slapped Selina in the face. They'd see her if she hopped out, and it would only be worse if she had that device. She returned to the truck and saw a series of fabricated wall pieces. She dashed to the side with the large board-like fixtures and wedged between two of them, just in time to hear the voices of two crew members near the rear gate of the vehicle.

"Why the hell is that heating unit unsecured? I tell ya, somebody's gotta get on these other shifts, man. I'm sick of having stuff going broke because we screwed it up."

Another voice, higher pitched, responded, "I'll get it, but I'm sure as hell writing a report up on this. I'm tired of cleaning up after people."

Selina's pulse rattled in her throat. After several moments of creaking and the sound of ropes tightening, the gate to the rear slammed shut with an obnoxious clang. Seconds later, the truck's engine burst to life with a deep rumble. The floor vibrated underfoot while Selina quickly slid from her hiding place. A medium-sized rope held the heating unit tied to the floor. Selina grabbed her knife and slid it across, popping the rope. Just then, the truck lurched forward, sending the Heating Unit and Selina sliding toward the back faster than she could've expected and definitely more than she wanted. She planted her feet to slow down, but it was useless. The heating device slammed the rear gate open. The unit then rolled out, and made a very abrupt landing on the Zormad soil, popping into several pieces. Selina landed nearby with a smidge more grace, rolling in the cool dirt until she came onto her feet. The truck continued, and Selina checked the unit out as Warrah ran up.

"Well, that wasn't the idea, was it?" Warrah chuckled.

"Um, no? I'm not sure how these things do on the Trading Markets when damaged, but you want to help me get this thing to the side of the road before they realize what happened?"

They managed to hide the unit behind the housing units in NewEarth. Later, Selina and Warrah sat behind Ward's Commissary. The location started as a typical dining facility for NewEarth, but over time became a gathering place for many reasons, and, in the case of Selina and Warrah at that point, it was a joyous celebration of, from all appearances, the heist they made it out of without being noticed.

"Thanks a lot for all the notice," Selina elbowed her friend. "I had thirty seconds not to get busted, real good."

"Well, I can't help it. I'm not exactly a mind reader, ya know."

"Yeah yeah. So, how much you think this will earn us?"

"Not sure. Fifty, maybe a hundred UA Credits if we're lucky?"

Selina gnawed on her lip. "You're gonna come with me and leave this place if we get enough credits to make it happen, right?"

"Of course I am. You and I, Selina." Warrah's wide eyes and warm smile further answered Selina's question.

The news about their potential score wasn't great for Selina, but at least it was progress. Their kitty was intended for one purpose: buying a starcraft for them to get away from NewEarth and Zormad for good. The colony may have meant a lot of things to its residents, but to Selina Ravencraft, it was a place of other memories made painful by loss, and the day she left NewEarth for good couldn't come fast enough.

After seeing Warrah off, Selina returned to her mother's housing unit. It was Selina's, too, for a bit longer. NewEarth residents were obligated to work on setting up their living quarters once in their late teens. Those structures came from a mixture of reused parts of *Intrepid*, the former ark ship that delivered humans to Zormad and Ling Galaxy in the first place, and other materials found on Zormad, including any gotten through the trading markets on the planet.

Selina would've been happier leaving Zormad than settling in with her place, as Zormad was where her father, Erick, died years earlier. Selina was young when it happened but old enough to remember and hold the pain ever since.

Selina entered to the sight of Laurina on the reclining chair. When her mother's eyes met hers, Selina knew she wasn't getting by with a simple hello.

"You've been busy again, haven't you?"

Selina froze. "What do you mean?"

Laurina stood quickly. "I got a call from Zed. One of the Regulation patrols spotted you with Warrah moving that heating unit into town."

A deep ache hit Selina's head. In her childhood, before her father's death, things were much easier between her and her mother, but in recent years, it was a string of disappointments and reprimands. Selina saw a lot of things unsaid through her mother's eyes. The majority of it wasn't necessary for speech, anyway.

Selina's throat clenched, though, and the urge to defend herself was too strong. "Mom, I'm just trying to get out of here; leave this place behind."

Laurina's eyes lowered. "You've said this before. So where do you think you'll go, exactly?"

"I don't know. We made it into Ling, and everyone seems happy here, but I'm tired of being where dad died." Hearing herself say the truth that had been her life for too long felt like a knife to the heart. Selina slumped into a nearby chair as her body rocked with sobs.

In the aftermath of Erick's death, Laurina raised Selina as best as a single mother could in a small community of humans desperate to rebuild a life of familiarity light years away from home. The nurturing came on a rotational basis when Laurina wasn't helping ensure NewEarth was as functional as possible. Then, as Selina gazed offward, she saw her mother approach her.

"You've been through really rough times. I've tried to give you as good a life as I could, but Selina, you can't steal any more. Did you ever think what your father would say?"

Selina swallowed a lump in her throat. It wasn't hard to imagine what a founder of the Regulation, NewEarth's law keeping group, would have to say about his baby girl being a thief.

Tears rolled down Selina's cheeks. "Mom, I don't know what to do."

Selina felt her mother's embrace as more cries choked out of her. "You've got to stop, OK? Right now. Tomorrow, you're going to return that piece to Zed. And then, it's over. I've done all I can do for you, and we've used up any goodwill we've ever had with Zed. He'll come down hard on you if this happens again."

While the hug felt good, there would always be a missing part of the picture for Selina and an imperfect home missing her father. But, as painful and dangerous as it was, she reminded herself that with a few more simple moves, she could get her way to a starcraft that would take her somewhere else and to a life where a new start might be possible.

TWO

THE NEXT DAY, SELINA AND HER MOTHER brought the heating fixture back to Zed, then they returned home for the usual chores. However, the itch that had begun earlier for Selina remained. Soon, she began scheming again with Warrah about another rumor of a visiting Mardak vehicle.

One of the conditions established for NewEarth to exist on Zormad was the partnership humans made with the Mardaks, trading goods back and forth. The bartering kept NewEarth alive and allowed them to bond further with their Mardak counterparts.

Selina and Warrah followed the Mardak transport on foot from a distance as it wound its way through the streets and pathways of NewEarth toward the main depot. The vehicle's appearance resembled the Mardaks: wide, round shaped, and with a series of blackish armoring covering the structure like an armadillo.

"I'm a little surprised the thing doesn't smell bad, like those Mardaks," Warrah chuckled.

Selina snickered while her eyes remained fixed on the Mardak truck. "They could use a bath. I heard them yelling at a few of our people once, calling them 'Xeno.'"

"Ahh yeah, our new nickname. Kinda nice we got labeled all the same."

The vehicle stopped to let a group of NewEarth residents cross an intersection while Selina and Warrah strolled towards it. Warrah commented, "I hear they're bringing in some converters this time. We must be trading something big to get those."

"Yeah, no doubt. That's gonna be tough to steal unnoticed, though, don't ya think?"

"Yeah, probably. But maybe there's some other spare parts we can grab. They might not be as missed and could be an easier sell at the Trading Markets."

Once Selina and Warrah agreed on their plan, they walked until they were a block from the Depot, passing by the Commissary. Selina caught sight of Ward, and she felt her face flush warm. Ward hadn't seen her, and at least Selina hadn't made eye contact with him; but suddenly she got a whiff of doubt.

"Look, let's double back. The Regulation usually checks this corridor. They already know about us, and if they see us looking like we're up to no good, they'll stop us quick."

They decided to run behind the next street over and, after a few more minutes, they were closer to the Depot and, unfortunately, even more out of breath.

"If I'd known we'd be getting all this exercise in, I woulda eaten more breakfast." Warrah gasped.

Selina patted her friend's back. "You can relax on the walk into Tas Ralong."

The entrance to the Depot featured a series of discarded containers, on which a crude but distinctive sign marked the entrance and the NewEarth crest, just in case anyone on NewEarth forgot where they were. The Mardak vehicle backed in toward the opening of the Depot, and Selina watched as a crew of Mardaks and humans unloaded two six feet tall, column-shaped structures.

"Those aren't converters; they're power generators. Wow,

NewEarth must've really cut a big deal. Did they give up any of our firstborn in trade?"

While the crews handled the bulky fixtures, a series of Regulation guards kept watch on the perimeter outside the Depot. Turning to Warrah, Selina whispered, "OK, the guards usually stay out watching for the goods to be moved into the Depot. Guess they figure they'll beef up security while everything's out in the open. Once that Depot closes, the Mardaks will probably be inside for a few more minutes, and the guards should go back to their other posts, like running through town. We'll have to be quick again, but I say check out the cab of their vehicle. They're bound to have some kinda navigation tools or something in there."

The two generators were safely moved inside the structure a few minutes later, and the guards left their positions. Selina saw one of them jump into a nearby vehicle, where they then picked up the remaining two. Selina took a steady breath and nodded to her friend, and they sprinted toward the transport. Twenty yards of a run later, they were at the vehicle's door, once again gasping for air.

"Seriously, can we steal a landcrawler or something next time? This running's gonna kill me, girl." Warrah managed a smile between heaved breaths.

Selina eyed the door and the window above them. "We're home free, dear; just give me a few-"

"What are you doing?"

The voice was deep, fierce, and most definitely Mardak. Selina looked into their eyes, not to mention the glowing red muzzle of the pulse rifle trained on her chest. Their armor showed Mardak Sentry markings.

Selina's mind raced for any reasonable explanation. But there was none, and Warrah's panicked look told Selina their options were zero.

Smirking, the Mardak grabbed for two restraints. "Yeah, that's what I thought - we got thieves like you among our kind. I'm not putting up with it from any damned Xeno. Let's see what your commander thinks about this."

THREE

SELINA AND WARRAH WOUND UP WITH Regulation command for discipline. Fortunately, they had no stolen property - which was their only saving grace. However, their known history of pilfering had them in more than enough trouble anyway.

Selina and Warrah were brought into a gathering room inside the Depot, seated and restrained in chairs. The two newly delivered generators stood untouched in the room's far corner. While Selina and Warrah sat, Zed and Aldric Porto, the Mardak commander, gazed over them.

Zed's frame was large, and his beard was thick but not enough to hide the deep frown on his face. "We've had a rough start in Ling Galaxy. We came here on a hope and a prayer in the *Intrepid* ark ship light years from home. Even getting us to land here took negotiations on a level neither of you can comprehend. Still, we made it happen. And we set up a community. But launching something like this isn't just risky; it's a hair away from suicide. A strange galaxy, with just a few thousand humans, not knowing what we're facing, not knowing if we can even produce food and water at first? Most logical beings would call all of that insane.

"But, we lasted. And slowly, we thrived. The way we did that was making partnerships with the Mardaks first and foremost. They allowed us to settle close to one of their cities, and we started trading with them. The only way that has lasted is because we were honest with them. Now, I know all about what you two have been doing, and I've been hoping you'd get bored and stop at some point. Selina, I knew your dad. And he's a big part of why we were able to land here to begin with."

Aldric grunted, his glare fixed on Selina like a sunbeam. "These Xeno should be punished. They're lucky our crew didn't catch them with any Mardak property."

Selina's eyes burned from sweat. The room was warm enough, but the glare of the reprimand did the rest of the job. She heard Warrah's silent whimpers.

Zed swiped the moisture from his face. "It's time you both learned your place. So, I've got two options."

Zed's snide grin clarified how bad the options were going to be. Selina wondered what kind of punishment awaited them but couldn't think of anything.

"Your choices are either join the Regulation, complete the training; or we send you to the retooling plant in Tas Ralong, where you'll be obligated to work until we decide your punishment is complete."

The Regulation did a lot of work covering NewEarth, protecting it, and fighting off any trouble-seeking types that sometimes visited planet Zormad. Selina was impressed by the Regulation, but she also knew more than a few died along the way. *Would I do any better than those people, who were mostly soldiers from before we landed here? I haven't fired a weapon in my life.*

On the other hand, the assignment in Retooling was sure to be a nightmare. With no end in sight, Selina figured that choice would lead to many long days, filthy conditions, and who knew what kind of treatment among the Mardaks, who were only interested in humans because their leaders said they had to be.

Selina and Warrah were given a few hours for their final decision, which they spent in the area outside the Depot. Selina's mother and Warrah's parents were allowed to see them for a few moments. The spartan surroundings of the main NewEarth warehouse facility featured a series of well-defined walking paths and not much more. Still, the decision that weighed on Selina's and Warrah's minds wasn't being distracted away by any scenery, no matter how picturesque. Selina and her mother held each other in a gentle and emotional embrace.

Laurina's choked voice came through the hug. "Selina, you're meant for better things. Grief hits everyone, but how we respond to it defines us."

Selina held her mother tighter and closed her eyes firmly. She'd had a few dreams of her father over the years, but there was never anything concrete, no message from beyond or secrets revealed. Selina's path was her own, made of all choices, good or bad, along the way. She found herself on a precipice; whichever choice she made from that point would define her.

Through teary eyes, Selina gazed at her mother for a moment. Neither choice was great, but at least one was more familiar.

"I'm signing up with the Regulation."

More tears came from Laurina's eyes. "At least you'll be with our people, not the Mardaks."

FOUR

SELINA'S DECISION TO JOIN THE REGULATION only further cemented Warrah's choice. The Retooling in Tas Ralong had every sign of being a gulag. Selina knew enough about the relations with Mardaks to know that would've likely been an early grave for her, especially if word got out about her past thievery.

While ragtag was the order for the Regulation, the leadership made every effort to form as rigorous and challenging a training regimen as possible. Selina's temporary home for her indoctrination was a crude set of barracks, formerly a portion of the *Intrepid* ark ship's individual quarters partitions. Gone were the once-plusher accommodations, however. The soft cushions and cozy furnishings were reused for the residential sections of NewEarth, and leftover was a menial series of rooms with only the barest of accommodations for sleeping and basic sanitation. The Regulation wanted their people hard and ready, and the simplistic offerings only helped to lower their expectations and raise their ability to survive with less-than-optimal options.

Sergeant Strong, the trainer for the Regulation induction, was anything but optimal as far as Selina was concerned. His uniform bulged out over his muscular frame from beneath, and a pair of darkened sunglasses capped off a rock-hewn face with a jawline that could've cut metal. In case that wasn't intimidating enough, his voice had a register of a set of low grinding gears with a pungent breath odor to complete the ensemble.

Selina and her fellow candidates had set up in their barracks, each claiming a bed when she noticed Strong observing them like a hungry vulture.

"OK, maggots, this isn't a rest stop. I want everyone out on the line outside in thirty seconds! Last one there will be my personal friend for the day!"

The recruits wasted no time scrambling for the door. Selina was at the far end from the exit but did what she could to snake her way through to be any place but last. Unfortunately, the narrow door and more sizable frames of several of her compatriots were not in her favor, and before she knew it, she was trotting to the line in last place. She caught Warrah's gaze - part compassion for Selina and part relief their spots weren't reversed.

After a quick glare from Strong, he strolled back and forth past the recruits, his arms folded behind his back. "Alright, you've got your rooms for the next few weeks. You are now all property of the NewEarth Regulation, recruit class 915. We're the last group of humanity anywhere. And we're in this galaxy with more than enough that either don't care about us being here, want to steal whatever we got, or just want to wipe us out because we're not the same as anything else around here. We've fought off raids, starvation, disease, and more. This colony lasted over twenty years because the Regulation made it so. Our officers protect, defend, and fight to the last."

Strong stopped short in front of Selina, and suddenly she got a full-on glimpse of him as he leaned into her face so much she caught a full reflection of herself in his glass lenses. After a few antagonizing breaths, he continued, "*Our* officers aren't quite you. Not yet, anyway. You're all here for one reason or another. Some of you, like

Ravencraft here, thought it'd be smart to try stealing parts to sell for money. I'm here to tell you that just because you signed up for this training doesn't mean you're automatically in. You better damn well know, if I catch any of you even thinking about stealing supplies, so much as a sip of a drink, you'll be outta here, and you'll be praying they let you clean the floors of a Retooling Plant in Tas Ralong with your bare hands."

Strong glanced back and forth on the line as he continued. "Every one of you's gotta hack it at Regulation standards, and you've six weeks to do it. There's thirty of you now, and we're only taking the top 20. So, work hard, do as you're told, and you damn well better not toss any lip to me or your other instructor, Corporal Ramsey, or you'll be in for a world of trouble. Just because the Regulation needs officers don't mean we gotta take any old jerk wad who doesn't care about anything. Understood?"

The troops gave a resounding "HUUH" in response.

Selina swallowed as Sergeant Strong's hot breath prickled her skin. "I got my eye on you, Ravencraft." Then, stepping back, he glanced over the entire group. "OK, let's get your blood flowing with a five-mile run. Ravencraft, since you showed up last, we'll just fit you with a 20-pound pack; see how you like that."

While Ramsey walked over with a smirk and her added baggage for the run, Selina wondered just how bad the Mardak Retooling service would've been after all.

The five-mile run was even less fun than Selina could've imagined. She was in the rear again, which would've been bad enough, but the extra 20 pounds of weight, not to mention Sergeant Strong's continual bellowing to her right about keeping up the pace, just lowered her experience to hellish proportions.

After a brief pause for hydration, the Regulation troops took to an obstacle course consisting of several stations, like a rope swing, chin-ups, a few climbing obstacles, and agility runs through giant pylons.

Selina met her friend outside the Regulation Training facility after the day's abuse slash training.

Sipping her decanter, Warrah swiped away the excess droplets from her mouth. "I think Sarge likes you."

Selina nearly choked on her swallow of drink. "Oh, what? Are we in the same training? He'd be perfectly fine if I washed out tomorrow."

Warrah nudged Selina as the two enjoyed more helpings of Aquand. The beverage, a close replication of water, was rationed for most of NewEarth. Still, the Regulation had a store of their own since their work meant a lot of calls and physical activities monitoring the security of the entire colony. Selina took another swig when she noticed a hulking frame facing her. Looking up, she saw it was Eber Cadwell. He would've won a height contest in their group, and it looked like he had a more than decent set of muscles to go with it.

Selina swallowed slowly as Eber's gaze held on her.

"Um, hi?" Selina said cautiously.

Eber's eyes narrowed a bit. "So, slow poke. Ready to quit yet?"

Selina smirked and traded looks with Warrah, who rolled her eyes a bit and glanced offward. Then, turning back to Eber, Selina said, "Nope, what's the point of missing out on all the fun?"

Eber's gaze remained unbroken. Clearly, he'd checked his sense of humor early on in the training process. "You keep up with the rest of us. I don't wanna be helping the slow ones in the group."

Eber's words gnawed at Selina like an insect bite. *I did keep up with the extra weight on me. You gonna forget that part? OK.* "I'm still here, aren't I?"

Eber nodded. "Yeah. You better buck up or stay outta my way." With that, Eber took another swig of drink and headed off.

Selina caught Warrah's surprised look again. "I see you met one of our hotshots. Eber's dad's in the Regulation and is a bit of a sharp-shooter. Guess he has a lot to prove."

"Well, he can go ahead and prove it away from me," Selina said.

Warrah's smile widened. "You're just making all kinda friends here on your first day, aren't you?"

The following days began a pattern: early wake-ups by Sergeant

Strong's voice booming against the walls of the tiny barracks, more runs, exercise. Selina became used to being at the rear of the pack for runs initially, not to mention the extra unwanted attention from the kindly Sergeant.

Their training activities soon progressed into advanced hand-to-hand combat. The troops were paired randomly, and Selina found herself on one occasion opposite Eber. His large frame towered over Selina's, giving the match-up a David vs. Goliath ambiance.

Eber jostled about Selina in the fighting circle, his arms in a fighting stance, his head slightly downward, and a deep glare in his eyes. The other recruits formed a ring around them, shouting remarks as unsupportive as they were noisy. Selina caught several jabs like "Take 'er head off!" and "Wash her outta here!" Finally, she caught Warrah's supportive gaze and heard her friend yell, "You got this, Selina!"

Eber lunged forward with a jab into Selina's chest. The blow shoved her back two feet, and she wobbled to keep upright. Sergeant Strong's voice pierced the loud din of cheers and jeers. "Size isn't important in a fight if you know how to attack an enemy's weakness."

Eber's protruding biceps, broad shoulders, large chest, and solid legs showed Selina nothing about weakness. She moved her gloves up to block a rapid-fire series of jabs. She stopped two, but another four found their mark. She felt an ache in her gut, and her breaths became difficult. They continued their dance of a fight, moving around.

Eber shouted his taunts. "Come on, slowpoke, let's see what you got! Are you gonna run around in a real fight or inflict damage?"

Eber's taunts hit Selina's ears like sparks on fuel-doused kindling. Selina felt the anger build in her. It came from many places, not just Eber's insults or those from the rest of her fellow recruits who weren't interested in any former thief joining the Regulation. Her thoughts about growing up without her father, and being unable to accept that Erick was not there as she grew up and would never be around for her. Her mind went to the image of Eber, earlier that day during a fall he took on the obstacle course. He'd slipped on one of the rope climbs and landed awkwardly on his right foot. He'd rolled it but true to form, Sergeant Strong pushed him to finish the race. But here he was, and Selina noticed he favored his left foot, keeping his right further back.

When Eber's eyes widened, Selina saw his shoulders flex, and his right arm pull back for a big punch. She quickly dove to the ground and kicked, connecting with Eber's right ankle. At once, his eyes opened wide, and he fell to the ground with a loud yelp, clutching his leg.

The crowd was silenced, except for Warrah. Sergeant Strong's eyebrows shot up. He knelt next to Eber for a moment, then looked up at Selina. "Alright, Ravencraft. It looks like somebody's been finally paying attention to what I've been saying around here."

FIVE

BY THE END OF THEIR SECOND WEEK, the original group of thirty recruits had atrophied to twenty-seven. The two male and one female candidates lined up on the same line Selina and the rest mustered to from their first day when Selina became Sergeant Strong's special friend. With little fanfare, they were dismissed, returning to NewEarth, and whatever alternate punishment or former lives awaited them.

Shortly after that dismissal, the remaining recruits entered the Depot for a briefing. They met in the large warehouse area with the regulation vehicles, Landcrawlers, and the armory. Selina smirked at how not too long ago, she and Warrah would've regarded the openly available hardware around as a target for stealing.

Corporal Nock stood before Selina and the rest. Nock's frame was lean, with a healthy layer of muscle wrapped around his upper torso. Not to be outdone, his bulging thighs and tapered midsection, even through his thick pocketed fatigues, gave the impression of a solid core.

"Now that's my kinda looking man," Warrah muttered.

Selina elbowed her friend while hoping no one else heard her chuckle.

Ramsey pulled up a holographic display showing the general map of Zormad, their home planet. "We're having a joint training exercise with a Mardak Sentry group tomorrow. Some of you may have seen them around NewEarth already. I want full cooperation. We aren't going to be the ones who start bad blood. I know there's a lot of strong feelings against the Mardaks, and I don't care what you think. You're not here to give opinions. If you want spirited debate, take a position on the NewEarth Council. I'm sure they'll be happy to entertain you there. Here, you deal with strength, courage, and force. The Regulation is all that stands between NewEarth and her destruction. And what is our motto?"

"We fight, we survive, for NewEarth!"

The briefing ended, and the recruits filed out for their daily ritual of abuse hardly disguised as their obstacle course. After several hours of rope climbing, jumping, running, and the side order of verbal abuse, the recruits were exhausted, sweat-drenched, and hungry for just about anything that would pass as chow. So, they headed to the small mess hall in the Depot for their meal.

Selina met Warrah with her fellow recruits as they shoveled in what passed for their rations. The metallic trays held an assortment of proteins and some off-colored piles that purported to be some kind of vegetable.

As Selina worked her food down her throat, Warrah cackled. "What the hell is this stuff anyway?"

"Hey, it's better than some in NewEarth eat."

"That isn't saying much. I wish they could've gotten Ward to offer his cooking up. Dude could make a knapsack tasty."

As Selina clinked her cup with Warrah's, she caught a glimpse of Sergeant Strong, who entered the hall briefly to refresh his drink before leaving.

"Oh look, it's your worst enemy," Warrah chuckled.

"Heh, I don't think he's anyone's hero anyway. I don't know what he sees in me."

"Oh, you know why. You're Erick Ravencraft's kid. Anyone with that kinda history has a lot to prove. That move you put on Eber in that fight earned you some cred. Sarge's probably just making sure you still ain't all high and mighty and are one of us regular folk."

CLASS 915 STOOD at attention as the Mardak Sentry vehicle stopped near the start of their parade grounds. The oversized vehicles with knobby tires coughed the occasional waft of black smoke from their undercarriages. After a few moments, the side and rear doors opened, and ten Mardak Sentries appeared. The peacekeeping force for the Mardaks, the Sentries, were part of the initial meeting with humans after their arrival on NewEarth. The Sentries weren't known for their diplomacy. Still, like the Regulation, their concern was keeping order, including ensuring the odd humans who decided to land on Zormad weren't out for anything more than a place to land and live in relative isolation.

Captain Hewlett Finer led the visiting contingent. He was tall for a Mardak, all of five feet two inches. His armor was dingy as the rest, but the officer markings gave the suit an air of class, if not experience. After a brief conversation with Sergeant Strong and Nock, the three stood between the two groups.

Strong stood in front, his arms folded together. "You're all going to be training together one on one today, and we'll have some time for target practice. You'll treat each other as equals. No squabbling."

Captain Finer added, "We're stronger when we work together, and the sooner you learn that, the better."

Selina caught Warrah's whisper in her ear. "Let's see how much they really wanna work together once we're paired off."

Selina's matching with Iona Yoke was as cordial as she could've expected. Iona's face had a series of scars, and the wild look in her eyes wasn't too assuring. She moved about Selina, tossing jabs. Selina managed to duck a few and blocked a right cross. Selina had play fought as a child with Ward behind the Commissary at night. It was a fond memory of her childhood, raised with a caring mother and a collection of would-be surrogate fathers in the wings.

A long hiss distracted Selina, and she realized it was something in Mardak.

"What was that?"

Iona's eyes narrowed. "I said I'm not sure why we have to train with you. You should leave our planet and go somewhere else."

"That's not your decision, is it?"

"It should be. My kind has lived and died on Zormad for centuries. We don't ask for anything. Then, you Xeno come and try to make everything your own. You might think you're welcome here, but you're not. Our leaders accepted you only because they think they can get something out of you."

Selina threw a stiff jab in response. Her blow landed on the center of Iona's chest, knocking her back. Iona's eyes opened wide, and she responded with a guttural growl. Whatever training exercise the Regulation and Mardak Sentries had in mind, things had just stopped. Selina held herself in a ready stance, waiting for Iona's next move. Selina registered Sergeant Strong's voice nearby.

"What's going on over there?"

Before Selina could explain, Iona lunged forward, and her large, coarse hands ran for Selina's throat. They tumbled backward and rolled over each other in the dirt. Selina closed her eyes as a bit of dirt fell in them, and she then felt deep sores from the series of blows Iona launched into her midsection. Selina wriggled to free herself, but so far, Iona held her on the ground.

Soon, Selina writhed enough that she was on her side and pulled her knee up as best she could, aiming for any spot on Iona. Of course, she had no way of knowing if the Mardak vital areas were remotely similar to humans, but she figured any blow in a fight was worth a try.

The scuffle went on for what seemed to Selina like another half hour. Then, the blistering sound of a pulse rifle fired in rapid succession several feet away stunned Selina and Iona into stillness. A moment later, Selina felt hands helping her up. Once back on her feet, she cleared her eyes to see the remaining troops surrounding Sergeant Strong and Hewlett Finer, both of which had very stern looks on their faces.

Sergeant Strong's jaw clenched so firmly it appeared it might snap off. But instead, he said, "I hope you all had good luck at this mess here. Because this isn't what we're about. There'll be plenty of chances for everyone here to fight, don't get me wrong. But you have to accept each other as allies. You don't have to like each other, but you have to accept. We're gonna run through drills as a unit with the Mardaks. I know you're hot, and teamwork with each other is the last thing any of you are even considering right now. I don't care. You're doing this, and you're making it work. Because one day, all our lives may just depend on it."

Selina dusted herself off and, after Sergeant Strong forced her and Iona into a quasi-handshake truce, they resumed their training as one large, not-quite-happy family.

SIX

BY THE END OF THE FOURTH WEEK, the recruits of class 915 were light years ahead of when they started. Twenty-two of the original group remained. Selina went from dead last to leading the pack on runs with her buddy, Warrah. Obstacles were still a challenge, but her sheer determination was undeniable.

The latter part of their induction involved more time on the weapons course, and Selina held her own with the others. One morning they were all set to begin another round of target practice when a loud klaxon sounded from the Depot. Selina traded looks with Warrah and the rest of their class. When Selina noticed the grim looks on Sergeant Strong and Ramsey's faces, their fears began to boil.

Strong glanced at the group. "Everyone, sit tight while we check in with command on the situation." Selina and the rest returned their rifles to the racks and held their places on the training grounds, awaiting further instructions. Fifteen minutes later, Sergeant Strong and Ramsey returned, their eyes slightly wider. Selina immediately noticed the fixed scowl she'd expected from

Strong's expression was gone. Instead, his face was ashen with a coating of fresh sweat.

The recruits gathered around as Strong explained the situation. "OK, there's been a raid in Tas Ralong. A group of Railen have come by, looking for trouble. They've already hit a few power generators and are trying to knock out the Retooling Center in town. The Mardak Sentries and their regular Militia held them at bay initially, but the Railen removed some of the Mardak force. We sent some of the Regulation over to assist, but we think some of our people might be down too. So, Regulation Command has asked us to pull some of you to help. You're recruits, but you're pretty damned close, and we can't let this facility fall. So, you're all coming with us. We've got a transport ready and heading into Tas Ralong pronto. So, each of you, get a weapon and meet me on that ready line outside your barracks in three minutes!"

With a resounding "HUUH," the recruits of 915 launched into action. Selina's pulse raced. The Railen were no strangers to her, as they were who killed her father. She wondered for a long time when she'd have the chance at a bit of payback on them, but she never quite imagined the scenario as it played out.

The Regulation Transport vehicle included armoring on the sides, but narrow windows allowed those riding in the back to see outside. Selina stood near one of the windows as their ride wobbled over from the pathways of NewEarth and then the streets of Tas Ralong.

Multiple wafts of smoke snaking up into the air were Selina's first hint that things weren't going well. Soon, the vehicle pulled over roughly fifty feet back from the scene of the fight. The Retooling Building was the source of most of the smoke, but several other fires nearby added to the haze in the air.

A grim tension hit Selina's gut when she saw the other Regulation vehicle on its side, partially in flames. A squad of Regulation troops was nearby, barricaded into a fighting position, firing volleys toward the Railen group across the street. Then, closer to Selina's group was another overturned vehicle. Selina recognized it as the Sentry vehicle that came by for their joint training session the other day.

The Railen group fired a relentless series of volleys toward the downed Mardak vehicle. The shots punched into the armored plating making a series of loud clangs.

Several Regulation officers in the downed vehicle stood behind it, firing pulse blasts in response. Sergeant Strong bellowed next to Selina. "Jared's over there. Eber, Ravencraft, follow me; we're heading that way."

Selina lowered her head and followed behind Strong as they fired several return volleys toward the Railen group. The air was heavy with smoke and the intense heat of the pulse blasts. Soon, Selina and company were behind the vehicle. Jared's face had a smear of grime, and a thin trail of blood oozed from his temple.

Strong ducked as a series of volleys peppered the vehicle near them. "Reinforcements, best we could do, sir!"

Jared gazed over Selina and Eber. "Better than nothing. The Mardaks had a series of ships on the far side of the planet when this thing started.

"You have an ETA on them?" Strong asked.

"Not sure, 15 minutes tops."

Shouts came from the Mardak vehicle, and Selina recognized the face of one Mardak sprawled out from the side. Iona, from the training. Blood from a cut on her head trickled past her widened eyes and trembling lips.

The smoke and flames from the vehicle grew. Selina leaned toward Strong. "Sergeant, we've gotta get those Mardaks out of there now. That heap is gonna blow any second."

"I know, Ravencraft. You see the heavy guns the Railen are using? That armor you have on isn't gonna help you if they zero in on it."

The Mardaks aren't that different than us. They just want to survive. They never asked for us to take up space, and they sure never asked for the Railen to blow them into the hereafter. Selina glanced over to Eber, who eyed the sight keenly.

"Hey, brawler. Whatcha thinking?"

Eber shrugged. "I think we can get that transport to act like a wedge for a while. After that, they should hold off the attackers for a few more minutes. Maybe Mardak air support will be close enough to wrap this fight up by then."

Selina caught a glimpse of a smile in her comrade. In the heart of a firefight, troop differences suddenly seemed less, no matter how big. Finally, they took off in a sprint toward their transport. Eber floored the engine, sending the vehicle on a beeline toward the Railen position, while Selina and Sergeant Strong raced to the wreckage.

Iona's eyes met Selina's gaze as they neared.

"Can you move your legs?" Selina shouted over the din of weapon fire.

Iona glanced down for a moment before offering a slight nod.

Selina gave a thumbs up to Sergeant Strong and said, "OK, wriggle yourself out the best you can. At best, we've got a couple of minutes to get free of this thing. After that, we're heading back toward the far end of the Replication compound. Air cover is inbound; hopefully, they're in time."

"And if they aren't?" Iona asked. Her tone was devoid of threat, with only the ambiance of fear behind it.

Selina gazed into Iona's eyes and saw the look behind the Mardak bravado again. They were a proud race because they had to be. But the daily threats worried them about dying far more often than any would admit.

Selina searched for an answer to Iona's difficult question. Finally, there was only one that came up. It was part of her training and was initially meant for the Regulation and NewEarth. But Selina felt it had a new purpose. "We fight, we survive. Together."

SEVEN

THE MARDAK AIR SUPPORT ARRIVED, but not before more damage to the Replication center impacted the facility. Nevertheless, Selina and her fellow recruits managed to save almost half of the Mardak and NewEarth Regulation troops first caught in the line of fire of the attack.

Back at the Regulation Depot, as the troops sorted the damaged weaponry for everything able to be salvaged, Selina noticed Sergeant Strong standing with Lt. Jared. When Strong's gaze met hers, he waved her over.

"Selina, it's about time you officially meet your new superior officer, Lt. Jared."

Jared still looked rough as hell but no worse than Selina did, she figured. He offered her a sweaty, partially dirty hand with a genuine smile. "Nice to see another Ravencraft joining the team."

Selina swallowed and paused. "It's Selina, sir."

"I know. We all want to make our place out there. You keep handling yourself the way you did in that fight and it's gonna happen for you. No worries."

Selina swelled a bit and snapped a salute to her lieutenant. Then, she headed back to the cleanup and resorting efforts, a lift in her step as she felt the specter of Erick release some of the weight that had pressed on her shoulders.

———

RECRUITING Class 915 passed their training and transitioned into regulars in the Regulation. Selina, Warrah, and her fellow graduates assembled in formation as the top cadre of the Regulation looked on. At the center stood Zed; his weathered uniform showed every bit of the pride on his face as he gazed over the troops. Selina caught a glimpse of Sergeant Strong to the right of the stage.

Zed said, "Graduates, you've taken a significant step. You all continue the legacy that started when we landed in this galaxy not even thirty years ago. Those who came before, those who fought, those who died, did so that you have a chance to live. And so it goes, your new job is carrying that torch, watching over those in NewEarth, and protecting this colony from all who would do it harm. We are relatively new to this galaxy, but that doesn't mean we aren't a threat. We've already seen the Railen cause trouble, so we must be ever vigilant."

The corps snapped to attention and offered the Regulation code in response.

The troops broke out into a line to receive their officer credentials. Sergeant Strong had the honor of handing the insignias out. When it was Selina's turn, she saluted and stepped forward. She extended her hand, and Sergeant Strong froze, his eyes narrowed.

"You ready for this, Ravencraft?"

"More than you know."

Strong's scowl turned to a grin with a slight chuckle. "You better be. Congratulations, Officer Ravencraft. Do your colony and your father proud."

"And then some..." Selina said as she walked over to Zed for a handshake.

Selina met Ward and Laurina at the end of the reception. Laurina wept openly, and Selina stroked her mother's shoulder.

Selina's stomach fluttered in the embrace with her mother, and soon her eyes stung with tears.

"I'm proud of you, baby. I know he would be too."

Selina squinted her eyes closed until they burned. "Thanks, Mom."

As Ward brought food out for the festivities, Selina saw Warrah approach with a wide grin, patting her shiny silver Regulation emblem. "Look at us, all respectable and all."

"Yeah, how about that."

Warrah's smile turned to a smirk. "So, I guess we're sticking around this place after all."

The crowd noise picked up as a few more recruits joined the party in Ward's Commissary. The smiles and warm conversations filled the room about Selina, reminding her of a time before loss was everything and family was all she knew. The love she'd lost would always be in her heart, but time showed her a new calling, and a chance to build again.

"Yeah, Warrah," Selina said, "We're gonna be just fine."

XENO RECKONING

ONE

SELINA RAVENCRAFT LOOKED OUT THE window at an arriving transport. It was mid-morning, but even the twin suns of the Zormad system hadn't managed to break through the clouds yet. On the nearby landing pad stood a collection of people waiting to be loaded aboard the arriving ship.

Selina lived with several thousand humans, refugees from Earth living on a colony on Zormad called NewEarth. She watched the groups of ten each, lined up and chained together on the landing pad outside. She wondered how much they second guessed what they did wrong or just what they messed up that had gotten them caught. These offenders were called Lookers because of their specific offense of crossing over dimensions, also known as Dimencrime. Lookers used their unique ability to commit Dimencrime involving theft, vandalism, and in some cases, murder. Selina hadn't any idea how Lookers came to do what they did, but regardless, she was part of the Regulation, an agency tasked with keeping order.

While in the past, 'order' meant a steady hand over the citizens of NewEarth and Zormad in general, more recently the issue of Lookers had become a prominent concern for all interested in upholding the peace, fragile as it was.

Selina hopped in her bio sanitizing unit to get ready for the day. Stepping out a few moments later, she slipped into her uniform and munched on some breakfast rations before she headed down to her Precinct.

Earth had become untenable for some time, and a group of brighter minds had had the foresight and ability to focus energy on an evacuation. The response from many wasn't unlike what a certain Noah had gotten many centuries earlier, but once again, preparation and perception won out over disbelief. A series of probes had pointed the human exodus mission to Zormad. With a climate close enough to Earth to be livable and a token offering of provisions to a world recovering from a great famine, the last of the human race were given a chance to start again on a system neither made for nor particularly happy with their presence.

Formerly a bustling system of industry, Zormad reeled from its most recent famine that left the choice of survival to those willing to do whatever to hoard the meager resources still left.

NewEarth consisted of a Network of cobbled together buildings, most of them constructed from the remnants of the former Ark Ship that humans traveled in to Zormad. The enormous craft languished in a state of progressive disassembly, its pieces gradually removed and arranged in Spartanesque towns of buildings with a definitive refugee motif in construction. The power reactor from the ship was also repurposed for town energy uses, and an agricultural area designated for crop production.

As awful as Zormad was for being a good or even decent destination for the last of Earth's human race, the original settlers of NewEarth remembered enough of their former home to know that even Zormad was a step ahead of the place they left behind.

Humans' ability to somehow cultivate rudimentary crops in the Zormad soil gave them the basest of acceptance on a system still in a pandemic of want.

Within twenty years on Zormad, humans' positions grew a little, and their initial baby steps on their adopted home grew in stride, where basic crop production continued on a small scale.

TWO

SELINA HEADED INTO THE REGULATION office but first stopped at the hydration port for a fill up of precious H_2O. One of the larger issues that remained for NewEarth, the arid land of Zormad left them scraping by for the aquatic sustenance they had in plenty on Earth. Selina was glad for her share from the Regulation office, which she gladly took away from the eyes of other NewEarth residents who still adjusted to the lower amount of water available overall.

Jared, her shift lieutenant, greeted Selina once she arrived. His burly frame slouched as he studied his hand-held digital readout screen of the latest report of Looker sightings. Among the sightings and crimes, a name surfaced over and over again: Malone. There wasn't so much as a face to go with the name, but he hadn't needed even that for the reputation he commanded.

"Morning, sir," Selina muttered as she leaned in a bit to Jared.

Jared's eyes met hers. "That it is. Care to explain this business from your last shift, Officer Ravencraft?"

There it was. Her breakfast had barely started digesting, and Selina was given her first serving of crap for the day. The good Lieutenant referred to the sighting Selina worked where a Looker appeared with a set of stolen artifacts and vanished, but not before making off with her weapon as well.

Selina felt the back of her neck go cold. She'd been on a routine run about the market in the NewEarth colony. She remembered the hairs on her arm stood on end and a strange sound, like the fluttering of insect wings, and before she realized it, she was knocked to the ground, and her gun was yanked from her grasp. She got a look at the thief, a bluish glowing figure with long hair and a beard. He gave her a smirk before he pummeled her gut and vanished, leaving her with no weapon and even less of an explanation for her shift supervisor. "It's not like I handed it to him, ya know. He snuck me with a tase and laid me out before I could get a handle on 'em."

Jared's mouth drew in a line. "Excuses, Ravencraft. Losing weaponry is bad enough, but when you're up against a Looker, you gotta be more careful than that. I know you're new here; how long has it been?"

"Six weeks." Selina was amazed when she realized she'd already been with the Regulation that long. It seemed like she had joined the ranks yesterday. A lot of people had encouraged it, especially her mother. Even though her father Erick wasn't around, Selina knew he would've been for it as well, as much as he'd done for NewEarth. Erick had a lot to do with setting up NewEarth's initial structure and government. He was in the first group of humans to set foot on Zormad. While they were the legacy bearers of that blue-green ball of life humans had called home for centuries, Earth soon became the talk of stories on its journey into becoming more of a fairy tale than a physical world. For the subsequent generations of humans on Zormad, Earth became little more than a series of legends, lessons carried over from a world forgotten by necessity, abandoned by requirement. The early colony of NewEarth took a lot of effort and diplomacy, first in managing to secure a location in the Zormad wilderness and to make contact with the locals and establish a presence. Through a combination of a little effort and much more persistence and stubbornness, humans forged a fragile but establishing presence on their new home.

Erick helped establish the Regulation, and even helped humans make inroads with their neighbors on Zormad. Selina figured it was her turn to chip in and make sure she did what her father would've wanted her to do. However, being daughter to someone like Erick also involved an eternal stay within a shadow of accomplishment, and Selina dreaded the day she was measured up to what dear old dad pulled off in his life, even though his was cut short when he was killed in a raid of NewEarth by Railen.

Jared offered a smile and patted her shoulder. He didn't have to be a clairvoyant to know Selina's history, and he always admired her resolve. "OK, Selina. Six weeks is still kinda green. But you've gotta understand, losing a weapon is serious. We have enough problems now without more tech getting into the hands of Lookers."

"I know, I know. There's just so much to keep track of, with the Railen and the Omegans milling around."

"Yeah, the Railen and Omegan fight has gone on way longer than our being here, but there's a good chance we'll catch some of that action too." He smiled. "I thought you had a lot of promise, giving who your dad was and all, and you were one of the best out of Training we'd seen in a while. Maybe, though, we rushed getting you out there solo."

"I made the cut, Jared, top level on marksmanship and tactics, and even your best boys couldn't dust me on the track." Even saying the word, Selina thought about how silly it was. The 'track' for NewEarth was essentially the perimeter of the colony, a decent 10 miles in distance, but long enough that all of the Regulation got more than a healthy workout running it.

"Selina, you got the fundamentals down, no doubt. But this job's about more than checking off a PT list. Our work's 98% instinct, and that doesn't come with a quick course time. There's plenty to throw down on out there. You need to have a solid grasp of the world we're in now. Trust me, there's any number of people, especially the

Mardak, who'd love to blame any old problem they have on us. Remember, we're the outsiders. Any problem that gets pinned on us is way harder to disprove." Jared chewed his lip. His eyes spun off in thought for a moment before a glimmer popped and he gave Selina a smile. "I know what."

As new as Selina was, she already knew when Jared or any of her superiors flashed the look like Jared's face showed right then, it was from an idea, and any of these were things she never enjoyed much, if at all.

"You're getting a partner. I'm setting you up with Wexan."

Selina felt her gut tighten and the roots of indigestion taking hold. "Really. You're gonna put me with one of them... now?"

Jared squared his shoulders. "Wexan's a decorated vet with over fifteen years steady service."

"He's also a Mardak." Selina folded her arms.

The Mardak were the primary race of Zormad when humans established NewEarth on the system two decades earlier. In that time humans managed a more or less fragile peace with the Mardak and other visiting beings. However, with the issue of the Lookers on the rise, and Railen and Omegan's posturing nearing lethal levels, tensions flared more each passing day.

The sentient races on Zormad like the Mardaks had, through decades of a lifestyle of plenty, grown more accustomed to an existence of receiving than of creating and giving when it came to the basics for survival. The famine left the more adaptable with the choice of what they were willing to do to live until the next week and beyond.

"Selina, I don't care what you think or believe about Mardaks. We've got way bigger problems to worry about."

Selina swallowed hard. She knew what Jared meant. In addition to the Lookers, and the turf war the Railen and Omegans seemed hellbent on, there was also a strange virus that had been rampant in the Galaxy. The contacts NewEarth made with the Mardaks on Zormad referred to it as "Veculus". They weren't exactly sure how it was transmitted, but humans were given plenty of warning and threats by the Mardaks, enough that gave humans the idea Mardaks considered them to blame for the strange illness.

Jared glanced up at a screen on the wall that displayed counts of NewEarth residents. It was both a status update and a goal, the silent hope of all in the Regulation that the number of NewEarth only increased over time. "It's not the time to be relaxed. The Mardaks aren't exactly thrilled we're here to begin with."

"What's that word they use for us?"

"Xeno. And you best get used to that, 'cause that's what everyone thinks of us. Dirty, stinky Xeno, who infected Ling Galaxy. Even with the regular shipments of crops we're sending to Tas Ralong and other towns, Mardak are dying to use any reason to remove us, up to and including blaming crimes and Veculus on us. We've gotta make a show of good faith to them that we're on their side working these problems in earnest."

Selina shrugged. "Yes, sir."

THREE

TAS RALONG JUT OUT OF THE POWDERY DRY land just to the east of NewEarth. Its wide array of streets snaked around large collections of buildings that thrust from the sandy floor like appendages of someone buried alive. While some structures soared several hundred feet into the air, others were humbler in appearance.

Once a prominent center of industry, Tas Ralong and its wide collection of denizens had since been well on a collective journey down the path toward oblivion. That trip lingered along enough so the devious had plenty of chances for swindles and cons before all life was truly sucked from the land. Tas Ralong was also a good place to go if you wanted to hide, provided you weren't out for trouble you weren't able to handle. A large number of smugglers and soldiers for hire found its somewhat loose concern for the law a nice amenity, similar to several other outlying systems in Ling Galaxy. Syndicates, groups of smugglers organized into even more disreputable fronts of villainy, hung their banners freely, especially on the Trading Markets that provided the closest thing to a sustainable economy Zormad had seen in many years. To the outsider, Tas Ralong had a feel of a great metropolis that had missed the memo about its obsolescence long ago.

The towering buildings still offered a good amount of occupancy, but the industry that once powered the town had mostly gone away, leaving a once proud but now crumbled infrastructure, where the economy of greed and the industry of the quick and questionable trading markets ruled supreme.

The Regulation of NewEarth had begun a cooperation with the Mardak Sentries. The Regulation assisted the Mardak patrols of Tas Ralong in exchange for a slightly better attitude by the Mardaks about several thousand putrid earthlings chewing up miles of real estate on Zormad. Together with the crop sharing gesture, it moved the needle on the Mardak attitude about humans a hair more toward the tolerance side, for some Mardaks anyway. As a slight gesture in response, the Mardaks forced the Sentries who were paired with offi-cers of the Regulation to learn basic English, which did two things: it created a group of Mardaks who spoke choppy and broken English, and it gave certain Mardaks even more reason to hate humans.

Selina and Wexan's introduction was handled without much pomp at all. She hated the quickness she was handed off to this assignment, and from Wexan's surly glance, she figured the feeling was mutual. They faced each other outside the Mardak Sentry post near a line of street patrol craft.

Wexan took his time notating things on his personal tablet device, then looked back at Selina. "What are you, ten years old?"

"I'm 25, dude. Nice shape you're in. Guess you don't miss many meals, including other people's?"

Wexan grunted with a glare. "Listen, Xeno. In NewEarth you do anything your little Xeno mind wants. Here in Tas Ralong, you do what I say. I got enough to worry about without a Xeno messing things up."

Selina swallowed and shook her head slightly. The sooner her shift ended, the better.

Wexan nodded toward a hover patrol vehicle. "Let's go."

The next fifteen minutes of their shift went down mostly in silence. Neither was crazy about breaking the void with conversation, when the only starters that came to mind were things like "How soon can your kind get the hell off my planet?" or "Why do Mardaks smell that bad; is it genetic or do you have to work at it?"

As a distraction from chatting, Selina checked the HUD in her helmet. The Regulation wore special digivisors that provided real time info on all creatures that came into view. Another aspect of the agreement with the Mardak allowed the HUD in Regulation gear to be loaded with the latest Mardak data on criminal activity.

Passersby on the paths near the street were identified on sight, and if the individual had any warrants, a reddish block appeared next to them along with an alert message to the wearer of the Digivisor. It was then up to them to figure out the best way to apprehend the person, how much force was necessary, and how much of a risk was involved.

Once she'd exhausted all reasonable excuses for ignoring her new partner, Selina decided work was the best topic. She looked at the Mardaks and other beings who walked on the street while her HUD cascaded updates on each that passed across her viewpane. "So, heard about any criminals here these days?"

Wexan snorted and coughed. For a second Selina, wondered if that was going to be his only contribution, but he soon found his gravelly voice. "Utility theft's the big problem. Stealing converters, energy supplies. Really putting a strain on what's left here."

"Any idea who's involved?" Selina asked. "What about the Syndicates?"

"No, that's too small for them. They're into Essence and bigger prizes like bulk vehicle hauls, UA Credit theft."

Selina nodded. The most widely accepted currency in Ling Galaxy, UA Credits were guaranteed on all worlds within the Universal Alliance and therefore were one of the preferred currencies of the criminal minded. This was especially the case on Zormad, where basic citizens were only concerned with their own survival.

Groups like the Syndicates dealt in UA Credits at the trading markets that held space in every major town on the system.

"What about Dimencrime; seen any in Tas Ralong lately?"

Wexan threw Selina a perturbed look. "You kidding? In just the last two years, they've gone from two or three cases in a month to four or five a week."

The problems with Lookers began with things as innocent as simple theft and public spectacles, as much as any theft was innocent, anyway. Jumping across dimensions allowed Lookers to bounce between locations hundreds or even thousands of miles away. Items like energy generation tech and weapons gave them plenty of theft options for sport, but the black markets sometimes requested more specific services, which brought on several cases of kidnappings and a slew of murders.

It was on the tip of Selina's tongue to talk about her own run-in with Dimencrime and the Looker, but she held quiet. The last thing she needed on her first shift with a Mardak was even more doubt of her worth.

When they stopped for cross traffic, Wexan sighed. "The hunt for Essence has never been stronger. At least the Nara were nice and careful to keep Essence hidden, or we'd be in for way more problems."

The only thing that could've possibly made life on Zormad worse than their current existence was the absence of Essence. The substance resided on Zormad, and every world in Ling Galaxy, as a source for life on its system. Essence was deposited on each world by the Nara since the dawn of Ling Galaxy as the life sustaining force and replenished periodically. The lack of Essence on a world meant its sure destruction.

Selina noticed an open field to the right of their path. The area was littered with a series of tents, and she knew by the way they were set up that it was a temp hospital for housing Veculus patients.

"What about Veculus then?" Selina muttered.

"You tell me, Xeno. I thought your kind buggered us all up with that junk."

Selina shot Wexan a glare. "Think again, dude. You know that crud was here way before us."

Many other worlds in Ling Galaxy had a better lot than Zormad and her fellow downtrodden, and had managed a life of moderate to greater happiness. But worlds of drought and lack like Zormad left many of her residents wondering about the Essence and the true nature of the Nara, and just how this source of life of all worlds existed, while so much suffering did too. Furthermore, others believed the existence of Essence and its usage were handled wrong, and sometimes redistribution was necessary to allow those who had less to at least know a life without hunger.

"You ever seen it? The Essence?" asked Selina.

Wexan scoffed. "Nobody getting near Essence and living to tell about it, unless they're a Nara. Remember that good, Xeno."

While Essence was kept on each world, finding it was nowhere near as simple as canvassing the system. The Nara constructed a repository on each world for holding the Essence orb necessary to sustain life and keep that world intact.

Locating this portal required the ability to shift dimensions, which made Lookers not only a threat to the lawful, but a tool for the nefarious.

Wexan swung their vehicle up a tight curve around an abandoned warehouse. "We don't need to worry about Essence. Besides, there's enough Energy Tech theft to worry about. How about we make ourselves useful, keep an eye on the markets, see where that stuff's turning up."

"You mean the ones outside of town?"

"Mmmhmmm." Wexan cast a slanted grin toward her. "You sound nervous. Think you can handle the rough types?"

Selina wasn't about to let anyone push her, especially a Mardak. "I'm up for whatever you are; just get us there."

Wexan chuckled. "Now you're talking. So, Xeno, tell me about yourself."

"Why do you wanna know?" Selina's midsection tightened. Wexan's sudden probe felt more like an interrogation than just co-worker chit chat.

Wexan's eyes narrowed. "Because we're partners. And one of us may have to save the other's ass. If that should happen and it's me, the more I know about your sorry Xeno self, the more likely I'll give a damn about saving you."

Selina shook her head and wondered how anyone from Earth ever got the bright idea humans would ever be accepted in a place like Zormad. "I was born after the relocation. About twenty years ago. My mom raised me. My dad, he wasn't around."

"What happened to him?"

"The Railen killed him." Selina's throat tightened with her answer. It was as much as she wanted to share with a Mardak for the moment, but truthfully it wasn't too far from everything she knew about her father's death. Like her fellow NewEarth residents, Selina had no idea about the conflict between the Railen and Omegans, other than it occasionally involved a close call for humans by one or the other. Selina knew both races were on a rampage to control Ling Galaxy, and on one occasion NewEarth found itself in the path of a Railen raid of NewEarth. Selina's father had led a group that held their own, though it later proved costly when the Railen returned for revenge. The reminder of that still stung, it always would.

"Is that right?" Wexan's gaze lingered on Selina for a moment, then he eased their vehicle on further through the streets of Tas Ralong.

Selina knew for her own sake anything she said, even if it was nothing at all, was better than verbal trips down her family history with anyone, especially a Mardak.

Selina had begun a mental note of exactly how many minutes were left into their shift when the vehicle console sounded an alert. "Incendiary charge activated."

Wexan grunted. "Where? Get location."

"Scanning. Quadrant 87, approximate distance, 2.7 miles, ETA less than five minutes."

Wexan slammed the shift lever down. The engine at the front of their vehicle roared angrily as they shot ahead.

Selina readied her pulse rifle. "Probably Railen; they've been rousing the Omegans lately."

"Maybe so. I'm gonna activate the tase net; see if we can pull them in for intel."

Selina shrugged. If it was Railen, she figured attempts at intel were as useless as painting a building with one fingernail.

A few quick turns and there they saw the scene. A former industrial district, the far end of the street wrapped into a cul-de-sac bordered by a collection of high-rise buildings. Several disabled vehicles were scattered around the center of the streets. Behind them were two squads, one Railen and one Omegan, each of which held opposing sides of the street in an active skirmish. Blasts tore through the tall buildings on the side of the street and sent shards of steel and stone through the air along with wafts of dust that hung over the scene like tattered drapery.

Selina ran a cursory scan with her Digivisor. The readout relayed a series of scans of the rubble scattered about the area as well as an assessment of the two groups engaged in a firefight of sporadic pulse weapon fire. Most important, Selina's HUD confirmed several building occupants aside from the brawling groups ahead of them.

"We've got bystanders in at least one building ahead," Selina muttered.

Wexan eyed the scene for a minute while he munched his lip. "This is more than a simple extraction. We're letting the militia handle this."

The ground shook with a blast. Selina ducked low out of instinct. "The militia? What week are they getting here? That fight just broke out. Those buildings have people in them; we have to clear anyone we can to safety!"

Wexan grabbed a handful of Selina's shirt and yanked her close. "Listen, rookie. You go out there, only thing you're gonna clear is a few pulse blasts into your body. Stay your ass here, I'm not filling out a lot of reports because you wanted to be a hero. This is a turf war; it happens all the time."

Selina eyed Wexan in disbelief.

Wexan narrowed his eyes and continued. "Think you're the only one who lost somebody here? We've lived with this for a long time, understand? Just like we've put up with Veculus, and even you Xeno. In fact, we dealt with these brawls way before Xeno ever came here. Railen and Omegans are trying to see who can grab more land. I can't tell you how many of these I've seen in all my years of service. The Mardak Militia's way better armed for this, and you oughta know that."

Selina grit her teeth. She picked up a pair of heat signals on the ground and sure enough, zoomed her viewfinder on two Mardaks huddled behind a transit station thirty yards ahead. She sucked in a deep breath and activated her armor. The nano metallic fibers wove themselves around her body in an instant, quickly fastened and became an airtight suit that included her visor. As she tapped the door release and leaped to the street, Wexan bellowed, "Get back here!"

Selina hopped before she shot Wexan a glare. "Sorry, but I'm not here to sit on my ass. Circle back the way we came; I'll grab those stranded Mardaks out there."

"Get back here, now," Wexan growled.

Selina smirked and cast another glance toward the fray before her eyes met Wexan's most disapproving glare. "Double back; meet you when I grab them."

Wexan barked something in Mardak that Selina knew wasn't a term of affection toward her. She grinned and darted towards the transit station. Her visor readout indicated the thermal detonation was imminent, based on the intensity of the signature.

Another blast shook the ground and knocked Selina on her belly.

She looked ahead and saw she was just a few feet from the station, so she scrambled up and slid under the small roof to find two Mardaks. They were clearly dressed like lab workers of some kind.

Selina activated her in-set translator so she spoke to them in Mardak and heard them in English. The Mardaks flinched at the sight of her but relaxed a bit when they noticed her Regulation uniform. "Hi there; want a ride?"

One of the Mardaks, heavyset with stringy gray hair, replied, "Yes, please, help us!"

Selina jabbed a finger back up the street. "My partner is that way. Head there, take a left at that first corner, and look for a Tas Ralong Sentry vehicle. I'll follow behind."

Not surprisingly, the two Mardaks needed no convincing and took off in a half quick trot. Selina crouched low as she jogged. A pulse shot seared the building slightly ahead of where the Mardaks ran, and Selina got off a few return volleys of her own back toward the fray behind them.

They were almost to the corner when Selina's display sent another message. "Detonator activated, shelter in place."

The blast knocked Selina to the ground and sent a cascade of rubble down the street in their direction. She strained her eyes through the haze until she saw the Mardaks. They were on their feet but gazed back at her confusedly.

"Keep going!" Selina bellowed. As she got to her feet, the dull thuds of pulse fire slamming into the ground sounded behind her. She looked and saw three of the Omegan squad had, for whatever reason, decided Selina was as good a target as anything. Maybe her rescuees were more than innocent bystanders after all.

She was fifty feet from the corner, and when the Mardaks disappeared behind it, she juked on her path, avoiding the weapon fire that spread from one end of the street to the other. The barrage ripped into buildings but also portions of the roadway a little too close to Selina for her liking. "Wexan, need help asap, taking fire."

Selina rolled to the ground behind a disabled vehicle and looked up. The three Omegans were on foot about twenty feet away. Their reptilian faces twisted in snarls, their reddish eyes shot back a cold and heartless look toward her. She felt the Omegans weren't so much living beings as they were some kind of drones, commanded and set loose on the world like an infection. The Railen weren't much better, but it seemed they had some sense of reason in their heads, even though that reason was pretty twisted in itself.

Selina activated her rifle and returned fire from behind her cover position. Her shots made contact on one of the Omegans, but it glanced off the armor, and aside from some stray sparks, they responded with guttural snarls of defiance.

The power store on her weapon was low, but she remembered from her training about the incendiary setting on standard weapons. It exhausted the power store in a few quick blasts, but if you were in a back against the wall kind of situation, it was a handy option. Several shots from the Omegans punched into the busted vehicle and knocked her back a few feet. She activated the incendiary round and slid from behind her cover. She quickly got to a standing position and charged, her weapon aloft, and a stream of brilliant white beams shot toward the Omegans. The nearest one was sliced in two from the shot; the others kept their fire up but were silenced when the remaining rounds found their mark.

Selina skid to a halt and tried catching her breath. She'd just looked at her handiwork when her HUD registered another alert, but Selina saw what it was without help from her tech.

"Wexan, the Omegans have a hovercraft; move your ass or I'm toast!" Selina hollered.

A few seconds later, she heard the familiar rumble of their vehicle. Once Selina dashed back and jumped in, Wexan pulled away.

Their sentry vehicle careened back down the streets of Tas Ralong as a Militia Vehicle roared past them down the street for the rest of the mop up. As Selina connected her spent weapon up to the recharge console, Wexan activated the privacy screen between them and their passengers.

"What the hell was that back there?"

"I dunno, your usual skirmish between the—"

"Not the fight. You and that hero stunt?" Wexan glared.

Selina felt a lump in her throat. Her years growing up without a father had taken their toll on her but also fostered a fierce sense of action. Her joining the Regulation felt right to Selina at the time. She never thought long enough where her drive came from, but she figured at least part of her attitude was wanting to show she was like her father: proud, determined, maybe a bit stubborn. In a deeper part of her mind lay the wonder if the reason she kept so active was coping over the pain of her father's loss, something she never addressed but had only endured so far. In any case, to Wexan, someone she'd barely known, she knew instinctively he neither needed nor deserved a full brief of her reasons, especially when she wasn't even sure of them herself.

"It's called saving lives, Wexan. See these two behind us? If I hadn't grabbed them, they'd have been vaporized by the time the militia arrived."

Wexan jabbed a shaky finger into Selina's face. "You don't know who we saved; they coulda been the ones who started that mess. Hell, they coulda been trying to find Essence. Your little sortie was damned risky. Militia's got platoons of boots for these kinds of fights. They take the big threats, the invasions, things like that. We handle small stuff, petty thefts, maybe smugglers if they aren't too big a threat. You best keep that in mind if you want to live much longer."

Selina shrugged him off. She figured on one hand he had a point; that fight could've easily ended bad for her pretty quick. The pulse rifles they carried were for pacification mostly, not military grade tech for extended engagements. But something else in her knew there was no way she'd have let those Mardaks go without helping them. As much as Mardaks and humans hadn't completely gotten over their tensions, she still felt like they at least owed Mardaks for the chance to start NewEarth, and without more efforts at working together, neither race survived in the end with all they faced.

They returned to the Tas Ralong Sentry precinct, where their next requirement was handing the Mardaks back for safe return to their residence once the militia returned an all clear for the area where the fight took place.

Wexan and Selina escorted the Mardaks to the holding area for refugees. As they walked over, Selina caught a glimpse of one of them, the shorter heavyset one, as they looked back at her with a bit of wonder. She just figured the sight of a human was a little uncommon for them.

But still, as they walked, she felt the Mardak's gaze still on her to the point she became uncomfortable. Selina stopped; her eyes locked on the Mardak.

Wexan, after a few steps, also noticed Selina's stare off.

"Move!" Wexan barked.

Selina's eyes were fixed on the Mardak. "Gimme a minute, Wexan; I'm getting a vibe here."

Wexan padded up, a lingering growl under his breath as he slowly shouldered his rifle. Selina activated her translator again and peered into the Mardak's eyes. "Is something wrong?"

The Mardak chuckled a bit. "Pardon me, I don't mean to stare. We Mardaks have a tendency to study new people we've

met, as our belief is in this grand universe we're all connected in some way. Pardon my rudeness, my name is Grisha Eld."

"Selina Ravencraft."

Grisha smiled warmly. "Suddenly a name makes one less ominous, no?"

Selina's lips curved up slightly. "I guess."

"You're the first Xeno I've met. I understand your kind came from a distant galaxy."

"Yep. And we didn't bring Veculus if that's what you're thinking."

Grisha chuckled. "Oh, I'd suspect the Railen or Omegans of Veculus before the likes of a Xeno."

Selina nodded. "We're just trying to make our way and help where we can."

"As are we all. In any case, Selina Ravencraft, the truth of the matter is you and my brother Mardak over there risked your lives for mine today, and as such I feel obliged to show you some act of kindness."

With that, Grisha pulled at his cloak for a moment. "I've found something that you might deem useful. I believe the Omegans were looking for it when they attacked the Railen back where you found us." With that he produced a slender device. The sliver outer coat of the item gleamed, even in the moderate light of the depot. It was shaped like a pistol with a greenish display at one end. He offered it to Selina.

The device felt cool in her hand. She held it up and examined it in the light. Wexan noticed her with the item and blurted, "How the hell did you get that?"

Grisha's eyes darted between Wexan and Selina, but he only managed a grunt in response. Wexan grabbed Grisha by his cloak and lifted him up. Grisha's eyes widened, and he let loose with a surprised whimper. Unfazed, Wexan leaned in.

"That thing's contraband if it's what I think it is, so start talking."

"It was dropped by a Railen. I swear, I'd never seen it before!" Grisha protested.

Selina held the item up. It could've been a pulse pistol, for what she knew. She felt a trigger where one typically would be. She held it overhead, pointed in a firing position and her finger slid toward the trigger.

She heard Wexan's warning, "Selina, better put that down!" but before she knew what else, a shock rocketed through her body and knocked her unconscious.

FOUR

SELINA WOKE IN THE MARDAK INFIRMARY. Monitors beeped around her, and the room opened into a larger area filled with the bustle of medics working on the sick. Wexan sat beside her bed but was on his feet soon after her eyes opened. "You're just determined to get yourself in trouble, aren't ya?"

"You're not gonna start acting like you care now, are you, Wexan?" Selina's attempt at a laugh quickly dissolved in a painful coughing fit. She grunted and tried moving herself up in bed. Her efforts at sitting up rewarded her with a piercing headache that bored through the center of her skull, and she lay back in a series of groans.

Wexan eyed Selina with a gaze she hadn't seen from him yet. She'd have sworn his eyes had a stain of compassion on them.

"Look, just because you're a Xeno and all... damn it, I'm responsible for anyone on my watch." Wexan coughed a bit before he blinked and glanced away for a moment.

Selina focused her breaths, hoping it calmed her aches. "What happened? Last thing I remember was—"

"Ignoring what I said about putting that device down. Maybe next time you'll listen. Well, our little friend we picked up was more than just a refugee. I had a feeling on that tech so I ran it, and sure enough. It's a Railen Tracker. They use them for locating Lookers."

Selina's eyes widened. "I didn't even know that was possible."

"It is, and whoever gets a hold of one has a huge advantage trying to find Essence."

"So, the Railen are tracking them?"

"The Railen are, plus anyone else with half a brain. First thing I thought seeing those two squads fighting was it was just another rumble between Omegans and Railen, you know, regular stuff. But this tracker, with these around now, it tells me they've got good reason to think Lookers are here. They can't catch a Looker without one of these. The tracker not only locates but incapacitates the Lookers and any other moron who doesn't know how to disengage the safety mechanism."

Selina rubbed her head and hoped the throbbing stopped soon. "Where's the tracker now?"

"Got it on me. I was gonna turn it into Central Security, but I thought better we hang onto it, and see what we can find out at the Trading Markets."

"Sounds good to me. How about the Omegans? They didn't look exactly happy to see us back there."

"Omegans are pissed from centuries of being someone else's errand boy. Former protectors of the Nara, the Omegans invested lots of time in their service and are ready to build their own empire. They've finally got it in their heads that in the grand scheme of things every race has their time to ascend to the top of the order and their turn is now. They've been getting bolder and bolder, and the Railen are one of their biggest threats, so go figure the two of them are gonna fight."

"How long 'til I can get outta here?" Selina wailed.

"They gave you some super dosage, so a few more hours at least. Before I turn in, I'll see if I can learn anything more about this tracker from my contacts. Tomorrow I'll get you and we'll get back on this together, alright?"

FIVE

A FTER A FITFUL NIGHT'S REST in the medical
facility, Selina was released the next morning. Wexan met
her at the front entrance, and they resumed their patrol.
They both agreed the Tas Ralong markets were a decent place to try
to find out if anything else like the Railen Tracker had showed up
recently.

The markets at Tas Ralong filled a tremendous abandoned warehouse on the outskirts of town. Once a huge facility for fabricating
structural pieces for buildings, and vehicles, the structure found new
worth with its large open space where rows of vendors hawked their
wares. From handy devices to weapons that were pretty useful if you
had a need, the Trading Markets filled the bill from basic groceries to
murder for hire and on the hush hush. Lots of the citizenry needed
one or more of the above on any given day in Tas Ralong.

Selina clasped the tracker firmly in her hand, determined to not
repeat her prior slip up. Wexan walked beside her. The Mardaks and
others in their vicinity gave them a wide berth through the crowd.
Sentry presence wasn't unheard of in the Markets, but it was definitely a wakeup call for everyone to hide any contraband they had

recently decided to test on the black market. While contraband wasn't a known term in the markets, the people who lived nearby knew that just because you had it there didn't mean you kept it if a lawkeeper saw it.

The rows of vendor booths were topped with banners that billowed like weeds in an open field. "There," Wexan said as he pointed a few rows over to a red and black banner with a triangular logo in yellow on it.

"The Syndicates are bolder than I thought. They always hang their shingle over here like that?" Selina asked.

Wexan flipped a UA credit to a passing food vendor and swiped a roll for himself. As they walked and he gnawed at his snack, he commented with a semi full mouth. "Lots go on here that slips by the average enforcement groups. The Sentries and Militia have an understanding with the Syndicate and the Markets. They keep their dirty business between themselves, and we don't come in and bust all this up."

Selina eyed Wexan and shook her head. "I always thought we were here to shut people like that down."

"It's not always that simple, rookie. Sometimes, you need to get a little close to the people you're after, spend some time with 'em and learn how they think. It makes it easier to know what they're gonna do next, and even more important, where they're gonna do it."

Selina balled her free hand into a fist. While she knew Wexan had a point, something in her burned at just being around so much criminal activity. But then, they rounded a corner where she saw a group of Mardaks in tattered garments; they picked out semblances of clothing from large bins. A little further down the row a few Mardak traded items for hot stew.

Selina noticed Wexan had stopped as well and watched her. "See? Not that simple. This market's a lifeline for people since most of the industry left this world. Add Veculus to that, and you got a real problem. Look in these faces; if you can't see the fear there, you're plain blind. If we shut all this down like good little lawkeepers, how many won't have clothes to wear, how many kids won't have food?"

Hearing the plight of the average Zormad citizen really drove home to Selina how similar humans were to Mardaks after all. All of them lay claim to a decimated home world and a lifestyle where the primary concern was living to the next day, and what it took for surviving that. Selina swallowed hard and dabbed at her eye as they walked on. She activated her in set translator in a feeble attempt at distraction from the squalor around her. They soon ended up at the flag with the Syndicate logo, where an older Mardak woman sat at a table with several metallic objects at it.

"Hi, Kreela," Wexan said warmly.

Kreela nodded in kind to Wexan, but when she saw Selina and the tracker in her hand, she recoiled in her seat. "What's she doing with that?"

"Not using it, for sure." Selina narrowed her eyes.

"Kreela, this is my new partner, Selina Ravencraft. We found this yesterday during a firefight between Railen and Omegans by the old mineral processing district. We're wondering if there's any more of these around and what you know about anything the Railen or Omegans are doing."

Kreela grabbed for a curvy piece of metal. Selina thought at first she was going to use it to examine the tracker, but Kreela just wanted something to fiddle with in her fingers.

After a few moments, Kreela furrowed her brow and exhaled incredulously. "You got me. Syndicate's got a low presence here these days. But I know Network has been all open on the Looker hunt. Word is a knocked Looker'll get ya three million UA Credits, no questions asked. I suspect you'll see a lot more of these sooner or later."

Selina had heard about the process of Knocking. It was essentially a lock put on someone's cerebral capacities, turning them into a drone. Catching a Looker without incapacitating them was as useless as catching a fly on a piece of paper. The Railen Tracker incapacitated the Looker for a few minutes, but the process of Knocking locked their mind up and turned them into an obedient drone, where whoever had control of the Knocked person could command them as they wanted.

"So, they get them to locate Essence that way?" Selina asked.

"Well, Essence still ain't that easy to get. But without a Looker, you aren't even doing that much."

Kreela's lips formed a line and, her eyes locked in with Selina's. At first, Selina thought maybe Kreela had some kind of tick or palsy that made her stare; the Mardaks seemed to do that from time to time. Selina then remembered Grisha's gaze on her and how it ended up in a conversation starter. Finally, Kreela commented, "You seem very familiar to me."

"Oh? I'm sorry, I've never seen you before in my life."

"Maybe so. But there's a connection somewhere; I'm sensing it." She turned to the Railen Tracker and worked it over in her hands. Focused on it, she continued, "People go through life, through this Galaxy on this ball, and they think they rule their own existence. They think they control their own path, when in actuality we are connected. The past, the present, the future. People who raised us and are now gone away from this life, people we've yet to meet."

Selina's jaw twitched. Her defense mechanism toward anyone who attempted prying too deeply for her liking sprung like a well-made snare. "What are you talking about?"

"There's something about you, Selina Ravencraft. You're not telling me, maybe not even telling yourself, but you've got something in you that needs to be seen by everyone. Until you do that, you'll be always in a state of unrest."

Selina stepped back from the table. *Unrest? She has no idea. I wonder how much unrest she'd feel if her dad was slaughtered for standing his ground.* Tossing a look at Wexan, Selina stammered, "I'm feeling a little woozy; think I'll grab some food while you two finish up."

As she hurried off through the aisles, she glanced back and

caught Wexan and Kreela as they chatted more about the tracker and probably Selina.

She arrived at a vendor who'd just served a crowd of Mardak and ordered a portion of Aquand, a concoction not far from Earth water. She plopped down at an empty table and sipped the slightly cool beverage. The partly sour, partly metallic taste tickled her tongue, but she was more interested in clearing her mind of what happened with Kreela.

Selina tried distracting her mind with their investigation, finding information on any Looker activity on Zormad and shutting it down when Kreela's words popped back into her head. *I've got something in me?* Selina thought. *Maybe she just meant my father and how he was killed. Of course I'm angry about that; who wouldn't be? That couldn't be it.*

Wexan found her twenty minutes later. "You keep bailing on me like this, I'm gonna ask for reassignment."

She finished the rest of her drink and swiped her mouth dry. "Sorry, Wexan, Kreela was a little hard to take."

Wexan gave a chuckle as Selina stood up. "Yeah, guess I should've warned you. Kreela's into UA Mysticism. Claims she's got the sight."

Selina nodded, her eyes astray from Wexan's. "Mmmhmmm."

Wexan shrugged. "Ehh, I never had much time for religion, me, but I know some swear by it. Like it's gonna resolve our issues one day. If that were the case, can't imagine all these people would be so hard up for Essence."

"I've no clue what she was getting at. I'd rather we get back to catching some criminals."

"Funny you say that. As I came over to find you, I got a notice on my comm unit. Energy theft in town. Perps just fled few minutes ago. Feel like a little fox hunt?"

SIX

SELINA AND WEXAN CORNERED THE PERPS on the Energy theft and saved a huge relay system from being knocked offline. They returned the pieces back to the Mardaks, who restored the fragile but lingering power grid in Tas Ralong to its current state, mediocre as it was. Her shift ended, Selina headed back to NewEarth for a two-day break.

The Commissary was a common meeting ground on NewEarth. The facility was built in the hope it gave NewEarth citizens the beginning of a routine for their day, even if it was just a regular place where they congregated, satisfied their hunger, and even percolated the smallest bits of gossip on their neighbors. The traditions of gathering from Earth were carried over.

The Commissary was run by Ward Dixon, a former maintenance worker who'd helped with the establishment of NewEarth and had decided to kindle that one portion of the human existence, the sharing of stories and times good and not so good over whatever meager rations were available.

Ward's Commissary was a business, but since UA Credits weren't quite that common around NewEarth yet, Ward happily adopted a more or less barter type system, trading basic items, or even the occasional credit type transaction—whatever it took so people's bellies were full and the NewEarth community kept growing.

Ward greeted Selina as she came through the food line. His large belly pressed close to the counter as he scraped food portions onto Selina's tray. "How's my girl doing?" Ward said in his inimitable booming voice.

"Eh, surviving. Just finished my first shift with a Mardak."

"Oh boy, sorry to hear that."

"Right?" Selina chuckled.

Ward nodded sympathetically. "They come this way now and then; seen 'em when we do crop transfers. Bunch a smelly bastards."

"Try riding in a hover with one." Selina smiled.

Ward laughed. "'Suppose we gotta play nice though. Keeping order takes all the help we can get. I'm still seeing some theft around these parts too, ya know. Don't understand how people are so bent on taking things from their fellow humans."

"We all want more, especially when we've got so little."

"Yeah, I guess. So, how's your mama been? Ain't seen her too much." Ward's lips drew in a line.

Selina's eyes cast down a bit. "Recovering. I've been trying to slip her some extra water rations when I can. Dehydration sickness isn't pretty."

"No, it ain't. Tell ya what, I got some extras from my food prep. See me on your way out; I'll give you some."

"Aw, Ward, that's for your business."

"My business is taking care of people. If we don't look out for each other, who else will?" Ward extended a knobby hand to Selina.

She swallowed a lump in her throat and blinked hard to bat away a tear that formed. She hoped the waver in her voice wasn't noticed. "Thanks, Ward."

Selina grabbed her tray and made her way to a spot on the far end of the large hall. She felt better with her back against a windowless wall. Ever since Regulation training, Selina was told to be ever vigilant, as even in a small community like NewEarth, lawkeepers inevitably became targets of those who skirted the law. Selina enjoyed her meal in peace as the wafts of conversations drifted around her. She mustered her courage; her next visit wasn't going to be an easy one.

SEVEN

S ELINA HAD MIXED EMOTIONS AT VISITING her mother, and she hated the way she felt about it. Her mother still lived in the same place where Selina had grown up. It wasn't so much the childhood memories that made it difficult; it was being where her father no longer lived that made the domicile a repository of grief and loss. Selina wished like anything that the memory of her father wasn't so closely linked with the place, but she knew that wasn't an option. This home was and always would be the reminder of what her life had been and painfully now wasn't.

Selina's mother Laurina lay back on a makeshift couch, made of former insulation from the Ark Ship and reshaped into a contoured soft recliner. Her tired eyes greeted Selina as she entered. "Hello, my love."

"Hi, Mom. How's the back?"

Laurina grimaced as if her back answered Selina's question on cue. After a few attempts at shifting, she gave a deep sigh. "Been better. How was your shift?"

"Eventful. Got hit with a Railen Tracker and knocked out for a few hours."

Laurina's eyes darkened with worry. "Are you OK?"

"Mmmhmmm. They put me up in the Mardak medical wing. I finished my shift, and I'm headed back there in another day. I've been assigned to a filthy Mardak for a partner. They think I need more training, I guess."

Laurina squinted. "They aren't pushing you too much, are they?"

"It's OK, Mom, I can handle it." Selina knew, even if she'd just uttered a big lie, it was the only proper answer her mom needed for that question. Selina assumed her mother's concern was in part out of a sense of guilt or maybe responsibility to her dead husband that their only child was taken care of, even after that child became a grown woman with every right and ability at self-reliance.

Selina glanced around the room and saw the monitor against the wall broadcasting a feed of activity on Zormad, reports from the Trading Markets, alerts on raids from groups like the Railen and Omegans, as well as a link to Network, the combined signal of open comm transmissions and warrants throughout Ling Galaxy.

"They're finding more Lookers around here. Some in Tas Ralong, but my boss at the Regulation thinks NewEarth could be hit again soon," Selina muttered.

"There's nothing here they'd want." Laurina managed a laugh that quickly turned into heaves.

Selina fixed a portion of water for her mother. At her bedside, she cradled her mother's frail body as she took sips of the liquid. "Ward says hello, by the way."

Laurina smiled at the name. "Oh, that sweetie. Gotta get out and see him sometime, I do."

Selina knew, much as she denied it to others and even herself, the days for her mother weren't long. Dehydration sickness had already killed a number of NewEarth residents, and though Veculus hadn't worked its way into the human population, their odds in Ling Galaxy weren't that much different from the one they left behind.

Selina pushed back at the thoughts of death and worry about the future. It had been her routine since her teen years. Her father being gone left her to look out for her mother. She regretted the move to her own place, but she also craved the independence. However, as much as the oxygen in her lungs, Selina always made time and room for her mother, in spite of the awkwardness she felt over the visits.

Having her fill of the water ration, Laurina slumped back down. "Listen, before you go," she said weakly, "there's something you need to have. It's from your father. I'd tried to figure out a good time to give it to you, but there never seemed to be one, and then you were away at Regulation training."

Laurina pushed herself up to a sitting position amid a series of groans. She pointed to the far corner of the room, where a collection of boxes leaned against the wall in a haphazard pillar. "It's in one of those. Your father wanted you to have this when you were old enough. I never felt like it was the right time. In spite of the fact I still see you as my little girl, I know you're out making your way, and I'd much rather you get this than some raider if it ever came to that."

Selina grabbed the first box. It wobbled a bit, and her hands ran over the warped heavy cardboard texture, damaged by water and just the general decay of twenty years. The boxes contained a lot of items that weren't useful anymore: manuals and some basic electronics brought to Zormad in the hopes their components served some use, even if just a simple bartering for spare or better parts.

The second box held a collection of cold weather gear. Zormad did have a brutal winter, so the heavy cloaks weren't completely useless, but Laurina's gaze told Selina she hadn't found the item yet.

When the third box was uncovered, Selina knew she found it. She still had no idea what it was, but the sight of it alone told her; she even sensed something that told her she'd found it. A dark steel box, she held it up for Laurina to see. Laurina smiled a slightly sad grin, her eyes closed in a trance of memory. "Bring it here."

Selina piled the boxes back neat and rejoined her mother at bedside, the strange box on her lap. Selina felt the coolness of the steel, even through the fabric of her pants. Laurina slid her hands over Selina's and their eyes met. "You know, your father was one of the very first from Earth to set foot on this system. We made contact with Zormad before we landed, but they weren't interested in us just arriving here. Your father made the deal with the Mardaks that allowed us to land. There's still a lot of people who credit him with saving us. If we hadn't landed on Zormad, there's no telling how much further our life support systems would've taken us."

Laurina slid her hand along the sides of the box, and at once the box responded with a series of electronic chirps and a glowing blue emblem appeared.

"Not long after we arrived, Zormad fell under a raid from the Railen. I was pregnant with you at the time. The Railen had come looking for supplies, energy tech, who really knows? The Mardaks warned us that the Railen made runs on Zormad from time to time. I suspect Railen saw our little group as an easy mark, strays from another world who even the Mardaks weren't too concerned with. Maybe the Mardaks figured it was better that we got hit instead for a change.

"Your father had formed the first unit of what later became the Regulation. Anyhow, they had weapons from Earth. We'd brought enough with us for protection. We weren't the scared victims the Railen thought we were; not that first time, anyway. Humans fought the Railen off, and even managed to kill a few of them. They underestimated us and came with way less than they should have that first time.

"This was taken from the Railen by your father; he removed it from the dead hands of one of the raiders. We later found out it was a grave insult to the Railen, taking this from them. Regardless, your father knew, like the rest of NewEarth did, unless humans made a stand and let it be known we weren't here to be picked off like lambs at a slaughter, we'd never survive anywhere."

With that, Laurina moved her hand in a clockwise motion over the now humming box and the lid rotated in a like manner, eventually opening and showing a glowing bluish cylinder.

Laurina took a shuddered breath. Her eyes winced along with

her voice, tinted with emotion. "I wish I could tell you more about this thing, but your father never had a chance to find out. Several days later, a bigger group of Railen appeared and targeted him while he was out with a group on an exploration of the further reaches of Zormad."

Selina started to reach for the device, but paused for a moment, remembering a little too well what grabbing a strange object did to her the last time. "Does anyone else know about this, Mom?"

"Well, Zed was closest to your father, and I know the two of them talked a lot about things like this. Check with him; maybe he can help you."

Zed was alongside Erick during the formation of the Regulation and was there that fateful day when the Regulation faced down the Railen threat. Since then, Zed assumed leadership of the Regulation.

Laurina's eyes were filled with wonder and a bit of sadness. She gazed at Selina though tears that lazily fell down her face.

"I wish your father were here to see you now—our little girl all grown up and in charge of the world."

"I'm a shift worker, Mom. So far I've been in charge of getting myself assigned to a Mardak on a constant basis."

Laurina batted her eyes and swiped a tear away. "You're a fighter, like your father. You're stronger than you know, and one day you'll realize just who you're supposed to be."

Selina glanced downward. "Can you give me a hint?"

"Only you can know that, once you find the answer. But if you really want my opinion, it doesn't matter what happens; you'll always be our little Selina."

Selina swallowed the lump in her throat. Laurina's words were equal parts heartwarming and also more than a little wistful. "I'll be back sooner next time, Mom."

"Will you?"

Selina coughed and did her best to strain the emotion from her response. "Of course."

EIGHT

THE DAY AFTER, SELINA BEGAN A NEW shift with Wexan. She kept the strange cylinder with her in case anyone, Railen or otherwise, came sniffing around for it. She slid the item into one of the inner pouches of her uniform. Before she began another day with Wexan, where they were scheduled for a pass through NewEarth, she knew she needed an answer about the device that cost her father's life.

This mysterious object from her father's past had grown from random curiosity to major mystery in her head. Selina wasn't putting it out of her mind anytime soon, and all the better to ask one of her own than chance any strange reaction from Wexan.

Like most areas in the precinct and NewEarth in general, Zed's office was a haphazard collection of equipment and hastily thrown together pieces of wall section cobbled from the Ark Ship remnants. A crude desk dominated the tiny office, a rare luxury only given to the upper tier of the Regulation.

Zed gazed at Selina's object on his desk. His palms were flat on either side of the cylinder. He eyed the item as if it were a holy relic and he feared his unclean spirit might combust if he touched it. "All this time, I thought he'd ditched it."

"Mom said you were there when he got it from the Railen."

Zed looked at Selina, but then his gaze rocketed past her into another realm. After a deep breath, he began, "We'd been on Zormad, I dunno, a week, maybe two? The Mardaks warned us about the Railen raids; said they came for anything good. It wasn't so much the Railen needed anything, they wanted to make sure everyone else had less.

"Erick knew as well as I and the rest that do or die, we had to hold up against them. We had a supply of weapons from Earth, of course, and so it happened; they sent a squad of Railen. I guess they'd sized us up and figured a colony of refugees wasn't worth much at all. But the Railen are scavengers, see? And, even the least threats have something of value, at least in the Railen mind. They walked into NewEarth, all high and mighty. By then we had a Network of tents while more permanent residences were being built. We did have the Ark Ship, which I'm sure was their initial target. We weren't as spread out yet, so it made the Railen easy to notice when they came calling."

As Zed continued with his story, Selina noticed his eyes lit up a bit. While the end was tragic for Selina's dad, she knew there was still a bit of pride, probably even felt by her father, over the stand that some lowly humans made in a strange Galaxy against an alien race that could've well decimated NewEarth, for all they knew at the time.

Zed continued, "I met them first, but it wasn't long before the rest of the soldiers came front and center. The Railen at the front was dressed a little nicer than the rest. I approached, and he asked if I was the leader. You have to realize, at that point we were all alone here. The Mardaks had given us just enough space where we had a place to land and figure out what the hell we were gonna do.

"The Railen didn't waste a lot of time; they started blowing up parts of the Ark Ship. We'd barely started unloading the thing yet. Erick saw to it we had a sentry system in place, and that was about the only thing that saved us from being wiped out. Our troops were never all in one place; they all powered up and put fire on the Railen quick."

It was interesting to Selina hearing Zed's description of how spartan the early version of the Regulation was. By the time Selina joined the force, their methods and tactics had been refined into a sub military operation.

Zed continued, "People scattered, tried for any cover they could find, but there wasn't much. The Railen weapon fire was everywhere. I'd gotten turned around but fired shots back when I wasn't looking after wounded close to me.

"And then there was Erick, your dad. He laid down fire on the Railen like the rest of our group did, and pretty soon that little group of Railen was all but dusted. After the fight, we approached them, their bodies just flung to the ground. One of them was still clinging to life, and he had this thing in his hands. He just lay there, wounded, bleeding out bluish green blood all over the place. He eyed Erick and me hard. I'll always remember that look in the Railen's eyes; I can't imagine what happened that gave him that level of hate, and especially to us, who'd just appeared on Zormad a few days earlier. He started to reach for another pistol to shoot when Erick stopped him, his rifle beaded on his head. Erick told him to stand down, but either he ignored him, or more likely, didn't understand English. Anyhow, he'd attacked us, and we figured there wasn't a solution that included a peaceful discussion, so Erick sent him to the great beyond.

"Anyway, whatever the Railen said was lost on us, but Erick kept the thing. He figured if it was that valuable to the Railen, it may come in handy, especially on the markets."

"Had you ever asked around? Maybe the Mardaks know what it is?"

"We showed it to a few Mardak Sentries, but aside from wanting nothing to do with it, a few more knowledgeable folks said it's a disruptor. It deactivates weapons in the near vicinity, but no one's said anything else."

Zed slid the disruptor carefully back toward Selina. "Given who Erick was and what he did for us all, I never felt right keeping this. If it's anyone's, it's yours. I'd keep it outta sight, especially from your Mardak partner over there."

Selina nodded. She returned the disruptor to its hiding place on her uniform. "Well, that's more than I knew before. Thanks, Zed."

Zed smiled in reply. "Your dad and I always looked out for each other. After he died, I tried to make sure you were OK. I gotta admit I wasn't crazy about you joining the Regulation. I had half a mind to reject your application. But we need all the help we can get. Besides, once I heard you ripped it up in training, dusting your classmates, I knew you had your daddy's spirit and you belonged here."

Selina swelled at the mention of her father, but also bristled a little at the comparison. She knew there was no changing her origin, but she hoped Zed and everyone else realized she had her own destiny and that it wasn't necessarily Erick's.

Selina rejoined Wexan in the NewEarth region for another leg of their shift. Her uniform had gotten a little tighter, as she included the Railen Tracker with the disruptor in another hidden location. Wexan decided he wasn't ready for handing it over, since the situation on Zormad after their run in with the Railen and Omegan brawl hadn't settled one bit.

Selina took the controls of their vehicle and guided them through the regions of the colony. As their time on Zormad continued into a third decade, humans learned more about Zormad and what kind of materials were available, which brought with it a change in the look of the living quarters. NewEarth housing soon took on a semblance of places like Tas Ralong, minus the towering facilities.

This wasn't lost on Wexan, who marveled at how Xeno scum managed to blend in with the Zormad architecture, if only slightly. "Never thought I'd see a bunch of filthy Xeno making their way here. I gave your kind a month, and look at you now," Wexan said.

"Don't count us out." Selina chuckled. "Hey, how did our last energy thieves do?"

"Oh, them? Mardak Council took care of them but good. They threw them in for some hard labor for three years, trying to make an example of 'em."

"Wow, didn't think Mardaks ever got that hard on crime."

"Things are changing, rookie. Got a new magistrate running things now, and they mean business."

Selina smiled. Zormad had full opportunity to slide into destruction and chaos, but since humans now called it home, that was never acceptable for Selina. At least, not until humans figured out their next move in their new Galaxy. She turned their vehicle up a straightaway alongside the gigantic hulk of the Ark Ship.

NINE

SELINA'S MIND HAD JUST ABOUT SETTLED into the humdrum of the ordinary when the vehicle comm disrupted their routine moment. "Units in immediate vicinity of Region Alpha respond. Repeat: units respond to Region Alpha; group of Railen spotted approaching."

Selina swallowed hard as she gunned the engine. Wexan said, "Could be a group of trollers, looking for useful trash."

"Inside NewEarth boundaries? I don't think so." Selina shot Wexan a worried glance. A dreadful feeling slid over her as their vehicle hurtled toward Region Alpha. She thought back to Zed's story, and wondered if the Railen were back for the disruptor this time. NewEarth wasn't a hot bed of production, and what they had back from the previous Railen raid hadn't improved much since—things were just more dust covered and worn out than before.

After rounding their vehicle around the broad side of the Ark Ship, they spotted the Railen group when they were still a half mile from Region Alpha. It was hard to miss; the Railen craft's huge wings rose a few hundred feet in the air. This collection of Railen was bigger than the one from Zed's story; the onboard computer identified a group of at least thirty, all heavily armed.

"This is an invasion," Wexan muttered. "I'm notifying Mardak Militia. We can't stop 'em here, and Tas Ralong's too close. I gotta call this in to my base."

Selina gunned the accelerator until they arrived where the Regulation troops had gathered in a defensive position across from the Railen. She pulled over alongside a grouping of Regulation vehicles. So far the Railen had just moved troops up but hadn't attacked yet.

Selina saw Jared making a report on the comm and headed over to him. "They hadn't said what they wanted, but they're standing in place. It's like they were ordered here by someone."

Selina felt the disruptor in its secret hiding place as it grew warm. And as if in sequence, she saw a group of Railen, with some kind of monitoring device ahead of them, yell and shout, pointing in her direction.

"That can't be good," Selina muttered.

One Railen stepped toward the gathered Regulation forces. He tapped a control on his suit, and his helmet vanished quickly into nothing. Selina gazed deep into the Railen's gray eyes, and she really got the irony of calling any one feature on a Railen gray when their entire physical form was a study in the shade.

"My name is Darrick Bruer, and we want what your kind took from us."

Jared cleared his throat. "You've got some nerve. The Railen steal whatever they want, from NewEarth and elsewhere."

Darrick's gaze shot to Jared; his eyes smoldered in response. Then he said, "Xeno scum, one day you'll all learn your place here, and it's not for you to decide what I need to explain."

"Start over, Railen trash." Jared shook his head.

Darrick took a steadied breath. His fingers gnashed together as his hands formed fists. *Whoever this guy was,* Selina thought, *he sure wasn't a chief diplomat.*

"It's very simple. One of your kind has a disruptor and it doesn't belong with you. We're here to take it back, even if we have to level your little settlement here to do it."

"Stand down and we'll talk." Jared's reply came through his gnashed teeth.

"Xeno, hear me well." Darrick pointed a finger to Selina. "We've confirmed a signature on her of the device we want. Give it, or her, to us, and we'll leave without further trouble."

Jared glanced slightly to Selina but quickly eyed Darrick again. "We don't negotiate with hostiles."

Selina felt her gut tense. She slid one hand over the disruptor's location on her suit, still hidden from plain sight. She'd never seen it in action, and wasn't about to pull a quick draw. The other Railen behind Darrick drew their weapons and, in a coordinated series of howls, trained them on Selina. The collective whine of activate pulse rifles filled the air, in a chorus of danger.

"Xeno, you really think we're the kind that looks the other way or just forgets a slight like theft? Your time in Ling Galaxy is sure to be full of painful lessons, I foresee."

Wexan grabbed for Selina and shoved her behind him. "This ain't a firing squad. Zormad's got a system, at least part of one. Only way we'll ever get peace here is through order. We aren't letting anyone blast someone else away just 'cause they suspect something."

But Wexan's words fell on deaf ears. The Railen to a one, opened fire on the gathered troops. The Regulation forces crouched and returned the shots. The air exploded in a sea of blasts from the Railen front with return fire from the Regulation. Selina rolled and returned fire herself; her shots landed a few glancing blows on the Railen.

Selina heard Jared yell and saw him fall to the ground. She scampered to his side, but he waved her back. He shouted commands to her and the rest of the Regulation in earshot as a thick ooze of blood trailed from his lips.

Wexan yelled over his shoulder to Selina. "Back to the hover, and get outta here! Mardak Militia's en route; I just hope they make it before it's too late!"

Selina and Wexan made a beeline for their vehicle as the rest of the Railen party advanced and fired at random at the gathered force of Regulation troops.

Selina and Wexan were almost to the hover when the sound of Darrick's voice to their side stopped them in their tracks. There he stood, the reddish glow of his weapon staring Selina and Wexan down like an angry eye.

"Not another step. Hand it over."

Darrick's gaze locked in on Selina. She thought about the disruptor, how her dad and mom held it all those years, and how her father was killed by a Railen because of it. She knew in her gut whatever this device meant to Darrick, for her it meant her father's life. That wasn't something she threw away on a demand. However, the sight of Darrick's rifle trained on her had Selina worried she was about to pay the same price Erick had.

Selina searched Wexan's face for their next move. Wexan eyed Darrick, then Selina, and she saw a look in Wexan's eye she'd never seen before. This Mardak, who sworn earlier her life wasn't even worth the paperwork it took to explain it, jumped in between Selina and Darrick, his rifle raised, but before he got off a volley, Darrick emptied a barrage into Wexan's midsection, littering the area with grayish Mardak blood and innards.

Time froze a bit as Selina watched her partner crumble to the ground slowly. She gasped at the sight of Wexan, the first Mardak she'd ever really known at all. To say she knew Wexan was a stretch too, but in their hours together, they'd managed a sort of ease with each other. Theirs wasn't a warm association, but their grouping had a kind of teacher-student familiarity, and suddenly Selina wondered about his last gesture and how much Wexan's earlier disinterest toward her was a front.

From the look of it, she'd be able to ask Wexan in person in the afterlife shortly.

A thousand thoughts flooded her mind. Plans unmet, promises unfulfilled, a future unlived. Selina felt though, if her death was here, she was ready. The rest of her crew were too far away, still engaging the Railen, and they wouldn't have made it in time. She pulled in a deep breath and waited for her end.

A crackling sound erupted around her. Her entire body tensed, a flash of light engulfed her, and then darkness and void. She tried to feel for something, anything, but instead of a sense of peace, an excruciating headache came over her. And then, her eyes opened and she saw she was in a room, but her vision was too blurry to identify anything.

A mechanical droning sound was a clue her surroundings had indeed changed. Furthermore, the way the room eased back and forth on occasion, made her suspect she'd somehow left Zormad altogether. She blinked her eyes, but the room was still too blurry and dark for making out anything.

Selina then noticed she lay on a mattress. It was moderately firm. She noticed a nearby pedestal with a digital readout display and thought, *Maybe it's some kind of sick bay area like the Mardak infirmary.*

A gruff male voice spoke. "Take it easy. You've been out for the past twenty minutes."

Selina looked around and saw an outline of a person, but her vision was still too fuzzy. "I had to grab you in a hurry; once I saw Darrick with a bead on you, I knew time was short."

Selina's eyes focused a bit more and saw the body that went with the voice. A pilot; from the looks of it. "My name's Ket Durban, but you can call me Ket. You're on my ship, the *Crimson Lance.*"

Selina rubbed her temples together until she realized it did absolutely no good at all. "What're you doing? You've gotta get me back to Zormad."

"Back to Zormad? Honey, you were in a big ass hot spot back there. If I hadn't grabbed you right then, you'd be a whiff of vapor right now."

Selina's throat tensed as she thought of her group, the Regulation, Wexan, Jared. They were under attack, and she'd left them. "You don't understand. They're my people, they're all I know, all I have. My mother—"

Ket looked on her with compassion. "I'm sorry, I would've stuck around longer, but me and the Railen go way back, and not in a good way."

"Uh huh."

Selina glanced about the room for anything she could've used to bludgeon Ket for a quick getaway. But nothing looked promising enough, and then he said, "So, what's your name?"

"Selina. Now that we're exchanging names, you mind telling me what the hell you were doing with a ship around Zormad and NewEarth?"

Ket's eyes widened. "Really? I save your ass from getting vaped, and you're questioning me? I don't know if Xeno have a saying like 'thank you', but that's a customary response when people in Ling Galaxy get favors like the one I just did you."

"You took me from a fight. My people were being slaughtered by the Railen."

"Uh huh, and you'd have been there with them, charred remains in that field." Ket's mouth formed in a line. "Look, that Clutch I yanked you here with can throw anyone for a loop. Just sit there a few minutes, get your head together, then I'll school you on gratitude."

Selina wriggled back in her seat, put off by Ket's cavalier attitude. She racked her brain over why she was taken, and not others. Could Ket have known about the disruptor? She sighed with relief when she felt it still safely in its hiding spot. Not only that, the Railen Tracker was still there too.

Selina lay back down. As Ket left the room, she activated her Digivisor. The reddish block over Ket's frame made her chuckle and wonder where gratitude ended and obligation began.

GAMBIT OF DARES

ONE

KET DURBAN WAS ALMOST OUT OF TIME. The bridge of his ship, the *Crimson Lance*, rocked back and forth with the blasts of exploding weapons fire outside. To his right, his robot co-pilot W915 relayed the latest damage from the ship systems.

"Rear deflector shield at 15% capacity. Are you going to do something before we get obliterated?"

"Working on it, Dub." Ket eyed the radar scopes that showed his pursuer, a squadron of Railen fighters. They swarmed about his ship and took random shots at his hull.

Saying things hadn't gone quite as expected was an understatement, but as of late for Ket it was more of a normal. He'd been on a smuggling run for the gangster Osten Chavis, and while he got his agreed upon haul, in the process he and Dub were spotted by a Railen patrol all too willing to make him pay for his theft with everything.

"Status on the transient warp drive, Dub!" Ket bellowed as the ship buffeted wildly. Sparks flew from the control board.

"95% charged. You might want to know, if they hit us one more time in the hull, we're done for."

Never one to wade into a dangerous situation without at least one ace, the transient warp drive had filled the bill for Ket on more than one jaunt. The sophisticated nature of the warp gave the cunning an extra edge over those capable of tracking a standard warp drive, making transient warp a choice option of those who wanted to remain gone from their pursuers.

Ket's eyes stung with sweat. The Railen weren't known for backing down, and given the cargo he'd just stolen, being vaporized would've been about the nicest outcome for him.

Ket swung the ship in a corkscrew arcing maneuver. It slowed the Railen ships down a bit, but only for a few seconds. He'd been in close calls before, but this one wasn't looking good for his survival.

"Divert remaining shield energy to the transient drive, Dub."

"Say again? It sounded like you asked me to remove our shields."

"That's what I said; do it. Give me a go when transient is at 100%."

Another pop sounded outside, and the ship console coughed a bit of black smoke. Ket swung the ship wildly to avoid the piercing laser blasts, each of which begged to be the one that sliced the hull of the *Crimson Lance* and ended its existence once and for all.

"Transient warp drive 100 percent," W915 sounded.

Ket wasted none of the seconds they had left. He flicked the release on the transient warp drive and activated the engage lever. The *Crimson Lance* shuddered for a moment, then the ship was surrounded by swirling trails of light as the ship quickly slipped into the transient warp layer and left their pursuers shooting at empty space.

THE FORWARD VIEW of the *Crimson Lance* changed to peaceful space, with a large system in the near distance. Ket looked at the bluish and red ball for a few moments.

"Dub, get our location from the onboard system."

Dub's robotic appendages went to work on the ship computer; multiple arms typed and manipulated holographic controls with no response other than assorted beeps and a glow on the console. As a 900 series robot, Dub was versatile in operating onboard ship systems for the *Crimson Lance*, not to mention hijacking the computers of other star craft. While a 900 was in demand for the massive amount of tasks the UA handled regularly, for a smuggler who sometimes needed a quick save for survival, the 900 was more than just a handy asset to have around.

"Approximate location is 17th sector of Quadrant 45, approximately 200,000 light cycles from our last position."

"Hmm, far enough from the Railen for now. How close are we to the Wenzo system?"

Dub worked the computer again for a few moments. "Approximately 2500 miles. Based on present fuel capacity, estimate three hours best possible speed."

"Lock us in; we gotta get somewhere with fuel first thing, even if we coast there on space wind."

Wenzo system was home port for a lot of smuggling types. That factoid wasn't exactly what would've been on a brochure for tourists frequenting the system, but the nefarious and shrewd knew well enough that if you're any kind of decent smuggler, you'll find a good amount of trade on Wenzo somewhere; just don't tell anyone or it's your ass.

While Dub locked in the necessary course for their trip, Ket launched himself up from his seat to stretch a moment. Time to think wasn't something he always had luxury for, and he figured he best collect his thoughts on what went wrong, and more so, what he was going to tell Osten Chavis when they met again, at least about the haul.

Ket headed to the cargo hold to view his stash. Thankfully, as close as he and Dub had come back there to buying it, their payload was left unscathed. Ket plopped himself on an empty crate in the corner and watched their cargo: ten reactor cores. They glowed with a brilliant yellow hue that was only dimmed by the protective casing enough not to be blinding. The cores were essential for a lot of things that included starcraft travel but also rudimentary power generation. In a Galaxy choked for energy, cores like the ones Ket had were way better than gold.

The job had gone OK for a while. As Ket would've put it, he and Dub had creatively inserted themselves into a Railen depot and liberated a few of their power generation inventory in the name of freeing inventory space. He laughed at how simple that part was, and he thought about how Chavis had shown him how to do it. The man was like a father figure to Ket, closest as he'd had anyway. Ket's real father wasn't a favorite topic of discussion, and the mere mention of him was known to provoke a pretty ugly reaction in Ket. Ket hadn't seen him in cycles, and he liked to believe his father was long dead. That was his hope, anyway.

Ket proceeded to the galley to see what rations were left. The typical job they went on included a meager supply of what they needed to finish the work, so things were near empty, but Ket figured a quick supply run at Wenzo would do the trick once he settled up with Osten.

After he had some food, Ket settled into a lounge chair near the galley. He'd nestled himself in and started drifting out of consciousness when the ship overhead comm burst to life with Dub's voice.

"Course plotted for the Wenzo system. Are you going to lie on your ass the whole way there and make me monitor everything?"

A yawn escaped Ket as he answered, "Yes. Keep an eye on the scope for any nasties. I'm grabbing a power nap. Wake me if there's trouble."

Ket drifted to sleep with visions of his payment and some pretty rude comments about himself from Dub.

TWO

KET'S SLUMBER WAS INVADED BY THE sound of an echoed electronic voice. What it said was muffled at first, but soon the words became clear and were punctuated with gentle shoves. Finally, Ket's eyes opened into the face of Dub.

"We're here."

Ket flung his arms about in an attempt to stretch. "You could've let me sleep a little more; I was having a good dream."

"I hardly think so. I've pulled into the fuel repository. They're a little backed up. We must leave it for now; ready in approximately two Wenzo hours."

Ket nodded and swiped a hand over his face. "Fair enough. I'm gonna get a drink. Wanna join? For the change of scenery?"

"I suppose." Dub's lower half reconfigured itself through a series of whirrs and clicks until a set of wheels appeared, and they headed off ship.

The town of Marwen on the Wenzo system wasn't much of a town—more of a collection of shanties and markets strewn together like a load of dirty laundry. The fuel depot was a popular spot, but also well frequented was the Dark Passage, equal parts dive bar, greasy spoon, and arguably the best place in Ling Galaxy for a troublemaker who wanted an ample supply of mischief.

Ket and Dub pulled up to the bar. While Ket got the attention of the barkeep, Dub adjusted his system to scan mode. It was a familiar practice for the robot, as historically Ket needed Dub's help on more than a few occasions in a scuffle. Dub always had handy a stat on the number of times Ket's scuffles were Ket's own fault, but Dub knew better than bothering Ket with facts Ket wasn't ready for yet.

Ket swung back around and watched the scene with Dub. It was an average crowd; the tables around the room were filled with collections of the typical bad sorts. Space pilots bragging about their latest blockade run, waitresses navigating the room and the wanton gropes from patrons in a mixed state of hungry, thirsty, and horny. A few other robots were around as well, since there wasn't any such thing as being too careful in a place like the Dark Passage.

"You sure the hold is secure, right?" Ket asked.

Dub's head swiveled slowly to look right in Ket's eyes. "Of course it is. What do you think I did while your lazy ass slept?"

"Hey, this is a big haul for us; excuse me for being a little paranoid."

"You might help that paranoia if you don't speak too much about that in a public place then."

Ket smirked and swallowed a gulp of his drink. He was about to ask Dub about any ship repairs when Ket heard a familiar voice to his left.

"What's up, asshole?"

Sidewinder flashed Ket and Dub a cocky smirk as he plopped himself down next to Ket. A bottle in one hand, he swiped his other through his mane of thick black hair. "So, whatcha got goin on?"

"None of your damn business, jerkoff. The hell you doing here, anyway?"

"Chilling, scouting out hauls, the usual." Sidewinder cast a look around and spat.

Ket and Sidewinder had known each other since their childhood as part of Osten Chavis' collection of lost children, an orphanage cum criminal enterprise where the most forlorn of young minds that ached for the love and protection of parents found instead a calling in the lucrative and adventurous field of thievery. Osten cared for them, and in return for the majority of the take from the kids' respective heists, they were given a place to live, food and the basics, and someone who they referred to as Papa Chavis.

Once he finished his manual and somewhat inebriated assessment of their fellow scumbag patrons, Sidewinder nudged Ket's shoulder. "So, how much did ya get?"

"Whatdya mean?"

"Ket, cut the crap. You're the best person ever to play poker with 'cause you can't lie to save your right arm. You got that twinkle going on in your eye. Unless you and Dub here just had a quickie behind the bar, I bet my right nut you just busted out a big score. Come on, man, out with it. We know it's going to Papa Chavis anyway."

Ket sighed. Though Sidewinder was for all purposes a brother to him, the endless competition irked Ket after a while. Once they'd graduated from the ranks of pickpocketing and small theft into interstellar smuggling, Ket took a modest amount of joy in the runs he made with just him and Dub, since they hadn't involved any amount of cockswinging that people like Sidewinder participated in for the hell of it. "Yeah, you're right, I'm bringing it to the Old Man, so if you're so hard up for scoop, why don't you bug his ass about it?"

Ket glanced to the front of the room again. Sidewinder gazed slowly and took a drink in thought. "Damn, Ket. I see how you wanna be. Well, don't let me pick you outta whatever funk your ass is in." Sidewinder stood up and nodded to Dub. "Hey, Dub, take care of this loser for me, alright?"

As Sidewinder sauntered off, Dub gave Ket the best disdainful look a robot could've ever hoped to pull. "Sidewinder isn't the childhood friend you recall, if any of the data I've come across has any merit."

"Oh? Do tell." Ket leaned closer to his partner.

Dub perused his back files while he executed a subroutine to continue his previous monitoring and collateral watching Ket's back. "I'm seeing evidence of him being an informant for some UA entities, but it's spotty reports so far."

"Damn, Dub, you telling me robots gossip too?"

Dub eyed Ket again. "We're well behind the less nimble-witted living creatures of Ling Galaxy when it comes to mindless chatter like gossip."

Ket marveled at Dub's news. He hadn't kept as close tabs on Sidewinder, but he'd heard that Papa Chavis had cut a few less than stellar earners loose, and the Syndicate had scooped up a few random hands for jobs here and there. But Dub's news was the first time Ket heard of anyone helping out the UA. What the hell kinda deal was there with the UA that was better than the smuggling and syndicate trade?

Another more pleasant voice called out behind Ket, this time a female.

"Well, if it ain't fast talking, no tab paying Durban."

Ket and Dub faced the bar and Dian, the regular bartender who made a practice of flinging out drinks as well as the occasional pearl of info to the lucky soul picked to receive it.

Dian grinned at the duo before she eyed the spot Sidewinder recently vacated. "Gotta say, Sidewinder missed a nice tasty bit of smuggler scoop, walking away like that."

Ket leaned closer. "Yeah? What's cooking? You got some good news for a kinda old flame?"

Dian batted her eyes and added a smirk before she reached for a few empty glasses that were actually clean. "Oh really, Durban? That's how this is? We hook up a few times, you get your pulse pistol off, I don't hear from you for a Wexian month and now you're all hot for what I got to say?"

Ket shrugged, and watched the dark brown liquid of his drink as it made a circular dance. "Aww, Dian, I don't know what to tell ya. I had to bust outta here quick; ya know the Railen have that death warrant on me and all."

Dian clasped Ket's chin between two fingers. "Ya could've called, smuggler boy. Anyhow, you wouldn't be into this kinda news. It's not your average smuggling job."

As Ket reared back in his seat, Dub amused himself at how easy his partner not only lost dignity, but hilariously failed at hiding his hurt ego.

"I'm not your average smuggler."

Dian bit her lip to stifle a laugh but failed and clutched the two glasses on the bar as she bowed her head in snickers. "Oh Ket, you're impossibly predictable. It's a good thing you're so damn cute, or I'd have you bounced outta here any old time."

Dian's wispy blonde hair flowed about her face, and a few of the locks drifted over her eyes a bit. But her eyes were fixed on Ket with a variety of colors. She wasn't exactly a one-man girl anyway, but Ket had thrown her for a loop in their tryst. It was a red-hot affair that ended pretty quick over the simple fact that Ket wanted to remain among the living, but that left many unanswered questions between them, a mystery they shared that looked to be unsolvable. The feelings that hadn't had time to take hold were instead placed below like so many cubes of ice in the bar to either be used or discarded someday.

"Come on, Dian. Look, if I'd have stayed around, it's a good chance you'd be talking to my grave somewhere. You gotta know I didn't mean to bail like I did."

Dian folded her arms. "Maybe you didn't, or maybe you did, we'll never know. It's kinda handy you have that as an out, though, without having to actually tell me to my face you weren't interested anymore. Anyway, I'm a big girl, and don't think for one second you're not one of a dozen flyboys popping in here, swinging your dicks around and looking for the latest piece. You've been around; so have I."

"Fair enough, Dian. Now, you gonna spill this news or am I gonna have to buy more booze from you first?"

Before Dian said anything else, one of Ket's stool neighbors a few places down called out a drink order. While Dian tended her business, Ket writhed his hands together tightly. The Dark Passage wasn't a stranger to the big deals offered to tradespeople willing to do anything for a haul. Ket hadn't even needed to ask Dub's take on this; Ket's manually operated swindle sense was tingling off the charts.

After a few more moments, Dian returned. "OK, so the other day I'm in here, the usual night. A fight or two, couple of pricks with their hands on some of the girls, yadda yadda. Then this guy in a heavy cloak and hood sets down at the bar. He's all alone and on the creepy side."

Ket's brow raised. Saying anyone in the Dark Passage looked creepy was quite a statement. "What did he look like?"

"Well, that's just it. He had this hood and never really lifted it up for me to see. All's I saw was these deep blue-green eyes glowing at me." Dian leaned a bit closer. "I ask him what he wants to drink, and aside from ordering some Grondian ale he asks about the smuggler for hire situation. As I'm pouring his drink, I ask him what he's looking for, ya know, type of cargo, security concerns, the usual."

"Yeah, so what was it?"

Dian leaned further to whisper into Ket's ear. "He's looking for Railen Trackers, and he'll pay top prices for them."

A chill shot through Ket. Railen Trackers were used to locate and capture Lookers. Lookers' ability to skip across dimensions made them extremely valuable, so the trackers were just as important. The Railen had created them for locating the Lookers to help with navigating back to Grondia, but word quickly got out on the devices. Ling Galaxy was fast on the bandwagon as well, and it meant an open season and uber bidding war on the choice bit of Railen tech.

"Dian, I know you're pissed at me, but you really giving me this tip now? As hot as I am with the Railen, if they find me with a tracker, my ass is beyond dead."

Dian squared her shoulders. "That's the scoop, Ket. You grab one of those, you'll need an intergalactic freighter to hold all the UA credits."

As risky as a move like grabbing a tracker was, Ket realized everything Dian said was true. Among the hauls he'd done over the cycles, none even came close to this in scale. Ket downed the last of his drink. "Alright, Dian, good seeing you again. Lemme get some grub to go; I gotta stop in on Papa Chavis before I do anything else."

"Alright, hon." Dian slid a scrap of paper over to Ket. "Hold onto this. You wanna take that offer up, you'll need to contact them."

As Dian went off to get Ket's food, he took a glance at the paper. The contact info was scrawled toward the bottom, but what shocked him was the name at the top: Malone StantonKet's mind tossed the name around like a beach ball as he headed back to the fuel depot with Dub for their ship. Was the stranger who talked with Dian working for Malone? It was too much to call coincidence that this Railen Tracker job's contact just so happened to have a note from the most notorious criminal in Ling Galaxy with it.

The name Malone Stanton was more than just familiar to Ket, of course. He'd heard it from time to time on his runs; it was spoken about with a boogeyman reverence or fear. Ket's dealings were on the small to medium trade, and he heard Malone's dealings were on the realm of galactic conquest. The latest on Malone was his search for Essence in order to manipulate and control it. Ket had also heard Malone planned a physical merge with the Essence and his body itself. Of course, details and reports over Network were just as rife with BS as with gospel truths.

What was wholly evident was the life generating and sustaining Essence was the ultimate power for anyone with the ability to control it. Any fears Ket had over someone like Malone with that power were balanced with his curiosity on the angle for himself, not to mention the hefty take involved if he played things just right in the Tracker Heist and anything involving Essence that may have been on the horizon.

THREE

ONCE KET DOWNED HIS FOOD, HE AND DUB flew the *Crimson Lance* to Osten Chavis' compound. The massive fortress stood alone in a wasteland area of Wenzo, with plenty enough visual space for identifying if approaching ships were friendly or not... a preferred amenity for life on the Wenzo system for anyone whose income came from anything but reputable means. Ket docked his ship at the adjacent port area and with Dub brought their cargo in.

Osten met them in the large entrance foyer. He greeted them both with open arms. "My boys, look at what you've got." He pressed his large belly to Ket in a bear hug and only released to pat Dub on the arm. "How was the run; any trouble?"

"You could say that; a squadron of Railen gave chase, but I finally shook them." Ket grabbed his neck.

"Must've been pretty dangerous; I hadn't expected them to be that active."

"Guess they're stepping up their security."

Osten nodded. "No doubt. I'm hearing stories about Railen Trackers on the loose and a lot of people going after them."

Ket felt an urge to mention his note from Dian, but something held him back. Dub eyed him with a bit of curiosity and said, "Actually, we just heard—"

"The Railen have been after the Omegans and are more active because of that." Ket eyed Dub.

Osten's eyes squinted. After a pause, he nodded a bit. "Oh right; you best avoid that pissing match. The Omegans and Railen want bloodshed and conquest. War's too messy. I like my income safe with smuggling and the like. Plenty enough of that still going on, especially if you avoid the lawkeepers. Well, come inside. I'll get your bounty for this, and you can stick around if you want."

Osten summoned one of his seconds to handle the reactor core haul and their payment. While Osten headed inside, Ket and Dub followed from a safe distance.

"Why did you cut me off?" asked Dub.

"Because we don't want the old man knowing about this other run yet," Ket hissed. He still processed the whole idea, and he figured it best he didn't let onto Chavis about taking the job for finding a Railen Tracker. The potential payoff would've set up a whole new future for Ket. As fatherly a figure Chavis had been to him, there was no way Ket was gonna slip by without a hefty kickback to the old man if he was in the know. Ket had done much in his time as a smuggler, but his thoughts lately had progressed beyond the capers, and millions of UA Credits sure seemed like a great start at a new chapter.

Ket and Dub headed to Osten's parlor while Osten verified the cargo and his people retrieved Ket's payment. Ket had spent a lot of time here in his youth, from when he was a boarder to when Osten broke him in as a pilot. The longer he sat in the room, the more he wondered if he was ready for what he had in mind.

Ket helped himself to some Wenzian liquor from Osten's stash. He slumped back into a chair and relaxed a bit until he caught Dub's curious glance toward him.

"What? You still chapped I cut you off back there?"

"No. For your information, I do a lot of calculations that have nothing to do with you at all." The digital board on Dub's center console backed up his retort, Ket noticed it flash a series of maps and what looked like coordinates for warp jumps.

"Well, fine. Then how about you do me a solid and let me know what the hell my co-pilot is up to? Otherwise, it looks like you're malfunctioning over there."

Dub's readout went blank, and he cocked his head. "If you must know, I did some preliminary scans on reports of Trackers in the surrounding systems. If we're going on this insane stunt of a run, I figure our chances, at least my chances, of not getting blown to bits, come down to locating the Tracker with the least amount of visibility on it."

Ket ran his hand through his hair. At times like this, he wondered if the idea of a replacement for Dub on the *Crimson Lance* wasn't so dumb after all. "OK, Brainiod. You gonna share the details so, you know, I can like, get us there when we need to?"

Dub's unit processed more but suddenly went quiet, and a moment later Osten's booming voice explained why. "OK, you're good. Twenty thousand UA credits, less my portion means six thousand credits for you. I'm having them loaded onto the *Crimson Lance*." Osten took one of the plush seats and leaned back, a chilled cocktail in his hand.

Ket took a sip of his drink. "That's great; thanks, boss."

"No problem. But there is one other thing I need to warn you about." Osten leaned forward, and set his drink on a nearby table. "Ket, I've known you a long time. I remember before you even had Dub at your side. You were one of my best learners and even better earners out there, running scams, skirting trouble and the law, and making your Papa Chavis proud."

Tightness seized Ket's throat. He'd gotten too comfortable and forgotten about Osten's listening devices in the parlor.

"Ket, I know you're planning on a run to get a Tracker. You don't get into a position like mine without taking all kinds of precautions, even monitoring your own home for people thinking of trying something foolhardy or even dangerous."

Ket clasped his glass tight; he felt his face flush. Osten was a kind man, but Ket and most people knew that mistaking that benevolence for weakness was pretty dumb.

Osten looked at Ket and Dub with the eyes of a disapproving parent. "You know, it's not so much your idea to set out on such a foolish run; it's the fact you tried hiding it from me that worries me."

Osten lightly grasped Ket's shoulder, but the look in Osten's eye didn't make him any less anxious about it. "Papa, I know it's risky, and you're right. I should've been more up front about it. It's just, I have to try this. You've given me so much; I won't ever be able to repay you fully."

Chavis nodded slowly. "Don't think I'm not aware of the bounty on the Railen Trackers, Ket. Even seventy percent of that take is the kind of money that will let you do anything you want afterward. Just think it over, son. What good's a reward if you ain't alive to use it?"

"Point taken, Papa, for sure." Ket nodded. Osten leaned back in his chair and eyed Ket with a sense of wonder. "You know, sometimes it's hard for me to not see you as that little boy you once were, thieving on the systems we went to."

Ket smiled at the memory. Some would've called Osten's arrangement with his kids nothing short of extortion and most definitely exploitation. It wasn't completely without consequence, though. Ket did several incarcerated terms for his dalliances. Besides the criminal penalties, Ket's work for Osten gave Ket the approval he needed, that feeling of belonging he never had from his real father. Besides his mother, Ket got the sense of being someone who mattered mainly from Osten. The memory also served to ramp up the guilt Ket had about trying to sidestep his mentor on the biggest job of his life.

"I'll cut you in on it, Papa. I swear."

Osten chuckled. "I've no doubt. Just take care of that ship and yourself; you've already got the Railen out for you. Remember, if you get your hands on the tracker and the wrong people find out, there's no army in Ling Galaxy that'll be able to save you, not even mine."

ONCE KET CLEARED THE AIR, he joined Osten and several other of the smuggler crew for a night's feast paired with a taste of Osten's gallery of wenches. His bodily needs met for a little while, he and Dub set out in the *Crimson Lance* the following morning, with Osten's half-hearted farewell. Ket knew, as much as Osten had offered his moderate approval of Ket's run, that he was on his own. On a normal smuggling operation, Ket as well as the rest of Osten's clan had the option of calling for assistance if things got too shaky. Ket had been on the verge of doing that when he was overrun by the Railen squadron, and had he not been able to warp out of danger, a call to Osten's Network was his last shot.

But this run was different. Ket had digested the logistics of it along with his prior evening of debauchery. While he still could've easily ignored the opportunity, he knew that as much as he bragged about the badass he claimed to be, if he grabbed a Railen Tracker, it would without any doubt cement Ket's status in the lore of smuggler runs as an all-time great.

Before fortune and glory were his, though, Ket knew he had to book the run. Once he returned to the *Crimson Lance* and Dub activated the blocking mechanisms to prevent location detection, he used the scribbled note and hailed Dian's mysterious patron on the *Crimson Lance* comm system.

A dark figure appeared on the hologram platform in front of Ket. A pair of glowing blue eyes glared back at Ket. Then, a mouth appeared on the face, a thin line that opened up as a third bluish glow. "Yes?"

"Um, I understand you're looking for Railen Trackers."

The face said nothing for a moment. Ket wondered if the connection had been broken, but then they replied, "What makes you think I am?"

"Because I heard from someone at the Dark Passage you came in looking for a smuggler to make a run."

Blue eyes chuckled. "Of course. Yes, I'm interested in getting a Railen Tracker. If you're willing to accept this run, I'll need a few details first, as well as give you a few instructions."

"You need details from me? Like my criminal record or something?"

Blue eyes narrowed their gaze into a sneer. "Don't be ludicrous. What I'm asking for is certainly highly risky, and of course the reward is commensurate. I'll need your ship tail code and information on your crew, so in the improbable case you are successful in this caper, I or my associates won't blast you into space dust when you make the rendezvous."

Ket swallowed hard. Some pep talk. "Fair enough."

The blue eyed meany continued. "This run carries with it a high probability of failure, and of that I'm nearly sure will be your result. That said, in the remote chance you are able to get this device successfully, I'm transmitting through this communication exact coordinates for you to deposit said tracker. Once it is in this location, I'll be notified and only then will the credits be transferred to you. Here's the part where you share with me where I should send your payment in the remote chance you are successful."

Ket shook his head. He'd had more encouraging pep talks from prison wardens. "Understood. Just keep your checkbook handy, blue eyes. Don't go buying a new cloak just yet."

Blue eyes deepened their glare in reply. "This shall be our first and only transmission. I suggest you don't cross me on this, as you'll be invoking retribution the likes of which you could scarcely imagine."

Ket had kept the charade up for a while, but the fact he'd made a deal that could've meant his life with this relative stranger had Ket a little twitchy. "Alright then. Good talk." Ket nodded and ended the transmission.

FOUR

THE *CRIMSON LANCE* HAD JUST REACHED suborbital status above the Wenzo system when Dub said, "I suppose you're ready for that info I had for you last night?"

Ket lined up the ship for its initial push into deep space. "Yes, dear. Please don't toy with my emotions any further."

"I've tracked several potential locations for Railen Trackers in nearby quadrants. If my analysis is correct, and I can't imagine it wouldn't be, much of these trackers are locked up with Railen military units. If we try to steal one, we will likely find ourselves in a situation much worse than the reactor core caper."

"Oh good, I was afraid you'd say it was gonna be hard," Ket muttered as he twisted the ship's steering yoke into position to avoid a cluster of approaching asteroids.

Dub continued, "However, there is one location that could give us a decent shot at a Tracker without much resistance."

"Go on."

Dub paused and checked some of the ship monitors on their console. "Of all the signals I registered, one popped on my scope. It's a fairly new update, so I'm wondering if this device had been inactive and suddenly turned on after a while."

"Sounds like a girl I once knew." Ket snickered. "Where?"

"Zormad system."

"Zormad? That junk heap? Sure you're not malfunctioning there, Dub ol buddy? Zormad's been the asshole of Ling Galaxy for a while; their main industry is junkers trading scrap for nicer scrap."

"I'm telling you, there's one there. The signature matches those I've verified in Railen possession."

Ket studied his mechanical partner and thought of all the times they'd pulled successful heists. There were plenty of busts in with the hauls, but Ket still fancied himself a gambler to take the risk. "It's a huge payday, Dub. Let's try your lead on Zormad. Besides, we've no way of knowing who else this Hood guy made a deal with, and I don't feel like being on yet another list. Set course for Zormad."

The pitch and yaw thrusters on the *Crimson Lance* adjusted to line the craft up for its warp jump. The first part of their trip, where the craft was aligned for its intended course, was manual. But once they'd entered the coordinates, the system took care of the rest. They were just there in case any manual overrides were needed. Ket patted the console as if the ship were a faithful steed, ready for its trek around a racecourse. "Atta girl, gimme some good money on this run; good luck's the tip."

Ket settled back into his seat. He'd earned the *Crimson Lance* from Osten. As part of his upbringing, as well as the other kids Osten nursed into a life of crime, Ket's earnings over the cycles went toward purchase of a starcraft. With each successful heist, from simple pickpockets to thefts petty and not so petty, Osten set aside a piece toward a ship for each of his kids. It was way more than benevolence, and the kids figured it out sooner or later. With a fleet of ships at his disposal and loyal employees he'd reared from diapers to deviancy, Osten's operations soon extended to the furthest reaches of Ling Galaxy in a generation or two.

Ket's memory of getting the *Crimson Lance* was impossible to

shake, and in light of his decision for making this run, Ket knew he had to make good by his mentor. Equally jarring though were the words of Osten about Ket being on his own. Ket knew this wasn't in Osten's mind when he gave him the *Crimson Lance*, but Ket also knew without making his bones on his own, he'd never be out from under Osten's shadow.

A series of chimes rang on the console. Ket smirked, knowing what the notification sound meant already, but of course Dub was one for proper procedure. "Warp Course confirmed by on-board navigation console. Warp jump in 3... 2... 1..."

An echoed thud vibrated through the ship bridge, and the craft shot forward at sub light speed.

Once the ship stabilized on its course, Ket got up again from the controls. "ETA for Zormad?" he asked Dub.

"Approximately one-hour, present speed."

"Good enough. I'm gonna check out the Clutch system, see if it's ready in case we have to make a quick grab and go." The Clutch system was a handy tool for any smuggler of note; it provided simple teleportation for objects up to a certain size. The only requirement was to be in near proximity of the item, at least within one mile. Ket activated the console for the device and began running through some diagnostics when a voice from out of nowhere startled the crap out of him.

"That's very fancy."

Ket flung himself to the floor and sprung up, pulse pistol poised for action. "Who the hell said that?" He searched the room, but after a few seconds it was obvious—a translucent, bluish humanoid form stepped toward him from behind several power consoles toward the rear of the room.

"Easy there; stay where you are!" Ket barked. His pistol shook a little. The form approached, and Ket made out feminine features.

"Hate to tell you, but your weapon won't do a thing to me. Besides, at your present velocity, I don't think firing a shot through your ship's hull is the best idea."

"Neither is letting someone waltz onto my ship and do God knows what." Ket's hand squeezed tight around the handle of his weapon. "Now then, who... or what... the hell are you, and how the hell did you get onto my ship?"

"What I am doesn't really matter to you, but if you're determined to know more about me, you can call me Julina. As for how I arrived here, I'm a little surprised at that turn of events myself. For all purposes, I wasn't supposed to wind up here—wherever 'here' is, anyway."

"At least we can agree on that. Here's the deal, Julina: this is my ship. I'm not UA Military, so there's no jurisdictional whatever here. You got five seconds to leave out the way you came, or we find out how wrong you are about me blasting your ass with this pistol."

Julina shook her head. "Oh. You're one of those smuggler types. Can't say I'm very surprised, given you're ready to shoot me even though I already told you it's pointless. Well, then, since I'm here, let's just see what I can make use of."

The next thing Ket knew, he was engulfed in a blue glow similar to the one around Julina, then it was gone, along with his pistol, and he was locked up inside the Clutch machine.

Alarms sounded on the ship, and when he glanced out into the room, Julina was gone.

Ket grabbed the comm unit on his wrist. "Dub, warning, we've got a stowaway aboard; seal the bridge."

After a second, Dub answered. "Oh, is that right? Maybe that explains what happened; our weapons systems are gone."

Ket slammed the door release, and darted out of the Clutch chamber. If Julina took any part of their ship, there was no telling what else was screwed besides their weapons.

"Damned Lookers, messing around where they've got no business," Ket muttered to himself as he stormed through access corridors and down levels until he was at the engine bay of the *Crimson Lance*. Once he surveyed the room for a minute, he contacted Dub on the intercom.

"Yeah, Dub, this Looker chick, she trashed the damned place. We best hope we don't get any action like we did from the Railen last time; ain't no shooting and scooting now. We're gonna have to run with no guns and hope no one gets a bead on us before we get away."

Dub's voice crackled over the speakers in response. "Affirmative. We're about another hour out from Zormad, present speed."

Ket reached for a piece of wire on the floor and flung it hard against the far wall. "I'll be up in a few."

———

THE *CRIMSON LANCE* finished its trek to Zormad. Dub activated the tracking system on the bridge, which displayed a reddish grid of their area. The Railen Tracker was marked with a glowing triangle. "We're near the outskirts of Tas Ralong. The Tracker is a few miles on the other side, some settlement called NewEarth," Dub reported.

"Settlements, huh? Think we'd find some good stuff for trade out there, like weapons system components?"

Dub eyed the map closer. "I doubt it. These settlements are typically for the dregs. People shouldn't assume a world is better just because they came to it from their last one."

"Easy there, Dub, you don't know what happened to them; their world could've been blown up or something."

Dub looked at Ket for a moment. "Or, their world was destroyed in a war of their making and they brought the fight with them." Dub pointed at the map, zoomed in to show a collection of troops and vehicles engaged in a firefight.

Ket leaned closer to the display. "Zoom in tighter; I wanna see who's there."

The map responded to Ket's command, enlarging the scene until it was clear. A group of people from NewEarth held their ground from behind vehicles and piles of rubble, but it was obvious they were outnumbered. Ket knew why; he immediately recognized the Railen insignia and the look of the ship in the background.

"The Tracker's in the middle of that?" Ket muttered.

Dub nodded in reply. "We go in there, I don't have to tell you how it'll go for us, do I?"

Ket rubbed his face. Every smuggling run, and all the petty thefts he did, all had some kind of risk in them. But the risk in those other jobs was mainly in getting away before being caught. A thief's life was more about deception and elusion. Ket had been in fights and held his own, but a brawl like this, with military action involved? Even if he wasn't personally known by those Railen, a simple run of his record would've displayed that death warrant plain and clear, and Railen were never ones that held back on something like that.

Dub's metallic tentacled fingers slid over the navigation controls. "We can bail right now, figure out some other job, and live to laugh about this another day."

Ket had a million thoughts pass through his mind right then, but he still held quiet. His mind offered several cursory images of Blue-Eyed Hood Guy, and whatever the retribution for Ket's failure might have looked like.

Ket focused himself with more positive thoughts. Easy, Ket buddy. Keep your head. Papa Chavis always said gotta play your hand nice and cool; wait until you see all the options. That's when the best one shows up.

Ket moved the view of the battle around on the screen, motioning with his hands to redirect the video before them. The scene twisted about until he focused on the NewEarth force. He froze on one of them. He wasn't sure why, but something made him look at this one. A young adult Xeno woman. Either she hadn't realized it, she didn't care, or no one else told her she should've been scared outta her mind, because she stood her ground and fired blasts at the Railen troops. Her black hair billowed around her as she aimed her weapon at the advancing Railen.

Ket froze when he noticed the marker on their console that indicated the Tracker location was over the black-haired girl. His eyes still fixed on her, he muttered to Dub, "Set the Clutch."

"Are you sure, Ket? I thought we had to be closer than this."

"We will be. Target that girl; it's on her. We don't have time to lock on just the device; better make a grab for her too."

"This is no time for harem building, Ket."

"Just do it, dammit!" Ket activated the steering controls at his console as Dub readied the Clutch. Ket rolled the ship wildly and gunned the engine. "Once we grab her, we gotta book out fast. Plot a course and stand by with the transient warp as soon as the clutch is complete."

They began their approach, shooting alongside a large transport ship in a state of disrepair. Ket gunned the engines until he and Dub lurched back in their seats. When they were fifty yards out, a few shots from the fray below slammed their hull.

"OK, they're shooting at us now. Dub, are you waiting for an invitation? Fire the damn Clutch!"

"A few more meters and we've got it!" Dub barked in response.

Several more shots pinged the *Crimson Lance*.

"Now or never, Dub!"

Dub smashed the control for the Clutch. A deep hum resonated in the cabin. Ket wrestled the controls on the ship as they entered the battle area. "We good?"

"Yes, cargo safely aboard," Dub replied.

With catlike reflexes, Ket wrangled the control yoke of the *Crimson Lance*. His eyes fixed on straight ahead, he muttered, "Hit it."

Amid a chorus of alerts from their ship console about various missile and gun locks on their craft, Dub activated the Transient Warp, and they zipped away from the scene instantly.

"Keep those engines at max, Dub, and find us a safe haven. I don't care if it's a friendly looking asteroid, we've gotta hide and fast, especially if those Railen find out what we took."

Ket took off for the Clutch hold, the repository for their haul. Ket had no idea how he was going to handle the girl, though. He wasn't in the kidnapping game; she was just extra collateral from the haul. One thing he knew—he had to make sure she was incapacitated. The way she handled herself in that fight, he had to make sure she was bound up. The one trouble-making female they already had on this trip was far more than enough.

Ket saw her through the portal to the Clutch repository. She was sprawled on her back, unconscious. Her outfit was either militia or lawkeeper, Ket wasn't sure.

He opened the portal to the repository and stepped toward her. She's as young as I thought she was, he thought. Wow, I'd have expected they left perimeter defense for more seasoned types. Xeno must just like wasting lives, he thought. As he got closer, he glanced over her frame for any obvious hiding places, but aside from the skintight envirosuit, the only clear possibility was beneath her chest. Alright, Ket, keep it together, no need to focus on the carnal instincts here. This is a simple pickpocket, just like you did hundreds of times for Papa Chavis back in the old days. Besides, your victim's unconscious so you won't have to subdue anyone.

The UA Crest on her uniform made him stop before he pilfered too far. As a seasoned thief, Ket knew well about the defensive mechanisms of the UA, and while rigging personnel uniforms with tamper charges wasn't exactly a known practice, Ket valued his appendages a little too much for rushing anything until they had more time.

Ket gently lifted the Xeno female up and brought her to one of the cargo rooms. As he laid her down on a spare bed unit, a barrage of static burst out from the comm unit on her uniform. Ket froze and listened to the garble that quickly formed into words.

"Proximal 1 to base, acknowledge."

"Base here, receiving full strength Proximal 1, proceed."

"Identified location of Railen Tracker and are proceeding on intercept course. Will update on progress, out."

Ket felt uneasy. So much for a simple getaway. Was that the Railen? Ket wondered. He called Dub on the bridge and warned him to keep an eye out.

Back on the bridge, Dub noticed on radar a squadron of Cerulak ships headed on an intercept course with the *Crimson Lance*. The Cerulaks definitely weren't Railen, which should've been a consolation, but Dub well knew what they were after.

The Cerulak race in general were known as one of the more notorious breeds of scavengers and smugglers in Ling Galaxy and definitely not ones to cross. Their standard MO for getting their target was to locate and even allow someone else to capture it before retrieving said cargo and blasting their ship into vapor.

Dub's worried voice crackled over the comm. "Our company has already arrived; you better get up here."

Dub engaged the ship's thrusters so they avoided the oncoming barrage of weapons fire. Blasts sounded about the ship. The door to the bridge flung open and Ket hopped into his seat.

"Did you get it?" Dub asked.

"So far, just got her name... Selina. She's wearing a UA Suit, Dub. Gotta make sure it's disarmed first," Ket replied.

A shot thumped the underside of the *Crimson Lance* and made the cabin buffet wildly. "Damn, we can't keep this up," Ket muttered.

"They're toying with us, I think," Dub commented. "They have sufficient firepower to vaporize us and yet they don't. Furthermore, we need time for the drive to recharge before we can do another Transient Warp."

Ket nodded. "I heard chatter on the Xeno's comm from our new Cerulak 'friends'. Seems we're not the only ones hot and heavy for Railen Trackers in these parts."

As if to confirm Ket's suspicion, the bridge comm signaled an incoming transmission. Dub activated the receiver and a voice boomed over the speaker. "Calling Zion class cruiser, acknowledge."

Ket tapped the control to open the communication. "*Crimson Lance* here; what the hell are you blasting our ship for?"

"It should be obvious. We've identified a Railen Tracker aboard your craft."

"The hell you talking about?"

"To whom do I have the pleasure of speaking?"

"Ket Durban, what's it to ya?"

"Ket Durban, you can call me Tarmun. I'm leader of this Cerulak squadron."

"Good for you," Ket replied flatly.

"I can assume you are a smuggler, or at least a thief of note?"

"That's among the nicer things I've been called. Suppose your equipment isn't off the mark and I have this Railen Tracker. What are you and your squadron gonna do, blow us all into space dust?"

Tarmun's chuckle filled the bridge. Dub looked at Ket quizzically. There were no ship maneuvers or warps out of this spot. This one required a bit of finesse, and Dub had doubts how much of that Ket had in reserve.

Tarmun continued, "Of course, we aren't interested in losing an item like that, but you need to know how serious we are. I hope you have intelligence to know avoiding a warp chase would be most prudent."

"OK, fine, I'm not an idiot. Don't punch holes in my ship, and we'll talk."

"A sensible response. Now then, as we speak, I'm having one of my ships tether to yours. We'll then board and retrieve the item from you before letting you, your ship and crew loose."

"Mmmhmmm. You heard where I said I'm not an idiot, right? Once you get this tracker, what's to stop you from blasting us into oblivion?"

"Oh Mr. Durban, surely you realize you don't have an option here."

The console lit up with a proximity alert, and the ship powered down.

Ket bolted back to the room where he'd left Selina. She was on her feet and started toward the door once Ket entered.

"Easy, tiger," Ket said, his pulse pistol drawn. "I thought we were gonna play nice."

"What the hell's going on? The lights flickered."

"Yeah, well, that's what happens when your ship's being tethered." Ket's eyes narrowed. "My guess is they fired a transit beam on our ship to temporarily deactivate it. Standard stuff."

Selina's mouth formed a line. "Sneaky stuff, you mean."

"Yeah, well. Look, Selina, we're in a spot here. Here's the truth. I only grabbed you because of that Tracker you've got. It's got a huge bounty on it, so that's what it is. I'd have gladly skipped yanking your ass with it, but time was too short; I had to grab and scoot quick. However, the situation's changed. You may not like it, but you're in this with us now. I don't know if you've come across Cerulaks before, but they're not the friendliest people out there. That device on you, that's all they want."

Selina folded her arms. "Uh huh. They sound the same as you to me."

"Yeah, well, I'm not about killing anyone who isn't trying to kill me first. But these guys aren't on that wavelength. Your Railen Tracker is what they want. Once they get it, everyone on this ship, including you, is space dust."

Selina grimaced. "How long do we have?"

"They're tethering our ship, so not much longer. They'll come on board and take it any way they have to."

"Let me talk with them," Selina offered.

Ket's brow creased. "Just what pray tell do you think that's gonna do?"

Selina jabbed a finger to the insignia on her suit. "My unit's affiliated with the Universal Alliance. I'll tell them I've got a warrant on you and I'm bringing you in."

Ket bit his lip, but the guffaw burst out anyway. "Oh, really? You're gonna tell them you're with the UA? Honey, wake up. The UA's a pipe dream. It's not about order out here; it's about control. That's not the same thing. You want to flash your badge thingy, like that's gonna make them cower and cooperate, but I'm telling you these guys only respond to firepower."

"So we'll give them that instead," Selina countered. "I'm

assuming you took my pulse rifle since it wasn't on me when I woke up."

"Well, yeah."

"Alright, flyboy, we just have to pull a little sneak on them. I'll hide myself somewhere close. Soon as they board, we blast our way out."

"Then what? We'll still be surrounded by people trying to kill us." Ket shrugged.

"Hey, smooth talking guy like you, you'll figure out something." Selina smiled.

"Something about you isn't right, ya know," Ket replied. "Alright what the hell, I can't imagine a better option, or any other option right now. Let's go."

The tethering process took several minutes. The Cerulaks docked the *Crimson Lance* to their ship and disconnected all its engine capability so Ket's space cruiser was little more than a floating metallic asteroid. They activated the exterior airlock and proceeded through the ship. Tracing the life form signatures aboard, they were led to an open area with a few tables in the middle. Ket and Dub sat at the far table, their hands folded, Ket with a glum expression on his face.

The first Cerulak into the area was Brynn Mak. He'd served for several cycles under Tarmun and had taken a liking to roughing up prisoners. He'd have risen up further through the ranks by the time he'd spend in the Cerulak military, but dishing out punishment, however much deserved or not, was just too damned fun for him.

Behind Brynn, equally as large and foreboding, was Zakk Goulden. Zakk was a mentee of Brynn's and pretty much echoed Brynn's take on the fun of beating up other species, especially ones that were too small or scrawny to give much resistance, of which description Ket and Dub certainly filled the bill in spades.

Ket swallowed hard at the sight of their guests and silently said a thousand prayers, wishful happy thoughts, and threatening curses that Selina was on the level about working with Ket and Dub, and she wasn't just going to sell them out. From the look of it, their survival chances were pretty slim, and Ket hoped with everything he had that Selina was as good a shot as he suspected from his brief glimpse of her in the firefight on Zormad.

Brynn gave his soon to be prisoners a greedy smile. "So, you're the ones who made off with that Tracker."

Ket shrugged. "If that's what your gear says. Me, I don't really know. Dub, you remember anything about a tracker?"

Dub's head swiveled to Ket, then back to Brynn. "Um, why no. We were just reviewing our last cargo and there wasn't a single tracker in there. Some power supplies, a little bit of rations we'd manage to spare for some less fortunate—"

"Silence!" Brynn's hand shot up. "We'll make a thorough check of the ship once you've been removed. Both of you stand, hands at your heads. Robot, all weapons disengaged."

Ket and Dub eased their way up and slowly complied. Ket wondered if something had happened with Selina, or was this her plan: figure out some way to rig the ship once they were taken and then hightail it back to Zormad? Or maybe she'd gotten stuck?

As Ket and Dub stood in position, Zakk attached binders to Ket's wrists, which brought Ket's arms down, behind his back.

Brynn nodded toward the airlock. "Robot, head out first."

Ket looked behind him for a bit, but instead of any signal he'd hoped for from Selina, he just met Zakk's fist with his face. Ket spun around and leaned over. A deep throbbing sore radiated over his head and his vision blurred for a few moments.

"None of that. We've got plenty in store for you, and there's no getting out of this, so get moving right now."

Anger hit Ket hard. He'd been in a series of gambits already, he made this run to begin with, he tried for the Railen Tracker even though their ship had no weapons for protection, and last, he trusted Selina to work with him. She was probably halfway out of the ship by now, ready to stow aboard with the Cerulaks and make her way back home. He doubted he'd ever see her again.

A loud blast thumped through the cabin, and Ket lurched to the ground. He let out a loud grimace in response. In the commotion, Ket heard a metallic clang he only assumed was Dub falling over as well.

Seconds later, he felt someone's hands as they worked on the binders around his wrists and soon; he was freed. He was lifted to his feet and stared into the eyes of Selina.

"You sure don't like to rush things, huh?" Ket shot her a glare.

"I had to make sure they opened the airlock, dummy. Otherwise, we're in a metal shell floating in space. You're welcome, by the way."

They helped Dub back upright. Zakk and Brynn's lifeless bodies were strewn about, and smoke still wafted from four-inch gaping holes in each of their backs.

Ket nodded at Selina's handiwork. "Not too shabby. Gotta let me fire that thing sometime."

"You had your chance. This gun stays with me. Let's get on that ship, we got seconds til they realize their boys aren't our escorts anymore."

The threesome padded gently into the adjoined ship through the airlock. A couple of twists and turns, and they located the cockpit.

"Cerulak Coupler Ship. Not much on the muscle, but it's got warp capability, which is good enough." Ket shrugged.

"Nice, but can you fly it?" Selina asked.

Dub and Ket eyed Selina in silence for a second.

Selina narrowed her eyes at her amused cohorts. "Excuse me if I don't wanna die on this thing because you bozos got into something you couldn't handle."

Ket winked at Selina. "We got this, sister. Just cozy up in that navigation seat. Dub, see what you can make of the interface."

Several metallic tentacles extruded from Dub's torso and connected to the console of the tether ship. In seconds, the console burst to life with a variety of colors and displays. "I'm cycling through access codes to see what I have; may take a minute."

Ket eyed his partner. "Better be less than 30 seconds." Ket slid into the pilot's seat and fumbled through the controls. He wasn't quite as sure as he'd let on, but he figured every step they made when they weren't captured or dead was a victory.

As Ket located the radar screen and activated it, a voice burst on the ship's comm. "Brynn, report. Are ship and crew secured?"

The radar showed the other Cerulak ships were close and in formation for a warp jump. Selina ducked down in case any Cerulaks focused on the cabin and saw them instead of their cohorts.

"Situation normal," Ket replied over the comm. He turned to Dub. "You got something, clunker?"

"Don't call me that. Few more seconds," Dub countered.

A few moments passed in silence, and then the voice on the comm responded again. "Say again, Brynn; we aren't reading you clear."

"Anytime, guys," Selina hissed.

The console glowed a solid green color, and a chorus of gentle chimes sounded. Dub said, "Access confirmed."

Ket smiled. "Fantastic, knew you could do it. OK, does this ship have a transit beam we can shoot back their way?"

"Got it, but we don't have time to target each ship," Dub replied.

"Just fire as broad a blast you can and get that warp ready to go. We'll have to hope it keeps them off our trail long enough." Ket worked the console until he found the warp mechanism, and together with Dub, plotted a course for Wenzo. "Ready to punch it. Selina, buckle whatever you got back there; we're booking out."

Selina latched the restraints on her chair and braced against the sides of her seat.

Dub activated the warp, and the Coupler took off instantly.

FIVE

"YOU'VE GOTTA BE KIDDING ME." Ket sat on a crate outside of the depot on Wenzo talking with Selina while Dub watched as well. Their quick escape, thanks to Selina's help, had gone off pretty well, but that left them with this hot device that was an easy mark for them to be ambushed and something they had to keep secret.

"I said I need to get back to Zormad, flyboy. This device I got here isn't coming out just yet. You want your big prize, help me first."

Ket knew he had a few options that didn't involve Selina, but he wasn't ready for thinking about them. He could've arranged something with Dub, but he just didn't see that happening either. He'd felt something from the moment he'd seen her and that hadn't gone away. If Dub was any kind of clairvoyant, he'd have assumed it involved Ket's groin area aka Ket just having the hots for her. Maybe it was just that, but Ket thought it went further. Ket saw flashes of it in Selina's eyes, the way she looked sometimes. Xeno as a race were loners in Ling Galaxy; since they arrived they had scraped for whatever existence possible. When Ket was a child growing up, he had Osten Chavis as a benefactor, but Xeno just had whatever deals they made with strangers, and the hope those arrangements were legitimate. Xeno's survival depended on the worth they proved to people and how accurate their trust was. Ket admitted at least with Chavis, he had a mentor who was already invested in Ket's growth, even if it was because there was a steady take in it for Chavis.

"What's so damned important on Zormad you gotta rush back there?" Ket asked. "You want my help, why don't you start with telling me what Zormad and NewEarth means to ya."

"They're my family, all I have left. You probably don't know, I'm sure you've got plenty of people you can depend on. My mother's there, and she isn't well; I can't just let them die."

Selina bowed her head and slumped down to the ground. Ket got off the crate and sat down beside her. She watched Ket with pleading eyes.

Ket's survival instinct swiftly kicked in and pushed aside the growing feelings he had about helping Selina. "Look, I'm a smuggler. I'm not in anything for the greater good unless it's my own. But the more I see these fights happening, the more I'm thinking if things don't settle, soon it's gonna be impossible to get anything done. Tell ya what; I don't have much of a family, but what I got I know I'd do anything for. You want to get back to your world, we'll help you. Give me that Tracker back when I get there, and we call it a deal?"

A tear snaked down Selina's face. "Deal."

THE TRANSIENT WARP DRIVE repair on the *Crimson Lance* took a day to complete, but the ship was then ready and back to its infamous glory. Ket and Dub aimed the ship back toward Zormad. Selina stayed below in the common area and checked her suit for any problems since her wild trip began.

Dub calculated it was a time for a CPU to heart talk with his compatriot. "Are you softening in your old age? The old Ket would've taken that Tracker off her and jettisoned her out into space in a standard minute."

"Yeah, well, guess I'm a moron then." Ket shot Dub a glare. "She kinda got to me back there."

"About her family? You know that was likely a ruse, right?"

"I don't think so, Dub. I got a read on her."

"Funny, I didn't."

"Dub, for a sophisticated robot, you don't know a lot about people, especially Xeno women."

Dub tilted his head indignantly. "And you do?"

"You're not the only one who checks things out. I'd heard about that Xeno colony, NewEarth. They came to Zormad in one ship, the last of a dying system. And they've pieced together whatever food and shelter they could get ever since. You saw her when we grabbed her; she hadn't backed down a bit from those Railen troops. She's all about making a stand, she's got that fighting spirit, man."

"Ket, sounds like you're still denying you have feelings for her."

Ket shook his head. "No, it's not that."

"Well, while we're talking about feelings we don't wish to discuss, may I be so bold to mention another?"

Ket eyed Dub. "Don't make me shut you down for the rest of this trip."

"Ket, we've been partners for cycles now. And as a sophisticated robot, as you say, I've kept myself aware of the goings on in Ling Galaxy; in particular, the ones with Essence. We can deliver this tracker and get our money, but I don't think we can deny any longer the problem that Essence poses to us if Malone does what he's threatening."

The name floated in the cockpit between them like a threat. Ket's hands grappled the ship controls as tight as he could stand, and the ship proceeded on its warp course without a comment for several moments.

Dub studied his partner, fully aware of Ket's agitation. "Ket, it was inevitable our exploits would one day bring us back into his path.

You must know that. I know your feelings on him are very strong, but we've got to consider, in this building conflict throughout Ling Galaxy, what our role will be. Essence powers the Galaxy, and if that balance is disrupted, there's no telling of the consequences."

Ket still remained silent. He hadn't tuned out Dub, and though he felt a strong urge to shut him down, another part of Ket, the one that felt sorry for Selina and agreed on a return trip, kept listening and realized that as agonizing as this topic was for him, his robot partner raised some good points.

"Dub, all I know here is we've gotta take this girl back to her home on Zormad and then deliver this device for our payment. After that, we'll figure out our next move. I'm not a soldier; I never was. I can handle myself in a fight, and I damn well know how to survive. You should know that, after all the scrapes we've been in over the cycles."

"Of course, but it isn't about avoiding a fight anymore, Ket. Even if we finish our run for the payoff, the bigger struggle remains. The fight is here, it's upon us, and soon it will be everywhere. I've scanned the reports on Network. Skirmishes are happening more often. The Omegans aren't backing down, and the UA is having more trouble keeping things under control. Lookers are out there; you saw one yourself, remember? They're looking for Essence. If they can get to it —and worse yet, hoard it—our entire situation will get infinitely worse."

"What if it doesn't? Dub, you never have to worry about dying, but plenty of people do. So if someone wants to control Essence to stop that from happening, I say we let 'em do it and see how we can work the angle on the side."

"Quite a risk, my friend. This is far beyond stealing reactor cores."

"Payoff, Dub, payoff. We're getting huge credits outta this, remember? Once I settle with Papa Chavis, we'll be set. Smuggling won't even be necessary anymore."

"Just think about it, Ket. The time is coming when we'll have to decide. You know Malone demands allegiance, if he comes to power like most people think he will."

"He's an idiot." Ket hadn't been able to even mention the name; it stung too bad. "What he's trying to do? Merging himself with Essence and making himself some kinda god won't work anyway. I don't know if his cover story about spreading Essence around is the worst idea I've heard, but him being in any kinda control is bad. That said, I'm really not dumb enough to try getting in his way, I'd rather get as far away from him as possible and spend our incoming loot in peace."

The ship console announced an update: "Estimated arrival at Zormad forty-five standard minutes."

Once Ket and Dub finished their discussion, Ket's insides still reeled from the talk, but he admitted, at least to himself, the considerations about Dub's arguments. There had been talk about a unification going on, even beyond the Universal Alliance, but Ket had doubts about that making any kind of difference. Malone was growing in strength, and the various lawkeeper and militia groups around were as much a threat to Malone as insects on a giant. Their problem was no coordination. Even on Zormad, Ket heard about the tribal lifestyle between NewEarth and the Mardaks. The Mardaks themselves were pretty Spartan and lived just for their own survival. Ket knew any resistance effort required lots of roots, and he wasn't any kind of commander who could've made that happen. His services were best employed in remaining alive and able to run other jobs or deciding when his last one was, which thankfully was now a possibility with his upcoming bounty.

Ket ran some cursory checks of Zormad for troop activity. He hoped the hotspot they had slipped through last time was a bit cooler, since with the Railen and Omegans around, the chances of either or both being there on the *Crimson Lance*'s return was a definite concern.

As the onboard console computed activity on their destination, Ket's mind reeled back over thoughts of Malone. As much as Ket denied it to Dub and even himself, Malone's name hung over him like a carrot on a string. And Ket knew one day he was going to have to bite it.

The name hailed from deep in Ket's history, a page in his book dogeared and left to age like an ancient relic. But there it was, fresh and new before him once again, and Ket knew he had to turn that page, but doing so meant facing Malone. The fire in Ket's veins over the idea made his face flush hot, but he knew that whatever happened with Essence, if Malone or even someone else took it upset the balance in Ling Galaxy, he had to find some sort of resolution with Malone, in case the escape he hoped for wasn't an option.

The two of them were in this game, and even though their goals weren't even remotely close to each other's, Ket knew their crossed paths were inevitable. Ket knew about the updates Dub mentioned. Ket was better at putting those ideas aside. But that was increasingly harder to do, and now it was time for Ket's acceptance that no matter what he did, how many runs he went on, how much he stole, how much money he made, how much fame he earned for himself, there was no way he could ever escape the fact he was the son of Malone Stanton.

QUEST FOR DOMINION

ONE

"THERE'S A VERY EASY SOLUTION TO all of this."

Malone Stanton's words echoed in his chamber. The Nara, Omegan, and Railen leaders surrounded Malone; the three holographic projections of his audience watched him intently, as they attempted to grasp what he'd just said. Malone smirked at the thought of how much his audience wanted to know just where he was. Malone had become a master of being invisible to many and was easily Ling Galaxy's most sought after criminal.

Ellene Ballo, leader of the Nara spoke first. "Are we to assume you refer to your plan to release Essence to those of your dimension?"

Malone gazed on Ellene with scorn that fermented for all the cycles of his exile into Ling Galaxy. "Precisely, Madame Hierarch. As all three of you know, we've been born, grown up, and died under an ancient system. The Nara claim to be keepers of the peace, but how can there ever be peace when so many go without? Are we really that bold to determine which mouths are fed and which go without? And, what about the scourge of Veculus, and all who've succumbed to that plague? Are we willing to sacrifice some, even a few, just for the sake of everlasting comfort for the rest?"

Ellene Ballo said, "Allow me to repeat the obvious for those present who are incapable of accepting reality. The Nara, since the dawn of time, have been keepers of the Essence. This energy and life sustaining force resides safely on Grondia and allows life as we know it to flourish in Ling Galaxy. The suns, the stars, energy, life itself is derived from the Essence. We produce and keep this flowing, and safely move it to your dimension properly. To insinuate that the Nara are responsible for famine or viruses is simply ludicrous. Malone Stanton is nothing short of a criminal. He's a charlatan of the highest order, and his only saving grace is his uncanny wit to avoid detection and capture."

Malone nodded with a devious grin, politely accepting the remark as if it was a greeting of reverence. "Yes of course, thank you, Ellene, and the Nara, for reminding me that while I am one of your native sons, my abilities and talents have finally exceeded even your wildest expectations. And let me say to the rest of you that the Nara have been very clever in selling their position in the universe for many centuries. Yes, they can take credit for all the goodness in Ling Galaxy. But what about the rest? There's plenty of going on in this galaxy that I'd be hard pressed to say is good. The Nara have the ability to change things, but do they? No. They just let things happen. Honestly, I'm offended the rest of you aren't entertaining my offer. I even made a point of not including the lesser races of Ling Galaxy: the Mardaks, Cerulaks, or the filthy Xeno."

"Why should we consider someone like you who'd probably hoard all the Essence to make themselves ruler of the universe," asked Ander Pimm, leader of the Railen.

"Because among you there isn't one with the ability or sheer resolve to do what I can. The Omegans and Railen have tried in some way to get to the Essence. But the Nara keep themselves cloaked in dimensions beyond ours. The Railen were in fact cast out of this world in the distant past. Your lust for power was your undoing. My proposal is an equitable sharing of the Essence as needed.

"Careful with your posturing," Ander Pimm growled. "Remember, Malone, you were once Nara just like the Railen."

Malone smirked at the jab. "Point taken, Ander. But unlike the Railen, I've evolved closer to my full potential."

"Malone, you've only evolved closer to full insanity. Regarding Essence, it is exactly where it needs to be and handled by the best suited for the task. We do what we can as it is now," Ellene Ballo retorted. "Malone is meddling with powers he can't possibly comprehend."

"And you think you do?" Malone replied. "You've only inherited that which was given to you. I've taken and studied this substance, and learned its inner truths. Madame Hierarch, you're using but a fraction of its potential. I offer you far more, if you weren't so frightened and short sighted not to see it."

"You're insane." Zakmar shrugged. "The Omegans are the best to handle the distribution of the Essence, and we will be the most proper stewards of this into perpetuity. We've got the capacity and the technology to best handle the Essence."

"You've got a lot of hard heads in this is what you've got," Ander Pimm said.

Malone reveled in the bickering nations represented by the floating images of their leaders before him. He hadn't expected much concessions with this conference he arranged. He knew full well the Nara would've never bowed to him. The Railen were half blinded by bloodlust for the Nara, and the Omegans wanted their own claim of Ling Galaxy. The three of them were mere pieces to Malone, parts in his symphony of dominance that would one day come to a conclusion with him as the supreme force over all.

Malone offered his agitated audience a snicker. "Listen to all of you. Bickering like lost children. Fighting amongst yourselves. I've got abilities none of you even dare hope for." With that, Malone reached into the case on his console and retrieved the orb. He palmed it and thrust it forward to his startled audience. "I see you recognize an Essence orb when you see one."

Random gasps came from the others as they stared in disbelief. Finally, Ander Pimm was able to speak. "You've gone beyond your limits, Malone." The others gazed in silence.

"My limits? Hardly. I'm just getting started."

TWO

MALONE SMASHED THE CONTROL THAT ended his conference immediately. The glowing faces vanished in an instant. He rose from his seat and flexed his arms. His elation was cut short by a brutal slice of a very familiar agony.

Malone's Nara physiology suffered several modifications, the first of which was punishment for his crime of attempting to steal Essence from repositories on Grondia. From there came several more surgical manipulations until, like the rest of the Nara Outcast, his abilities to travel to Grondia were removed completely and he was thrust into Ling Galaxy like an unwanted bastard.

He turned and saw Frey, leader of his army, at the entrance to his chambers. "You summoned me, excellency?"

"I did." Malone folded his arms in thought when a piercing pain jammed its way through his body and settled on his brain. His large frame flinched from the agony, and he clasped his head. Malone had the option of using a serum to combat the attacks, but he mostly did without. In his mind, each attack was a reminder to him of what he'd lost and what he'd one day claim again for all time his own.

Malone's mind still hammered out details and orders while his body grappled with chronic agony. "Frey, I want you to find out all you can on planet Agmon. I want to demonstrate the power we have through Essence."

"Agmon, sir?"

Malone's eyes narrowed. "That's right. Outer planets are a perfect place to continue expanding our family."

Planet Agmon wasn't remarkable for anything. While its derelict state wasn't unique among Ling Galaxy, Malone knew it was as good a place as any for his first spectacle of commanding Essence. It was more about the act than the destination for him.

The wave of pain subsided a bit, enough that Malone's vision focused sharply again. "Get my children ready; I must speak with them."

"They are assembled in the Great Hall, ready for your bidding."

Malone placed his cloak over his shoulder and strode out with Frey following. Segredo, the moon where his facility, organization, and followers were located, was less than a footnote to most knowing beings in Ling Galaxy. This minor distinction made the satellite a prime location for Malone as he began his mission away from the prying eyes of the Universal Alliance and all others who threatened his quest for dominion over Ling Galaxy.

Segredo wasn't the destination Malone had originally planned for himself, but once his breakout from prison was successful, the search of possible planets made the small moon that orbited the Bimlok Major planet a perfect candidate for someone with goals as lofty as his. Besides, Bimlok Major's worth in Ling Galaxy was little more than a focal point for Segredo's orbit.

The earliest currency for Malone was his charisma, and he wielded that as the wealthy with stores of precious jewels at their disposal. He recruited a number of brilliant but discarded individuals with expertise at construction, and through their efforts managed a gigantic subterranean network on Segredo for housing Malone, his followers, and his grand visions for Ling Galaxy.

Malone collected the unwanted, the forgotten, and the never realized. Being a discarded soul himself, he sought comfort in commiseration with the other forgotten beings in Ling Galaxy. These downtrodden souls who begged for some purpose, for some chance, were caught in Malone's offers of not only a place to belong, but a parental figure who knew they mattered. For their undying allegiance, Malone gave them what no other life available to them had.

Malone fit his followers into his plan with care. He managed a network of soldiers of fortune that served as a burgeoning army. Still, another group, known as his 'children', were the beneficiaries of a series of bodily enhancements Malone oversaw in coordination with his network of surgical artists. By examining his own physical state after the Nara procedures, Malone was able, to a degree, to restore dimension shifting abilities to himself. Not yet being able to restore his access to Grondia, Malone did find the formula to transfer himself elsewhere across Ling Galaxy.

Malone's intent initially was self-serving; he merely sought locations of existing Essence stores on each planet for holding them hostage. But time and a sense for the devious offered Malone other uses for his gift. A Galaxy of limited resources often demanded thievery for survival. The ability to shift dimensions and teleport into and out of locations in the galaxy was as handy a tool as any decent thief could've ever wanted.

Malone walked onto a parapet overlooking the floor of the Great Hall, where two hundred of his children had gathered. The ones who spotted him began cheering until the rest saw, and the entire group shouted praises to Malone.

He stood for a moment, accepting the devotion and the love. These lost children, found under his providence, believers in his cause, servants to his demands were his.

Malone silenced the group with his hands. "My children, I thank you. Your Great Supreme sends tidings to each of you. You've all prospered and grown here, each of you given lives that Ling Galaxy denied of you."

The group shouted and applauded excitedly.

"The time has come now for your Supreme to ask of you a request."

Shouts came in response. Several from the group thrust their hands up, as if they reached for Malone's grip to hoist them up into whatever he needed of them.

Malone silenced them again. "Ling Galaxy despises you. There are many who search for you and want to take you away from this family. But fear not; your Supreme watches over you and will keep you protected. All you are asked in return is simple."

Malone's children knew what he was going to ask before he said anything, however. As soon as they were raised to the point of understanding speech, it was drilled into their heads. Like the food and drink they were given, his plans and mantra coursed through their veins and filled every fiber of their being.

"Hail the Supreme; his will be done!" The shouts came first in a jagged repetition of voices from the floor, but the chants soon synced up until the entire body shouted it as one. Malone thrust his palms aloft and basked once again in the adulation.

It was his meaning, his purpose, and calling to accept all their love that he knew he dearly deserved.

"My children," Malone said, quieting down the chants. "I task you with two things. The first is simple. The second, not so much. First, I charge each of you to canvas Ling Galaxy. Use your abilities and what you've been trained to do. Wreak havoc. Steal from whomever you can, whether it is food from a child, a weapon from a soldier, fuel from a city. Take, thwart, disrupt. This Galaxy has abandoned you. Show them that was a mistake.

"The second is about Essence. Its life sustaining force has been horded and kept out of reach by the Nara. The same kindly race who manipulated her own citizens and cast them out. These shunned Naras' only crime was they dared to ask 'Why is Essence not given more freely to those who need it?' Essence is essential to life in Ling Galaxy, but it cares not for quality of said life. So many people are suffering. Your Supreme has a purpose and a mission. I want to collect Essence, so we ourselves decide how it is best used. We don't need anyone telling us the state of the Galaxy we're in is just OK. Ling Galaxy needs direction, and that we will give; once we have Essence, absolute rule over Ling will be ours!"

The crowd rippled with excitement. Malone lifted his arms in response, as he savored their energy before he quieted them again.

"I am just like you. I was told my ideas were all wrong. That the people didn't deserve a chance, that the Nara knew best in all the Galaxy on how to divide the Essence up. I've seen the suffering around Ling Galaxy: the wars, the disease, the famines. We can stop it. We can make a new Order where all those in the Galaxy will have their fill, through our providence.

"Finding Essence will be much more difficult than your task of havoc. You'll need to search much harder for that, my children. You have the abilities for the task though, and I know you can do it. The gifts I have given you allow you to seek Essence where once only Nara tread. When you find that Essence, use the receptacles you've been given, and bring it to me. In fact, consider any world you liberate the Essence from to be a collection of your new siblings. The residents of planets in Ling Galaxy will become part of our extended family once all realize that the Essence they seek comes from their Supreme on High. They must swear faith to our cause to get their Essence to continue surviving."

Malone watched his eager followers. He'd spent cycles with them, made sure his history and his treatment by the Nara was drilled into the heads of each of his children and his soldiers until the hatred his followers had of the Nara rivaled his own.

He'd taken time to operate on his children and instilled in each the ability to shift dimensions. Their skills at jumping gave them the name "Lookers" to most in the Galaxy. The Railen, also kin to the Nara, were well aware of the dimension ability, and they had been stripped of this just like Malone was. But their path took them on one of conquest. Their reasoning was, if theirs was now this existence, they would rule and conquer and one day storm Nara to reclaim their homeland, for the Essence but also for the ultimate insult of their expulsion.

Malone's desires lay solely in Essence itself. He considered his family to be the Lookers as well as the devoted army he cobbled together through sheer will of domination.

"So, my children, that is your command. Your quest will begin soon; I will send for you when it is time! Be ready, for it won't be much longer!"

Malone departed with the roar of his followers shouting his praises in unison. The church was healthy, well fed, and ready for its patriarch's bidding, no matter how extreme a task it was. He savored his plan and the faithful he'd assembled for its execution, while his thoughts reminded him of his old friend who made it possible.

THREE

AS MUCH AS MALONE RELISHED AND and savored every bit of what he and his followers assembled in very short time, he still had to admit his fortunes came in part through the help of his friend Pietro. Malone and Pietro were once part of the rising class of future leaders in Nara. They'd shown distinction through their cycles of upbringing and instruction, and were poised to assume the mantle of leadership in their respective areas. Pietro's work on the delivery and usage of Essence brought him in direct contact with the substance regularly. With access not even all Nara citizens could claim, Pietro found himself enamored of the life-giving Essence, and over time his analytical mind opened doors that weren't considered by many. Pietro's thoughts and musings gave way to questions until he found himself amid a series of experiments using the Essence.

All good discoveries only became greater when shared, so Pietro brought Malone into his study for a display.

Malone listened to the ramblings of his over ecstatic friend, who rattled off obtuse jargon with the ease of a bird soaring through the air. "Pietro, you're talking a mile a minute. Focus. And ease up on the gibberish, please."

"Malone, I'm telling you, the Essence we've been sending throughout Ling Galaxy isn't just something that we can process this way. It can be harnessed for more and different things."

"Different?"

"Watch." Pietro activated the lights in the rest of the room, illuminating a series of targets at the far end. He eyed the objects eagerly before he stopped a moment to glance back to his friend. "You may want to duck behind that shield there."

Malone cocked an eyebrow. He'd seen his friend do a number of experiments, but a lot of them had gone south, especially in their earlier cycles. He still laughed at the memory of when Pietro fried the hair of one of their teachers.

The blast thundered through the room and knocked Malone back fifteen feet onto his back. He clutched his head, which had a severe throbbing, and glanced back toward where he had stood. There was Pietro, his uniform slightly singed, but behind him, the series of targets were nothing more than smoldering remains.

Pietro jogged back to Malone, who'd managed to get back to his feet.

"Well, how about that?" Pietro gushed.

"What in the world did you do?" Malone said.

"It's the Essence. I've figured how to channel it."

Pietro's response hung in the air like a loose thread. Of the many thoughts that began to fill Malone's mind, pulling at that thread was utmost and at the top. The Nara had at their very disposal a colossally lethal weapon. The Galaxy that had survived under the Nara was at war, and Malone's desires swiftly overtook his designated life of fueling. The Galaxy had her food, but Malone wanted the Galaxy to be shaped. And anyone with such desires for control of the Galaxy had no problem with adding 'by me' into every passing thought about it.

FOUR

MALONE RETURNED TO HIS CHAMBERS. On the glowing console near his desk displayed a map of the known Galaxy, including the supposed location of Grondia. *If only it was that easy to get to,* he mused. He stared at the yellowish ball that represented his former home world, the place he learned so much early on. He was a promising young rising star on Grondia. Malone rose up in the ranks for Essence production tasks on Grondia, and he learned all he could about its properties.

He thought about the times he'd accompanied Loaders on their trips to worlds around the Galaxy. Traveling to each world, Loaders moved the Essence orbs into place, replacing the previous ones, as had been the case since the dawn of Ling Galaxy.

From early on, the idea hit Malone about how Essence was underutilized. His first attempts were to change the minds of his fellow Nara about the Essence delivery system. He remembered the day he approached Ander Pimm about it.

"Ander, we've got to do something better about how we handle the Essence," he said. "We can correct so many problems in Ling Galaxy: famines, wars, illness even."

Ander's large forehead creased in thought at one of his pupils who dared question eons of Nara process. "Malone, all living beings possess in them a choice for good or evil. The Nara aren't a court system or a governing body. We allow the galaxy to unfold as it is; beings have it within them to make their own choices."

"Understood, Ander. But the illness, the poverty, the famines—why do they persist if we supply the life force to all?"

"Life is finite, Malone. It starts with birth, continues with growth that leads into decay and then death. This is not something we can circumvent. It is ours to know this cycle and do our best with what time we've been given, however great or little."

MALONE SETTLED into the soft chair in his lair. The lights were dimmed low, but his mind was alight with thought. The locations of Essence orbs were an annoying mystery to him, but he figured his children had a decent chance at finding them.

He reached for the Essence orb at his desk. It hovered to his outstretched hand, obeying the unspoken command he willed toward it. The orb landed softly in his grasp. He shuddered at the touch, which sent a million sensations of electrical stimulation through his body. He'd been able to hold the orb for a little at a time since he obtained it but had been working at holding it longer.

The gentle shocks of the orb continued, but he'd learned through practice how to better tolerate the sensations it produced. Soon he entered a trance, where he saw before him a temple that arced into the air for thousands of feet. He smiled at the realization the temple was on Grondia, and he'd managed to travel astrally to his home world. Before him stood a collection of Nara Ancients. The creatures of Nara served them as the providers of the Essence that the Nara distributed.

"Ancients, I ask your guidance in my matters," Malone said through his thoughts.

A booming voice echoed through Malone's mind with a harsh tone. "Malone Stanton, the powers we grant are not for those with their own shallow ends. Our power extends life to the galaxy, and with that life comes a price. You must choose wisely, for this course you seek has been tried by some in the past, with the common result being collective doom."

"You're wrong, Ancients. I've proven my worth, surely; I've gotten an Essence orb."

"Malone, your possession is solely the result of theft. We know well your transgressions, and you will not return to this world by any means. The Nara Council has seen to it, and the Ancients forbade you as well."

"But you cannot stop me from seeking my own truth; you cannot stop me from making my own."

The Ancient's face drooped in sorrow. "Malone, no course you take in this matter will end well for you. The Ancients, in addition to the bounty of Essence, have sight in all matters of the Galaxy. Consider yourself warned. The beings of the Galaxy are already on the move to usurp you, and if your pride isn't brought under control, it will one day be your undoing."

Malone clasped the Essence orb tightly. Its gentle hum gave way to an angry roar as he felt its energy course through his veins. "You'll see, one day, you'll be coming to me for guidance and mercy. Be afraid of just how little sympathy you'll get from my hands. Your rule over the Galaxy has lasted for millennia. I will end it in hours."

The Ancient's face steeled up in response. "Malone, begone; our council has spoken."

The Ancient snapped their arms together, sending several rays of brilliant light slamming into Malone's form. He fell to the floor, and just that quickly, he was back in the dark room of his lair. The Essence orb was on the ground to his side.

"Pompous fools," he muttered. "They've no idea who they've toyed with."

FIVE

ALONE SUMMONED HIS CHILDREN TO an Outcropping, at the end of the gathering area. The rock sloped upward toward an opening out into the cold darkness of space.

The Lookers randomly activated their powers, teleporting off the ground and becoming thin trails of light until they were all gone. Malone watched the scene with great pride; his second was next to him.

"Have you sent all of them?" Frey asked.

"No, I've kept a few here with us. There's too much going on to put all my children on one task."

"But the ones who left – you think they'll be able to find Essence?" Frey asked.

"I do. I raised them; they'll get it for me. In the meanwhile, we've other issues to address." Malone cast a glare at Frey, who swallowed hard. Malone's true plans for the Galaxy were close to what he'd told the Lookers, but the full truth included others to contend with.

"Emperor Zakmar of the Omegan empire has sent a message to you with an offer of collaboration," Frey said.

Malone's brow raised. "Those goons want to work with me? Funny how my little display swayed some minds so quickly." Malone laughed. "Wonder what they're offering?"

"I will arrange a contact with them so we can discuss terms."

Malone mulled the thought as he steepled his fingers. Having two of his enemies engaged with each other was never a bad idea. With all he faced from the UA and even the Railen, if the Omegans were under his direction, it meant a considerable advantage.

"We'll hear the Omegan deal in time. In the meanwhile, there's a pesky situation with the Cerulaks we must address. Ready my ship."

While Malone had the ability of physical travel through open space by himself, he knew it was best he kept his appearance as menacing as possible, which meant a large presence of craft. There was no point to any of his plans unless they invoked as much fear as possible, and the small but menacing fleet Malone commanded was all about that. He assumed the bridge on his ship, the *Aeon Impaler*, a battle cruiser, along with a collection of starcraft, each equipped with the dimension shift capability of the Lookers.

Once aboard, Malone contacted the detachment of crafts from his bridge console. "We are proceeding to a known outpost held down in a deep space quadrant by the Cerulak fleet. As you may already know, the Cerulaks are among the many seeking to locate and capture Lookers by way of those Railen Trackers. Our purpose is to eliminate this outpost and all there as a signal for Cerulia to stop their present course of action. Rules of engagement are standard: be swift and merciless. There'll be no prisoners, no escape, and no survivors. Any who fail in these parameters will be disciplined solely by me, and I'll be as merciless to you as I will be to the Cerulaks."

The grouping of starcraft pierced through deep space like a razor through paper. The *Aeon Impaler* was in the lead; their course was direct, their purpose clear. Their warp jump complete, the ships settled into an orbit around a moon where the Cerulak outpost stood.

The Cerulaks used random locations as waypoints in their search for things like the Railen Trackers. Canvassing the Galaxy for Railen, and in particular their trackers, was a long process. Staking out locations for regrouping was as much a convenience as a necessity. Malone feared ignoring the tracker issue would've led to them being used to locate himself eventually.

"We'll descend into sub-orbital trajectory. Focus on the base, and eliminate the starcraft you find. Leave communications open," Malone directed.

The starcraft in Malone's convoy descended like a hive of angry hornets. The swarm of starcraft each maneuvered on a swift coordinated attack. The Cerulaks fired back on Malone's ships in response, the random bolts of pulse energy rocketing around the billowing craft.

"Stay your course, and destroy those ships," Malone ordered.

A shot found one of Malone's fleet; the starcraft's wing burst into flame and careened offward, back out into deep space, before it exploded completely. Malone eyed it for a moment, but continued on. The bigger casualty in a fight was cowardice, he always believed. He told that to all his crews and the Lookers. Their mantra had remained a life serving Malone until a death that glorified him.

The Cerulak base was a collection of buildings with an accompanying space port made for short trips and a place for refueling afterward. Malone's fleet broke off from their initial approach and proceeded on a direct run toward the Cerulak facility. Several Cerulak starcraft made it into the air and gave chase, which Malone's starcraft squadron gladly entertained. The air was punctuated with blasts and weapons fire. Malone wasn't concerned with the fray though. He knew his people got the job done. Instead, he ordered the *Aeon Impaler* to land and then proceeded to the largest building on the surface.

He activated a lock burst on the large facility, which sealed it electronically and prevented escape. Then, he directed his crew to keep the *Aeon Impaler* in a ready position. Together with two of his Lookers, Malone was engulfed with a crackling glow of yellowish light, and with a loud pop, his surroundings changed and he was inside the facility.

Once Malone's group was inside, the Cerulaks nearby opened fire in response. The blasts ricocheted about his body as Malone walked through the room unfazed. His senses felt the weapons fire around him, and he directed the volleys so they missed him and his team.

"I demand to speak with the commander here," Malone said amid the shouting and running. "Tell me who it is before I kill you all."

"Go ahead!" shouted a Cerulak nearby. Malone faced her, a female with a rifle trained at his chest. Her uniform had officer markings on it. Malone approached her. Her greenish skin prickled as he neared her.

"Dear child, do you think your weapon will stop me? You must know by now, I'm the universe unfolding. All of you are my children. Realize that, or suffer."

The officer clutched her rifle tighter. "Not another step!" Her voice betrayed a slight tremble.

Malone salivated as a predator with their mark fully in sight. "Fair enough." With that, he transported himself until he was at her back. With one swift move, he ripped her rifle from her hand and tossed it to one of his Lookers. Retrieving a long blade, he eased it up to her throat. "Tell me now, what is your name?"

"Zaratha," she said amidst hurried breaths.

"Zaratha, I admire your bravery. I admit, I'm impressed by all you did to stand your ground. It leads me to think you're a person of importance here."

Zaratha said nothing in response but offered a slight nod while she continued her huffing.

"The simple solution here is to let me state my case. I want a communication to the Cerulak high command so I can explain a breach of decorum."

Zaratha paused. Several other troops had gathered but were under watch from Malone's people. "If I do this, will you let us go?"

"Of course, my child. I'll let you and yours all go if you do what I ask."

Zaratha agreed and led Malone to their broadcast console. As Malone sheathed his blade, the Cerulaks opened a comm channel and hailed their high command. After a few moments, Pon Ebnora, high ruler of Cerulia, appeared on screen. She was a slender female with skin a slight shade darker than Zaratha's.

"Zaratha, this communication is highly unusual."

"It is indeed, highness. As you can see, I'm not Zaratha, but a passerby who wishes to speak with you."

Pon Ebnora's face reeled back in shock. "Malone, what are you doing there?"

"Simply put, I'm doing what you denied me. I requested numerous times an audience with you in person to discuss the most distressing news of the Railen Tracker situation and your people's attempts to obtain them. You've left me no choice but to contact you directly once I had some collateral you'd be interested in."

Pon Ebnora's jawline twitched. Her eyes darted about with the deviancy of a child caught off guard without the time or ability for a cover-up. Malone savored the look of concern and worry. He knew his next move and relished the knowledge of how few options Pon had for retaliation.

Malone once again freed his trusty blade. He held it down, like a winning card. He wanted the moment to play out at first. It was no good killing the Cerulak until he learned all he could. To Malone, the idea of the Cerulak deaths was enjoyable, like a meal savored by a victorious predator. The information was the sweet dessert he truly craved, however.

Pon Ebnora wasn't a rank amateur though; her uneasy twitch steadied after a few moments, and her composure returned to one of a resilient leader. "Malone Stanton, you really think I don't know what you're about to do? I'm frankly surprised there's anyone alive there now."

"Highness, we both know what's about to happen with the Essence, and your feeble attempt to get a foothold will be dealt with. You can dawdle all you want, but you'll waste the lives of the rest of your people on this outpost and beyond if you don't tell me what I want to know."

Pon looked at Zaratha as she writhed under Malone's firm grip. Behind them, the rest of the Cerulaks still at the base had been rounded up. This round was over, and Pon knew it. She ached at the sight of her fellow Cerulaks under the knife, but as bad a loss as these, she comforted herself in the knowledge the bigger fight remained, and any advantage Malone gained then made the larger victory that much more difficult.

"Malone, I've nothing to offer you. You want to make a bloodbath, that's your choice. I can't stop you, but I can stay ahead of you, and we'll find your Lookers, no doubt."

Pon ended the transmission. Malone gazed at the blank space where Pon's image had hovered moments ago. He was stunned. The mere idea of someone who denied him bit into Malone like hungry vermin. He already had a long list of those he owed retribution to for slights far too many to number, and Pon Ebnora had easily added herself to the list with distinction.

His glance still on the blank space, Malone's arm flexed in one motion, which brought the knife across and severed Zaratha's throat. Her lifeless body draped to the floor amid a chorus of shouts and curses from the other Cerulaks present. Malone spun to his crew, their weapons at the ready.

"We've got more work to do. Finish up here, and make it bloody."

SIX

ONCE THE CERULAK POPULATION WERE reduced to minced remains, Malone returned to his starcraft for a journey through the nearby planets. He figured any Cerulak outpost made the immediate area worth a closer look.

His wandering eyes perused the screens before him, a holographic depiction of the sector they traveled in, when he was interrupted Osmun Myer, one of his crew and one of the many tangents in the paramilitary machine Malone had assembled among the mercenary dregs for hire of Ling Galaxy.

"Master, we've located a strong signal for one of the trackers on a starcraft near our quadrant.

"Identification," Malone said.

"It's a Zion Class cruiser, sir," Osmun replied.

A series of thoughts overtook Malone, and the report from his crew member was muffled in the process. In this sea of concepts, a name appeared, and he blurted it out in response. "The *Crimson Lance*."

Osmun paused. His Tillian ancestry kept his emotions from

being too pronounced, but in spite of that, a healthy look of surprise washed over his face at Malone's clairvoyance. "That's correct, sir."

Malone smiled confidently. "Passengers, cargo?"

"Minimal."

"Show it on-screen," Malone commanded.

The forward display on the bridge shimmered for a moment, then a full view of the *Crimson Lance* filled the monitor wall. At first, Malone eyed the starcraft like a hunter regarding its prey: passionless, only sizing up of the mark, a cursory glance for weakness, and a burning desire for it. But then, the display Malone watched changed, and the forward command portion of the starcraft appeared on-screen with a familiar face in view.

Is it true, he wondered. *Could it really be my son?*

"Analysis of crew aboard!" Malone shouted.

Osmun checked several monitors at his station for a moment. "The ship appears to be piloted by two. One looks to be of Outcast Nara ancestry, the other a robot."

Malone had long considered his son lost, a casualty of Malone's punishment and one of the many reasons for the path of revenge he'd chosen. While he was still a proper Nara citizen, he'd tried to get his son and wife to join him on his quest, but his family hesitated. Even they had their doubts. Malone refused self-reflection at this; instead, he blamed the Nara for what he considered a clouding of the minds of those he loved the most. Regardless of any conspiracies that may have been in effect, plans made in the shadows weren't an easy sell, even to loved ones. Malone's cycles since his exile were filled with many thoughts, and while his son and wife were high among them, his grief over their separation faded once the urge for revenge had taken hold of every fiber of his being.

"Track them."

"Already are, sir. They appear to be headed for a planet called Zormad toward the far reach," Osmun replied.

"Then set course for this Zormad. We've got much to take from them, especially now that it appears a reunion is most in order."

SEVEN

OF ALL MALONE'S WANTS AND DEMANDS, he'd never considered his son to even be an option among them. To Malone, his life with his son and wife seemed to have taken place a thousand centuries ago. Malone's efforts with the Nara had served him but also helped his family reach a status of preferential treatment. He'd never known such happiness, but once his growing ambitions caused concern for the Nara upper echelon, the Nara did what they could to stop him. Found guilty of attempts at Essence manipulation, Malone's transgressions were unforgivable under Nara law. The Nara had previously reached their hand out to Malone and desperately attempted to correct his eyes from his path, but he was too far gone. His wife Ursula was kidnapped as well as his son, which only fueled his distrust and contempt for everything the Nara held dear.

Deciding further, the Nara declared his wife and son among the Outcast, and sent them to distant reaches of the Galaxy, but not before destroying his wife's memory of him. His loves were removed like locks of hair. Malone in turn underwent modification and was thrust out of the dimension forever.

Alone in the Galaxy, Malone's mind went to work on many things. The retribution for those who'd done this to him, the worry and anguish of his lost family. He was a soul that searched in a Galaxy of those who knew nothing of him and were indifferent. His life post expulsion was a slow climb, starving and stealing for food, and learning many illicit trades. Eventually, he decided on a course for himself. To him, his early transgressions were a call to overthrow the true tyranny of the Galaxy. He knew that for him, and his family if they ever survived, his course lay in the dismantling of everything the Nara and Ancients stood for.

AFTER THEY ENGAGED their jump capabilities, Malone's posse of starcraft entered the atmosphere of Zormad. Osmun straightened up in his chair, excited with an ID of easy prey for his master. "Excellency, we've identified a troop massing on the far side of the planet."

Malone gazed ahead at the map. He ran a finger back and forth over his upper lip in thought. "This isn't a sightseeing trip. Give me data, armaments, everything." He glared back at Osmun.

Flustered, Osmun opened several holographic screens and did a number of calculations. "Troop size 10 thousand approximately. A small fleet of starcraft at the ready as well. Sire, they show Railen Markings."

"Ah, the marauders are here." Malone snickered. "That means our prey is more valuable than I already sensed. Soon enough I'll sic my new lapdog Zakmar and the Omegans on the Railen fools and the UA. We don't have time to serve their punishment now. Do you have a fix on the *Crimson Lance*?" Malone muttered.

"Sire, yes, we do."

"Excellent. Proceed on a direct run. Fighters, use your shift abilities and disable any starcraft in immediate range. I'm getting the *Crimson Lance*, however possible," Malone writhed his hands together in delight. Whether or not his son was interested in joining

Malone wasn't a concern of his right then. Malone had been chased by so many entities, fights like this had become regular sport for him. Evasion of their measly pursuits was so effortless, it teetered on boring. However, finding his son after all these cycles alive and well made things quite different and new.

Malone's fleet formed ships in a large V, with the *Aeon Impaler* at the head. They shot toward the amassed area of Railen ships with lightning speed. As they approached, several Railen ships broke off the main group into defensive formations. Malone contacted his pilots with further instructions.

"Engage them, but don't worry about a slaughter for now. There'll be time for that later. Wound them. Once you get an all clear from me, reconvene at the rendezvous point and we'll make our warp jump home together. For the greater glory of your Supreme!"

The pilots replied their acknowledgment to Malone. Ship to ship, fire rumbled about the scene, and Malone saw the *Crimson Lance* through the forward view.

"Target that ship's engines; don't let it escape!" Malone said.

However, Malone's crew was a hair too late with grabbing the errant ship. In a brilliantly colored flash, the *Crimson Lance* vanished from view.

Malone stared blankly at the spot where the *Crimson Lance* had been moments earlier. He blurted out to no one and everyone on the bridge at once, "Someone tell me we've got a trace on that ship's warp path!"

Reige, who handled analysis on the *Aeon Impaler*, said, "No, Supreme, it appears their warp was transient type. Those are more random and difficult to track. I'm afraid we don't have a solid trail on this one."

The realization of what happened was clear to Malone, but he still hadn't grasped the fact that it was reality. Things slipping away from Malone wasn't a common occurrence, and this took a little longer for him to accept.

"Reige, in my quarters. The rest of you, canvass the Galaxy. I want that ship and its passengers alive!"

EIGHT

THERE WERE NO JUDGE AND JURIES coming to rescue the good Yeoman Reige. His guilt was predetermined, his sentence grim and forthcoming.

Still, Reige found a sliver of courage, enough for a feeble attempt at an excuse. "Sire, we failed to identify the ship warp capabilities; the number of ships in that area made the scan inconclusive with the small time we had to work with."

Malone eyed Reige with curiosity. He'd been accustomed to the pleas, the begging of the guilty, the cries for mercy from those who knew well it wasn't theirs for the asking, certainly not for the taking. Reige took a different tack. Malone hated to admit his admiration for such a play, and he wondered if he may have misjudged this move of discipline.

"Reige, your points are most valid." Malone folded his arms. "And I do agree, we were in a tight position. Even with our capabilities, that fight was not ours to command. We had to be swift and leave the area, and such a short amount of time leaves much to go wrong."

Beads of sweat formed on Reige's forehead; he blinked nervously and nodded with Malone.

As Malone paced about, the yeoman shifted his weight between his feet, uncertain what his next move or choice of words was. The only thing he knew was absolute agreement with Malone was the smartest course for the moment.

Malone swung back to the yeoman, a twinkle in his eye. "Yeoman, I've got just the thing for you."

Reige's midsection tightened, and terror shot through him as he braced himself for whatever was about to happen. Malone was fond of the knivery for his dirty work. The idea of a knife twisting its way through his midsection gave Reige a decent amount of nausea, and he soon felt dizzy.

Malone steadied him with a hand. "Easy there, yeoman. You've got more work to do. Your post on this ship is terminated, but don't worry. Your time among the living isn't over yet, I've got one more mission for you to do. Think of it as a penance and also a comeuppance. Whatever you want to call it, just know your choices in this matter are nonexistent."

ONCE REIGE WAS DISPATCHED, Malone returned to the bridge. His plans had many sides, and he couldn't have wasted too much time on just one of them in finding his son.

The ship's warning system blared an alert, but Malone had sensed what it was without seeing it on the screen. The Railen were as close to kin for him as the Nara, and their presence sent an unnatural shudder through his system.

The *Aeon Impaler's* ship's comm hailed an incoming transmission, and moments later, Malone stared into the face of one of his former brethren on-screen.

"Commander Viro, I trust this isn't a social call," Malone muttered.

"Hardly. I'm on a mission of mercy from Ander Pimm. Malone, we have a common enemy. If you'd only listened to Ander's numerous offers of cooperation, you'd be much better supported with our fleet at your disposal."

"Vengeance and retribution are hollow goals, Commander Viro. The Railen want to reclaim their inheritance, and I certainly understand that. But, I seek something far deeper, a far richer meaning in this existence that neither the Railen nor the Nara can comprehend."

Viro eyed Malone. Theirs was a chess game, and Malone knew better than to dismiss someone like Viro, who'd been in his share of scuffles. Viro was among the leaders of the insurrection of Nara where so many of the citizens were outcast.

Viro sighed. "Malone. Realize that we're hellbent on our return, and we'll go through everything and everyone we must to get there, including you. Believe me, I for one would rather work with than against you attacking the filthy Nara. I'm starved for my return, and Malone, no matter what you say, you can't deny in your being some missing fiber of that. Ours wasn't meant to be dwelling in this dimension among the lesser races of Ling Galaxy, but to rule, to control, to preside over existence with our kindly benevolence toward all."

Malone mulled Viro's statement over in his head. It wasn't a lie, and Malone knew part of him wanted that return to his home world. However, what he'd seen in his visions into Essence told him that his place in the Galaxy wasn't determined by the planet he once called home, but instead by control of Essence itself. As much as Viro may have been genuine about an offer of brotherhood to his former fellow Nara, Malone knew there would come a time when Malone's control of Essence was the driving force that made Viro seek Malone's death.

"Viro, old friend, I'm not interested in backstepping. I have much more pressing matters at the present."

Viro sneered for a moment. "You'll regret this one day, Malone. Know that."

Malone ended the transmission. "As if." He turned to his crew. "We've got minds to win, hearts to heal. To planet Agmon!"

NINE

LIKE HER NEIGHBOR PLANETS IN LING GALAXY, Agmon had endured times of sustenance and periods of want and utter despair. Lately, the scales tipped to despair and stayed there. A famine had rocked the planet, leaving a large portion of the populace without necessary food and water.

Veculus had also ravaged Agmon, and a collection of abandoned makeshift hospitals that littered the surface told a tale of loss and death that spanned many cycles back.

The more resourceful citizens found escape from the planet via their own starcraft or by trading passage on a number of transports, sometimes for money, sometimes for possessions, and sometimes for physical favors. Poverty awakened the basest of instincts in citizens of Ling Galaxy. The excess want also revised the viewpoints of many on how much of one's personal dignity would be traded for another breath of air and day of life.

Malone knew how decrepit Agmon was. He was ready to show the rest of the universe why all needed his protection. After all, rhetoric fell flat without a visible example of action now and then.

He watched the map of the Galaxy on his console as a giant

studying a pile of ants. *So many lifeforms*, he thought. *Some already have seen the way, but how can I show the rest what their only true path is?*

While the Galaxy spun on its continuing course through the void, an idea planted in Malone's mind. It was one of many, and it hadn't arisen until he took time to study the Galaxy and its worlds. *I must get the message out. To claim and to promise is the stuff of politicians. I'm far beyond that, but unless I show people what I can do, I'll never achieve my goal*, he thought.

He summoned Frey to his side.

"Frey, I'm going to perform a demonstration at Agmon. The Galaxy can fear me, but if they don't believe in me, we'll never accomplish our goals."

Frey glanced at the map of the Galaxy, then back to Malone. "Perhaps they need to see more of our firepower. We can double back on Zormad with more ships and send a strong message to those stupid enough to defy us."

"No, Frey, there'll be plenty of time for battles. The wretched Nara, the pompous Railen, the devious Omegans, the conniving Cerulaks—one day they'll all be at our mercy. Before that happens, though, we need to curry favor with the masses of the Galaxy. We'll rule with diplomacy in the end."

Frey clenched his jaw. He'd been ready for a fight, especially since being dismissed from the Omegan military. Citations for extreme recklessness in the Omegan military like the one Frey received were a prime example of intergalactic irony. Frey had on numerous instances bucked authority and had led his ships into dangerous situations. His success rate was difficult to argue, but eventually the Omegans grew tired of the risks he subjected his crews to. He then found himself adrift, a soldier of fortune until Malone cast his eyes on him one day and not only offered him a new start, but a chance to feel useful, and even important once again.

"Agmon, it is." Frey nodded before commanding the navigation team on the new course.

"We will be broadcasting Galaxy wide as well. See to it our signal is sent to all the Galaxy corners on Network."

"Aye."

THE *AEON IMPALER* with its associated escorts descended on Agmon with little fanfare. The derelict planet's resources left it with no military presence, nor any strategic resources of note. Its citizens existed in a series of shanty towns, surviving off barters and starving for what little hope any of them still had.

Landing near one of the towns, Malone directed Frey toward the ship's external broadcast system. The unit would send a feed of their activities throughout the Galaxy. Some saw their message as it happened while others would view it after it was shared. Nothing seen by Malone Stanton, as wanted a fugitive as he was, would ever go by unnoticed.

Once Frey nodded that their signal was being sent, Malone activated the ship's external address system.

"Citizens of Agmon, I bring you good tidings. The Galaxy has forgotten you. The Nara, mother to all Ling Galaxy, have forgotten you. However, I, the Supreme, have not forgotten you. I bring you new life and a chance to become what you were always meant to be. Those within my voice, come forward to my ship and meet me. I offer you life."

With the Essence orb in a container, Malone and Frey left the ship with a group of soldiers following. Malone walked ahead unprotected. Some like Frey had warned him about such moves in public, but Malone shrugged them off. He felt a strong wave of invulnerability over him, fueled by his powers but also stoked by his control of Essence. He knew that he'd been able to do what so many others hadn't and in their eyes, couldn't, even wouldn't.

Frey checked the broadcasting system and confirmed all was still sending. "We should leave within 15 standard minutes to prevent anyone from locating us and making this planet," Frey warned Malone.

Malone shot him an annoyed glare. Frey swallowed hard but held his gaze on Malone.

"Fine, but these people and the Galaxy will see me and know I was here."

Malone looked out to a collection of Agmon's citizens. They were a mixed group, one Railen, several Mardaks, and some other Tillians, the once proud race native to Agmon.

Malone thrust his arms outward. "My children, the Supreme has heard your suffering and has come to ease your pain. Please come forward."

One of the Tillians, a short and frail female, stepped closer. Her voice cracked with sadness. "We've been without food for weeks. We eat the roots we find and drink whatever moisture we pull from the air."

Malone neared the female, his brow furrowed. "My child, your suffering is terrible and unnecessary. Tell me your name."

"Taru... Nosova," she whimpered.

The rest of the group lowered their heads when Taru spoke. Malone knew their stories were similar to Taru's without even hearing any others. Their collective despair burned into his mind with the rays of a million suns. He held his hand up. To the derelict dwellers, it looked like he beckoned them closer, but Frey knew better. He checked the equipment for a proper angle and view of Malone with the Agmon dwellers.

Malone embraced Taru. Her thin frame twitched with sobs of weakness and despair. Malone soothed her, his face twisted with the sadness he felt whenever he found someone who, like him, had been forgotten. When he spoke again, his voice was also choked with emotion.

"Today, I liberate this world, and fulfill a promise to you that the Nara have failed at for centuries. You will no longer want today, you will no longer thirst; you will thrive, you will be reborn, you will be my children. Your Supreme offers you this."

With that, Malone released Taru. He produced the canister with the Essence Orb in it, and held it aloft. "Today, in my name, this world of Agmon is reborn." Malone twisted one end of the container. The device lit up with a series of blue glowing patterned lines, and a deep hum filled the air.

Within moments, the arid land of Agmon became fertile ground, and around them various trees bearing fruit appeared. The derelicts looked around them in amazement. Several fell to their knees in disbelief, and soon all of them glanced everywhere, tears in their eyes and the deepest awe for Malone.

Malone savored their look, their unspoken gratitude, for a moment before he turned to one of the cameras controlled by Frey.

"The Nara have failed this Galaxy, but through me, we will all be reborn. All the Supreme asks in return is your belief and support."

TEN

THE *AEON IMPALER* LEFT AGMON, a planet renewed with life. As they neared the jump to deep space, Malone lounged in his quarters with Frey, and they watched the replay of Malone's presentation.

"This was received by no less than 60 percent of the Galaxy via Network," Frey commented, a beaming grin on his face. "Your message will soon cover the remaining portion of the Galaxy once people see the results of your kindness."

Malone studied himself on the video and nodded with Frey's statement. "It appears so. Tell me, what have our enemies been up to?"

"Nothing too out of the ordinary. The Railen are massing against the Omegans, and they continue their efforts on tracking your children down."

Malone gnashed his jaw. "The Railen are too consumed with their own pride to be a concern for us."

Frey slipped a quick smirk at Malone's ironic comment about pride, but caught and steadied himself quickly. "I'm more concerned about the threat of the Omegans anyway. Perhaps it's time we consider their offer."

Malone arched his brow when he heard the tone Frey took regarding his former brethren. "Do you really think we can trust them, Frey?" Malone asked. "I figured they're only in it for the bloodshed."

"They want what you want, like the Railen do as well. This Galaxy has been without a decent ruling body for many cycles. Even with Nic Sava leading the UA, they've still struggled with establishing order. There are moves in developing the UA again as a more standalone body; several in the systems have been in support of that. The unit we saw on Zormad looked to be similar to what I've heard of in that regard."

The UA had reformed a bit, but as spread out as Ling Galaxy was, many hadn't given it much concern. A coordination that large took not only many cycles, but a number of like-minded souls determined on order. Long distance partnerships suffered strain of many things, and the state of Ling Galaxy wasn't fertile ground for cooperation yet. Unity gave way to survival more often than not.

Malone watched the on-screen video of his embrace of the Agmon citizens. "Have you sent a communication to them with our requests?"

"I did," Frey said. "They're ready for your bidding."

Malone smiled. He enjoyed the news of more converts, and he also anticipated the time when the number of devotees he had grew by more than a handful at a time.

"Keep me posted on my children. I want first notification when one of them has secured an Essence orb. We'll show this Galaxy who is in command."

While Frey worked on a communications link with the Omegans, Malone settled back, and once again his thoughts meandered toward his son. He'd come so close physically to getting Ket in his grasp again. There were other ways to reach his progeny though. It was time to put his mind to use and attempt a link to his once lost child.

MALONE FOUND himself for the first time possibly ever without a clear thought on what to say. Over time, Malone's thoughts had gone from hope to finding him again to the grim realization he'd perished like many of the Galaxy had, from one catastrophe or another. Famines were common in Ling Galaxy, but so were conflicts.

Yet his son was there, within reach. He activated the comm on his ship and broadcast a signal toward the *Crimson Lance*. He had to hear his voice.

"Ket, are you there?"

No response.

"My son, it is your father."

Still nothing in reply. Malone scowled a bit at the screen; he realized perhaps his son was in a similar state. But then a response.

"Hello."

"I can't believe you're alive."

"Yeah, I am. And so are you."

"Are you OK?"

"I'm a lot of things, I don't think 'OK' is one of them. What do you want?"

The question stung Malone in a way he wasn't accustomed to. His minions offered him undying loyalty, but his son hadn't been able to. Malone steadied himself, and he knew that the barrage of questions that flowed from his mind were going to take some time for resolution.

"I thought you were dead. Once the Nara cast me out, I looked everywhere I could, but there wasn't anything."

"Mom and I were sent away. Later, she came down with something. I figured it was a reaction to the Disconnection. Whatever it was, she... didn't live long after that."

A trail of moisture oozed from Malone's eyes. He stared at Ket on screen. The pain in his son's eyes was clear, and Malone's thoughts

careened through memories of his wife, and now yet another griev-
ance toward the Nara.

Malone was about to ask where he'd been when Ket asked, "So is
what I heard about you true; you're harvesting Essence?"

"It is. I'm working on saving the Galaxy from the Nara."

Ket bowed his head and chuckled incredulously. "Are you now?"

"Yes. In fact, I've already gotten an Essence orb."

"You mean you stole it."

"Essence is the right of every living being; there's no reason we
have to live any longer in a system that demands our blind allegiance
to the Nara, who have hoarded Essence."

Ket bit his lip. "The reason is reality. And, you're not healing the
Galaxy; you just want Essence for yourself and whoever becomes
your slaves."

"That's not it at all, son."

"Don't call me your son." Ket thrust a finger toward Malone. "I
haven't been your son for a long time. I heard about your experiments
with Pietro. You couldn't stop even when they took us away from you.
We weren't even worth losing your glory, were we?"

Malone clutched his fists. "Ket—"

"Save it. You really think I buy that story about looking for me?
Your son vanishes, and you just give up the chase? How do you
expect me to believe that?"

"I was genetically modified, Ket."

"So was I; all Nara Outcast were. You don't hear me whining
about it."

"But it went further with me, because of what the Nara considered my crimes to be."

Ket shook his head. "A father doesn't abandon his child. Anyhow,
keep your distance from me. Any moron can look out there and see
all the warrants you've got piled up on you. Of course, I can't say I'm
without my own, so I guess we have that in common... people want us
dead." Ket frowned and glanced off.

Malone clasped the side of the screen. "I never wanted it to be this way." As he heard himself utter the words, Malone realized what he truly meant. He had no control over losing his son; even Ket had to agree to that at some point. Malone's true lament was his son's lack of belief in Malone's present course. Of all the converts Malone sought, his son was the one he most needed, but was the most out of reach.

ELEVEN

WHILE MALONE MULLED OVER HIS missed chance with his son, he knew another deal was close, and he readied himself for more intense negotiations.

Emperor Zakmar of the Omegan Empire had formally reached out to Frey with an offer to join forces with Malone, in exchange for some concessions. Aside from Frey's glee at facing his former countrymen as a removed Omegan, he had to admit the deal being offered was at least discussion.

Frey eyed the comm controls before he turned to Malone. "I've already spoken with Zakmar about what he wants."

Malone smirked. "Let me guess, the width and breadth of Ling Galaxy, and a few nearby systems as well?"

Frey shrugged. "He's certainly got his needs and he wants in on your Children."

Malone seethed at the notion. All the time and care he'd taken into finding the lost in Ling Galaxy and giving them purpose was lost on most individuals who weren't part of his collective. He relished the thought of them being filled with purpose again, and that purpose was a life of freedom in Ling Galaxy. Of course, service to him was a given, but considering the abilities they received in trade, it didn't seem that big a requirement to ask.

Malone was very cautious about any attempt to sway his children, especially from a nation who hadn't quite signed over to his side yet.

"Zakmar never ceases to amaze me. We'll just see how much that's worth to him."

Frey nodded. "I'll reactivate the comm so you can hear their full terms."

Several moments later, the screen flickered again and there was Zakmar. His reptilian skin was wrinkled with his advanced age as well as the stress of leading the Omegans from subservience into their present position of burgeoning power. The Omegans were hungry, as eager as Malone was. But unlike the Railen quest for revenge or Malone's quest for dominion, the Omegans wanted their own stake. They wanted to be regarded as a dominant force in the Galaxy. Their period of serving the Nara had brought them recognition as faithful stewards, but even the Omegans grew weary of their thankless level of subservience to Nara despotism.

Zakmar's gravelly voice boomed through the on-board speakers of Malone's ship. "Malone, what do you have to say about my offer?"

Malone took a measured breath. "I found it interesting you failed to mention this offer in my earlier meeting with you, the Railen, and the Nara."

Malone amused himself at the teasing of Zakmar, who favored the discreet negotiating. As much as the Omegans wanted to be known as the dominant force, Malone relished their secret insistence on under the table deals. Survival in Ling Galaxy sometimes made even the most elevated of rulers resort to a back-alley deal or two.

"I would think someone with your history of recklessness would appreciate a bit of strategic maneuvering now and then. Besides, I'm not the one with a number of death warrants on my head," Zakmar countered.

"Fair enough. Now then, I understand you want some of my children in return for your military forces to combine with mine?"

"Precisely. Malone, even you can't deny your maximum troop strength is at very best a decent third behind the UA and our own. Even with your shifting ability, that won't further your aims against the UA unless we work together."

Malone tapped his fingers on the console in thought. Images of his ships on the Cerulak raid flashed in his mind. They'd been cocky, a bit too aggressive maybe, but the truth remained that Malone needed at least some help to reach his goal, and a cooperation with the Omegans, for the time being, seemed a decent bet, given their history.

"I appreciate your dedication, and I know, like you, many were duped by the Nara. Your race had the greater misfortune of being in service to the Nara, stewards of the Essence. But when your usefulness was brought into question, you were removed from duty, relegated to a level of survival like the rest of us. I can tell you that my children are at work retrieving Essence from the corners of the Galaxy. Once they have it, they will hold any number of worlds hostage. I'm content to provide the Omegans with a quantity to use."

"Afraid I will need more than your word on this, Malone." Zakmar shook his head.

"What more can I provide?"

"Give us some of your Lookers as a sign of good faith." Zakmar smiled. "If you're so eager to fulfill your part of the bargain, it won't be a problem for you to part with a few of your children."

Malone clenched his teeth. He shuddered at the thought of even one of his Lookers out of his reach and in the hands of a race with whom he had an alliance, shaky as it may be. But he knew that they were a means to an end. He had so many of his children to command, and losing any of them weakened his position a bit, but the greater value was in the enhanced military. The Omegan fleet offered the best attack against the UA arsenal, and for Malone to have a big enough spear at attacking the UA was worth so much to him.

"Just how many of my children are you demanding?" asked

Malone.

Zakmar mulled over the thought for a few moments. Then he eyed the screen again. "Send me thirteen of your children."

"Oh no, that's far too many. Zakmar, you have to consider the abilities of just one of my children."

"And you have to consider the abilities of my fleet. My people are crying out for their own portion. This Galaxy is ruled by those who dare take action. Now then, we can bargain and barter all day long, but the fact remains that your cause isn't going to succeed without more help. You think you can stop the UA military alone? Your fleet of craft can give them a chase for a time, but even your shifting ability won't give you much to stop them. And especially if that Railen tracking works and your children are all incapacitated. We can seek out their trackers and remove them, giving you the power you want. We'll make sure the UA has more than they can handle. Now, I say again, Malone, thirteen of your children in exchange for my fleet. What say you?"

Malone steeled his jaw and locked eyes with Zakmar. Malone knew that while his gaze provided a measure of mind control over the average citizen, Zakmar wasn't a lightweight. But Malone also knew that in any negotiation, the first offer was never the best.

"Five of my children is my counter," Malone replied.

"Ten," said Zakmar.

Malone's face twisted in a scowl. "Are you insane? Have you any idea of the efforts involved in producing one of my children? Do you know the insult you're giving me valuing them so lowly? Five."

Zakmar's eyes steeled. "I'm aware the service of the Omegan military has considerable value as well. Eight."

"Seven."

Zakmar took a measured breath. "Seven."

Malone's brow relaxed and he smiled. "Agreed. I'll send them your way. Now then, I've got operations for your fleet; I'll send coordinates and you let me know when you've got Omegan starcraft en route."

Malone ended the communication and slapped the console in celebration. He'd gotten his army, even if it he gave up a measure of control. It was inconsequential, though. His children were all but too eager to die in his service. And their presence with the Omegans was just a brief delay. Malone knew his next moves had to be swift. The UA fleet already engaged the Omegans, but with Malone's plans and ability at foreseeing moves, he knew the upper hand was soon his with this new arrangement.

He contacted Frey again. "Frey, we need to do our best to remove the UA resurgence. Set course for Zormad, and relay to the Omegans. I want to drive a spear down the UA's throat once and for all. We'll start by removing Zormad from existence. It stands as a beacon of hope, a place the Xeno started a new life in. We'll show Ling Galaxy the only hope is in following me. Once you get to Zormad, take all who are there: Mardak, Xeno, or any other race. We'll offer them a chance at conversion, and failing that we lay them to ruins. The war for Essence is upon us. We cannot hesitate, we cannot waver on our quest. Our purpose is just, our calling true. We will earn our place in the Galaxy."

Malone leaned back in his chair with confidence in his cause. Frey bowed and contacted the Omegans again regarding the coordinates. Malone eyed his crew, ready to proceed on their course. Malone found himself with tinge of wonder about his son, and in the midst of his eager energy about his dominion of Ling Galaxy, he struggled with thoughts of his son, and just what it was that made his son doubt his father's quest. Malone steadied his resolve with other thoughts. *This is a time for action, and now the Galaxy has seen my intent. They'll follow me wherever I go, and one day they'll beg me for the scraps that I hold. All will be my subjects. Even the Nara, and I will delight in Ellene Ballo's head under my blade. She'll beg me, much as I did when they expelled me. They are my bane, and I will show all that no one in this Galaxy can question my rule. This was my purpose, this is my only course. The Galaxy will be mine.*

QUANTUM OF DESTINY

ONE

ELLENE BALLO WASN'T SOMEONE who took threats idly. She leaned back in her chair and pondered the one she'd just received from Malone Stanton. As Hierarch, supreme leader of the Nara for over five decades on their home world of Grondia, she had come across more than her fair share of problems. Several individuals and groups wanted more Essence than they were given, and they weren't afraid to press any number of buttons on Ellene to make their wishes happen.

But Malone Stanton wasn't the typical pusher who wormed their way in amid a threat of destruction that could easily be dismissed. Malone was a renegade who had big ideas, bigger plans and an even bigger mouth. Ellene knew the traditional Nara policy of ignoring the threat in this case wasn't going to be successful for long.

Ellene recalled Malone was given every possible chance, maybe even more than the typical Nara dissenter. She debated inwardly though if the taking of Malone's wife and child from him overstepped her rightful bounds of authority.

Still, the way Malone worked himself into his situation concerned her. As much as anyone who'd broken Nara law, Malone was first labeled a Violator and subjected to Disconnection, the procedure that altered a Nara's physiology to prevent them from reaching the dimension in which Grondia lay. Furthermore, Malone was restricted to a maximum-security prison off dimension in Ling Galaxy. Ellene mused they should've removed his voice; maybe that would've been the most appropriate punishment for him.

Ellene gazed at another file on her console. It had grown steadily for a while, and it contained reports of Malone reaching Nara students in Instruction, speaking with them telepathically and encouraging them to break from the Nara procedure, steal equipment, whatever they could to help him. The incidents went from mild annoyance to serious threats in a short time. The Nara production of Essence had always continued, but Ellene knew, as much as these things happened more rapidly each passing day, the threat to Nara's purpose and the Galaxy at large was too big to ignore Malone Stanton, as much as some of her brethren preferred it that way. Besides, they had other challenges before them: Railen, the Omegans, the needs of the UA in general.

She stretched her long slender limbs before focusing on her machine access. "Scan data for activities of Malone in connection with syndicates known and suspected."

A hologram burst out and hovered above Ellene, and she watched the display as it morphed around her. Grondia was in close proximity to Ling Galaxy, and Ellene knew what Malone had been up to was focused there. Ling was vast, with plenty of civilizations, people, and more importantly, want, that someone like Malone knew how to work to his advantage.

As Ellene spoke details about her query, maps came into focus with specific locations marked in jagged lines. Collections of fugitive photos along with news updates on various heists around the universe.

Ellene's mouth formed a line as she saw the pattern whiz past her. Ellene still had a stubborn hope this was going to be a simple fix, where she quietly dispatched someone to take care of this thorn in her side.

The system completed its assembly, and a flat male electronic voice gave the update. "Stanton, Malone. Convicted of theft of Essence approximately 25 cycles ago. Escaped from UA Penitentiary and at large for past 23 cycles."

Ellene steepled her fingers and stared at the text that floated before her like a friendly aid who brought supplies hoping it pleased her. Malone had been a prized student in his day, one of the promising future Nara, and Ellene knew from back then how crafty he was. What she needed to find was going to take some work, as Malone was more than capable at covering his tracks.

"Update, provide most recent news." Ellene wondered what else he'd have been up to that he'd made such a bold call to her and the rest of the leaders. Not only that; his ability to hold Essence himself across the dimension was a bigger threat.

The electronic voice continued. "Malone has partnered with Gamma Network, a syndicate running a variety of lower-level front operations, smuggling, arms distribution. They have affiliated with Railen but not exclusively."

"That figures," Ellene mused. The Railen were also outcasts of Nara, but unlike Malone, they chose the way of collective rebellion instead of personal vendetta. Many Railen were former Nara military. Once tasked with the homeland security of Grondia, home of Nara and repository of the Essence, they became weary of Nara policies and thought they were better suited to handle the Essence themselves. This of course met with a stern and quick exit from Nara, with Disconnection from their former home world.

After a few minutes in thought, Ellene hailed Bates Rocke, head of Nara Security.

"Yes, Hierarch?"

"Bates, I'm looking for more details on Malone Stanton's activities of late. I'm getting more updates on these contacts he's been making."

Bates paused on the line. Any news like this was a slam on Bates, and as much as Ellene liked letting her people know she always had her eye on things, in this case her concern overshadowed her enjoyment. "It seems, Hierarch, that Malone has been able to forge some access through the dimensional barrier, and he's targeting our youth."

"Any idea what he wants?"

"Typically, it's sabotage level stuff. I've interviewed several of the ones contacted, and it usually involves suggestions of them acting out, stealing equipment, things like that."

Ellene said, "That's not all he's on for. He's also interested in Essence, as you are aware."

"Yes, but he's not getting that through any kind of neural or telepathic access."

Ellene leaned back in her chair. As much as Malone tried, she knew it was only a matter of time before even the dimensional barrier wasn't an issue to him as well. "Bates, I'm concerned about our position here. Malone is already corrupting the minds of our students, and that's how revolutions start. The more who think our work isn't the utmost important, the more dangerous he grows. And if Malone Stanton is allowed to harness Essence for his own purposes, you realize what that means, don't you?"

"I'm well aware, Hierarch."

"Good, I would hope so." Ellene drummed her fingers on her console. Malone's moves weren't clear to her, but she felt he had something in the works, and it was time she put some plans of her own into place.

"Double your watch on the student population, Bates. I want immediate notice of any Violators. I'm going to talk with Perdita Auer about the state of our military to see what can be done there. I say again, I want to know right away if anyone has been contacted by Malone Stanton and especially if they are a Violator."

"Consider it done." Bates said.

ELLENE ENDED her call with Bates and watched the display a few moments longer, then swiped her hand, which closed the holographic display completely. Malone was a lingering concern for her, but not her only one. She was due to meet with some of the students in Nara Instruction.

A Nara's childhood was free from any rigid training. As youth, they had chances to socialize and develop bonds with peers while under the watchful eyes of Nara elders. Family units provided organization and routine for the Nara, but all learning at early stages of life was done via parental guidance and social interaction.

While there are no formal class activities for youth, all Nara from the age of 13 cycles, roughly 16 Earth Years, are brought into Nara Instruction by the process known as the Acquiring. This process allowed the Nara elders, with some input from the Ancients, to assess the Nara as they've been monitored from the early stages of their lives. The ultimate tasks for the Nara revolved around the production, handling, and distribution of Essence. Any part of that process involved a great number of Nara, and no part was without a certain level of risk.

The duty of the Nara, and the reason for their existence, was handling Essence. The substance resided in an area of Grondia known as the Spring. The source of Essence had the appearances of a calm lake of water, with an effervescent glow about it. Essence was dealt with in two stages, processing and delivery. Both were equally important, each with their respective risks as well. Once a Nara passed the Acquiring, their training began. After they were initiated, they had to decide which path they took.

Ellene put on one of her more imperial cloaks and strode out of her residence toward the Nara facility. The azure hue of the exterior of the Nara Compound greeted her as she took in a breath of the cool misty air. She turned for a moment to watch the temple of the Ancients, an adjacent building on the Nara Compound where the spirits of Nara who had passed from existence resided. The entities were a continual guidance to Nara, especially the Hierarchs.

Ellene offered a demure bow toward the Ancient temple. "Guide my way," she said softly. It was part of her routine. The phrase was a customary one the Nara spoke toward the Ancients. While it was sometimes just a routine to Ellene, on that day, she felt a deeper than usual connection to the timeless mantra. Another lingering glance toward the Ancient temple and she was off to her day's schedule.

As she walked past fellow citizens, they offered the customary greeting toward the Hierarch, a bow with the right arm across the chest. Ellene responded to the greetings with a polite smile or wave. Soon she found herself in the Headmaster's quarters, readying for her encounter with the future of the Nara.

Iden Combes had been headmaster of Nara Instruction for at least 60 cycles, by Ellene's best estimation. When she assumed the position of Hierarch, he had offered his services to her for the transition, and they'd began a friendly contact. While they hadn't seen eye to eye all the time, she figured Iden to be one of those who would always give her the honest truth.

Ellene reclined in the chair in Iden's quarters as he gave her the rundown on the class statistics to date: number of students in each path of training, the general progress, any problem areas. But Ellene wasn't as interested in the updates as she'd been before.

After a few minutes of Iden speaking, she thrust a hand up, quieting him. "Iden, we've got a problem."

Iden's brow creased. "What are you talking about?"

"A problem with a name. Two words that shout a thousand details."

Iden froze. He'd seen enough Nara Violators that he knew exactly who Ellene meant. Like many who knew what this name was, Iden hoped the mere avoidance of its mention was enough that it disappeared. "Malone Stanton."

Ellene nodded slowly. "I had a most troubling contact with him a short while ago. I, along with leaders of the Railen and Omegans, was contacted by him."

"What did he say?"

"What he said isn't what concerns me. No, what concerns me is the fact he's evidently been able to harness Essence on his own in addition to reaching Nara students telepathically."

Iden's head bowed. Malone had once been a most promising Nara, a bright student full of remarkable potential. But a brilliant mind faced a huge number of possibilities, including ones that used their remarkable abilities for destruction. Iden remembered Malone's swift progression and handling of tasks with the Essence that students several cycles ahead of him struggled with. Iden only ever admitted to himself that he once considered Malone as a possible replacement for himself when he was ready to relinquish his position. But all that promise and potential was lost when Malone chose his eventual path.

"We should've seen his threat much sooner, before he became what he is now," Iden muttered, his head still downward.

Ellene rose slowly. She placed her hands on Iden's hunched shoulders. "Old friend, we've been deceived. Malone has taken the power of his ancestry, and with his diabolical mind he has betrayed all Nara. That doesn't mean, however, that I plan on letting Malone Stanton have any more victories."

Iden's head raised slowly until his eyes met Ellene's. "What do you intend to do?"

Ellene's eyes narrowed sharply. "I'm not discussing that now. Just know I will give this a lot of thought. And, while you have done an admirable job in your cycles here, know this... Violators make their choices because the stewardship of their direction hasn't been watched closely. That stewardship begins here, under your watch. I say to you, Iden Combes, get your institution in order. The flagrancy of Violators is a mark upon the Nara, and if these transgressions aren't kept in check, I will be looking at you to pay the price, along with your core of instructors."

"Yes, Hierarch."

RANDOM STUDENTS WERE SELECTED out of Nara Instruction to meet Ellene as part of an interview process. While it originated in Nara tradition, Ellene tailored the practice so it kept her feelers into the school, and any students with potential for higher assignments, like potential Hierarch candidates for future generations. Traditionally, this took the course of an informal conversation, but over the cycles Ellene had learned how to pull out certain details from a student by what they said, and in some cases, what they hadn't said at all, at least verbally.

Leaving Iden's quarters for a more public area, she set herself up on one of the large class halls in the Nara Training Center. The rooms were auditorium style, with a large holographic display at the focal point of the stage. To the side of the display tech was a series of chairs, set up specifically for Ellene's meeting.

As she waited for the students to be brought in, Ellene wondered if she'd be able to tell if any of them were contacted by Malone, and just what was his criteria for reaching them. Was it completely random, or had he chosen a certain aspect? She figured any students selected for Essence Delivery service would be of great interest to him. However, the fact he'd gotten a piece of Essence had her wonder if the very students responsible for producing Essence were his main target.

Ellene reclined in a comfortable seat on stage, where an instructor normally presided over a class. A free chair waited alongside her as a stream of randomly selected students were brought in. Questions were mainly standard until an answer provoked a nonstandard response, and Ellene jumped into the conversation like a ride down a river rapids, savoring all the unexpected jolts and turns that went with it.

She was nearly done for the day when a set of bright eyes amid a deep auburn mane of long hair made her pause. The female was led to the open chair by Nara Guards, just like the others, but Ellene felt off for some reason.

The student gave the customary bow to Ellene before sitting, then crossed her legs and offered a polite smile, waiting for Ellene's process to begin.

Ellene extended her personal data screen, which displayed the student's information. "Sarika... Tholl."

"That's correct, Hierarch."

Ellene gave a slight nod in response. She then perused Sarika's student and citizen file for a moment. Clearly, whatever had caught her off guard was in there somewhere.

But after two minutes of searching, Ellene was no closer to the answer than when she began. "So, tell me, what do you think about your training so far?"

Sarika shifted a bit in her seat. "Well, it's fascinating. I've always wondered how the Essence orbs were made. My parents used to tell me stories, but it's kinda obvious they were just trying to get me to go to sleep back then."

They shared a laugh. Ellene closed her data screen, then eyed Sarika. "For some reason, I'm feeling something about you. It's as if I've seen you before or something."

Sarika's brow creased. "N-no leader, this is the first time we've met. I'm sorry, but I'm not sure what you could mean."

Ellene clenched her jaw. Sarika's response wasn't out of insolence, and Ellene knew she wasn't being combative. She decided to press on through the questions.

"You mentioned Essence Production. What aspect of that have you enjoyed the most?"

"Oh, the delivery, of course. Being on the teams that send the orbs to the Galaxy."

"That's quite dangerous, you know. We've got plenty of safeguards, but there are people out there who are doing everything they can to get to us."

"I know that. But getting Essence to the worlds that need it and keeping life existing in the Galaxy is worth the risk."

Ellene marveled at Sarika. Her eyes were as bright as any new student, a young Nara full of hope for what she could bring. Ellene couldn't help but feel a little melancholy over the spark in Sarika's eyes and tried her best remembering a time when she felt that same zest for the Nara. She loved her position and her job of leading and guiding the Nara, but she had to admit her cycles had stolen some of that vigor she once had that was now staring back at her through Sarika's gaze.

"Sarika, you've been by far the most interesting student I've spoken with here today. There's no doubt in my mind you'll be a fine addition to the team, and if Delivery is what you want, I suspect it will be yours in very good time."

Sarika beamed at the praise and started to rise from her seat until Ellene clasped her arm. "Not yet. There's still a little more."

Sarika's brow furrowed and her skin flashed a lighter pink hue for a few moments as she lowered back into her seat.

Ellene clasped her hands together. "Tell me, have you heard anything about students being contacted?"

"Oh, in their housing units during sleep? A few things here and there; no one I really know that well though."

"I see. We've been trying to figure out what's going on there; have you heard anything more from these students at all?"

Sarika's brow crinkled, and she glanced downward in thought. "No, I'm sorry, Hierarch, I can't offer any more right now than what I said."

Ellene held her gaze on Sarika, and Ellene peered deeply into her eyes. Ellene's mind followed suit and searched the thoughts of Sarika. They were simple, thoughts about school, a few male Nara who Sarika fancied, but nothing of what Ellene had hoped for.

Sarika, feeling the probe, stiffened a bit, her skin flashing a pale tone during Ellene's mental peer into her mind. Once Ellene realized what she was looking for wasn't there, she released.

Sarika let a gasp out and leaned back in her chair.

"That's all. Thank you for your time, and I wish you the best," Ellene said as she motioned Sarika toward the exit portal.

TWO

SARIKA THOLL TRIED HER BEST to get comfortable. The firm back of her seat pressed her flesh harshly, but she wondered if that pressure was just tricks from her overworked mind. She was in the first phase of Instruction in her future life as a Nara. The training was mandatory for all citizens as it prepared them for the production, handling and distribution of Essence to the entire Ling Galaxy.

The classroom was modest in size but was one of many to handle the two thousand Nara of the age of 13 cycles. The training was intense and long, but was necessary to handle the delicate process.

Sarika stretched in her seat. The bluish tint of her limbs darkened as she strained her muscles away from tightness as best she could. At the head of the class stood Razak Frankum, their instructor. His bluish Nara complexion was a darker hue, typical for Nara of the older generations. Sarika wondered if his scowled complexion was the norm as well.

"Class, the next eight cycles will not be easy, I can assure you. But as we all place our trust in the guidance of the Ancients, you can be assured your work here will be vital to the survival of Ling Galaxy.

You are expected to participate, learn, and apply. Your Galaxy needs you, and as a Nara, your life is about service."

The tolerance of the Nara for troublemakers wasn't anything Sarika nor her fellow students needed a lecture on. They'd heard stories of the likes of Malone Stanton and Ander Pimm, among many who let the idea of what the Nara's work was truly about get clouded with their own selfish dreams of galactic glory.

As Razak's introductory speech droned on, Sarika noticed a message on her classroom portal.

Here we go, huh?

Sarika smirked and glanced to her right, catching the eye of Alda, her longest and closest friend, sitting next to her. Sarika shrugged and nodded to their instructor, making a sick face.

Alda let out a guffaw, catching Razak's attention, and he stopped short.

"Excuse me. You there in Row 13, is there a problem?"

Sarika swallowed under Razak's glare. She looked at Alda for help. "N-no, sir. Sorry, nothing at all."

"Well, then, why don't you tell the class what was so important you had to interrupt valuable Instruction time?"

Sarika felt the eyes of everyone on her, and she noticed the skin on her arms turning a shade pinker. The Nara's emotions were easily registered, at least when it came to things like embarrassment, which turned their complexions varying shades of red. It made them easy to read, which at that point was the worst trait Sarika could've ever wanted.

"She was describing a dream!" Alda blurted out.

Razak's gaze shifted to Alda, then back to Sarika, who nodded, her head cast downward.

"Kindly keep your conversations about personal matters to your free hours. Both of you, see me at the end of the day for the appropriate disciplinary measures."

"Yes, sir," Sarika and Alda replied in unison.

The class continued in silence, with Razak running through a number of screens relating to Essence Production and Delivery. The class was designated as Delivery candidates, so they were going to be on the hook for a lot of processing and running about the Galaxy.

Sarika met Alda in the common area of the Nara Training facility for lunch. They grabbed two spots at one of the lengthy tables and relaxed a bit over their rations.

"So, you going to tell me how she was or what?" Alda asked, playing with her rations.

Sarika shrugged. "I don't know. She was nice, I guess."

"You guess? You meet the Hierarch, and get a half hour with her—"

"More like fifteen minutes."

"Ok, fifteen minutes with the Nara Hierarch, and all you can say is she was nice? Come on, give me more; what did she ask? What did she say?"

"We talked about what I wanted to do after Instruction, and she asked me about my family."

"Standard stuff." Alda's brow dropped a bit, disappointed Sarika didn't have more juicy or intimate details. She wasn't able to figure out why she hadn't made the cut to be interviewed by Ellene. *Maybe they were afraid I'd have asked about getting her job*, Alda mused to herself. It wasn't too far of a stretch to consider.

Baldric's shaky voice interrupted their chat.

"Can I join?"

"No," Alda said, sending a playful smirk toward him.

Baldric's brow creased, and he eyed Alda. Sarika shook her head. "Sit down. Don't mind her; she's on some kinda trip today."

Baldric placed his food down, and it was clear right away he wasn't there to play little flirty games with Alda. He took a huge gulp of his beverage and eyed the room. The rest of their classmates were deep into their own food and conversations, providing more than a decent amount of background chatter. Still, Baldric edged closer to the girls, motioning them to do the same.

"I heard from someone last night."

Alda cocked an eyebrow. "Ooh, someone special?"

"No, not some—look, I really need to talk with someone, and you're both my closest friends."

"So talk," Sarika said. "We're here. I doubt anyone else could hear you over the chatter in here."

"Maybe. But I'd rather not risk it, given who this was."

Sarika felt her midsection tighten. Baldric's tone, his worried look, and the fact he was scared to even tell his two closest friends about something in public worried her. She lay her hand on his arm. He eyed her touch then watched her eyes, tinted with concern. "It's OK. Meet us after school at the library. I'll save us a study room."

———

THE NARA LIBRARY was a huge complex that adjoined the Instruction Center. The tall edifice held the complete archives of the Nara, the history of Ling Galaxy as well as the texts of the Ancients, which dictated the purpose of the Nara as well as the edicts that all Nara lived by. It also held information about the punishments Nara faced for sufficient violations of their law.

As promised, Sarika grabbed a study room for the three of them. This wasn't an unusual practice; during their time of Instruction, the three had often been together after hours, studying their course materials, even playing games to break up their mood.

This evening had a much different spin, though. Baldric's mood from lunch hadn't gotten much better, and Sarika was beyond anxious to hear his story. She only figured the record amount of time Alda went without knowing Baldric's news already must've had Alda on the verge of combusting.

Baldric sat at the table in the center of the room with Sarika and Alda opposite.

"So, out with it. Seriously, I may just drop dead if you don't start talking in the next five seconds," Alda gasped.

"I heard from Malone Stanton."

The name seemed to stop time, at least in the room, as if it were a magic spell and the simple uttering of the words activated a cataclysmic freeze of space time.

After what felt like ten minutes had passed, Sarika managed to ask, "How?"

Baldric shrugged, his eyes darting off for a bit. "It was late; I was about to sleep for the night. I heard a voice. At first, I thought it may have been my father; he'd spoken with me a few minutes earlier. But the voice persisted, and I soon realized it wasn't in the room, or even in the housing unit."

Alda and Sarika shared a worried look.

"He spoke to me via my mind, and the weirdest thing is I realized I could speak back."

"You talked. With him," Sarika said.

Baldric nodded. "He told me about Essence, and what Nara's been doing that we don't know about."

"What's that?" Sarika asked.

"The Nara send Essence out, but they're also using it to keep themselves living longer with less disease. Haven't you ever wondered why the rest of the Galaxy has so many problems like Veculus, yet we live in an endless paradise, with no illness whatsoever?"

Sarika and Alda looked at each other. The Nara had been essentially disease free, but it was attributed to the proximal location of the system, away from the rest of the Galaxy.

"There's no way of knowing that this was the reason for our health condition," Alda said.

"I know, but it was enough to get me thinking." Baldric shrugged.

Sarika watched Baldric. His eyes darted between her and Alda for a moment. "What did Malone want to talk with you about?"

"He wants to return to Grondia."

Sarika's eyes opened wide, and she grabbed Baldric's shoulder. "You know who he is, right? You remember the talks about him in

Instruction? He's an enemy of the state. If you help him, and they find out, you'll be sent for Disconnection. Do you want that?"

"I don't know; it's almost like I feel bad not helping him." Baldric's head sank. Sarika was moved at the sight of her childhood friend so torn. She and Alda went to his side, their hands grabbing his shoulders and hair softly.

"Promise you won't tell," Baldric begged.

Alda's lip twitched. "I won't say a thing, I promise."

"It's not that simple," Sarika advised.

Sarika stood and paced, while Alda and Baldric eyed her. Sarika's long dark hair swept downward past her face, her hands together at her mouth as she stepped around the room. Deception was beyond complicated for a Nara, from a physical standpoint alone. Sarika understood their challenge better than her friends, but she also found her mind thinking ahead even more.

"Promising isn't enough. We need a cover story. We have to practice it and keep it just between us if this will work."

"How do we even do something like this?" Alda asked.

Sarika said, "Every day after Instruction, we meet here. We use an hour in our allotted free time and work on this. Do everything you can in the meanwhile during Instruction, whenever a teacher singles you out for anything, play it calm and collected. We've only got one shot at this, and we have to make it count."

"It goes also we should keep ourselves on our work. The more we comply and follow the rules, the less chance we'll be picked out to begin with," Baldric said.

Sarika smiled. They had a chance, but she knew it was going to take everything they had in themselves, and possibly more they knew they were capable of yet.

THREE

AFTER A MONTH OF INSTRUCTION, the exceptional among the crop of incoming Nara had distinguished themselves. Sarika showed notable promise on the Essence Delivery side while Baldric proved himself well suited for Essence Production. Nara custom not only identified those with accelerated talent, but it also incorporated that talent by giving the standouts advance looks at their ultimate responsibilities post-graduation.

For Sarika, that meant following an Essence Worker on one of their runs through the dimensional barrier to replenish Essence on a system in need. She admitted to herself the work was even more fun than she'd imagined. But the lingering sense of danger had her afraid more than once. She'd heard the stories about the Nara who paid for their work with their lives, and she was determined to figure out what she needed to do so that never happened to her.

Baldric immersed himself in the workings of Essence Production. He was brought to the Central Plant, where he gazed on the Source, the never-ending pool of glowing green fluid that was the purest form of Essence. While not even the Nara were able to touch it without proper protection, an imposing structure encased a huge section just adjacent to the more rugged and undeveloped location where Essence originated.

Another aspect of Essence Production involved communication with the Delivery teams via the Nara Net, a communications Network capable of spanning dimensions, to contact Nara on their runs to relay and receive information. While Nara are essentially on their own once they cross the barrier, a lifeline in the Nara Net gives them the chance to call back home to relay information about conditions, or in extreme cases, a distress signal can be sent in the event of a horrible turn of events.

In keeping with their agreed plan, the three met regularly in the Nara Library, where their discussions ranged from what Malone's messages to Baldric were to the new information about the previews of their eventual responsibilities.

Alda huffed. Never one to hold in her frustrations, she relished the chance to vent to her two closest confidants. "I don't get it. How come you two get Advance treatment when I'm just sitting back with the rest of the group?"

Sarika managed an awkward grin. "I don't know. You'll be there soon enough, you know."

"Yeah, I guess. Would be nicer if I could be there now."

Baldric huffed. "Advanced or not, we'll all be deployed to our jobs soon. I have more bad news."

Sarika and Alda eyed their friend in anticipation.

"Malone's asking me to help him adjust the Nara Net."

Alda said, "You know that's what they use to contact the Nara in the field, right?"

"Yeah, I do, but he's saying they're all in danger."

"What kind of danger?"

"He said that what the Nara are teaching us isn't helping Ling Galaxy. In fact, it's keeping it enslaved. Malone wants to free the Galaxy so everyone has all they need instead of letting a few Nara decide the way for everyone."

Sarika said, "What you're suggesting goes against cycles of teaching. You've heard this and we've been taught it—the Nara are the reason Ling Galaxy lives. If Essence gets out, and squandered until it isn't available, where will we be, where will all of this be?"

"But we're isolated; doesn't it make you wonder why we've never been shown the outside Galaxy, except for a few glimpses? Malone has shown me things, taken me places, revealed the suffering throughout Ling Galaxy. Do you want to be part of a system that lets people suffer, Sarika? Because I don't."

They sat in silence over that. Baldric wasn't being swayed, and Sarika held her side of the dispute up pretty well too. Alda found herself in the middle, as she wondered how much of what Baldric said about Malone had merit.

"Can you show me; can Malone show me these things?" Alda asked.

Sarika grabbed Alda's arm. "Are you nuts? He's already in danger of being labeled a Violator, and now you want to find out what our biggest threat is up to?"

Baldric shook his head. "He's not our threat, Sarika. Why can't you see that?"

Fear latched itself to Sarika's core. For the first time, she saw how clearly she and her friends were headed down divergent paths. She stood and attempted to collect her emotions, though her voice was still very strained. "What I can see is my two closest friends going down a very dark road. Don't you remember the history of the Violators? OK, maybe there isn't always peace and happiness in the Galaxy, but without people willing to work towards that, it'll never get there."

"Don't you even want to think about it?" asked Alda as she reached out for Sarika's hand.

Sarika leaned away from her friend. "Resolutions aren't always absolutes. I think people can and will be greedy. If Malone gets to spread Essence around, who's to say that's even what he really wants? I also heard he broke out of a prison, and I can't imagine he'd have been there in the first place if he was just some misunderstood soul. You two better think about that and what you're about to attempt."

Baldric stood as Sarika turned to leave.

"Sarika, you're still feeding off the truth the Nara have given us. There's another way. Please, come back!"

But Sarika had said her piece; she was done. Alda and Baldric just watched her as she left the room. Though their lives had begun together, they realized the painful fact that their time together had just met a swift end.

FOUR

SARIKA SKIPPED THE MEETINGS WITH Baldric and Alda from then on. Even Instruction periods she shared with them became a regular challenge of ignoring the contact attempts Alda and Baldric made toward her. Sarika's thoughts on them were avoidance at all costs. Her fear was of what Ellene really knew, and especially if she'd had any inkling of Sarika's link to Baldric.

One day, Sarika's luck of staying away from Alda ran short, and she was cornered between Instruction periods.

"Baldric's going to do it," Alda said. "He's going to contact Malone."

"What do you want me to do about it?" Sarika asked. She looked at her friend and was surprised how different Alda looked to her in just a short amount of time. Sarika had chosen the way of the Nara, and she felt guilty that she hadn't been able to report her friends sooner. She hoped it wasn't too late. She shrugged her friend off. Whatever Ellene knew or didn't, Sarika realized her best bet was if she got out ahead of Baldric's schemes before Nara Security got wind and began a trace of all his contacts.

Sarika found a Security contact after one of her classes for the day.

"I need to report a Violator."

The officer quickly escorted Sarika into the Administration Wing and took her into a briefing room. The walls were bare, and she knew she was only in there for one thing. She wondered if the room was used for other things, like Disconnection, and just what happened to those people. She swallowed when she realized those people now included one or maybe two who had been close to her for a long time.

After a few minutes, Bates Rocke appeared. "I understand you've got some information on Violators for us."

"Yes, that's true."

Bates pulled out a series of digital files and laid them on the table. "Your willingness to come forward helps your standing in this matter. We're looking for even the associates of Violators, and the fact you have personal knowledge of some leads me to wonder just how much you're connected."

"We were friends since before the Acquiring. I knew them as children."

"Did they ever express any thoughts to you in early cycles about not believing in the Nara's mission?"

"No."

"Have you ever seen them doing anything regarding the Nara Essence facilities that isn't in a manner directly related to our purpose?"

"No."

"What are the specific violations you're reporting here?"

"Attempts to use the Nara Net to contact parties beyond Nara."

Bates narrowed his eyes. His hue turned a darker red as he leaned toward Sarika. The sour smell of Bates' breath slid past Sarika's nose. She tried moving back, but the seat was rigid. Soon they were only a few inches apart. Bates eyes looked directly into Sarika's.

"You're going to tell me everything, because if you don't, I'm going to pull your mind and get it anyway. The more you tell me now, the easier this will all be for you. So, give me everything you know, Sarika Tholl. I want to know what these Violators were up to."

Sarika managed to swallow after a few moments. She felt the pangs of lost friendship as she began from what she knew. She hated everything about the experience, but most of all, she hated feeling like she had no other option but to bury her former friends.

FIVE

E LLENE WAS LOST IN THOUGHTS ABOUT Malone
and how to handle the growing threat he represented when
she heard someone clear their throat behind her. She
turned to see Bates Rocke.

"I can't say I'm not surprised at your presence."

Bates took a careful step forward. "Apologies, leader. But we've
caught another one."

"Violator." She knew it was that, but she still had to say it, as if
a small portion of her being wished it was something else. She
wondered how many past Nara hierarchs had such dissension to
deal with. She took a long breath and braced her hands on her
desk.

"What have they done, and what is their name?"

The name is Baldric Frier; he's a first cycle student. He was
caught attempting to signal the outside."

Ellene clenched. The rebellious nature usually festered among
students and didn't surface until at least the fourth cycle. The early
cycles of Nara Instruction covered the basics, and the dangers only
rose once the students began to work closely with Essence. The

substance had a way of corrupting even the most resilient minds with the possibilities it contained.

"Where is the Violator now?"

"In general holding. Shall we proceed with Disconnection?"

Ellene studied the walls behind Bates where several tapestries hung. They depicted scenes of ancient Grondia, when the Ancients taught the earlier generations of Nara, when their society was less formalized, and the Nara had even fewer concerns over their own selfish gains. The corruption that had grown in the Galaxy wasn't even a thought in ancient times. She held a gaze on the fabrics and wondered if a time like that was ever possible again.

Bates began to speak, but Ellene cut him off. "I wish to speak with him. See to it."

After Baldric Frier was moved to a less secure location, Ellene proceeded with Bates for her meeting. She'd spoken with Violators before. The typical exchange included a number of threats against the Nara, and especially a strong rebuke over the nature and the attitude perceived in training. The benevolence and care of the Nara was often dismissed by the typical Violator as self-serving and grandiose while ignorant of the true needs of the Galaxy.

Baldric was restrained in a chair. Once he saw Ellene, his eyes widened. She knew Baldric was still too young to be a physical threat, but knowing what she did about Essence and those who managed to harness its capabilities on a personal level, she insisted on the precautions reserved for the most physically strong offenders.

Ellene strode about, refusing the seat made available for her. Bates kept an eye toward the back of the room as well as two Nara guards for safe keeping.

Ellene's head was downward as she thought for several moments. Once she arrived in front of Baldric, she began. "So, care to explain yourself?"

Baldric's hair was mussed, his eyes wide with many thoughts, fear over what was going to happen, anger that he was even caught, regret he wasn't able to get more people to join him. "We have a—"

"Moral imperative; yes, I've heard this before." Ellene spun around and walked more around the room. Bates eyed her with concern. Baldric's reason seemed to be the stock answer of many Violators, and while Ellene had grown a little too accustomed to hearing it spat back in her face, no matter how many times it was recited to her almost verbatim, in her inner soul she knew there was never to be a time where she found that line of gibberish acceptable.

She paused for a moment, then charged up to Baldric until her face was mere inches from his.

"Madame Hierarch!" Bates said, but Ellene ignored his warning. Instead, she gazed into Baldric's eyes. The youth hadn't yet mastered the skill of handling intimidation. His shell of bravado had just begun its process of hardening, and Ellene almost savored the easy challenge of dissecting the youth's will.

Ellene narrowed the gap between herself and Baldric until she swore she saw the vapor of her breath condense on Baldric's cheek. "Tell me now, what did you share over Nara Net."

Beads of sweat formed and trickled off Baldric's forehead like drops of rain. His complexion became a variety of hues from light pink to darker red. As much as Ellene savored Baldric being uncomfortable as he obviously was, she was afraid of just how much information Baldric had shared.

"I don't have to say anything," Baldric stammered.

"But you do, and you want to. Talk now."

The name was in the room even though it was unsaid. Everyone there knew it, just like the rest of the Nara and even the Ancients knew. Malone Stanton's deeds had reached beyond that of mere violation into threatening the very fabric of their Galaxy.

Baldric looked around, but Bates gave him no inkling of assistance. This offense was his to bear.

"It was about deliveries, the schedules for Essence."

"So, you've seen him? Or at least you've heard from him? Baldric, you're meddling with powers you and he cannot begin to comprehend."

Ellene pulled back. Now in addition to getting her precious students to wreak havoc from within, Malone had a pipeline into the delivery of Essence itself. His reach was far greater than she'd even dreamed possible.

"You're not telling me the entire truth; I don't even need to pull your feeble mind. Enough of the charade. I want to know everything you've told him. You'll provide details in full, and you'll do it now!" Ellene eyed Baldric with considerable disgust.

Ellene's gaze stayed locked on Baldric, but thoughts raced through her head like a rushing brook. This youth was conniving and resourceful, but someone so young wouldn't be able to manage a violation like this without assistance. And Ellene suspected the collaboration wasn't with a peer. For Baldric to have the kind of access he needed, that required help from someone higher up.

She shuddered at the realization that the break in security happened with assistance from someone with Elder status. As long as she had the youth here, she had a chance to pull and pry and procure every pertinent fact, and she at least savored that part of the entire calamity.

Ellene backed up a moment, and Baldric's breathing slowed a bit. His eyes were still tinted with fear, and his skin hue had gone from a mild pink into nearly a mauve shade.

"You're too young to have done this all on your own. I know you're not the only Violator we've yet to catch. I want to know who else you're working with." She said it plainly, not unlike the way a Nara instructor might ask a student if they had any questions about an exercise, or if a Nara worker processing Essence had checked with a fellow Nara for the proper handling protocol. But her question cut deeper, and Ellene caught the change in Baldric's face as her question pierced his false bravado into the underlying agony of what he'd tried to conceal.

Baldric said nothing, but Ellene saw the beads of sweat forming on his face along with his darkening complexion. "Deceit is not a trait for the Nara. I say again, who are you working with?"

Annoyed with the continued disrespect, Ellene focused her mind into Baldric's, and a slew of images shot forth into Ellene's vision. Random classmates mostly, but the girl with the dark hair Ellene spoke with showed up several times... Sarika, was it? She'd note that. Any personal ties were easy ammunition; they cut deeper than the sharpest blade when an uncooperative Nara was being questioned.

Baldric's mouth opened and shut several times, but he only offered wordless grunts, nonverbal cries for help from someone, like a thirsty man at a well with no water.

Ellene clenched her jaw and circled around Baldric. Her next option was at the ready, but using it just ratcheted her temper up to a boiling point. "Computer, access Trainee files for Frier, Baldric; list known contacts."

"Wait!"

Ellene swirled on her heels back to Baldric, who'd managed a weak smile along with a return of his powers of speech. "Instructor Frankum helped me."

Ellene felt an ache in her gut. She begged the Ancients the youth was lying, that it was the desperate act of a condemned Nara, tossing any and every possible name out in the ridiculous hope it meant some menial bargain, some pathetic last-minute deal that gave him a chance to avoid the most painful punishment paraded before him through Ellene's eyes.

Ellene recovered her agitation so her once cool countenance showed again. "I see. You say Razak Frankum, our long-time instructor and most faithful of the Nara, who himself led the revamping of the Essence process, who has on numerous times sworn his undying allegiance to the Nara, has decided to turn on us?"

"Not turn. Be awakened."

Baldric spoke with the confidence of a prized student, which worried Ellene all the more. "You're too young to know just what you've done. Baldric, you reprogrammed some Nara systems to broadcast critical information detrimental to the sole purpose of our race. There's no possible reason for doing that unless you're trying to help someone find Essence, and we both know you were trying to help Malone Stanton. Answer me here and now. If you're truthful, I may find it in my heart to be the slightest bit merciful."

Baldric bowed his head, his huffed breaths continued. "Yes, it's true, I did it for Malone. For the Supreme's greater glory."

"Don't you call him that!" Ellene watched Baldric with contempt, shaking her head. It was clear to Ellene at that point, Malone had worked his way fully into the heart of the youth. She'd seen the reports, the updates, Malone helping worlds caught up by famines, restoring sustenance in exchange for devoted followers. His followers, some of them former Nara and others who underwent surgical augmentation in the hope of traveling to the dimension where Grondia lay, were a threat she knew had to be addressed.

Ellene searched Baldric's eyes, in hope of some reason, some justification for the dissension of Nara that continued and only seemed to be on the rise. Was ignorance of their purpose ever considered justified?

"Someone so young, so full of promise. You were just beginning your path toward your ordained purpose. The Nara aren't meant to live a regular life in this Galaxy because our lives are in service to the Galaxy. You had at your fingertips the power to offer life to billions, and instead you squandered that opportunity in the service of one."

Baldric's brow furrowed. "He's promised me things, to show me ways with the Essence."

"A false claim, and a fabricated truth."

Baldric's eyes got a wild look in them. Ellene braced herself. She hadn't heard of any attacks by those Malone had reached and infected with his ideas, but she figured she'd better be a little wary.

Baldric took a slow breath, his eyes filling with anger. "He reached me and my brethren here. I've seen a vision; his is the glory and always will be. He won't rest until you and this place are ashes. He'll keep you alive to let you watch your world burn, the Nara—old, young, infants—will be massacred. Blood will flow across Grondia, and he'll save you for last, cutting your throat as the final sacrifice of this failed experiment."

"You're testing me, and I don't think you're aware of what you're pulling." Ellene retrieved a slender cylinder from a pocket in her cloak. She thrust it overhead. The lights in the room blinked off, and when they came back on, the small cylinder had become a blade formed of a translucent series of beams. Bates froze, his eyes widened. Ellene had learned from her time with Nara Security that sometimes, an uncooperative interrogee needed a little persuasion beyond verbal threats.

She waved the shimmering weapon near Baldric. His breaths picked up in response, and he eyed the blade as Ellene worked it closer to him.

"I'm not beyond making the rest of your short time on Grondia very painful, Baldric. I'm giving you a final warning here—the more you cooperate, the more likely you'll leave here in one piece."

Baldric nodded quickly. Ellene smiled and continued. "We'll get the details on what you leaked, but I want more from you. I want to know where Malone is headed next. Has he mentioned anything to you?"

"No, not at all."

"Are you sure?" Ellene lunged forward, her weapon a mere inch from Baldric's skin. He trembled violently. "No, not at all! He calls us his children, we're in service to him; I don't know any more than that."

Ellene withdrew the weapon. She sensed the youth had offered everything. She did have one last option at her disposal. Focusing once again on his eyes, she drove her mind into his and attempted to reach past Baldric's subconscious into the realm of where Malone had called him. It wasn't something typical, and Ellene knew it was a longshot, but the place she was in, long shots were more on the order of the day.

Baldric's body jerked and twisted as Ellene's mind probed his. She found shreds of the Baldric's contact with Malone amid his various thoughts. She weaved through them like weeds in a field. She thrashed about, but the only thing she saw in return was his image. Perhaps Malone had known about this possibility and covered his tracks too well? After a few minutes of this, she released her hold, returning her mind to her own self. Baldric slumped backward in his seat.

"Tell me about Sarika Tholl, Baldric. I saw her in your thoughts."

The name roused Baldric again, his face basted in panic, he lunged forward against his restraints. "No, she's innocent! She's a friend of mine from before the Acquiring; she's not involved!"

"But she's in your thoughts; do tell."

"I told her about the contact. I had to make some sense of it, that's all!"

Ellene hadn't even needed the mind grab to see the feeble attempt of Baldric to hide his friend. She made a note to visit Sarika immediately. The infection of the Nara was growing, and she was determined to stop it above all else. The only thing she was concerned with about Baldric at that point was retrieving all the information he had. His account was almost empty, and she was hell bent on closing it in full.

As Hierarch, Ellene had the privilege of being judge, jury, and executioner. The simple life of the Nara meant their transgressions weren't typically plentiful, but when they happened, they were dealt with in the most complete and definite way possible. No witnesses were needed, as the Hierarch answered to no one, except for guidance from the Ancients.

Ellene hated admitting to herself she felt bad for Baldric, being deceived so intensely, but she still felt regret for what was to come of him, especially since it was on her to order it. At the very least, she learned to look deeper into her own upper echelon for another source of rebellion. The youth had the more malleable minds, but she worried if this meant that Malone had gotten control of the upper echelon of Nara. Her handle on her society was slipping fast, and she needed to do something to right the ship before it was too late.

Baldric tensed. Oftentimes for the Nara being Disconnected, the procedure happened at the end of an interrogation. The intense badgering was in part a process of getting all possible information about the infractions, but it had an added effect of physically exhausting the Violator for the next phase, the Disconnection, a surgical process that in itself took several hours to complete. The Nara were ruthless with the Violator at that point, performing procedures without any anesthesia and broadcasting to the general population. The intent was for all to see the dangers of breaking Nara law. Anyone who dared break Nara law knew well the consequences were swift, dire, painful, and permanent.

Ellene bowed her head. Baldric was done. She was most certainly finished with him as well. She'd collected her information; it was part of her ongoing siege that she herself knew had to come. Her hope was that the rest of the Nara saw how necessary it was that they take the unprecedented course she had in mind. But that was another day. This day, she only had a serving of justice to administer.

"Baldric Frier, son of the Nara. Your crime of attempting to aid a known enemy of the state places you in violation of Nara law. By the powers vested in me from the Nara council and the Ancients on High, I sentence you to removal from Grondia forever and Disconnection. Bates, see to it the procedure happens at once."

With that, Ellene left the room. Baldric's cries echoed loudly against the walls. She passed Bates with no other regard for his presence; her edict was clear, her punishment resolute. She brushed a bit of moisture from her cheek as she left the room, and a young Nara's once promising life shattered under her hand.

SIX

PERDITA AUER BELIEVED IN ACCURACY. From an early age, she processed all she saw and was keenly aware of her surroundings and those she came into contact with, always interested with making sure all things were neat and in order. Her parents deserved a healthy share of credit or blame for this as they raised her in a stringent method while still adhering to Nara custom.

When Perdita got Ellene's summons, it took her a bit by surprise at first, but Perdita had good ideas on the reason for the sudden contact. Perdita was in the top echelon of Nara society who were notified of serious events like a breach from a Violator, and she'd been seeing the reports via the Nara Net of the rise in incidents. She wondered how the discipline at Nara Instruction had laxed to a point that made all the dissensions possible.

Perdita stretched her limbs for a moment as she sat at the table on the observation platform overlooking the Essence generation process. She ran her hand along the neatly pressed seams of her uniform cloak. As military leader of the Nara, Perdita prided herself on a crisp appearance, an expectation she placed on every soldier in her command. While the Nara Military wasn't a force that actively patrolled Ling Galaxy anymore as in cycles past, their place as a de facto garrison among the Nara required they keep their vigilance up. For Perdita, the image of a polished force was as important as the physical might it showed when provoked.

From her time as an upcoming officer in the active Nara Military, Perdita's exploits in Ling Galaxy had gotten notice rather quickly. She ascended through the ranks of Nara Military, in part because of her stellar training record, but also, her ability to think and hold her own in hostile situations proved her most valuable as a fine example and leader. After a string of attacks on Essence deliveries, Perdita formed a task force of the best Nara soldiers and conducted a series of operations securing delivery of Essence. It gave her accolades from the Nara and an equally impressive series of bounties on her life from the lawless side of Ling Galaxy.

The Essence workers walked about on suspended platforms several levels below Perdita's seat. Multiple large containers moved the Essence through a transformation from the shapeless glowing liquid to the small orbs used to transport Essence to the Galaxy. The process had been part of the Nara culture for centuries. While Perdita knew enough about it from her childhood, it was different seeing the Essence actually being produced in this case. It gave it more of a tangible feeling instead of a story shared between Nara parents and their offspring.

The group Perdita watched moved a large apparatus directly over the Essence container, where a series of claws grasped the Essence in one of its processed forms before its final state. Nara were unable to touch Essence. The substance caused burns on the skin of even the Nara. Enough steps had been taken, however, that allowed them to handle the substance without any concerns. Perdita noted the count of the workers as they paused between tasks. Every part of the process was a planned out mapped dance, a carefully choreographed series of moves that had to be repeated verbatim. The risk to Nara and the Galaxy in general was far too great otherwise.

After several moments of watching the crews, Perdita returned to her table and tablet in front of her. A message onscreen stared back at her, the reminder of why she was at that particular observation point, as if she needed the notice. She tabbed through the message, the collection of Violators discovered in Nara society recently, as an uneasy tinge worked its way through her midsection.

Oftentimes, Nara allowed their young more flexibility. Their time before service, known as the Acquiring, allowed Nara a chance to grow and socialize and learn without the forced Instruction that came later as their life paths became rigid.

Perdita found herself challenged at making friends in her youth, but one bonded with her from an early age: Ellene Ballo. This connection blossomed and grew through their cycles of Instruction, and remained to the present with their respective appointments, Ellene as Nara Leader and Perdita as head of the Nara military.

After Perdita hugged her longtime friend, they both took seats and enjoyed the sight of each other, not always a daily occurrence with their respective busy schedules.

"How's your arm?" Ellene asked.

Perdita glanced down at the brace on her right appendage. "Healing alright, I suppose. It's good for the spirit to keep a hand into the action somewhat."

"I never understood why you still rotate into training cycles for Nara Military and Security, but everyone has their own agenda in the end." Ellene smiled and shook her head at her friend.

"A good leader passes their eyes around now and then, for morale and just for good faith."

Ellene nodded. "Leaders should, but the Hierarch is more about diplomacy than pure leadership."

They shared a laugh. Perdita wasn't about to argue with Ellene's assessment of her position. Perdita also never envied Ellene's list of responsibilities. The Hierarch was the interface between Grondia and Ling Galaxy. The Universal Alliance met with her on a frequent basis about the situation throughout Ling Galaxy. While the Nara under the Hierarch had little to do other than provide Essence orbs, that little work amounted to a lot of activity for the Nara.

"You can play diplomat all day, Ellie. I'm an old soldier. Though in recent cycles, I've felt more like a soldier without a mission."

Ellene reached for Perdita's healthy arm. "But your loyalty and faith are as valuable as your physical strength, Perdie. That's why I keep you close, and why you're the one I'm coming to now for help. He's at it again," Ellene muttered, her gaze locked on the Essence workers in their task.

"Malone." Perdita spat the name out like a curse. There were a few names that fell into the category of vile expletive, and Malone's was right at the top. "If he'd only stayed and focused that energy of his on our purpose instead of his own ego, he may have been Hierarch."

Ellene's brow arched, and her face flashed a deeper blue complexion for a moment. "You think so?"

Perdita winced, annoyed at herself that she'd let a comment like that slip out unchecked. Perdita gasped at what she'd said, clasping Ellene's arm. "Oh Ellie, I'm sorry. I just meant Malone had so much potential, and for a Nara to waste that when our purpose is so much greater, it just makes me sick."

"It's OK. I'm sure he would've been a person of importance. But the truth is, he's gone renegade, and the idea of what he may try next bothers me."

"He's crafty. Not as bad as Faraz Len, but he's unfortunately got potential."

Ellene sighed. "I remember, Perdie. Faraz, first Nara to be Disconnected, but not before he disrupted a huge Essence delivery and caused a lot of famines in the Galaxy."

Perdita nodded. "That's right, and Ling has never fully recovered. The Hierarch at the time was so desperate to regain control, they developed the Scion project. All it amounted to was taking some good Nara and plundering their physical beings for a horrible outcome."

Faraz Len's exploits had happened several cycles before Ellene and Perdita were born, but by the time of their Instruction, the lessons of Faraz were a regular topic in their class, not to mention among conversations with their friends and even their parents.

Ellene snickered. "Faraz was in league with a lot. I still remember stories of how he sealed off the Essence plant for a time, demanding an audience with the Ancients. Fortunately, he had the dumb idea he was physically able to merge with Essence, and that took care of any punishment he'd have gotten."

Faraz's lack of consideration for how lethal Essence was hadn't diminished the seeds of dissent his actions planted in the minds of the likes of Malone and the others who rebelled against the Nara.

Ellene spied the Essence workers on the platforms as they pulled the finished Essence orbs into their final receptacles for transport. *Another batch about to head out to the Galaxy, would any of these fall into Malone's hands?* She turned back to Perdita. "You know, we caught another Violator."

"I heard. A youth, wasn't it?"

"Mmmhmmm. Contacted by Malone. I don't know how he's getting to them so young."

"What did this one do?"

Ellene leaned back in her seat. "Tampered with the Nara Net, tried to raise a signal to Malone."Perdita gaped.

Ellene noted her friend's reaction. "I've been trying to tell people; Malone is more than just a meager threat. He's got above all the desire to get us, hit us where we live, and show us just how wrong we are."

"You really think he can do that though? Tampering with the Nara Net is a notable infraction, but with our scrambling capabilities, it would take more than a rogue student or two to send any kind of message like that out."

Ellene's brow creased. "I know it sounds farfetched, but I can't dismiss it anymore. I'd rather get a better handle on this situation than dismiss it outright."

"Well, what then? You catch them and then Disconnection?"

Ellene nodded silently. The punishment wasn't entirely accepted by all Nara, but no one argued the treatment wasn't effective at removing Violators from Nara forever.

Ellene inhaled slowly and leaned back, her eyes shut. "I've overseen thirteen Disconnections so far as Hierarch, Perdie. It's a necessary process, that's for sure. What we've learned from the Violators is questionable at best."

Perdita folded her arms. "You can't expect the condemned to be contrite when they know the punishment they're getting for their crimes. Disconnection is brutal, but it serves its purpose.

A Violator has no place in our world, and the longer they remain, the stronger their threat to our safety remains."

Ellene marveled at Perdita's composure as she spoke with blunt truth about the disciplinary system at Grondia.

Perdita glanced back at the screen near her on the table. The count of Violators was a regular statistic, shared with the Nara Council and ranking authorities like Perdita and Ellene. But Perdita had focused herself on the art of interrogation and pulling out every bit she was able to from the Violators. As trends went, however, even Perdita couldn't have denied this steady rise wasn't anything that could be ignored for much longer.

"The Ancients have assured us time and again our place in this Galaxy is not only vital but secure. Are you doubting those who went before us yet remain as our eternal guides?"

Ellene glanced off in thought. She knew everything Perdita said was true, and she had a difficult time arguing back, but she found her emotions telling her something very different. She smiled at Perdita. "I called you here because we need to discuss Project Scion and activate it again."

Perdita blinked in silence, then angled her body slightly back from her friend. "Did you say what I think you just said?"

"Perdie, I've been Hierarch for 50 cycles, and I couldn't imagine a better leader of the Nara Military than you. I know the Ancients assure our safety. But they knew a Galaxy from earlier cycles, with less corruption and danger. These are not those times."

Perdita took a steady breath and grasped Ellene's arm. "There has always been corruption, Ellene. We were just too young to either care or even know about it. Project Scion, the weaponizing of select Nara, was extremely drastic, not to mention very dangerous. I know you heard the stories, because I sure remember my parents telling them to me."

"Perdie, you were in one of the last groups deployed into Ling Galaxy, don't you feel the urge to do something more than follow the Ancients rule of passive acceptance?"

Perdita's brow creased. Ellene saw a spark of the soldier in her, something she'd hoped to have stoked to a full blaze. But Ellene had underestimated Perdita's reserve, the cooler demeanor of a military leader not so obsessed with active operations, but with defense and security of their position.

Ellene had hoped for a much different outcome, asking her friend for this favor. It wasn't a very realistic or safe thing to ask, and Ellene had to admit that Perdita's concerns were true. In Project Scion, the Nara were actually selected for the process, but when exposed to such a high concentration of Essence in their systems, the overwhelming force triggered a series of horrible mutations. While there were some successes, many affected Nara perished soon after the procedures took place.

"I know I'm asking something a friend should never ask. And I know about the Nara who already paid the ultimate price for this. But I beg you to remember who I am and how long we've been together. And you know Malone; he was your student at one time."

Perdita winced a bit at the memory. "Go on."

"The Nara physique was never intended for Essence, but we're obliged to process and deliver it to the Galaxy. My thought is that we enlist those from another race."

Perdita's brow raised. "You want to get others to have this power?

Just how do you think one of the lesser kinds can handle this unruly energy when the very Nara who work closest with it cannot?"

"I've studied beings in the Galaxy. I think we can find some to help us. I'm going to speak with someone at the UA and get this process started."

"I think you're forgetting something, dear friend," Perdita said. "A Hierarch must reach out to the Ancients before anything of this nature can be done. No Hierarch has attempted Project Scion since the incident, and you can be very sure the Council won't accept its adoption without a whole lot of convincing, not to mention blessing from the Ancients."

Ellene nodded, sipping her drink. "I've got my work cut out for me. Just give me your word, on the support from the military on this. If I can get this started, we'll need to mobilize quickly; I don't want to give Malone any more time than the abundance we've already given him."

"You've got my word as Nara Military Commander and your friend. Just make it count. There's plenty riding on this, way beyond our respective reputations."

"Good. I'll deal with the Ancients. You're right, I have to do that. But how much have the Ancients held back on us? They think that this world can persist for eternity, but look at the famines that have hit Ling Galaxy. Systems like Zormad and Agmon were without food for several cycles. Races like the Railen prey on things like that, and now with Malone in the mix, it would be rife for revolution. The UA has maintained order for many cycles now, but not without bloodshed. We can offer help; we can extend a hand to help stem the tide away from destruction. Don't you think we should?"

"Ours isn't to dictate the course of things, Ellie." Perdita's gaze was tinted with worry. "The moment we interfere, we are that much more vulnerable to those who want to exploit what we have and what we are. We must be careful. We cannot save the entire Galaxy."

Ellene thought back to her youth when she and Perdita were students in Instruction. She knew about one Violator back then, because she'd seen the Disconnection procedure. It gave her night-mares for months afterward. But in all, the cases of Violators were few. It was enough for her seeing the lecture about Disconnection, and certainly the image of the treatment stuck firmly in her mind.

Ellene studied her old friend and again had to admit the truth in her statement. As much as she knew the proper course for handling Malone, she needed the Ancients' blessing. The Hierarch ruled Nara, but it wasn't without council.

Ellene knew a visit to the Ancients lay ahead for her, but not before she got all her facts together, which included research into the suspects and their associations presented to her from Baldric's forced confession.

SEVEN

ELLENE REMEMBERED HOW SARIKA LOOKED. Her hair alone was memorable enough. She heard from Bates on Sarika's involvement with Baldric, but that hadn't settled Ellene's lingering curiosity. She waited in the concourse outside Sarika's training session for when her class was released.

Ellene knew that others worked on the issue. Bates did things about the rising threats to the Nara, as was his job. She knew Perdie was on it as well. Still, Ellene felt better knowing directly that things were being done, and that Violators were monitored and tracked. It wasn't necessarily the place for a Hierarch, but Ellene dared anyone to tell her different.

The electronic tones indicating the end of the session echoed through the hallway. After a few moments, entry portals slid open, and a steady procession of students oozed from the various room entrances, as if the classrooms were severed arteries hemorrhaging Nara into Ellene's vicinity.

Ellene worked her way through the oncoming students. Most who saw Ellene did a hurried version of the salute to acknowledge her, but Ellene wasn't really concerned with decorum then. A group of students nodded and quickly slid out of Ellene's path, bringing her facing Sarika. Sarika's hair was not as neat as the last time they'd met, and her eyes had a sparkle of something behind them. Ellene thought Sarika's interrogation by Bates could be to blame; they weren't exactly kind and gentle in extracting information for the most part.

"Hello, Sarika. I wonder if you'd grant me the pleasure of your company for a few moments."

Sarika eyed Ellene's extended hand nervously. The greeting was equal parts kind and fake. Ellene's mind lasered in on a task when the situation called for it, and her request could've been better worded as 'If you'd like to remain among the living, get your ass over here before I shoot you down.'

Ellene took Sarika to a quieter area of the Instruction Facility. As determined as Ellene was to drain Sarika's mind of any details on her and Baldric's association, she figured it would be better for the time being to stay in a place comfortable to Sarika. Failing that, Ellene would've happily proceeded on a similar course the likes of Baldric had gotten, but she was OK to play it calm for the moment.

Ellene ushered Sarika to a table in an empty workshop for their discussion, and the two took seats opposite from each other. "Your friend Baldric was subjected to Disconnection," Ellene began. The news wasn't a surprise to Sarika, but she still flinched at the idea of her longtime friend's fate.

"This isn't the way we wanted this to go; I hope you can understand that."

Sarika swallowed with difficulty before she was able to respond. "I know. I wish he'd have been smarter and not listened to Malone like he did."

Ellene traced her finger over her lips. "Indeed. I know you've spoken with Bates about your involvement with your friend, but I was hoping we'd talk a little more."

"I've already told Bates everything I know." Sarika blinked quickly.

"I hope you can understand by my presence here how serious this situation is. While Baldric isn't the only Violator we've dealt with, I still need to find out as much as I can about what Violators are doing, and especially anything he's told you about Malone is crucial. Our way of life is dependent on a series of activities, events, and tasks that are now in danger of being disrupted, or worse yet, stopped altogether. Malone will destroy Grondia if he returns here. Essence grants life, but the abuse of it is a very serious concern. Malone isn't a benevolent force. Behind those grand gestures is a cold calculating heart. You must realize if he's allowed to proceed on this path, he can unmake not just Grondia, but all of Ling Galaxy."

Sarika's complexion changed to a mild red. She kept quiet, her lips in a line.

Ellene continued, "Essence isn't an unlimited resource, much as Malone may think it is. He's got his stage for now, but I'm concerned where this all will lead if we don't stop him. He can grow worlds, and he's doing that quite well. But he also expects allegiance."

Sarika nodded. "Yes, I know. My friend Alda, have you spoken with her?"

Ellene's mouth drew in a line. "Yes, she's under tight surveillance too."

"Well, they did tell me he's creating an army he calls his children. He's working on the ability to travel across dimensions for himself and his followers."

Ellene froze. She knew dimensional travel was the also first order for the Railen once they formed their own society. The Railen purpose was to take back their own birthright, the Grondia system, and repay the Nara for the insult of their expulsion. It made sense Malone wanted the same thing, although his motives went deeper than basic revenge.

"I'm sorry I didn't say this the other day; I guess I forgot." Sarika's head sunk, and a deep mauve tint came over her complexion.

Ellene broke from her moment of strategic analysis and clutched Sarika's shoulder. "My child, I sense a great deal of honesty in you.

That is an asset, but be careful. There are several among us who see honesty as a weakness to be exploited as much as possible."

Sarika nodded. Ellene, satisfied, waved Sarika away. Sarika happily launched herself from the table, heading down the concourse at a double speed without looking back.

As Ellene watched Sarika's hurried exit, she mused over the options she had available. A visit to the Ancients was definitely on the scope of the reasonable. As much of a formality as it was, she knew that to get the support of the Council and the underlying military backing from Perdita and Bates, she had to play along with the process set forth eons past.

EIGHT

ELLENE RETURNED TO HER CHAMBERS for some mental digestion of Sarika's story and just what Ellene's case to the Ancients would be. In her sanctuary, Ellene began another search on her console when the display flickered. At first, she thought she may have imagined it. But it began again, and then the display of maps and news updates regarding Malone Stanton were replaced with the face of Malone and his symbol. She heard the shrill alarm from her console, and checking the readout, she noticed an outage message from elsewhere in the Nara control facility.

"Contact Control, what's going on?" Ellene yelled into her comm.

"Hierarch, we've had a breach. We're working to address it but we're not sure."

It's him. Of course it is. What else could it be?

Ellene flung herself backward from her desk, and she realized she had a method to reach him already.

Since her youth, Ellene had learned the stories of the Nara Ancients, and how they used their minds to explore and connect with people and places throughout the Galaxy. But she also worked at it herself until she too had the ability. She felt any Nara Hierarch needed all possible faculties in keeping track of all she was responsible for.

Tuning her mind, she flung herself past the confines of her physical form, past her chambers in the Nara Control facility, into the ether and beyond.

Malone, I know you're out there.

No response at first, but then a regrettably familiar chuckle filled the void.

-Now that's more like it. What's the fun of speaking like the sentients when we can speak in the spaces between like the Ancients do.-

You're not even worthy to say their names, Malone.

-Oh Ellene, your respect for that ancient and dying order is touching. It will be a great pleasure to see it all come to an end. It will soon, you know. As will you.-

Not if I can help it. Just what are you up to anyway?

-Really, Ellene. You think I'd share details like that? I'm afraid you'll have to find out on your own. You're intelligent enough though; I'm sure you'll figure it out.-

We have already; we've caught one of your so-called children, and don't think we won't catch the rest too.

-You won't. My children multiply daily. You'll be best to stay out of my way; the only thing you'll earn chasing me is more of your precious Nara killed.-

Ellene paused for the shudder that passed through her. Even with the might of the Nara Military in their present state and Ellene's own control of Nara, she felt limited in the fight she faced with Malone. She believed in her heart the Scion Project had to happen if Nara and Ling Galaxy stood a chance at all.

She strained her mind with all her strength but had no luck finding Malone's location. She knew it had to be possible to find him if she worked at it hard enough. Thoughts all originated from a physical body, and that body had to be somewhere on a physical plane. Ellene had been a quick study when she was a student and had shown a lot of promise. But that was many cycles ago, and her mind was a bit older, and clouded with many more concerns and obligations than from the time of her youth.

She would find him at some point, and she knew she would. Because she had to.

NINE

THE ANCIENTS RESIDED IN THE TEMPLE, on the Compound area where the Hierarch's residence lay. It was in clear sight to all Nara and stood as a continual reminder of where their race originated from. The grand structure had sweeping columns that balanced a foreboding roof and gave hints of both religious temple and governmental building.

Ellene navigated the long series of steps to the entrance, where she was greeted by two guards. She bowed to the shimmering spirits, who, like the Ancients themselves, weren't in the physical form. All beings in the temple remained as advisers to Nara. A Hierarch ruled all Nara, but tradition dictated any move with a real risk of catastrophe to Nara and Grondia in general was only actioned after a blessing from the Ancients on High.

Ellene was escorted to the central chambers, where she waited for the Ancients' arrival. After several moments, two wisping spirits joined her in the room, Nathifa Turay and Hu Golovina. Before long, a collection of spirits floated in and assumed positions in a series of seats in a semi-circle. Ellene stood behind a podium at the center of the arc and faced the spirits. It was the place for anyone with a request of the Ancients and something a Hierarch had to be used to, if not tolerant of.

Nathifa held the center seat among the Ancients. She still bore the military distinctions from her time as a Nara military leader. Four places to her right, Hu Golovina's vestments included markings of academia, from his time as head of Nara Instruction.

Nathifa's voice boomed against the walls of the room. "Ellene Ballo, what do you wish to discuss with the Ancients?"

Ellene felt an itch in her throat as she attempted clearing it first. "Ancients, I implore your counsel and blessing on what I am about to request. First, allow me to explain the situation. In recent cycles, the Nara have come upon attacks on an increasing scale, primarily while delivering Essence to the Galaxy, but as of late, through telepathic suggestion."

"Is this Malone Stanton of whom you speak?" asked Hu Golovina. The name brought forth a low rumble among the assembled Ancients. Malone's notoriety was common knowledge for Nara both living and deceased.

Ellene cleared her throat. "Yes, that's correct. We've learned of several instances where Essence workers were attacked, and in some cases killed from the efforts of Malone Stanton or his known associates. It's only by grace that more Essence hasn't been taken yet."

"How are you certain this is the work of Stanton?" asked Nathifa.

"The methods seem to be all the same, not to mention the images posted all carry the same markings. As you know, upon Disconnection, all affected Nara are given a brand once released from this dimension. The scene of these attacks all carry that marking in some form, often in the blood of the deceased."

"How could you be certain? There have been many among the outcasts."

"But none with the reputation of Malone Stanton, blessed Ancients."

Nathifa's eyes narrowed. "You've told us this, but you forget our vision reaches beyond Grondia and this dimension. We too have seen the threat the Nara have faced. You have yet to ask us for anything, even guidance. Ellene Ballo, speak your mind; tell us what you want."

"I want to activate Project Scion again."

The room erupted in shouts as several other ancients cursed even the mention of the name. After a few moments, Nathifa quieted the assembled group and faced Ellene again. "What you ask is extremely dangerous. Are you aware of the trouble Project Scion brought to Nara in cycles past?"

"I am aware, Ancients, but I'm afraid the time will come soon when the greater danger of doing nothing will lead to our most certain extinction. Going by what I know, I think Project Scion was misguided at first. That's why I plan to combine Project Scion with a search for the One from Without."

Jumah Contos was among several Ancients who lurched forward. "Prophecy is about belief, not a to do list, Hierarch!" he shouted. Ellene clearly had come to play hard with her requests.

Nathifa silenced the uproar among Jumah and her other peers before she eyed Ellene again. "And now you mention Ancient Prophecy. Ellene, do you dare suggest we haven't considered all aspects of Nara history in our advice?"

"I do, of course, with all respect. From my youth I've heard about the One from Without, who channels Essence to all worlds, restoring balance. I know what I ask is risky. But I think we'd agree Malone Stanton is aware of this prophecy as well, and while I find it deeply troubling that he may be attempting to exploit this legend for his own purposes, I think it illustrates just how dangerous this world can be, and I think unless we take more steps now, we'll be looking at the catastrophe of fighting Malone Stanton on our own soil."

"Malone is a cast out; what can a cast out do against Nara?" Jumah asked.

Ellene replied, "A cast out who wields Essence, Blessed Ancients."

Hu Golovina said, "A trifle. He's gotten a foothold, but he'll perish if he attempts to do anything further."

Ellene clenched her jaw. Their dispute over Malone seemed to be nearing a stalemate.

Claud Kos sat on the far right of the assembled panel; a deeply cynical gaze etched into his face. Of all the Ancients, Ellene hated dealing with Kos the most. It seemed to her Kos was always determined to undermine or discount anything Ellene had ever said.

"You really think the threat you're facing is that serious? We've seen wars, young Hierarch. Systems split apart, brave legions of troops fighting only to be decimated by the thousands. This Malone Stanton is a harmless insect. He's effective at getting noticed, I'll grant you. But in the end, like all insects, they make one move too many and they're crushed."

"With respect, I don't think it's wise taking a chance Malone Stanton will somehow do himself in one day."

Nathifa said, "You come to us for guidance because for now your knowledge only spans your life. Ours, on the contrary, reaches back millennia. You'd be well advised, Hierarch, to respect the council of this chamber, in the manner all who have come before you have done."

Kos strode about the chamber floor. "Since our esteemed subject has forgotten a thing or two about our history, allow me the space, assembled party, to educate this one."

Kos threw a glare at Ellene that she happily returned. She bit her lip as he swung back toward the Ancients, his arms raised as if a preacher about to perform the homily of his entire ministry.

"Essence is not for anyone to touch. It is our reason since the dawn of time to deliver this to the Galaxy but only as stewards. Essence is not for us to control; it is for us to provide. The ruling Hierarch at the time, Den Montez, thought as our subject here does. That we had the ability, and furthermore, the right to take action. To stop tyranny. To make ourselves more than we were. Our divine purpose must not be avoided nor tampered with."

Ellene clenched her fists. The Ancients' expressions while listening to Claud varied from basic interest to the occasional glance toward Ellene. She didn't need any powers of thought delving to see their looks toward her weren't quite the warm support she'd hoped for.

Nathifa's face mellowed into stoicism as she spoke slowly, as a judge who read a verdict. "Project Scion failed because the Nara cannot physically handle Essence, Ellene. You know this."

"That's why I'm proposing we reach outside our race this time."

"Such as?"

"The Xeno."

Nathifa shook her head before she responded. "You're risking a lot. Ellene, the Ancients don't believe this will preserve our way as you seem to think it will."

"What about the deliveries disrupted? The Galaxy is already teetering on the verge of disaster. We have to try something, Blessed Ancients, to avoid catastrophe."

"Disaster is a part of life, as much as death is, and corruption. For millennia, Ling Galaxy has seen cycles of prosperity and destruction. Essence provides life, but it is up to each individual to do what they can with that life. Some choose to grow and build honestly, while others seek the quick and easy path. We cannot and will not ever be able to guide individual choice because it is for the individual."

"Besides, what makes you so sure the Xeno are that One from Without?" Nathifa asked.

"I've studied their kind. They're hardy, and brash. They traveled a great distance to Ling Galaxy and have managed a foothold with very little help from any, save their neighboring Mardaks. Also, their physical makeup is completely alien to Ling. We've tried Scions of Nara, but even our forms are corruptible by Essence. We need a pure vessel, and the Xeno are the best candidate I've seen in a while."

Nathifa said, "One person's prophecy is another person's weapon. We do not approve your decision to act upon this while a known enemy of the state like Malone Stanton is at work. We must allow for Essence itself to handle this. Malone will overstep, and Essence will prove his undoing. Trust in our word."

"I am here by obligation, my duty to uphold Nara law and traditions. Am I hearing from the Ancients that I must pursue a path beyond their guidance?"

"The Nara Council is yours to rule, Ellene. We are advisors, but I must warn you, taking steps with the Scion Program is fraught with danger. There may come a time when you'll be unable to control the effects of what you'll be starting," Nathifa said.

"I understand. My bigger fear is controlling what happens if I don't take my own steps now," Ellene said.

Nathifa said, "Remember, Ling Galaxy lives with us, and it so shall die with us."

"But we are here to ensure life, are we not? Respectfully, I argue we can take steps now, albeit risky ones, to ensure our purpose is fulfilled. With respect to the Ancients, I humbly ask what course you suggest I pursue regarding this threat. You must see the Violators. By Nara law, I'm acting for the good of Essence and our mission—to protect. But the time for defense won't be much longer. We can defend an enemy who isn't yet on our soil with our present course, but I tell you, there will come a time when we'll be face to face with Malone and the army he's assembled," Ellene said.

Nathifa quieted the grumbling Ancients. "The Universal Alliance maintains order within the Galaxy. I see no reason why we cannot provide some of our military for support to their efforts. That is certainly within our grasp."

Ellene chuckled to herself, thinking about Perdita's assessment of their meager strength. "Our military hasn't even handled skirmishes in recent cycles. How effective do you really think they'll be?"

"More effective than handing our most precious asset over to a group of untested individuals. Ellene Ballo, your request for council has been heard, and this chamber has spoken. I advise you to retire to your chambers to decide how best you can have the Nara military aid the greater cause of Ling Galaxy beyond the dastardly Project Scion." Nathifa smiled.

Ellene's exit from the temple was much more difficult than her arrival. She bit her lip and waited until she was back in her own quarters before uttering curses about the Ancients. She was never more certain than she'd been about this, and while the Ancients weren't in agreement with the danger they all faced, she knew it was time for action of her own.

TEN

SLEEP WAS THE FURTHEST THING FROM Ellene's grasp that evening, which said quite a lot. Her restless mind ran through many things. Scenarios for handling the Council, the resistance from the Ancients and Perdita, and how many more incidents of Violators were yet to come. She racked her brain hard for all possible options, and she knew the best one she had was handily with her. As Hierarch, she was obliged to address the Nara community from the Instruction facility on the state of Nara. It had been the custom of Nara for many cycles, and she'd obliged the task much in the way she did a lot of her duties. But this time, the menial chore carried the weight of the Galaxy on it, and she knew this was her chance—she was determined that her speech planted a seed in everyone's mind that would soon grow into the real action she knew Grondia and Ling Galaxy desperately needed.

Ellene's mind was a swirl of thoughts, thinking about Nathifa's stern response to her request over the Scion Program, her childhood friend Perdita's answer to her request for help, and just the faces of the Nara she saw daily, a mixture of relaxed compliance and doubt. The seeds of uncertainty had been planted long ago, and she knew that no matter what the Ancients or others in the power structure of the Nara figured, something was coming to a head.

THE GRONDIAN SUNS cast their light over the exterior of the Instruction facility and Arena. Ellene prepared herself for the day with her customary regimen of meditation and nutrition. She knew, as much as this speech was ceremonial, its ultimate intent was anything but ordinary, and what she was going to say to the assembled could change the course of her civilization, hopefully for the better. She knew above all that it was time that everyone knew about the severity of the issue. It was one thing showing Disconnections to the populace for the sake of showing the consequences of non-compliance. But she needed to mount a ground offensive by the Nara unlike any in their history. Anything less than support for that meant a dire and short future for the Nara, Grondia, and Ling Galaxy.

The Nara Arena stood alongside the Instruction Facility. It was a common gathering point for ceremonies, including the Acquiring, Commencements, and the Hierarch's addresses. Rows of seats arranged in six columns flowed out from the stage, and in the near distance, an arced collection of raised seats tied in the area. Ellene glanced over her prepared notes for her public address, conditions of Essence production, the usual boilerplate. Ellene grinned to herself at the one piece of information missing, the one she hoped would stir her fellow Nara into overwhelming support for her and the choice she knew they all needed for their survival.

Her thoughts meandered back to when Malone was officially removed from Nara society. Of all the enemies of their people, there was no one who made a more public and vicious exit than Malone did. Ellene recalled the day of his Disconnection. Additional security was brought in to handle Malone, as he'd managed a gigantic disruption in Essence production. There was no stay, no waiting period for reprieve of punishment. Malone's sentence was deliberate, public, and final.

To keep him from exercising his great weapon of persuasion, Ellene had him gagged, and ordered the sentencing and Disconnection to happen on a broadcast loop to all Nara.

She faced Malone, with Bates nearby, and began. "Malone Stanton, son of Nara, your crimes against Grondia, the Nara, and the civilized Ling Galaxy are too numerous to list in complete detail. Utmost in severity is your flagrant attempts to disrupt and control production and distribution of Essence to Ling Galaxy, thereby endangering the life of the Galaxy itself. You will from this moment forward be subject to Disconnection. Due to the level of knowledge you hold over Essence, you will not be released into the general population of Ling Galaxy but instead will be sent to a maximum-security facility where you will be subject to a mental cleanse. Your knowledge of Grondia, the Nara, all you know and have learned in your life, will be swept away. Your greatest weapon, your mind, will be decommissioned. This is the penalty—the price you must pay—for the trust you've broken and the crimes you've committed."

A layer of sweat covered Malone's face. His eyes bored into Ellene's to the point she became uncomfortable. But she steeled herself; it was important to her showing resolve even facing Nara's public enemy one.

The Disconnection of Malone proceeded shortly after. Three robotic techs swirled about as the pedestal Malone was attached to rotated to a flat position. As the androids probed Malone's body with a series of needles and electronic probes, he replied with muffled screams and curses. Ellene clenched her jaw as she watched. She hoped all Nara understood the reason for this, and anyone else who had even a slight idea of insurrection had immediate second thoughts of crossing her in the future.

PERDITA AND BATES sat to the left of Ellene at the arena. Two thousand Nara students were ushered in to attend the speech in person, giving the Hierarch a ready-made audience of enthusiastic respondents. After all, every speech always benefited from some hardy cheers in support. The Nara students were, of course, accompanied by a selection of Nara instructors and other dignitaries, such as Essence production team leaders and other administrative representatives from various districts of Grondia.

As Ellene watched the crowd filling in to the seating area, she felt a tap on her arm. Perdita's mouth was in a line, her eyes filled with worry. "You're not going to bring up the Scions, are you?"

Ellene started to respond but caught herself. "The Ancients have advised against it. Why should I?"

Perdita's mouth curved in a smirk. She knew her friend way better than she let on. "Just be careful. Remember, no Hierarch has ever crossed an Ancient."

Ellene nodded. Perdie was right, but Ellene realized also that the Hierarch was the ruler of the Nara. And a ruler sometimes made tough choices and difficult moves. It wasn't always about following the rule of law; sometimes it meant guiding situations and people at risk. Ellene knew first, however, she needed to see where she stood with her people and where they stood. There had to have been rumblings about the attacks. The Nara's sole purpose had been brought into jeopardy, and there must be sympathetic voices out there.

Perdita took the podium first to introduce Ellene; per the custom of the Military Leader, the caretaker of safety of all Nara, ushered in the Hierarch. "Gathered Nara, in person and throughout Grondia, I bring you well greetings. In keeping with the customs of the Nara, on this, the first day of our new cycle, we hear from our Hierarch, Ellene Ballo. Give tribute for our leader!"

With that, the gathered crowd erupted in loud cheers. The youthful students supplied a healthy majority of decibels of yells and whoops in response to Perdida's command, with the older and more reserved Nara offering enthusiastic applause and affirming gestures.

Ellene smiled to the crowd, making sure she gave a lingering grin and wave to the cameras present as well. She basked for a bit in the adulation, then quieted the crowd down for her speech.

"Citizens of the Nara, our work for Ling Galaxy is its lifeblood. While we reside adjacent to Ling, under dimensional protection, we are vital to its survival. You cannot see the fruits of your labor, but I assure you, the Galaxy only lives because of what each and every one of you commit to every single day."

The crowd responded with shouts and cheers again. Ellene, ever the polished and practiced orator, paused for the response. She knew she needed every iota of goodwill for what she was about to suggest to her people.

"I look into this crowd, and I see these young faces, so full of hope and energy. You are the future of our race. Like those of my generation and those gone before, the Ancients, you are preparing for your time of responsibility, when each of you will pick up the mantle of the Nara and continue our task. You bear our future, and together with your assembled instructors, I salute you and pledge my all to helping you reach your full potential!"

With that, the assembled Nara instructors faced the students and gave them thunderous applause and cheers. Ellene applauded in kind as well.

"I am honored to have been your Hierarch for fifty cycles, and with the good faith and support of the Ancients on High, I hope to be around for at least as many more. As your leader, it's incumbent on me to always keep the care and interests of all Nara most important in my mind. And while our overall purpose and mission remains vastly successful, I cannot ignore the fact that some of our operations have been compromised."

Ellene noticed from the corner of her eye as Perdita shifted in her seat. The crowd's overall responses of periodic cheers quieted down.

"I know this may trouble some of you. You must understand, I along with others with access to see what happens in Ling Galaxy, have noticed several of our Essence deliveries disrupted, and in some cases, destroyed."

The crowd's response turned more negative, downing the idea of anyone disrupting Essence shipments.

"Let me tell each of you, I am here for you even if times aren't great. And regarding these attacks on our people, I have a plan to handle this. We have the benefit of a dimensional gap, as you know, but our brethren who risk so much of themselves are in need of assistance. We face many threats. Enemies like Malone Stanton, who want to dismantle everything we stand for and our very existence.

"Therefore, I say to you, we will harness the power of Essence channeled through a few brave souls. I intend to restart Project Scion in the near future. The Scions will be our best defense going forward for a secure Grondia and a safe Ling Galaxy. I will send out these Scions as an aid to our Essence deliveries, as well as seek out and neutralize any of our enemies who attempt to reach our world and do us harm."

Shouts from the crowd increased but they were mixture of cheers and angry retorts. Ellene held her hands up to quiet everyone, but that time they weren't as cooperative. Perdita shook her head slowly at her friend. Ellene turned to say something but instead felt a burning stab in her shoulder. Ellene slumped to the ground while the crowd exploded in a panic. With the swift reflexes of a tigress, Perdita jumped over her collapsed friend and braced her down with one knee while she swiped her pistol and pointed it aloft.

Perdita's military demeanor never showed even a blemish as she bellowed into her comm unit, "Security, clear the area and alert medical; the Hierarch has been shot!"

ELEVEN

ELLENE WOKE UP ON A BED IN THE NARA medical facility. She noticed stiffness in her shoulder, and when she reached for it, she felt the layers of coverings over her wound. At that point her injury reminded her of its presence with a nasty throb.

"Easy," Perdida said from Ellene's bedside. "The wound was superficial, but you'll still need time to heal. Well, you were right. I'm afraid to admit it, but you were. I'm sorry; I shouldn't have questioned you so much, but it's real. In fact, it's more than just Razak; several others in Nara Instruction and even some military leaders have been reached by Malone. We're quarantining them now and having a mass Disconnect procedure done when we're ready."

"Uh huh." Ellene slumped back down on the bed. "So, do you have an ID on who or what did this?"

Perdita nodded. "Another Violator. This one had writings, more like scrawling, from Malone on the walls of their quarters."

Ellene bit her lip. She savored the fact this incident gave her cause weight but was also terrified of what the course ahead meant. "Have you spoken with anyone else?"

"Only Nathifa, and while they remain highly concerned about Project Scion, they acknowledge the Hierarch's discretion. Looks like you got your wish."

Ellene edged herself more onto her side for a better look at Perdita. She'd kept a pretty faithful vigil by Ellene's bedside, only leaving to speak with the Ancients about the actions going forward.

"Where's the Violator who did this now?"

"We've isolated them and are planning to send them to a secure holding facility off dimension."

"Better get a good one; better than where we sent Malone." Ellene huffed a bit. "So now what?"

Perdita took a steadied breath. "I've talked with Bates, and I'm looking into what we can muster in the way of troops. Our fleet of starcraft is still in service but in a reduced capacity. I can muster up a small cruiser for our travels; it can hold up to thirty people."

"Kind of a small contingency. What if we're spotted by Malone?"

"We've been able to upgrade our shroud technology. Assuming Malone hasn't perused that on one of his little mind explorations, we'll be OK."

"That's a risk I suppose we'll have to accept for now," Ellene said.

Perdita checked her comm unit. "I've summoned Bates; we'll need protection out there."

"I thought that's what you're for." Ellene laughed amid a series of coughs.

Perdita steadied her friend until their eyes met again. "Protecting someone like you is never a one-person job. If it comes to it, I'm taking a shot to save you. But given where we're going, I think it best we have all the help we can."

"Agreed." Ellene worked herself back down to a prone position.

"The problem is also we'll need to cut off ties to the outside world for now. It's a precaution. I know it leaves our people in Ling Galaxy vulnerable, but the greater risk of Grondia's safety can't be ignored any longer."

Ellene nodded at her friend. Perdita's eyes were weary. The fight ahead for them was a long one, and both knew it. Perdita's days as active military leader were far in the past, but with this turn, she was thrust back into the heat of the action, with a fraction of the prepared force she'd had last time.

"Perdita, listen. You're my oldest friend. If I didn't think anything of your opinion, I'd have never even asked you for it. Believe me, I didn't even want to think about this problem for the longest either. Malone was, I thought, a problem we'd dealt with. But he's infecting Ling Galaxy, and my great fear now is that we've let it go on too long to stop. But we're in it now. It's time the Nara have peace, and we need to be the ones to ensure it."

Perdita said, "It's a large Galaxy, and we're vastly outnumbered. What can we do?"

Ellene said, "All beings in the Galaxy know Essence. They may not all realize it, but their existence is solely based on it. The problem is if we just take any of them, their innermost beings will not be able to handle the incredible power of Essence itself. Even the Nara cannot. But if we can harness some of the transient lifeforms that journey to our Galaxy, just maybe they can be taught and shown the way without the dangers of corruption."

"And just what transient race do you have in mind?"

"I've been following a group known as the Xeno. They've managed a foothold in our world from a distant Galaxy. They're a small group, but rugged. They've carved a civilization out of the wasteland on Zormad, which couldn't have been easy. They've faced attacks from the likes of the Railen and Omegans, but they persist. Why? Because they have to. I think they'll be able to help us."

"But why Xeno, Ellie?"

"They're new to this Galaxy. They haven't had time to be corrupted by the possibilities of Essence. If we can harness them with Essence, we may have a chance. I'm not even talking about prophecy here; this is just hope. But it's what we have; we can't let that go or what else is there, Perdie?"

Perdita shook her head. "Just what do you propose we offer them?

There's enough want in this Galaxy, Malone won't have to push very hard to get converts to his cause. How do you know the Xeno won't want the same?"

"It's a feeling I have. I wish I could say more, but sometimes a good idea is all you have to build hope on."

Perdita eyed Ellene for a while. "I'm putting my faith in you here, Ellie. I hope you're not wrong."

"I'm as sure as I can be for now. Good enough?"

"It'll have to be."

The dull thud of a boot smacking the floor disrupted their conversation, and they noticed Bates in the doorway, fixed in a salute. Ellene returned the gesture, and Bates relaxed slightly. "Are you alright, Madam Hierarch?"

"I've been better, but I'll make it." Ellene smiled warmly. Perdita waved Bates into the room. He stood opposite Perdita at Ellene's bedside.

"Bates," Perdita began, "since the Hierarch is still not 100 percent, I'll speak for her a bit. We're going on a mission out into Ling Galaxy, and we need additional protection."

"Is this a military maneuver?"

"Hardly. We're seeking out candidates for the Scion program."

Bates face went pale. "I thought that was forbidden."

"Not anymore," Ellene muttered. "We're going to look for candidates to be enrolled. Honestly, I wish we'd have started this much earlier, but it seems I had to get shot for people to finally take me seriously."

"What can I do, Hierarch?" Bates added a bow to his reverence.

Ellene said, "We'll be using a small ship, but we'll need something of a contingency to follow us. We're taking a risk, but sending all our ships out as protection is the surest way to arouse suspicion or worse yet, antagonize someone the likes of Malone before we're ready. Right now, Malone is comfortable, he's on the move, and I want to be as far off his radar as I can. He's already got his sights on Grondia, he needs to never know we're out in the open or he'll make us his top priority."

"We start looking for Scions. You have any ideas where?"

"We start with the Xeno colony on the Zormad system."

"Zormad? That scrap heap?" Bates scoffed.

Ellene pointed a shaky finger at Bates, and he quickly collected himself. "The least of beings in Ling Galaxy is worth more than any overconfident about their place in existence. I want the lowly, those who have possibly never known more. The less they know about our true selves, the easier it will be to convince them to become a Scion."

"Are we even sure it will work?" Bates asked.

"As much as we can possibly be." Perdita shrugged. "We're at a point where risks of this level are standard play."

"What's our plan?" Bates asked.

Ellene said, "We'll use one of our spare Disconnection chambers, and reconfigure it. The Disconnection process was used as the basis for the Scion program because it impacts the physiology in a similar way. So, load it onto one of our cruisers; we'll take a small unit of your best." She looked at Bates and Perdita before adding, "I want top soldiers. Periods of service no less than 10 cycles. We've got to hope none of them were touched by this maniac."

Bates said, "We probed the Violator who shot you. They had more than written or verbal threats for us. It seems they had a collection of coordinates. We can't be certain, but they appear to be rendezvous places of some sort."

Ellene nodded. "We'll worry about giving chase when we've got a bigger stick to swing. But good info, Bates. Keep it secure. Once we get candidates, we'll begin the conversion process. We'll need a secure location for doing so."

"How will this work with the Essence; how long can it take?" Bates asked.

Ellene replied, "We can expect the implantation to take several hours. After that, we'll have to watch the subjects carefully. The first several hours post procedure are crucial. If they can survive that, we may have a shot."

Perdita asked, "So the idea is we get a squad of these Scions and then locate Malone?"

Ellene replied, "Indeed, but that in itself presents several challenges. Malone's abilities are ever growing. He's already mastered the mind reach of the Nara pure, and from what I'm told, he's already included dimensional travel in his cache. We must figure out a way to hit him where and when he won't expect it, even though he is likely on the verge of being able to sense thoughts and predict actions."

"For a moment, I thought you were going to say this would be difficult," Bates muttered.

Ellene was far from her podium at the Nara Arena, the pedestal with the Ancients, and her seat ahead of the Nara Council. Regardless, for the first time in her long run as Hierarch, she felt something firmly in her hand. The reins of control, yanked from her grasp by Malone, were firmly in reach again. She had her cache of lieutenants like Bates and Perdita, a small but hopeful group of Nara soldiers, a plan, however rooted in hope and chance as it was, and a target, pure and clear. Malone wasn't the endgame, she knew, though. It was in minds the width and breadth of Ling Galaxy. They'd know the Nara by the time this was over. Their existence was a product of the Nara's work, and while they never asked for any recognition, Ellene felt in every part of her being that Ling owed far more than they knew to the Nara, and it was Ellene's mission to make hers a position of indubitable power once this Malone Stanton business was settled once and for all.

VENGEANCE DIRECTIVE

ONE

ANDER PIMM SMASHED HIS FIST on his console. On the video screen in front of him was the frozen image of Malone Stanton, who'd moments before made his announcement to Ander, the Omegan and Nara leaders about his threat on Essence. Ander wasn't angry because someone made the kind of challenge Malone had. Rather, he was furious someone else beat him to the punch.

He'd have gladly gone in with Malone in cycles prior when they were comrades in the Nara Military. But Malone was on his own path, and taking Essence as he did was rather bold, given the physical risks Essence without containment posed. Malone's brazen attitude about showing it told Ander that Malone had slipped past the level of vengeance into full on megalomania.

Ander ran his hands over his arms for a moment. His coarse gray skin, one of several byproducts of his Nara Disconnection, itched with the touch. The discomfort was better than thinking another moment about Malone, or even the Nara. But those thoughts were always at the ready in his mind.

Ander summoned Darrick Bruer, his lieutenant. Darrick's large frame filled the entrance to Ander's chambers. Darrick's booming voice filled the room, and he looked on Ander with fiery green Railen eyes with the eager gaze of a bloodhound on the prowl. "Yes, excellency?"

Ander glanced at Darrick for a moment, then returned to the screen. "Darrick, Malone Stanton has taken drastic steps with Essence. Not only that, he's brash enough to state his intentions and broadcast it for others to see."

"He's always been about spectacle, sir. I wonder, though, if the front he presents conceals a lack of substance, or maybe, lack of preparation?"

Ander's annoyance was suddenly interrupted by a jolt of agony up his side. He grimaced and clutched the aching area. The pain wasn't new; it was all too familiar to all Railen. Another of the "wonderful" side effects of their surgical alteration involved periodic pain. Each Railen dealt with the discomfort in varying amounts.

Seeing his commander's unease, Darrick rushed to his side. "Sir, the treatment?" He grasped a cylinder of bluish grey steel and offered it to Ander.

Ander's breaths became labored huffs. Sweat beaded on his forehead, and he looked angrily at his lieutenant at first, but then remembered the treatment Darrick offered was the one thing that kept the pain at bay. Ander yanked the vessel from Darrick's hand, extended the short straw from the top and sipped the elixir with generous gulps.

The medication needed a few minutes before it took hold, but Ander knew it was coming, and his tensed body eased a bit out of anticipation.

Once Ander's system relaxed from the attack, his breaths slowed until his mind cleared again. "I'll deal with Malone soon enough. He's not our only problem though."

"No, sir. The Omegans, they've been massing in a zone of Ling Galaxy near ours, in particular the Bertold system."

So, Darrick's been keeping an eye out for threats. Good, he's not as useless as I was beginning to fear, Ander thought. He returned to his console and activated the display of Ling Galaxy, which showed a spotty map of their location as well as outlying areas. The Omegans had been on the move to claim more space in Ling Galaxy and were all too eager to take care of those who stood in their way. Their latest efforts brought them in close proximity to the Railen, and Ander knew the Railen were an easy target for the Omegans, given the state of the Railen people and their history with the Nara and Omegans.

"Omegans should realize their place. They were guardians to the Nara for all those cycles, but they were discarded by the Nara like us. Instead of considering a strategic partnership, they went their own way of conquest. Ling Galaxy isn't theirs to rule, and it never will be. What's our current troop strength?"

Darrick replied, "Building, sir. Viro's whipped up a decent sized force of three hundred Railen. Too small for large engagements, but enough for causing trouble, along with the modest fleet we've got at the ready."

Ander nodded. "It's time we send the Omegans a message. I want Viro leading a swift and direct attack. Summon him to my chambers at once."

———

AS DARRICK CONTACTED Viro for an audience, Ander returned to the screens in his office. The crude monitoring and scans available to him only showed activity in areas immediately beyond Delfina, the remote system the Railen had called home since their exile from Grondia. While it annoyed Ander, he knew improvement of Railen technological strength was a daily chore for his scientific minds. Sometimes, the state of their shoddy resources made Ander think about the arsenal he had back when he and the Railen were solid Nara citizens.

Ander hated how nostalgic about his Nara past he felt at times. The feeling crept over him without warning, and there was never any specific trigger for it. But his entire physical makeup was geared for recalled memories, whether he admitted it or not. As leader of the Railen, Ander performed a variety of jobs. He bolstered his people's morale wherever possible, which was usually a pretty big challenge. The Railen were all cast out of the Nara. Their participation in a failed coup to overthrow the Nara government managed to get them all labeled as Violators, and subject to the largest mass Disconnection the Nara had ever seen, reducing the Nara population by nearly two thousand.

By provision of the Universal Alliance, the Railen were given a place to live on Delfina, their decimated culture forced to reforge in the home of a world strange to them, among strangers who neither knew nor cared for their existence beyond the strain the Railen residency placed on existing resources. The UA also provided medication that included the elixir that helped the chronic pains of the Railen. Of course, it never seemed to be enough, and usually the Railen ran out between shipments.

Ander's quarters were a commandeered portion of the facility the UA begrudgingly gave the Railen as a place for them to begin their new society. The Railen Complex was formerly a research facility, long since abandoned from its original purpose. Ander often mused how the public disregard of the massive structure gave it an odd kinship with the Railen plight.

Aside from the monitors in Ander's quarters stood the Count, a series of numbers scrawled on one bare wall. Ander updated it and made it well known to their people. The Count was the number of days since the Railen had been exiled from Grondia. For twenty cycles, Ander endured his people's suffering through their new existence. As time went on, the Railen found a shred of industry, learned to barter on the sparse markets on Delfina, and made periodic trips off world in limited numbers, as much as the small number of ships the Railen had available offered them. Through the efforts of the most hardened and survival prone, the Railen cobbled together a fleet. What ferocity and intimidation the craft themselves lacked, the burning desire in the heart of each Railen, stoked by the mighty reputation of Viro Peralta, made their rising military strength an unavoidable threat. Ander knew this determination was the key element they needed for their existence and future.

Ander's rule hadn't been a constant for the Railen, however. He swiftly replaced Alistir Stone, original leader of the coup on the Nara and original leader of the Railen. Alistir carried charisma like the petals of a rose, and he endeared a large number of followers. Ander had been content to be Alistir's second, but once the exile from Grondia happened, Alistir became obsessed with revenge more than most Railen, which was quite a statement. Once the UA relocation of the Railen to Delfina was completed, Alistir knew what had to be done in his eyes. Alistir grabbed a group of former Nara Military who were part of the new Railen race and set out on a trek for the Nara sent throughout Ling Galaxy to work out a hostage situation. Their weapons were minimal, and they'd managed to get a few basic weapons that made for a threat level a few shades above pathetic. They filled in the gaps with their drive and ferocity, however.

Unfortunately, Alistir's anger and desire for revenge clouded his judgment. Besides leading to a fateful encounter on the Zormad system, Alistir's bloodlust brought a heavier price for the Railen: a Disruptor developed post exile, a copy from memory of some Nara tech that offered a potential for finding the location of Grondia, was stolen. The Railen also lost ships and several of their better fighters.

The blow could've been the beginning of their end, but Ander rallied the Railen instead. He used the example of Alistir as a reminder that while their end goal was the same as Alistir's, the approach required a more planned effort.

So, the Railen waited. Their home on Delfina became their cocoon, where their slow and steady rise began. Powered by their shared desire of retribution, and guided by Ander, strides were made slow and steady. But any fire needed fuel, and the Railen had slim pickings for cycles. The Railen post Alistir period was marked by a tremendous amount of scavenging, with a more than healthy measure of hope.

The environment of Delfina wasn't any friendlier to the Railen than their other circumstances. The arid system's three suns kept the surface at a much higher temperature than the cooled world of their birth. But the UA wasn't in the business of hospitality, especially for a race like the Railen, which many still deemed to be the dreg variety based on reports from Network and warnings directly from the Nara. Surrounding the Railen complex was a crude network of towns and some independent trading markets. The Railen were allowed to use the mostly scrap collection of the complex as their own, and some of the more enterprising determined ways of trading the scrap for slightly more attractive scrap. For basic sustenance, the UA sent meager provisions to the Railen periodically. The intent of the meager gesture was less about the Railen thriving and more about prevention of reports on how the UA held a race of refugees on the end of a rope. While not a charitable institution, the UA wanted the appearance of a law keeping one, which forced its hand into a low order of generosity.

Ander stared at two words scrawled on the wall opposite his desk, near the Count: Rebirth and Journey. Those were his making, his sermon to his congregation of downtrodden brethren, desperate for a direction. Ander learned well from Alistir's blind vengeance directive that while the goal he had was lock step with Alistir's; it had to be attempted in phases. The blade that did the most damage was the one that took its time over cycles to weave through the sinews of opposition, the veins of order, and the organs of organized society.

TWO

VIRO PERALTA WAS ANDER PIMM'S trusted military leader. Their cycles together spanned back to when they were faithful Nara citizens, both with Nara Military under Perdita Auer. Viro was one of the exceptional sons of Nara: swift and able in physical combat, and more than capable with weaponry. Like all salty Nara Military, Viro and Ander endured the pains of being decommissioned from active field service, relegated to a ceremonial guard status.

Disuse soon gave way to unrest among some Nara faithful. When the attempted coup over Grondia and the Nara happened, Viro stood strong alongside his longtime friend, Ander, and their superior, Alistir. However, their movement fell short on support in the end, and they were among the cast outs once they were Disconnected.

In their exiled location, Viro threw his energies into developing the Military Wing, the section of the Railen complex devoted to building up a fleet and arsenal of troops as secretly as possible under the UA's eyes.

Viro strode into Ander's inner chambers with a dignified gait. Even Darrick avoided eye contact with the military leader, as Viro had a long-established reputation of stoking the fear in those who followed him. Ander knew if there was anyone up for the task of a swift and definite message to the Omegans not to mention any other races who dared cross the Railen, it was Viro.

Viro entered Ander's room to the sight of Ander fixated on a display screen. A number of images floated about, among them, Malone's face and a readout of the nearby Bertold system.

"Planning more operations?" Viro asked.

Ander tossed a pained glance back to Viro. "If I had even a fourth of the scanning capabilities we had with the Nara, we'd be well on our Journey now. How are you, old friend?"

The two hugged for a moment.

"Adjusting." Viro's one-word reply resonated a volume of stories and struggles. It went further than the typical pains the Railen endured.

Ander squeezed his friend's arm as the memory of Carmita lingered on his mind. "I haven't forgotten your lovely wife. We owe it to her and the others to finish our Journey."

Viro took a shaky breath. "I know. I carry her love with me. It fuels my drive to return our punishment to the Nara one thousand-fold."

"Indeed, we will." Ander motioned Viro to a seat as he returned to his. "Anything else on your mind, old friend?"

"I'm well as can be, but I am a bit hungry." Viro shrugged.

"Hungry; is that what you are?"

"Yes, hungry for action. And for blood."

Ander felt a childlike giddiness at the look in his military leader's eyes, who still ached for a brawl. "That's my general. It just so happens we've now got options unfolding that we never had with that madman Alistir in charge. Our wonderful Joanna created something special. It's a tracker for locating Nara traveling in Ling Galaxy, and she's ready to implement it. I've every confidence we'll find one or more of the Nara couriers very soon."

Viro beamed. "That's wonderful, my friend. But you know, that's not the only problem we're facing. With our increasing audio and video monitoring over Ling Galaxy, I've caught some spotty reports from Network, as I'm sure you have, too. The Omegans feed their own hunger for power more every day."

"I'm well aware, Viro. That's where you come in and why I've asked for you." Ander motioned Viro to a seat as he returned to his console. "As you said, the Omegans are indeed on the move. We've located them in the zone adjacent to ours, and for my taste, that's far too close. Not only that, the Omegan installation is housing for a future troop garrison. I think you'll agree if we let this go unchecked, it won't be long before we're visited by them with a choice of Service or Death. We have to send them a message."

Viro's eyes sparked at the idea of a military campaign, however small it was.

"I thought you'd never ask," Viro snarled. "If the Railen are to be supreme in Ling Galaxy, all must know whoever stands in our way does so at the cost of their own destruction. Tell me, how did you get this detailed information about the Omegans? Our monitoring is still way too crude to tell you all this."

It was Ander's turn for a twinkle in his eye. "My friend, I've got a spy on the inside."

"Brilliant."

Ander laughed. "It's their science lead, he's apparently feeling... neglected."

"So, you've been feeding him?"

"Scraps so far, but I know he'll be wanting the main course soon. I just hope it's on our menu." Ander shrugged. "So how is our military strength; what's available?"

"We've got a small force." Viro's mouth formed a line.

"Right, but if you're swift and surprise is on your side, you'll cause a good amount of damage. I, for one, know the kind of destruction you can manage with even a little effort."

The two shared a laugh. Ander continued, "So then, my request is this: ready your forces to attack the Omegan outpost on the Bertold system. Our source indicates they haven't reached full troop strength there yet. When you strike, Emperor Zakmar of the Omegans will know the Omegan reach will never overstep ours."

"Consider it done, excellency."

Viro stood, and Ander followed suit. Once the compatriots shared a warm glance, knowing their period of dormancy was nearly over, Viro snapped a salute and exited Ander's room.

THREE

THE RAILEN EXISTENCE INCLUDED a measure of hope that the UA hadn't noticed their steadily increased levels of energy development over time. The fact was that while the UA had the Railen on a steady monitoring schedule that included periodic unannounced inspections, the entirety of Ling Galaxy stretched the UA's ability to keep a constant watch on the Railen. Still and all, the Railen were noted as being in need of checks due to their prior history.

After he finished with Viro, Ander went to the Science Wing of the complex and the laboratory of Joanna Yamak. Once a prominent member of the Nara's technological group, Joanna had provided a number of services in the processing of Essence as a Nara and the general betterment of Nara society. But she grew frustrated over time, once the realization set in that her efforts would never be properly recognized or even utilized.

Joanna suffered from the same thing many with brilliant minds who worked in a system that corralled their energies did.

Her thought process only concerned the free flow of new ideas. But Nara, and especially Ellene Ballo, had pruned Joanna's brilliance

down to a level of maintenance worker. It wasn't until two Nara—
Ander Pimm and Malone Stanton—reached her that she saw any
other possible opportunity for developing her capabilities to the
fullest.

She'd been seduced by Malone Stanton and Ander Pimm at
different times. She was drawn to both, each because of their
powerful personalities. It was Ander who finally offered her the best
deal. Joanna knew Malone's quest was about his own personal glory,
and Ander gave her what she'd wanted for so many cycles: recognition for her work and, more so, a very reasonable way to use it
unfettered.

It was Joanna, alongside Ander and Viro, who formed the top tier
of the insurrection below Alistir Stone, the group that led to the
attempted coup over the Nara. Their revolution sent messages
through Nara society however they could, and festered doubt and
suspicion in the hopes Nara broke rank from their occupations, their
assignments, and overtook the Nara Hierarch. The coup was
definitive but ultimately short lived. Joanna took up her place with
the rest of the conspirators, and once their exile was complete on
Delfina, she returned to what she knew, with Ander's encouragement. As expected, the original aspirations of the former Violators
turned Railen sunk many levels after their exile as priorities of shelter
and food overtook plans for Essence. Ander and Joanna agreed at
least having her continue the work she started was the best way to
honor her true purpose.

Joanna straightened her Nara uniform. A series of discolored
areas adorned the upper right chest at the location where Joanna's
various Nara Military decorations had been removed. While the
condition of the once proud garment had taken on more the look of
thrift store discard, Joanna still kept and wore it with pride. As much
as they all wanted to return to Nara, she saw her uniform as a symbol
for being flaunted in front of her Nara oppressors as their own crimes
back for retribution. Her outfit tattered and decorated with a series of

stains, scorch marks and tears, Joanna adjusted her protective head-gear as Ander sat with her at one of her worktables.

Ander clasped her hand gingerly. "How's my brilliant beauty today?"

Joanna managed a slight grin but nodded quickly to a covered item on her table. "I've got something special to show you."

Ander bristled at Joanna's choice of words. He'd known a lot of what she'd worked on. Her food sourcing and power generation projects had given Railen a more solid foothold than what the UA had done for them. But in truth, their end goal revolved around one missing piece.

He eyed the covered item on the table. "Is that what I think it is?"

Joanna said nothing but offered a coy smile in response. She reached for the item, her hand over the cover, and continued. "Journey is most of what I think about these days. All we've been through because of the Nara—they need to pay, and I'm determined to make sure they do. If we can find at least one Nara courier, we've got a chance."

Joanna removed the cover, showing the silver-plated item. Its shiny metallic surface gleamed in the room light. It looked like a pulse pistol. She clutched it firmly. A patch of green light lit her hand, a reflection of the display from the piece. Joanna swiveled it around a bit, with the slightly awkward manner of someone quite technically adept but without basic weapons skills.

"Our Rebirth has been slow and difficult, but I'm seeing some-thing here that tells me the crawl we've been on in our Journey is about to become a run." Ander's eyes widened. "I knew you could do it, dear. That's sensational, how does it work?"

Joanna tapped a control on the device. In response, it emitted a deep hum and a bluish glow lit up on one end. "I call this simply the Railen Tracker. It can not only locate the presence of Nara couriers, or Lookers traveling in Ling Galaxy, but it can incapacitate them for a time, long enough for capture."

"That's just what we need—capturing them for the extraction

process." Ander gazed on the tracker with wonder. "This is how we'll win; this is what we needed."

Joanna beamed at Ander's adulation of her.

"How many of these can you make and how fast?" Ander asked.

"I've already begun a run of fifty and will prepare more afterward."

Ander planted a kiss firmly on Joanna's forehead, her face darkened for a moment at the attention. "It's time to address our people. They deserve to know we are ready to rise on our Journey. There's been enough talk and foolish missteps in our past. Our faithful have suffered long enough under promises of their deserved glory. It's time we surged toward our goal."

Joanna offered the tracker to Ander, beaming. "Use this, show them!"

FOUR

ANDER INSISTED ON SPEAKING WITH his people directly when the time came to give them news or any information about their journey. They all referred to it as such: 'Journey'; their return to their home, one they all knew they were destined to make, and the thing that kept them going through the lean times, the foraging for food, and combining forces to ransack others to get enough just to sustain themselves.

The Railen compound was arranged like a wheel, with the Gathering Hall in the center. The Railen had copied some customs of their Nara origins, with a regular meeting place to join and share, in the hope of being able to help those less able to carry on their Rebirth. The outer ring of separate buildings of the compound offered a network of locations, many used for housing. But one location was reserved for the developments of Joanna and her group. Ander knew that as much as the military Viro commanded would be the spearhead of Journey, the efforts and work of Joanna was equally important, and it was she who was the ultimate driver that determined just when their final destiny would be achieved.

In addition to Joanna's warehouse, a safe hiding place for the burgeoning Railen fleet was kept on a nearby satellite of Delfina, disguised to look like random space trash.

Ander wore his regal cloak, a former Nara Dress Uniform and a tattered reminder of his time with the Nara, much like most Railen had outfits that had some reference to their ruptured ancestry. Their pride lay in the fact that in spite of all the odds they faced, the painful process of Disconnection, and the life they'd been subjected to, the two thousand strong Railen civilization stood firm. Their existence was a continual reminder to the Nara that the transgression of letting this many of Grondia's own blood be left to suffer and die wouldn't be forgotten at any length of time passage.

The Gathering Hall was a bustling place for Railen. Some handled armaments like they were a child's toys, checking and holding them up, examining all their intricate pieces. The Railen managed to acquire weaponry during the initial time of their exile, but enough in their group showed the promise to build weaponry of their own and, combined with the deadly military might and knowledge of the former Nara security in their midst, the Railen soon had a very impressive arsenal of destruction at their command.

The room, used for briefings by research teams on mining developments before the Railen occupation, was rechristened a gathering place for the Railen. While the support they had from the UA and others was minimal, they learned to lean heavily on the bond of their own brethren. Their shared plight gave them fuel to strengthen their bonds, and while some mistakes had been made, the belief was that their goals would be accomplished faster by their cooperation with each other, let the outsiders, including the UA, be damned. The room was lined with benches, arranged in concentric circles, like an amphitheater in the round. At the center stood a pedestal and disabled holograph projector. Ander knew the slipshod equipment didn't matter for this speech though; what he had to share and tell his people, a million digitized holographs couldn't have shown a better picture.

Ander strode through the hall; he seemingly floated about on the shouts and praises from those present. While the Railen had plenty to be angry about, one thing they agreed on was the quality of their leadership post Alistir. The fate of exile was shared by all of them, and Journey was their uniting cause, their rally cry, and Ander Pimm directed that chorus with the might of a seasoned conductor.

As he proceeded through the crowd, Ander stopped at times, embracing fellow Railen in his path, holding some of the youth, the offspring born in cycles post exile, and thrusting his arms up at other times, rousing a series of cheers in response. Finally, he made his way to the central pedestal and was ready to speak to his beloved people. Viro and Joanna stood to his right.

"My friends, my family, for many cycles we have suffered a grave injustice. The Nara, in all their wisdom, have seen fit to throw us away. To make us the fodder of Ling Galaxy, to scrape by for whatever sustenance we can afford. They've stripped our very birthright from each of us. I know you feel the pains of that as I do."

The crowd noise rose up with a steady pallor of growls. Ander's mouth pursed in a slight smile. He knew his people's agitation and was only too eager to stoke it, especially when he had an engagement planned for them that required their utmost commitment.

"You put your faith in me, and for that I am eternally grateful. Because, like you, I know how it feels to be misled, and that we have been for far too long. We let the Nara show us their way with Essence. Then, they told us our desire, our need for more, was not in the interests of the Galaxy at large. Then, our former leader, Alistir Stone, taken with his own purpose, was so eager to strike back, he endangered our very existence and sent us even further downward into our Rebirth than we'd been before. For twenty cycles now, we've regrouped and rebuilt. You've seen your lives improve, day by day. The new generations of Railen give me hope that, in fact, our climb back has been steady and undisturbed. I'm here to tell you now that our Rebirth is drawing to an end, and our Journey is about to begin."

"You've been called much. Railen... less than... Violators in the eyes of Nara. But here and now, I say to each of you, the entire Railen race, you are destined for greatness! Your path leads where we were removed, our true birthright: Grondia. We head there on our Journey, where we will make those who have lost sight of the true power of Essence pay for their flagrant disregard of the true purpose of our kind!"

Ander spotted a Railen youth, his arms thrust into the air and shouting. Those born after exile from Grondia were fed the story about the Railen exit from Grondia and fostered a belief in Ander as their savior. The life of a Railen was hard, but focusing on their eventual destiny made things a little easier.

"Our fleet grows with our every effort. The scrap that industrious Railen have collected is being reforged, reworked into a deadly fighting force. Hiding our fleet off the surface of Delfina, we allow our rebuilding progress to happen out of the watchful eyes of those who only want to keep us down. Our plans for Journey are simple: we will be sending teams into Ling Galaxy. Once our long-range monitoring has been restored, we will find the Nara sent on their errands to deliver Essence to the Galaxy. Once we've gotten a Nara, we will extract our birthright, steal back what was brutally ripped from each of us, and return ourselves to what we never should've lost. We will take our homeland back and make Ellene Ballo, the Ancients, and all Nara, adult and child, know what happens to those who dare disrespect the Railen. They rejected us as Nara, and so it shall be. Proud Railen we are, and we will be always!"

Ander paused for the swelling of shouts and cheers in response. He took in the crowd's energy and briefly glanced at his cadre nearby. While Joanna's eyes were lit with excitement at the idea of the Nara being summarily punished, Viro kept his cool military demeanor. He preferred to show his enthusiasm in results, not to mention body counts.

Ander continued. "But our Journey won't always follow a straight path. We have other concerns, other challenges that are in our way at a more serious level for the time being. The Omegans, the bastard race of warriors, have been massing forces around Ling Galaxy, and in fact have been setting up a base on nearby Bertold System. They are on their own quest to stake a claim. They want to rid Ling Galaxy of all threats, and do you know what they think of us? We're a challenge to their existence. And you know what else? They're absolutely correct! They'll try to move on our encampment here before long and take us out, because they see us as the roadblock to their power that we are. So, to fight them, and protect you, I've ordered our great military leader, Viro Peralta, to take a force to Bertold and give the Omegans a clear message what happens when they overstep their boundaries!"

Viro's stoic look gave way to a warm nod toward his friend, and several Railen Military in the hall thrust weapons into the air along with howls of pride.

"While our spear Viro and his group are sharpened and ready, our technical reach will be improving steadily. Thanks to our brilliant scientific minds like Joanna, we are able to hide our growth and Rebirth from the prying eyes of the UA. They aren't our friends, my people. They lie and serve the lying Nara out of fear by treating us as a malady, a wound to be covered and forgotten. We will not be forgotten anymore. And we will start by letting the other races of Ling Galaxy know we will take what is rightfully ours."

The audience once again responded with loud yells of support. Ander clutched Joanna's device under his cloak. The steel cooled against his hand, and he squeezed it tight before he thrust it overhead. The crowd paused for a moment.

"With these trackers our technical minds have developed, not only will we capture Nara, but we will finally bring an end to millennia of tyranny at the hands of the Nara, and we will finally have peace in Ling Galaxy!

"You've heard talk, I'm sure, about Malone and his doings. That he's making strides and soon the Galaxy will be his. My dear Railen, our former brother is out for vengeance, and that favors us, but his aims are far different. Our intent is reclamation of our homeland and Essence, while Malone's misguided crusade is to merge himself with the Essence. The success of any race in Ling Galaxy hinges on its ability to control Essence. We will provide a fair but firm method for Ling Galaxy. Those we deem worthy will be given their share. But it starts with ourselves. We will be the ones to forge our destiny!"

Ander launched his arms up, and the crowd responded with cheers. He savored their energy and knew he had to deliver for them soon. As he turned to leave the room, he approached Viro. "General, it's time. Execute your raid with all the force you can muster."

"Your word is law," replied Viro. Ander watched Viro signal his troops to follow him, then left the Gathering Hall, the room still in the afterglow of promise and hope. Ander was as hungry as his audience for results. He knew they'd waited so long, and he silently feared that without some more concrete results soon, how many of their resolves would waver.

FIVE

ANDER AND DARRICK MET IN ANDER'S chambers to watch the scene of the Railen attack on the Omegans. The lights in the room were dimmed, and a large projection on one wall displayed the area of the Omegan stronghold.

Ander had dreamed of bigger victories, but he knew even big plans sometimes started with small accomplishments.

Ander activated his bank of monitors and switched views to the Railen fleet. The ships, repurposed abandoned craft, were rebranded with a Railen insignia, and colored black. Ander marveled at the ferocious look his growing fleet suggested. He deliberately advised Joanna's team on the appearance of their craft. Ander knew the first goal in any assault was undermining confidence of the opponent through appearances, along with swift and blunt force. As for the opponents, to Ander that meant all beings except Railen.

Ander leaned back in his chair, his hands folded, a defiant grin on his lips. His pride in the nation he had grown was obvious to anyone with eyesight. "Now, we'll show the Omegans just who's in charge of Ling Galaxy." He leaned over to the comm and activated his private channel to Viro. "I don't want any prisoners; just send them a message. Be swift and deliberate, General."

"Your will is law," came Viro's reply moments later.

The Railen ships swept around the location and fired shots indiscriminately at the structure. The Omegans scrambled and managed to get several craft in the air in response. The scene morphed into a chaotic skirmish; Railen and Omegan crafts soared about, while platoons of Railen ground infantry landed and engaged the Omegan garrison in armed and unarmed combat.

"See their strength, their determination. Those are Railen virtues." Ander's eyes beamed at the sight. The Omegans weren't an easy foe by far, though. Surprise had been a great advantage, and the Railen wielded it like the mightiest sword of an ancient knight. While Ander remained fixed on the scene on the monitor, Darrick split his attention between the unfolding attack and the reports on Network from elsewhere in the Galaxy. Ander's first focus was on this attack, but Darrick knew well that his attention would be back on Ling Galaxy at large soon, and it was best they kept as many steps ahead of the Universal Alliance and all others in Ling Galaxy.

Network consisted of the connected series of comm broadcasts, official updates from the UA on developments in the Galaxy, and the taunts of those like Malone Stanton. While intended to ease communications, one fallout of Network's platform was it fostered loud cries from across the Galaxy by the phony tough or crazy brave who relished the power of threats made from unknown places that provided them the safety of retaliation that only further fueled their bravado.

After several more minutes, the fighting in the air had dwindled. Some Railen ships were grounded in the attack, but the majority in the air still were Railen. The area surrounding the encampment was mostly barren, but Ander knew better than to have dismissed it as that. The Omegans had been cleverer than most in developing subterranean facilities to hold their stores and house their citizens.

Ander activated the comm to Viro again. "Do a swift search; sweep the area. I want to know all they've got."

Ander savored the feeling of control, of dictating the course for his people. He turned to Darrick. "Our next phase starts soon. Do you have our hunters?"

Darrick nodded. "Picked from the best and most able of our youth with some seasoned military along for guidance."

"Good. And the trackers from Joanna?" Ander eyed Darrick and waited for his lieutenant's reply.

"Trackers are ready; I'll assemble our crew of hunters in the Gathering Hall for your orders and meet you in there."

SIX

FOR THE CREW OF NARA HUNTERS, Darrick favored the younger, spryer Railen, many who'd grown up post exile, per Ander's advice. The two agreed that the mission of searching for Nara was likely a prolonged one, and while any of these hunters would've done well under Viro's group, their best shot at grabbing the Nara was through the energy of this mostly youthful detachment.

The hunters stood in formation before Ander and Darrick, their unkempt appearance a sharp divide from their fixed and hungry gazes. Ander strode around the group of vainglorious Railen, males and females, ready for the task. He felt a surge of pride at the sight of the troops.

Ander spoke as he walked about. "You'll be sent into Ling Galaxy hunting for the Nara couriers. When you find one, use your trackers to capture them and return them to me here. We've reserved several small craft for you to use. Follow your plotted courses; they'll get you fairly far through Ling Galaxy. I will reward the first capture of a Nara hand-somely, so be thorough, and ruthless. Everyone has counted us a dying race; you are the first message we send to Ling Galaxy that the Railen are far from a forgotten breed of outcasts. We are the Prime beings who direct the course of life in this Galaxy from this time forward.

"What I ask of you could mean the end of some or even all of you. But, as your leader, I say remember our cause. Our Journey sometimes demands sacrifice, not unlike our Rebirth did. Do I have your cooperation?"

The hunters shouted in unison, "Hail, Ander Pimm; your word is law!"

Ander felt confident about their chances, which was far stronger that he'd felt about anything they'd been involved with for some time. He gave the detachment a salute, to which they snapped to full attention, and returned the acknowledgement. With a swift breath Ander shouted, "Go now, and do your job!"

DARRICK AND ANDER stood at the launch of the unit armed with trackers. All had been said to these souls, Ander wanted one last look on them though, so they felt in their hearts that Ander was behind them completely.

As the ships departed, Ander gazed around the exterior of the complex. The afternoon light had dimmed a bit, and a firm breeze wisped about them, carrying the faint stench they'd come to expect from the Delfina climate.

"I want daily reports and updates," Ander muttered.

Darrick nodded.

"The moment any of your crews find a Nara, contact me directly, even if I'm asleep, understand?"

"Of course," Darrick said.

"This time he won't win."

"Who, sir?"

Ander eyed Darrick with mild contempt. After a moment

Darrick caught himself, wincing at his obvious blunder. "We'll make Malone Stanton wish he'd stayed with us, sir. Count on that."

Once Darrick and the teams of hunters left, Ander strode about the compound through the winding corridors. He was passed by fellow Railen; some carried meager food supplies, others had tools. All who passed Ander paused for a quick salute for their leader. *I owe them so much,* he thought.

A notification tone rang on his comm unit from Joanna. The message was plain but made Ander stop in his tracks:

COME SEE ME NOW. SOMETHING GREAT HAS FALLEN IN OUR LAP.

SEVEN

ANDER ALWAYS ENJOYED A CONTACT from Joanna, since that usually meant she'd reached some new development in her efforts of improving the technical capabilities of the Railen. However, on this occasion her news was more of the third-party variety.

Joanna's hair was still tousled, but her eyes had a gleam Ander hadn't noticed before.

"Excellency, we've got something new from our friend, the spy."

Ander's face lit in response to Joanna's report. She beckoned him further into her lab, where she approached a large container with a small window in one side. She pointed Ander to the window, where he saw a rock formation. It cast a green hue that filled the rest of the space beyond the rocks themselves.

Ander marveled for a few moments before he asked, "What am I looking at?"

"The Omegans call it Brescar. It's an experimental fuel for them. They've been working with it as a source of energy. While it has some stability problems, they've used it successfully in starcraft flight."

Ander's eyes widened. "Any other applications?"

"Unfortunately, it doesn't have the potential we know Essence has. But this Brescar could get us along our Journey faster."

"What are the stability issues?"

"They largely affect space time, and only if containment isn't kept in check. I say it's well worth a try, using it for our starcraft. Considering my work done on containing Essence as a Nara, handling this new substance should be easy."

"How were they able to break this much off and slip it to us?" Ander asked.

An alert beeped on one of Joanna's computers. She took a moment and checked the device. Ander smiled a bit. She wasn't rude, just ever absorbed in her work, and Ander knew it was that attention to detail that had gotten the Railen as far as they'd been to date on their resurgence.

The issue resolved, Joanna returned her attentions to Ander. "The Omegans are tough but short-sighted. They want their hands on Ling Galaxy. They aren't focused on development of tech; they want conquest, not creation. Our spy has the dubious honor of being in the scientific wing of the Omegan machine. Their efforts toward military might are heralded while those geared on things like energy production are considered less than."

"Sounds like you have a kindred spirit, an underutilized and unappreciated brilliant mind." Ander smiled.

"Yes, and thanks to our improved flight capabilities, I've been able to work out a delivery system. We can't replicate Brescar, I'm afraid, as that level of activity will surely reach the UA, and we can't hide that like we did our growing fleet."

Ander's brow furrowed. Their need for replication became a more serious priority each passing moment. "We really can't do that here?"

"With our setup, no. There's a chance we can ask a nearby settlement, but I don't really want those Cerulaks nosing in too much on us."

Ander nodded. Even with the diminished monitoring capability they had suffered for decades, he'd heard enough warnings about the Cerulaks. If they scavenged enough, they'd have found out way more than they needed to see from the Railen. "How do we make replication possible?"

Joanna smacked her lips. "I suggest we try the Far Reach territories. The mining is much better out there. I don't want the locals on Delfina learning too much about us. They're devious in their own way, and the last thing we want is to much about us. The Cerulaks here are devious in their own way, and the last thing we want is to start courting those thieves. We also don't want to alert the UA any more than we have already."

"What does our spy want?" Ander's lips curled in a smile. It bothered him that Joanna hadn't yet mentioned any requirements in the form of payment, and he hoped the bill wasn't beyond his limits.

"Simple, excellency. He wants a secure facility for replication. He wants to set himself up as a supplier, and he wants our resources to help make it happen."

Ander nodded. "It's time I meet this spy."

"Of course. I'm due to check in with him anyway. Sit tight; I'll raise him on the comm."

After several minutes, Joanna reached the Omegan spy, and Ander got his first look on their furtive partner. He wore a cloak with elaborate crests on either shoulder. Aside from the regal looking garment, his appearance was definitely haggard. Ander wrote much of the spy's scattered expression off as him having a hurried and occupied mind, similar to that of Joanna's.

Ander spoke first. "Hello."

The Omegan waited a moment before nodding. "Oh, Joanna, I see you've got a guest."

Joanna nodded. "Findlay, this is Ander Pimm, our leader. He wanted to meet you."

Findlay nodded. "Greetings. I trust you've received the package."

Ander leaned back in his chair. "I did. I understand there could be more. I'm just wondering about the payment terms."

Findlay glanced about, his face uncertain, but then a knowing look came over his expression. "The first part of my payment is revenge. I'm sure Joanna already informed you, I've been relegated to the dregs of Omegan society. While they've provided for me and my family, I can't bear to think all my efforts have only been meant to have a roof over my head and comfort. After all I've tried for, and all the Omegans have taken from me, I want to know my work is affecting lives. In addition, I want suitable starcraft for a hasty exit from my home world when the time comes."

Ander and Joanna shared a look. If Findlay was away from Omegana and cut off from the Brescar supply, he would've been infinitely less useful. "Why should I help you escape? Aren't your capabilities of giving us Brescar contingent upon you being among your people physically?"

"It is, for now. But even with your help, it won't keep prying eyes away forever. Distrust is a way of life in Omegana. Our arrangement for now will soon be difficult, if not impossible, to continue. I can't keep making supplies vanish without raising questions, after all. If you want a steady energy supply, you'll do right to get replication capabilities for me."

Ander figured his association with the Omegan wasn't without a measure of payment, and he hoped the toll for this link wasn't too steep. "Our fleet is on the rise, and you'll realize soon if you haven't already that the Omegans won't last against us once we reach our full strength. I think we can accommodate you as long as you're willing to parlay."

"We both know UA Credits are in jeopardy, especially in the event of a full-scale war. I want twenty million in Wenzo crystals for payment, assuring our agreement is legitimate."

Wenzo crystals, a precious but rare item, promised the best value for anyone into illicit trade in Ling Galaxy. Their certainty in value was inversely proportional to their availability, however. While Ander and the Railen had made fast work of cobbling together a fleet and military complex, choice currency such as Wenzo crystals required a special effort for those who acquired them.

Ander gnashed his teeth. The sting of Findlay's bargain jabbed at him worse than the pains of his post Disconnection wounds. "That's rather steep. Would you consider ten million?"

Findlay chuckled. "Control of Ling Galaxy comes at a price, Ander. Besides, I would think you appreciated the sheer risk I'm taking on my end. I do have a family to provide for, assuming I live long enough."

"Then you need to consider the gesture of the Railen assistance toward keeping your cover and getting replication capability for you to the best of our ability. Ten million. Remember, we're growing our own network with Syndicates in Ling Galaxy. For twenty cycles now, we've fostered relationships so we can offer the protection you're looking for, provided you continue to help our cause."

Now it was Findlay's turn to bristle. He'd been well into the negotiation game, since the Railen were the first in a long line to more than just entertain his offers. But Findlay's race of keeping several steps ahead of the Omegans wasn't one he could've ultimately won, and compromises became an ever-bigger part of his survival.

"Seventeen million," Findlay said amid a low groan.

"Deal," Ander replied.

Ander ended the transmission and leaned back in his chair. Findlay was a most valuable asset to him, but the price tag was still a little higher than he'd hoped. It was up to his people to do the work that made this possible.

"Wenzo Crystals. He could've made it a little easier, like developing an Essence Production facility for him," Ander scoffed.

Joanna lay a hand on Ander's thigh. "It's workable, Ander. We can make it happen."

Ander eyed Joanna with warmth. "As we shall."

EIGHT

ONCE ANDER LEFT JOANNA TO HER WORK, he amused himself with searches on Network for any hints of activity by the Nara delivery groups and the Lookers. Those who wanted their hands on Essence made it a regular part of their day: a half fun, half crazed attempt at finding that prize. Ander felt that if he just kept at his watch, eventually, by sheer odds, they'd have found something.

After a while, Ander left his chambers and headed to the Gathering Room, where he met Viro, back from the raid. After a brief embrace, the two settled into chairs in a private area. "Have the ships been stowed?"

Viro wiped his brow before he gave his friend a smirk. "Really now, have you forgotten how I like to run my operations this quickly?"

"Aha, of course not." Ander laughed. "What's your report?"

"We definitely caught them off guard. Only a company of their fighters was on site. They gave us a little struggle, but our surprise was enough to get them under control before long.

I think they were massing for an activity. I can't say if it was a direct assault, but for them being that close, we needed to show them who was boss."

The lights in the room flickered and went off. Ander reached for his comm as he heard Viro growl orders to his ready troops via his own comm unit.

Ander bellowed into his comm, "Report!"

A frantic voice replied, "UA Force at the front gate!"

ANDER AND VIRO headed to the complex front entrance, where an assortment of UA ships had landed. A company of UA troops stood in front of the craft in the distance, their weapons out and at the ready. A small group stood at the entrance of the compound, and Ander recognized their leader quickly.

"Hal Miro, what a pleasant surprise." Ander hadn't bothered hiding his sarcasm when he dealt with the UA, as their visits to the Railen had progressed quickly from the periodic to the frequent.

Hal Miro stood every bit as proud as a third-tier officer who led a contingent of military on a follow-up mission for a race of discarded beings could've been. "Alright, Pimm, you know the routine. We've noticed unusual energy production levels from your facilities of late. We need to inspect what you've got going on."

"But the Galaxy is in dire straits, is it not? Surely you can't hold me responsible for wanting to give my people a little extra comfort wherever I can."

"We can do this simply or the hard way." Hal pointed to the heavy guns on the craft in the distance.

Ander salivated at the UA craft; the shimmering silver of its phaser cannon sparkled under the Delfinan suns. *If we just had one of those, I bet our Journey would be done in no time at all,* he mused.

"Of course, we don't want to be accused of criminal activity." Ander offered the phrase "criminal activity" like it was a ridiculous trinket to keep a child quiet. He turned to Viro and said, "Escort Mr. Miro and his detachment to our facilities; show them around."

Miro stepped forward. "Oh Ander, how about you lead me through. I'd feel that much better if you were around, so we can ask you any questions we might have along the way."

Ander eyed Hal's taut hand on the handle of his rifle. He sized up the group before them and his own while reciting a number of prayers that the ships from Viro's fleet were in fact hidden properly per their usual precautions. The Railen were surely outgunned, but Ander knew with a little prodding the Railen would've thrown in good for a fight. It would've been poetic too, showing the UA just how little their help over the cycles really meant to the Railen. But he steadied himself; it wasn't time yet. Instead, Ander focused on selling the situation of his people working to better their meager lot, of carving out a survival in the wild as best they could to keep their race from extinction.

Ander led his crew to the far end of the facility toward the Military Wing. He passed Railen as they made their way to the commissary. Some Railen worked on fixing the feeble roofing or construction of their facility, shoring up walls that were never meant to have lasted as long as they had for that purpose.

They arrived at the location and met Joanna. Ander tapped his left cheek, in a previously arranged signal with her. Viro had relayed a message to disassemble enough of their facility to cause enough doubts on what they were trying to accomplish.

"As you can see"—Ander gestured to the pile of materials—"we scavenge whatever we can from what's available to fabricate a better life for our people. The Cerulaks near our settlement have worked a barter with us: our labor in exchange for basic fuel cells they mine, and then there's the kindliness of the UA for the rest. Our first priority is in developing enough facilities to hold our growing population."

Hal nodded. "What about those converters? Looks like you've got far more than you need for simple urban existence."

Ander caught himself and gasped. "Do I have to remind you and your UA superiors about the plight my people suffer from? I hope you never live to see the day where you or those you care about suffer from even a half of the afflictions that affect the Railen on a daily basis. Our genetic disaffection has given us a life of many ailments. Pains that come unannounced and last for days, sometimes weeks. Our existence demands more than the meager supplies allotted to your average citizens. We're going to need better standards of care for our people. I'm afraid that's simply the way it is."

Hal chewed on his lip in thought. "We've got no data on the needs of your race, but we need to monitor you closely, given your past history."

"As you do and as you shall." Ander offered a slight mocking bow in reply. "Just know we need every bit of the energy you see here."

"Those parts look to be from starcraft; care to explain that?" Miro frowned.

Ander slowly inhaled. His fists balled at his side, and his neck stiffened as he worked out as measured a reply as he was able to. "We need the finest materials to rebuild, ones of durability and strength. What better than the armaments on craft that travel the deep of space? I'm afraid with our situation, there aren't many options for us to be choosy in our development; I think you'd at least agree with me there."

Hal nodded. "Ok, Ander, but I'm putting you on notice. The UA is sending a detachment on a satellite basis. In the future, you'll be hearing from us far more often."

"Like good parents, you're making sure all your children are loved and watched after," Ander said.

Miro glanced about the room for another moment before offering a moderate sigh. "We're done here for now, but we'll be back."

AS ANDER, Viro, and Joanna watched the UA units depart, Ander sucked in a breath through his gritted teeth. Viro, his eyes fixed on the craft as the flew off into the sky, responded, "I know, old friend. We'll get them; have faith in that."

"Indeed, we shall. We'll get them, and everyone else." Ander turned to Joanna. "Have you progressed on the Brescar project?"

"Making progress. I hope to be ready for a demonstration soon."

"Good, I'm tired of waiting on and bowing to these UA fools."

NINE

AFTER THE INITIAL VICTORY OVER the Omegans at their Bertold compound, the Railen morale took a big leap forward. The hope of their Journey not only being possible, but probable, helped even the most doubtful renew their belief that Ander one day delivered to the Railen their true destiny—their homeland and purpose regained.

Darrick returned after several days with reports to Ander about the progress of their hunt for the Nara. There'd been some close instances, but so far none of their hunters had made the mark.

While the Railen dreams crystallized a bit more each passing day, Ling Galaxy drifted further into chaos. The Omegans, undaunted by the Railen threat, continued on their own journey of conquest. Their goals weren't any lesser than the Railen, and they faced the Railen on several systems as the Railen reach into Ling Galaxy deepened.

The Railen moves weren't without problem, however. On one trip to the Zormad system, the Railen squad encountered heavy opposition from an Omegan unit, and before the Railen secured their tracker, it was lost. Ander pressed Darrick for its recovery while he kept his eyes on Ling Galaxy, with the enhanced monitoring abilities from Joanna that allowed Ander a deeper glimpse over his eventual domain.

While Central systems in Ling faced the most serious damage and threats from the marauding nation systems of Omegans and Railen, outer systems dealt with a whole different threat. Seen as useless by many except for the most enterprising, the trading markets on remote systems proved a fertile ground of opportunity. Ander knew that they weren't supposed to avoid such places, as much as their environments left a lot to be desired. As desolate as Delfina had been for their initial home in Ling Galaxy, places like Zormad weren't ones that he could've dismissed.

Ander called his top cadre together into his quarters for plans on their next move. Viro, Darrick, and Joanna sat around a table in Ander's planning room as they reviewed their situation. The hunt for Nara had continued for weeks, with little response other than several encounters with the Omegans and other groups around Ling Galaxy like the Ceruleaks out scavenging.

The skirmish on Zormad brought the Far Reach system front and center to their attention, however. And Joanna had taken an extra interest in it on a scientific level.

"Zormad provides a definite edge," explained Joanna. "It's easily got one hundred times the mining capacity of Delfina, not to mention more than a lot of other systems much bigger than Zormad in size. If we get a foothold there and perfect our replication capabilities, we'd be virtually unstoppable."

Ander ran a finger under his chin. He eyed the rest seated with him. The military logistics of Joanna's idea weren't far out of reach of the current Railen force, but Ander knew Viro wasn't as brash as Alistir. Viro only signed off on any operation like seizing Zormad once it was carefully vetted.

Ander's jaw twitched for a moment. "Zormad may be useful for replication, but let's not forget why else we should be looking there: the lost tracker and what we're doing to get it back."

Darrick swallowed; his head tilted downward.

Ander slammed the table. Darrick flinched, and Joanna gasped. Ander silently stood, his arms folded and his head bowed slightly. "I see my lieutenant is lost for words about recovering our lost asset." Ander strode about the room, his hands clasped behind his back. "You all may have also forgotten the Disruptor Joanna built for us with just a scrap of our capabilities, only to have it lost by Alistir. Well, enough guessing about what's on Zormad. Joanna, you've seen the latest from our improved scans of Ling Galaxy; what exactly do we know about this system?"

Joanna fumbled through a few pages for a moment. "Zormad, class Rylen system. Approximate population, two million. Climate varies from temperate to hot. Once a place of industry, mining structures now are derelict. Chief industries are trading markets. Minimal agriculture. Its bartering economy allows citizens the opportunity to trade for living essentials."

"Military presence?" asked Viro.

"Notable, but minor. The most prominent forces are the Militia and the Sentries of Tas Ralong, a paramilitary police unit tasked with preserving order. If we send a large enough unit of Railen, we should be able to handle them."

"But then there's the Omegans." Ander leaned toward the table, bracing himself with his hands on the flat surface.

Joanna continued, "Of course. While they've been confirmed with an encampment on world, it seems to be a way station for them. They're on the hunt, and they use these locations for regrouping, for keeping their deployed units available around the Galaxy for more coordinated operations."

Viro shrugged. "I'm familiar with the Omegan Horde system. They're pack hunters; that's their style. We have to remember that and strike swiftly. The longer we're engaged with the Omegans, the more chance they'll call in supporting units from nearby, and we'll be outnumbered, or at the very least in an unfavorable outflanked situation."

Ander let the advice from his trusted cadre sift through his mind.

He'd seen Alistir pause in silence during meetings, and once Ander took the reins, he fully understood the process. Theirs was a series of moves; while their goal clear and simple, the path toward it was anything but.

Of all the aspects of their operation, Ander knew one of the variables that was the biggest risk to them. He stood upright again, his back turned to his crew, waiting for their answer to his next question as a priest hearing a confession.

"And then there's the Xeno," Joanna added.

Ander winced at the name. He spun on his heels and looked into Joanna's widened eyes. "The Xeno. What about that filth?"

Joanna stammered for a moment. "I've heard, as you all probably have, about their development on Zormad. They seem to be growing into their own entity."

"They're more of a disease than this Veculus we've heard about," Ander scoffed. "I've hated the Xeno ever since we saw reports of their arrival in Ling Galaxy on Network. How, not unlike us Railen, the Xeno arrived here, but instead of the hasty delivery to a rusted-out piece of forgotten slab, the Xeno were featured as a race from outside Ling Galaxy, one of curiosity. The attention they were given drove me nuts. Evidently, it helped tip the scales on Alistir into full-fledged madness. You may have forgotten about the Disruptor that was lost, but I haven't. We've never been able to locate it, but every fiber in my gut tells me it's the dirty Xeno's fault."

Several moments of quiet passed. Ander saw the looks his cadre gave each other. It was Darrick who first broke the silence. "They'll be dealt with in due time."

"Will they?" Ander spun and locked his glare onto Darrick's startled expression. "Strange how quickly you say we'll handle the Xeno when our very leader was taken down by them."

Viro replied, "Those were different times, Ander. We were flying blind, led by someone more consumed with blind vengeance than the Journey back to viability that we've taken since." Viro reached his hand toward his friend.

Ander eyed Viro's offered hand for a second but returned to Darrick. "Make no mistake; our path toward Journey won't be interrupted anymore. As much as the Omegans threaten our goal, the Xeno are a thorn in our side. The mere fact that the Nara have taken an interest in them tells me they're either now or soon will be another threat to us, and they also will be eliminated. Once we control Ling Galaxy, the Xeno, to a one, will be extinguished. No souls will be left unturned. Male, female, young, old—we will make the mention of their name a crime, we will remove them from existence. Am I in any way unclear?"

"No, excellency," the others responded.

TEN

ANDER CONCLUDED HIS MEETING WITH an order to Darrick to visit Zormad with a detachment and get the lost tracker. Ander then returned to the Gathering Hall. The great room wasn't half as full when he addressed his people. The Railen day was filled with a lot of tasks and chores, and gatherings weren't always a part of that. Ander relaxed in thought on a chair down in the crowd area. He noticed some Railen examining spent weapons off to one side of the hall.

Darrick promised a secure mission to capture the Nara couriers. I should've known better to trust him. He's greedy and eager to impress, but he hasn't the drive that Viro has, nor the record of success. Maybe I gave him too much responsibility before he was ready.

After thinking about the state the Railen Journey was in, Ander left the hall and strode outside the Railen compound. He needed a different view for his thoughts. They'd been so directed on their Journey, or he at least thought so. The lack of replies from his hunters worried him. He managed to keep his people's spirits at least mostly up during their time, but he knew they expected some other results soon. He wasn't as brash as Alistir, but even his goodwill from his people had an expiration date.

On Ander's meandering walk, he ran across Joanna, herself on a break from her latest round of enhancing the Railen monitoring of Ling Galaxy. She joined Ander while he strolled the hallways of the complex.

"I can't promise I can locate that Disruptor, but the tracker is a simple signature to pinpoint."

Ander smiled and placed his arm around Joanna. "I've no doubt you'll do your best. How's the Brescar adaptations going?" Ander asked Joanna.

"Well, excellency. I expect full functionality with the engines before long."

"Amazing." The ideas for Brescar usage blossomed in Ander's head, and he wondered if the applications for Brescar could one day extend past simple ship fuel. "Any possibility we can use this to find a way back to Grondia?"

"Doubtful. I don't recommend too much tinkering with this. Brescar has been verified safe for simple fuel, but I'm concerned about going too far with modifications."

"What's the risk? We're not in danger now, are we?"

"Keeping its applications for fuel is enough for now," Joanna said. "Findlay had a brilliant idea, but his Omegan ancestry showed in the rush to completion. Brescar does have some volatility, but only when tampered with."

"Fair enough."

ONCE ANDER and Joanna parted ways, he returned to his quarters, his mind still ablaze in thought. There was plenty to worry about anyway. From the news updates on Malone's exploits to the moves of the UA hard pressed to maintain order in the Galaxy and the

Omegans ever on the rise, Ander was never lacking in things that needed his attention.

Ander was wafting through his schemes, both those in play and potential ones, when his comm sounded out a message. The sender was unfamiliar to him, but the message framed everything he needed to know:

NARA SEIZED. PROCEEDING TO DESIGNATED RENDEZVOUS AS ORDERED.

Ander let out an uncharacteristic whoop as he spun with the grace of a dancer. The breakthrough he needed, and wanted, but was only slightly sure would've ever happened. He summoned Joanna to meet him in his quarters immediately.

Joanna was in close competition for being most excited about this news, and Ander only felt right that he shared it with her first.

"Was there any difficulty in the capture? Did the trackers perform well?" Joanna wrung her hands with the giddiness of a child about to get candy.

Ander chuckled softly and swept Joanna up into a hug. She grimaced and awkwardly smiled as she eyed the room while Ander spun her for a moment before he set her back down and responded, "My dear, you've done exactly what I needed. Now we've got a leg up. Now, we will hit the dear Nara right at the source."

"What a relief," Joanna said, quickly straightening her uniform before she took her seat next to Ander at his console. On screen was a preliminary mapping project Joanna had begun, using the basic Railen physical makeup and alongside it, a preliminary one of the Nara. The exact knowledge of the Nara genome wasn't known to many. Even Joanna had minimal knowledge of the physical map, which she had put together from memory. It was more than they had at the start of their mission, so Ander was fine with the work-in-progress it turned out to be.

Ander nudged Joanna to access the console as he spoke. "We'll sedate the Nara and run preliminary scans for viruses and, of course, any surprises. We don't want to get too far in only to find a wired-up explosive, now do we?"

"Of course not." Joanna nodded quickly, her eyes glued to the display as she worked. Her hands became a jumble of motions as she directed the on-screen display. Helixes twisted, formed, broke apart and formed new combinations as she looked at her work. "Having the Nara in front will help me fill in the missing pieces."

"I've no doubt they will!" Ander rose and planted a kiss on her forehead as he strode about and checked his comm for an update on the arrival. "They are en route; ETA in two Delfina days."

Joanna wiped her brow. She knew this job easily replaced all her other duties. Her work on this mapping and the surgery that came next could've moved the Railen Journey from a rhetorical battle cry to a reality as their bastard race finally claimed their comeuppance.

ELEVEN

A LARGE CROWD GATHERED INTO THE operating theater in the Science Wing. Ander, out front, observed a lone gurney at the middle of the room, surrounded by a series of chairs. The process of finding the Nara and, furthermore, experimenting on them was of great interest to a number of Railen, so much that the procedures were televised using the crude but still functional closed-circuit monitors at the facility, so all Railen had a chance to see the event. Every Railen shared the ache and the pains of their exile, and the idea of them being able to return to their home world was of great importance to them.

A pair of Railen guards stood nearby on the stage. While Joanna had enough tranquilizers on hand to euthanize their unwilling subject, the unknowns of this procedure had Ander order the extra protection, just in case.

Joanna consulted the hovering surgical robot that wafted around above the Nara patient. The complexion of the Nara on the table was a darkish red. Joanna checked the contacts between the robot and the Nara to make sure all were intact, and the Nara was receiving a healthy dose of tranquilizer.

Joanna turned to Ander and the assembled crew with a flourish. "The crucial part of this process is at the beginning. I must make sure that the Nara's system is brought to a slow arrest but kept alive. Our research has suggested that the key genetic makeup can only be harvested within the first few minutes of this process."

She returned to her work, moving swiftly around the table. Ander eyed her and her robot, looking up now and then to see that more Railen had gathered. He wanted these procedures left open to his people in the hope that it kept up their morale during the long periods of little to no progress.

The monitors on the robot broadcast a series of beeps and pulses, and Joanna raced to the Nara. She checked the robot again and confirmed the Nara was near the arrest point. She retrieved a blade and a series of small needles and kept them at the ready. The room was quiet except for the occasional response from the medical robot.

As Joanna sliced into the Nara, the room fell into a deep quiet. Even Ander himself felt his body go taut.

The mood was shattered by the sharp scream of the Nara, who flailed about and managed to break one of the restraints on the table. Joanna rushed to send more anesthesia through the Nara's system, but the Nara managed to knock Joanna down before the Railen guards nearby subdued the Nara. After a few more minutes, the Nara began to breathe very rapidly, then their reddish hue faded to a pale gray.

Joanna picked herself back up.

"Everything OK?" Ander asked, but Joanna said nothing at first. She studied the needles in her hand for a few seconds, still not acknowledging Ander. Then she turned to him.

"We've got it."

ANDER AND JOANNA gazed at the vial that contained the genetic data from the Nara. Ander admired the colorful swirled liquid substance as an ancient relic. For all their exile, it was their hope, their goal, their driving purpose. All those who were with him, all who'd left, all who had died, they all deserved this moment. His arm found its way around Joanna, and he hummed softly. "My dear, you were wonderful."

Joanna demurred slightly, but her joy about her achievement got the best of her and she replied, her voice strained with emotion. "Thank you, love. Where do we go from here?"

"We need to replicate; once we have the ability to do so, we work on implantation. I've asked Viro to give me ten candidates. The best and strongest. I don't mind letting the first generation have a chance, but I'm suspecting we'll need to go to the post exile born Railen. Once we implant them, we send them as our heralds, bringing messages to the Nara. They'll infiltrate Nara society. Once we've confirmed success, we'll begin a mass conversion. We'll all be given the genetic code, and then we'll be ready to complete our Journey."

Warning sirens broke up their serene moment of achievement. While Ander knew the UA could always be counted on for an unexpected visit, he sensed something else at play. He jumped to his feet when the first series of explosions sounded, a collection of dull booms that gradually grew louder. Ander activated his comm to Viro. "What's going on up there?"

Viro's agitated voice replied, "It's the Omegans, they're striking back."

TWELVE

ANDER RACED TO THE MILITARY WING, where several were already gathered. The on-screen display of their exterior confirmed the worst. Several squadrons of Omegan fighters were swarming their facility while bombers back in the distance carved a deep and wide trench around the Railen compound, leaving even escape by foot impossible. Ander winced at the scene; his discomfort only eased slightly by the sight of Railen craft airborne in a counterattack.

Ander found Viro amid a collection of his subordinates. He bellowed orders to any in earshot, which included most in the room.

Ander locked eyes with his General in a gaze that told him the gravity of their situation without a further report. "How long do we have?"

"At this point, minutes."

"Ships left in the wing?"

"A cruiser and a few transports."

Ander swallowed hard. The moves and sacrifices the Railen had made to get to their place weren't in vain, but for a good number of citizens, the road ended with this attack. "Get all the able-bodied you can to their ships, we'll make a jump to a safe distance."

Viro looked at Ander through strained eyes. "We cannot take everyone. There's only room for about a third of our numbers."

"At this rate, we won't even have that many left. What's your plan, General?"

"I've got my best armed up and putting what fire we can on the raiders, but it's just going to be a holding tactic. We've got to evacuate now to the transports. Once we get off Delfina, we can get to our craft, but only if we can take out enough of their ships first."

Ander glanced past Viro to the monitor and saw the size of the Omegan contingent. It was enough to level their facility. *Why aren't they demolishing us?* he wondered. *They've got the ships, and their numbers are way ahead of ours.*

Ander's comm crackled to life, and he heard Commander Chun's voice.

"Ander Pimm, I presume."

Chun was someone known as much by his tone than by his voice itself. A battle proven warrior, he made his bones with his aggression. His reputation came from how little mercy he showed his victims. And while Ander had to admit the Railen weren't blame free, given their recent raid on the Omegan outpost, the attack the Omegans made against the Railen was the equivalent to storming the Omegan home world of Omegana and laying it to waste.

Ander steadied himself, only barely secure in the knowledge the Omegan offense in this case was to maim the Railen for the sake of teaching them a lesson. "Chun, this aggression is highly unbalanced and beyond reasonable for even the marauding Omegans. What's the purpose of all this?"

"Oh, we've followed you and have kept our eyes on your doings for some time. You and the rest of Ling Galaxy will learn your place, as the Nara will too. Under our rule. We've united with a dear old friend of yours, Malone Stanton, who sends his regards, by the way."

Ander swallowed hard. "You think a deal with that megalomaniac will stick? The only thing you've aligned with is a new master. You'll see that in time, I hope before it's too late."

As if on cue, another face appeared next to Chun on the comm. Ander gasped. "So, it's true."

"Indeed," Malone said. "I'm honestly a bit offended at your lack of respect for a former brethren Nara in your presence, Ander."

"We're brethren in genetics only. In the matter of goals and destiny, we couldn't be further apart."

Malone mocked dismay as he chided Ander. "Be that as it may, our purpose here is only to further cripple you. We can't have a fleet of—what's that you're calling yourselves now, Railen?"

"That's correct, and it's a name you'll respect in time." Ander sneered.

"Oh come now, that's no way to earn anything. It may start with words, but it ends with actions. Now, as payback for your attack on our Bertold System colony, we're going to remove your facility from existence. But just so you have enough chance to see your new home destroyed, we're going to allow you five standard minutes to vacate the system before we reduce your structure to ashes. So, you will live, all the better for you to see what I've got planned for Ling Galaxy. You'll be serving new masters in time; count on that."

The comm terminated abruptly as shots continued to fall around the complex. Ander bellowed into the comm, "All available head to transports before they eliminate our facility!"

THIRTEEN

AS CHUN PROMISED, THE OMEGAN FLEET destroyed the Railen facility. Barely eight hundred Railen left the Delfina facility before it was demolished, leaving another sixteen hundred as casualties for the Omegan onslaught. The Omegans evidently began requiring interest on their payments for blood, and Ander relished the day when he settled accounts with them for good.

The Railen fleet, weakened by the Omegan attack, assembled in deep space after a series of warp jumps. Reports to Ander indicated heavy losses of over 60% of the Railen population, although several fighters and his cruiser remained.

Ander sighed as he made his way through the hold of the cruiser where the remnants of his brethren lay. He cursed a thousand things to himself, about how he could've let this happen to his people and if they were ever going to trust him again. They had put their entire existence in the palm of his hand, thinking that his words, his belief about their future, were not just empty thoughts, but a path, a directive, a series of events they simply had to follow him to experience. But here, the fragments of their existence, he wondered if any of them would ever look at him the same way again.

"I'm sorry," Ander muttered to no one. He strode slowly about the room, his eyes downward. Joanna caught up with him several minutes later.

Ander eyed her sadly.

"The Nara code is safe, dear. Don't worry about that. We'll get to it in time."

Ander nodded and offered a weak smile in response.

ANDER FOUND a quiet alcove on the ship for a meeting with Viro and Joanna for a recap of their situation. His two strongest allies showed more than a little concern and fear on their faces as together they discussed the pitifully few options ahead for the Railen.

Ander said, "The Omegans are an opportunistic bunch. They thrive on the chance to get more than they have, which doesn't make them really any worse than most of the citizenry of Ling Galaxy. But the Omegans have a certain ruthlessness that if directed can be a very powerful resource. We need to get all advantages we can now on our side. We'll head for Zormad."

Joanna nodded. "The comm on this cruiser can't reach there yet, but we'll have to take a shot that he's still there."

"Yes," Ander said. "And our spy; I hope he's still safe."

"He is, as of my last communication with him a day ago."

"Do you still think we can trust him and that he's still got good cover?"

Joanna shrugged. "I'm as sure as I ever was. Besides, we do have a bargaining chip we can use if we need it."

"What's that?" asked Ander.

"His child; we know of his child. Should things turn south, we can always exploit that weakness."

"I suppose that will do for now," murmured Ander. He decided he needed a speech; as much as his people may not have wanted one at that point, he knew the tone had to be set, even as another dark hour came on them. He activated the ship comm, broadcasting to the cruiser and transports, in a small convoy headed for the distant system of Zormad.

"My people, we are once again nomads. Not given the chance at what we deserve. But my fellow Railen, those who get what they deserve do so by taking it, and that's what we shall do. I've ordered our course set for the Zormad system. We'll make our way back through the markets, through the trading, because that's what we are. They haven't completely crippled us. I only want you to remember the faces of those who did this, and remember that no matter what happens, we are on a crusade, and what was taken from us will be ours once again."

BALANCE OF RETRIBUTION

ONE

"**W**HAT'S YOUR NEWS?"

Findlay Mantisword handled questions far more involved than that on a daily basis. In his position as Chief of Scientific Development for the Omegans, his nerves endured a consistent test every day, from Emperor Zakmar down to the science staff under his lead. He handled things as well as one in a position like his could, but even Omegans had their occasional outbursts when the benign or ridiculous was too much to handle with a simple shrug of the shoulders.

But this time, it wasn't as easy. It wasn't the nature of the question so much as it was who asked it. "You're dying to know what it is, aren't you, Charista?" he smiled.

Charista wrapped her arms around the back of her chair. "Come on, Dad, you can't build something like this up and keep me waiting."

Findlay chuckled. "Alright, alright." He grabbed a seat next to her and stroked her shoulders. "You remember that energy project I worked on, right?"

"Brescar, yes." One of Findlay's many research projects had involved the search for a suitable replacement for Essence in Ling

Galaxy. As tall an order as that was, Findlay knew if he ever found a reliable substitute for Essence, that would've flipped the growing unrest about energy and controlling Essence delivery in Ling Galaxy on its head for sure. Unfortunately, Zakmar cut Findlay's hopes off, at least initially, when the Brescar project was ordered scrapped.

Findlay smiled. "I've found someone interested in working with me on Brescar besides Emperor Zakmar."

Charista's brow creased. "I thought that project was canceled."

Findlay shook his head. "More like delayed."

"Then who's working with you, another group in Omegana?"

"Not Omegan at all."

Charista froze. The idea of her father working with someone off world bothered her as much as the worry over if the news got around Omegan society and back to Zakmar himself.

"Dad, who?"

"Ander Pimm of the Railen."

Charista's eyes widened. The sworn enemy of the Omegans, the Railen were on their own quest for domination. But, while the Omegans wanted control of Ling Galaxy itself, the Railen aimed their sights on recapturing their lost home world of Grondia and Ling Galaxy by proxy. However, lofty goals were only dreams without the tools that made it happen.

His daughter's unease fairly obvious, Findlay said, "I know Zakmar doesn't take kindly to treason, which I'm sure includes dealing with the Railen. But I've thought about our situation and I feel like we're in a holding pattern here." Findlay's plans for their future included stability and freedom, neither of which seemed on the menu with being a solid Omegan citizen, as high up as he was in their chain.

Charista collected herself enough to speak again. "Is a deal with those ragtag bastard outcasts worth the risk?"

Findlay smiled. His daughter had very successfully reiterated the line fed to all Omegans from their collective education. "Don't forget, dear, the Railen were also outcast from the Nara. Omegans can't claim a genetic heritage with them, but our race served the Nara as guardians for centuries. As for the Railen, the race you learned about in school isn't the Railen race of now. Their resourcefulness made them a force to be reckoned with in short time. Remember, they have the key element a warrior needs: hunger. I believe they can get us where we want to be: a place of our own, hidden from Omegans where we can finally be free."

"Dad, I know you're no loyalist to Omegana and won't be heart-broken if we end up leaving here for good, but are you sure the Railen are our best bet?"

"I am, dear. I've met with Joanna, their scientific head. Our lives here are under a microscope. I'm followed and observed more each day. Zakmar's will to power is only checked by his chronic paranoia."

"What about Nic Sava and the UA? Maybe there's a chance for us there?" Charista asked.

"Sava and the UA are more politicians than anything. Sava wants to keep the status quo. He wouldn't ditch Essence; he's making too much money to do that. He's appeased Omegan aggression and Railen hostility for a while now. Besides, I'm hearing rumors Malone Stanton is interested in a deal with the Omegans, so no telling what changes come with that lunatic in the mix."

"What are you going to do then? There will be a war coming soon at this rate."

"I've no doubt. But wars mean opportunity for the clever. That's why I want to establish myself as an energy supplier, neutral, working for the highest bidder."

Charista marveled. While Findlay had typically been more of the scientific mind, Charista relished her father speaking more practi-cally, even strategically, for a change. Findlay's world and work involved more formality, like regular meetings with Emperor Zakmar and other heads of state in Omegana. He had access to privileged info, but that came at a price of enhanced monitoring of his work by Omegan Security.

"But Dad, providing energy supply as an independent... you need protection for that."

"Of course, and that's where you come in. Once you complete training and get assigned into an Omegan military unit, you'll work yourself into a leadership role. Once we make our exit from Omegana, with your military might and my abilities, we'll build our own corner of Ling Galaxy that no one will ever be able to take away from us."

Charista's eyes widened. "Lead? Dad, that won't happen very fast. I'm just a graduation candidate right now. I'm barely known; definitely not a leader."

"The deal I'm negotiating with Ander Pimm will take at least a few months to come to fruition. Dear, are you forgetting how you brought in top marks in your training? Believe me, you're every bit the fighter your mother was. With the right effort and time, you'll be noticed, and soon."

Charista smiled at the thought. Her military future was still bittersweet, not having her mother alive to enjoy it too. Charista had faint childhood memories of her mother, Winola. The footage Charista watched of Winola addressing troops and leading Omegan detachments defending Nara on Essence runs were things she cherished very much.

Findlay said, "If the Railen come good on my first deal, that gets us money to start. We can look for soldiers for hire at first; and then, when we prove our worth, I bet more will join us."

Charista nodded, her brow furrowed. The mood overtook her sometimes, when she thought of her future and how she was cheated of sharing it with her mother.

Findlay, sensing her melancholy dip, grasped Charista's shoulder. As he'd done many times in the cycles since Winola's death, he felt himself putting out the good thoughts of what could be so the dread of what actually was stayed in the background. "It won't be easy, but I just know for us, no future of hope involves service to the Omegans."

"What about you, Dad?"

"I'm not much of a politician. My best work is done in research and science. It's better I worry about the logistical side of our plan. You, on the other hand, have your mother's charisma. It's best we fight this problem from two ends. I'll make my arrangements with Ander Pimm, and you propel yourself further into the ranks militarily."

"I'm one of dozens graduating, Dad. Everyone wants the choice details."

"Do your work. Make contacts. Volunteer for the tough assignments. You'll get there faster; I just know it. The Omegans will be moving into more systems soon, and they'll need able bodied field leaders like you."

"Somehow, I thought your news was going to be a cure for Veculus." Charista sighed. "My friend, Phoebe, has it now."

'It' was sufficient enough a pronoun for any citizen in Ling Galaxy to understand it meant Veculus. The horrible virus had mysteriously circulated the Galaxy for many cycles and infected a large number of citizens from various races. Only a few, like the Nara and the Railen, showed immunity from it to that point. This fed wide speculation that Veculus was a biological weapon sent into Ling Galaxy by the Nara in an attempt at maintaining control over their operations.

The Omegana system had joined the ranks of worlds infected with Veculus long ago, and Gajanan, the capital city where Findlay and Charista lived, was no exception.

Findlay clutched Charista's shoulder. "Phoebe, huh?"

"She's been placed with the quarantine."

Findlay shuddered. The quarantine was the last ditched effort in a fight with no reasonable option. Large portions of the Omegan population infected with Veculus were brought off Omegana to a distant moon, where they spent all their time in an isolated community made of sectioned areas. The mere description of it sounded more like a prison than a medical healing facility. To many, the thought of being sent there was one worse than death, especially given the low number of patients who were ever known to have returned alive from the Omegan quarantine colony.

Findlay hoped Charista hadn't noticed the fear he felt as it simmered in his gut. "How long has Phoebe known?"

"A few days. When the fever didn't break for a week, she had herself checked, and they confirmed it."

"I'm sorry, dear. I know the latest attempted vaccine failed to stop it." Findlay quickly got to his feet.

Charista was soon at her father's side; it was her turn to be comforter. "I know, Dad, I know." She wrapped her arm around Findlay's drooped shoulders. They both knew the next part of the story; it went unsaid as they both paused in their memories. Besides a few video clips, Charista only had Findlay's stories about her mother to cling to, one of them being her death from Veculus.

Findlay felt buoyed by his daughter's love as, together with Charista, they relished his lost wife and her lost mother. "She was a good woman, tried and true, one of the best Omegana ever produced."

"The best." Charista echoed his words through a whimper before her tear-filled eyes locked with Findlay's. Many of Charista's memories of her mother were through the stories of Findlay, as Charista was a young child when Winola died.

"She gave her all for Omegana, and there isn't even a statue or a plaque for her. How could they just forget her like that?"

Findlay said nothing at first, but only slipped his arm around his daughter. "Zakmar likes to paint his own history, and whatever doesn't make him out to be the savior of all Omegans gets pushed aside. Don't think for a moment I've forgotten what happened to your mother. Not for one instant. Every day I get up, go to my work, meet my marks, satisfy quotas, and keep in the back of my head that one thing above all: to honor her. She wasn't worth the time to Omegana, but she will be honored by us. We will both do that, in our time."

Charista nodded and slunk downward into a chair in thought. She was almost at the end of the adolescent phase of her Omegan development, and with it came a marked degree of impatience. She activated a holo screen as a distraction. The display leaped in front of her in a midair projection that displayed a collection of games available.

Findlay lay his hands on Charista's shoulders, kneading them softly. She smiled at the gesture of affection. Findlay had struggled to fill the gap left by Winola, and he did as much as he could, sometimes to Charista's amusement. But she couldn't have denied feeling the love her father showed her through all the cycles without her mother.

"It's all going to work out." Findlay smiled. "Ander's willing to set up a plant to distribute the Brescar once he can secure proper replication capabilities. And feeding him tidbits on what the Omegans are up to has given us a pretty good entry point with them."

"Are you sure the Omegans won't get wind of what you've been doing? It's pretty dangerous, Dad."

"Sometimes danger is a necessary risk, my dear." Findlay shrugged.

"So, why can't you replicate here?"

"Because, Zakmar commandeered my replication facilities. They're only interested in making weapons and crafts for their exploits. Brescar is less than an afterthought. They don't like the instability."

"Instability?"

"I've seen it lance holes through the time spectrum, even space spectrum. I've been interested in exploring those, but not while Zakmar's waving the war banner. I've been put on notice for assistance in weapons development, and if I'm going to keep up this charade with the Omegans and still get my part of the bargain with the Railen, I must act as though I'm playing along, at least for now."

Findlay took a calming breath before he continued. "Of all the things I've done, setting up your future is my top goal. Your mother and I..." Emotion finished Findlay's thought as he clutched his midsection in a sob. Charista hugged her father, and sadness for his and her situation flooded her, along with a hatred for the indifference their government showed at their situation.

"You're taking Brescar for this plan; don't you think they'll notice enough of it missing to be a problem for us?"

"No, I've got a reserve quantity for development. Anyway, if you listen to the likes of Chun, he's only interested in conquest. Fuel is a minor concern, as much as Essence in Ling Galaxy is in dispute. My position with the Science Wing of Omegana doesn't carry enough weight. There's too much for them to focus on in Ling Galaxy without worrying about my developments. They'll gladly fuel their ships up, but the interest and gratitude stop there. My friend, Joanna, has seen to it to make this deal possible, and I think it's the best we've got so far."

Charista shrugged. The loss of her mother was too great for her to shake off, and she resented Findlay at times because he seemed too little emotionally ravaged externally for Charista's liking. But she knew, in time, her turn for making plans would come. Whether it be with the help of the Railen or by her own doing, vengeance stayed in Charista's sight, even if it was still out of reach.

"For now, my dear, we've got to keep going. Every day, think of Winola, what she'd want for us, and make it happen." Findlay saw both sides of the Omegan machine and the Railen as pawns in his own game. His only fear was in discovery before his position became powerful enough.

TWO

THE FOLLOWING DAY, FINDLAY MET with the other heads of Omegana for their regular session with Emperor Zakmar. Over the past thirty cycles since their separation from Nara service, the Omegan race grew at a very healthy pace. Their abilities and physical strength at least extended their survival in Ling Galaxy, a place where want was more known than satisfaction.

The Omegan goals were uncomplicated. Their history was filled with subservience to the Nara. From early times, the Omegans served as protective force for the Nara, once the Nara deemed their own security an overreach of their mission. The Omegans provided protection to the Nara on their missions of Essence delivery in Ling Galaxy.

Omegan service to the Nara had lasted for centuries, and while it wasn't without trouble from bands of marauders and smugglers trying to grab some of the precious element to Ling Galaxy, the Omegans prided themselves on a regular run of service until the Nara released them.

Like other races in Ling Galaxy, the Omegans dealt with their own trials and sufferings. Illness hit a large portion of their population and, while potential medications existed, the width of Ling Galaxy and the number affected made treatments for all beyond reasonable. The Omegans counted their dead, and when the numbers grew too large for them to tolerate, they took action.

Zakmar led the charge for change. Staging a coup, he overthrew the existing Omegan ruler and established a firm presence for the Omegans. No longer would they be known as former hand servants of the Nara, following and obeying their directions. The Omegans' new purpose was of conquest, of order, and of domination in Ling Galaxy.

Never one for modesty, Zakmar reclined against his opulent chair and gazed on the faces of his military and scientific heads. "We've come a long way. Omegans no longer stoop in service to others, but have stood in declaration of our superiority. We've spread our empire to other systems in Ling Galaxy, and every day our foothold increases. But our path forward isn't always clear. We've got obstacles, and there are those who want more than anything to see us fail. I want to know what happened at the Bertold system."

The room went deathly silent. Part of the Omegan conquest involved setting up encampments on strategic systems in Ling Galaxy for coordinated operations. The mission of the Omegans was clear: capture, raid as many systems for supplies as possible, render any opposition encountered inert. The UA forces fought the Omegans to a point, but the stretch of the UA in Ling Galaxy left many of their units less able to hold off the Omegan onslaught. Nic Sava with the UA opted for a policy of sanctions against the Omegans, a punishment Zakmar regarded as a mere taunt. While the Omegans hadn't yet tipped the balance of systems in Ling Galaxy to their favor, Zakmar's primary goal was making that happen as soon as possible.

The Omegan pack hunting method had proved successful; at the very least it gave them a handy supply of reinforcements for those who ran into trouble they weren't able to handle on their own.

However, one of these operations was disrupted by the Railen attack on the Bertold system. What further concerned Zakmar was the utter secrecy of the operation. Not even the average Omegan citizen knew about military operations like the one on Bertold, at least not information specific enough for an ambush like this required, so the betrayer among them was part of a select group.

Findlay swallowed hard. While he wasn't on the immediate hook for answering his leader, he knew full well his part in the Railen attack. He tensed his midsection and attempted his best at invisibility. He'd felt himself in this position more and more since his deal with the Railen had begun, and he leaned on a mantra when his fears reached a point he was afraid might have caused him to break down and reveal himself. He sucked in slow breaths and repeated to himself: *I am safe, I am hidden, I am fine.*

Findlay's meditation was broken up when Yul Mailey managed to clear his throat. At once, the attention of the room shot to him.

"Colonel Mailey, you have something to share with us?" Zakmar completed his sentence with a deep-set scowl.

Yul nodded and, after a slight stammering, began, "My Lord, we were fortified in our defenses; we'd begun deployment of our heavy weaponry when we were caught by surprise. I'm afraid our forces were unable to respond quick enough, and the encampment was lost."

Zakmar steepled his fingers and eyed Yul. Zakmar found it best, when he received a report on a failed operation, that he first allowed the responsible party enough time for their brief on all information pertinent to what went wrong. "I see. So, you claim your defenses were set and strong. So then, how is it that you were overrun, engaged, and defeated by a group like the Railen?"

Yul's brow creased, and his breaths quickened. Zakmar thrust a palm in Yul's direction. "Do we all know the Railen? I'm assuming we're aware of them. As strong as the Omegans are, surely we're aware of any of the races who pose a mild threat to us."

"A race of renegades," Commander Patrach offered, giving his junior officer a brief rest from the hot seat. "Bastard children of the Nara, expelled for crimes against Nara society, genetically altered and thrown into Ling Galaxy to forage and find an existence permanently cut off from their birth home."

"Renegades," repeated Zakmar as he stood, his hands flattened against the table and his head facing downward. "Given a meager existence from the UA, barely enough means for even the simplest space travel. How then did they even get word of our location and manage this attack?"

"They're destitute, but hardly helpless," offered Patrach. "Some of the better minds from Nara were in that group. The lost yet resourceful can find their way with the right kind of effort. We cannot discount their inventive spirit. Our own scouts have come across the Railen, organized off world into several sub fleets."

Zakmar arched a brow. "Go on?"

"Their ships are mismatched, but their desire and skill are indisputable. We're also talking about some of the best Nara military produced, as we may remember, the very race that once trained ours. While I won't speak for their worth against Omegan muscle, they aren't the cowering wretches we'd like to believe. We should never count them out, with all due respect, my Lord."

"Fair enough," Zakmar growled. "But aggression against our own never goes unchecked under my rule. The Railen grow in power, this I accept for now. That doesn't mean I choose to flat out ignore it. They've struck at us; so we now revisit that transgression with every bit of vengeance I know lies at the heart of every Omegan. It's that desire for retribution that led me to assume control; it's that hunger for power that made me want to lead this crusade."

Zakmar aimed his eyes back to Yul for a moment. "Omegans are destined to rule Ling Galaxy. One day it will be reality, not just words. That said, we will not achieve rule if we cannot hold our own against lesser races. Are you comprehending me, Colonel Yul?"

Yul nodded quickly; his eyes cast downward.

Zakmar stood and walked around the room. Findlay felt beads of sweat itching their way down his scalp and forehead. He thought back to the times of Zakmar's inspections of the Science Wing. The reviews of even the scientific developments by Zakmar were extremely detailed, which always had Findlay worried he'd taken care of everything.

Zakmar kept a very hands-on approach throughout his rule. Findlay figured it was because of the nature of how Zakmar assumed power. A ruler crowned out of deceit lived with the possibility of a coup done in kind back to him.

Findlay felt his heart seize when Zakmar passed directly behind him. Like his fellow attendees, Findlay searched the words and even the tone of Zakmar. These meetings were known for being displays of discipline for any who stepped out of line in their emperor's eyes.

"Our efforts will continue. We keep our Horde deployed, groups in close proximity to each other. Our operations to overtake Ling Galaxy continue. Tell your troops to a soldier to do all that is necessary: infiltrate, take, destroy, capture the able bodied for our slave work. The phony benefactors of the UA and the smug Nara will one day kneel before Omegan might, of this I'm sure. The Railen think they deserve some recompense for their slight. While I've no love for the Nara, the Railen will learn the price of crossing the Omegans."

Zakmar stopped his circular procession once he got behind Yul's chair. With one hand on the seatback, Zakmar pawed the handle of his ceremonial Omegan blade. It was the customary adornment for Omegan rulers. As the story went, the weapon's steel had etched markings of early Omegans and tarnishes from bloodstains added by Zakmar when he did in his predecessor at the height of his coup.

Zakmar glanced across the table to Findlay for a moment before he looked to Commander Chun. "Commander Chun, take a company of Omegan ships and ground troops to the Railen settlement. Teach them a lesson. Let them know Omegan blood spilled will be revisited tenfold."

Chun grinned hungrily. "It will be a pleasure, my Lord. We'll eliminate them from existence."

"No," Zakmar corrected his liege. "Kill many, but leave some intact. I want Ander Pimm and his kind to see the result of their foolish move."

As Chun nodded, Zakmar pulled the blade from its sheath, and in one fluid movement, jut the blade through the back of Yul's chair, until the tip of the blade burst through Yul's chest. Yul responded with a loud yell as he slumped forward, his body drenched with a gushing pool of greyish blood on the table. The others seated nearby gasped. Those closest to Yul's fresh corpse recoiled from the spray. Findlay felt a tremor through his core as he attempted to swallow the lump that remained in his throat.

"Let this be an object lesson for any who doubt my orders in the future," Zakmar muttered blankly before he sheathed his blade and exited the room.

THREE

AFTER THE MEETING WITH ZAKMAR and the other Omegan heads, Findlay returned to his private communications chamber where he contacted Joanna. Unlike when he spoke with Ander Pimm, where the feeling was filled with worry and doubt, with Joanna there was an ease, a calmness. Joanna was a kindred spirit, an intellectual type like Findlay, and she was under appreciated in her past position with the Nara. She knew what it meant to be important to someone.

Joanna had also been a bright spot in the mostly worried hours of Findlay's life. She even showed concern for how Findlay was handling Winola's absence. Findlay was still amazed how they initially ran into each other.

Findlay's designation as head of the Omegan Science Wing gave him flexibility similar to the Omegan military. Trips off Omegana were common for Findlay, and his craft was designed to indicate scientific research far more than military aggression. As a result, he was typically ignored by the marauders and other warlike types in the Galaxy.

Findlay made a lot of excursions in his search for the elements of

Brescar. Initially working on a suitable alternative to Essence, he began to look for more exotic matter and found several locations of it in Ling Galaxy. His mining spots were typically on remote moons and far less traveled places, making his work rather isolated and lonely. He comforted himself with his end goal: the substance that all races in Ling Galaxy, even Omegans, would be unable to function without. This alternative to Essence would then establish Omegana as the ultimate power.

Findlay had been off on a scouting mission, mining for precious elements in his work on Brescar, when he happened upon a Railen expedition as well. His Omegan background had him on guard at first, as the Railen were also. It was Joanna, leader of the Railen expedition, who eased his mind. Something about her relaxed him. Findlay thought perhaps it was a look in Joanna's eyes that he'd seen in Winola's that gave him an island of warmth in his sea of cold scientific search.

He had managed secret contacts with Joanna since that day, and it was she who gave Findlay an in to the Railen Network and meeting Ander Pimm.

Findlay felt an odd kinship with Joanna on many levels. Their respective scientific distinctions from their diametrically opposed races gave them more than enough for endless conversation, but they both shared a bond over their placement in the realm of the unappreciated.

Findlay even found a place of bonding with Joanna on the subject of his wife's demise. The more he spoke with Joanna, the more comfortable he felt with her, but it never eased his worries about what the contact with her meant to his own government and the punishment he faced if caught.

"How are you holding up?" Joanna asked.

Findlay chuckled for a moment. "Hardly anyone asks me that. I'm surviving. I keep my eyes on the end goal and tell myself everything I'm doing will get Charista and me there. I just have to believe in the deals I made."

"And how is lovely Charista?" Joanna asked.

"Fine. Fit. About to graduate and take on the Galaxy. She's her mother's daughter, no doubt."

Joanna studied her friend for a while before she continued. "Have you told her?"

"About my deal with the Railen? Of course. She deserves to know."

"No." Joanna's eyes bled compassion for her friend. "You know what I mean."

Findlay froze. Of course, he knew. Joanna's reminder wasn't necessary. She only brought it up out of her growing concern for Findlay, someone whose contact had over time gone the way from amiable colleague to emotional partner.

"I haven't, I can't tell her that, I—"

"It wasn't your fault, Findlay." Joanna clutched the screen. Findlay smiled weakly at the gesture. It had happened naturally between them. Their initial professional demeanor gave way to a tension-filled relationship of subterfuge, where she offered something Findlay rarely had except with Charista: a confidant unjudging and concerned for his welfare.

Joanna's eyes pleaded with him. "Zakmar made you inject Winola with a Veculus culture under threat of killing Charista if you didn't."

Findlay winced from Joanna's words; he sank back into his chair as a wave of grief cascaded over him. "Every day since I've had to live with that. Every moment I wake up and know she's not with us and I'm the reason why. Each time I see her eyes in my daughter's—how can I tell her I'm the one who did that to Winola?"

Joanna's mouth formed a line. "Listen to me, dear. You're a scientific genius. Your life's desire is for discovery and for making the world around you better. Is there glory in that? Sure, sometimes. Regardless, you want to rest your head knowing you made a difference. Winola wanted the same thing, to make a difference for her people, the nation she loved. But she saw her leader going out of control, and she did what anyone who loved their nation would've... she tried to stop him."

Findlay desperately wanted to believe the things Joanna told him, about his place and how his work wasn't to blame, but he wasn't ready to believe it yet.

Joanna continued, "You're given us a chance to expand our reach, and that won't go unrewarded, I can assure you. I've got the ear of Ander Pimm, consider me a direct line to him."

Findlay nodded.

Joanna continued, "With our improved ability, our presence in Ling Galaxy is continuing. All we need from you is more information on the movements of Omegans, like the Bertold System maneuver. We will work out of their sight as much as possible, confronting them with force only when necessary. We've already located a place for you and Charista. It's secure and, with the Replication technology we plan to acquire on the Zormad system, we will soon be in a very desirable position."

"Sounds good to me. And our arrangement stays in effect?" Findlay swallowed hard. While his plans of being a major energy supplier were largely driven by his scientific urges, he knew in the end, a solid funding source and the ability to hire enough of a garrison for his safety was the key ingredient he needed. The financial aspect of his agreement with the Railen was the last bit of his insurance policy over his goals.

Joanna paused for a moment then replied, "Our deal is intact, as much as I can say."

Findlay tensed. Any uncertainty tested him. "Joanna, I have to know we're solid. I've given you fuel in good faith; don't forget I can make that unavailable very quickly."

Joanna's brow arched. "You have to understand, Ander gets more driven daily. He gives me new directives all the time. The best I can tell you for now is all is as it was. Please believe me."

Findlay sighed. "I guess that'll do for now. Have you thought about my other offer?"

Joanna demurred slightly. "Joining you?"

Findlay nodded.

Joanna glanced downward, then back. "I do think about it. A lot has to happen first before I can do more than think about it. Please keep the faith, dear. We'll be in touch."

Findlay rubbed the sides of his head in thought. "We're in a place, aren't we?"

"Absolutely. Remember when it was just about the science?"

Findlay ran a finger down Joanna's jawline on-screen. Her smile deepened. Findlay then recited the mantra they'd made together, as a way of focusing their anxieties about the dangers ahead. Joanna joined in as he spoke, "Our futures aren't set, but with faith will become reality."

Findlay kissed his palm and touched the screen. "Until later, my love."

"Bye for now." Joanna nodded.

Regardless of what became of Findlay's plans with Joanna, the Railen, and his Omegan subterfuge, he knew Charista deserved the truth. He hated how he'd kept it in for so long, but the practice became just another one of his many running deceptions.

FOUR

F INDLAY PLAYED BACK THE MEMORY in his mind often. While the pains he felt over how he lost Winola were strong, he resigned himself to the pangs being something he deserved. In Findlay's mind, no one who did what he'd done deserved any measure of peace.

Since Zakmar had assumed rule of Omegana after he dispatched Anton, the former Emperor, he'd devoted his energies and those of Omegana to canvasing Ling Galaxy and establishing Omegana as a proper ruling entity. This brought them in contact with the Universal Alliance on more than one occasion, with the associated skirmishes and, sometimes, full out battles as a result.

Among the ranks, leading troops as a proper Omegana general, was Winola Mantisword. She carried out her duties according to her oath. But even the most devoted soldier suffered the occasional bouts of second guessing, in particular when the homeland population of Omegana began suffering with more cases of Veculus.

After many discussions with Findlay and seeing firsthand Zakmar's devotion only to conquering worlds without caring for his own, Winola made her attempt at assassinating Zakmar. Unfortunately, the support Winola drummed up among fellow military wasn't nearly enough, and she was caught before her plans were ever carried out.

Zakmar insisted on addressing her personally, and after an in-depth session with Winola and Findlay to determine exactly the depth of the insurrection, Zakmar knew he needed a public display and a statement. The Emperor needed his people to know that even a high ranking General of Omegana wasn't immune from the most severe punishment for treason.

Zakmar had Findlay escorted to his private chambers, where Findlay stood, his innards knotted up with fear he'd never felt before.

"I can't have officers doing things behind my back like Winola was," Zakmar began. He paced about the room, his eyes narrowed in deep thought, while Findlay was frozen in place.

"I've seen the reports that you weren't involved in this coup. However, being the spouse of the offender doesn't exactly get you off without a mark."

Findlay swallowed hard. "I understand."

"I give you a choice, one you can discuss with Winola. We need an example of how this betrayal won't be tolerated at all. The choice you have is Winola's life... or yours."

Findlay's legs buckled. A million regrets shot through him... *why did Winola even try what she did? If she'd gotten more support, could it have worked? I can't lose her! No, take me, please!*

Zakmar, smiled slightly at the sight of Findlay in a horrible game of bargaining with himself. He decided to sweeten the pot even more.

"Director Mantisword, I'd accept the life of your daughter instead."

FINDLAY TOOK a break from his memories, worries, and plans. He walked into the storehouse area of his facility, where lay his prized creation, Brescar. Other than his dear departed wife and devoted daughter, nothing roused more pride in him.

The greenish liquid swirled around in the large containers that held it. Findlay stared at his creation through the windows of the holding bins and wondered just where Brescar was going to take him. He'd lost his faith in his government, but in his family and his creation, he placed the fate of himself without question.

While Essence was the ultimate jewel in Findlay's mind, many relied on the standard fuel cells in Ling Galaxy as a dependable source of energy. The challenge with standard fuel cells usually lay with supply, however; while the UA had the majority of fuel cells, they weren't altogether safely hidden. And the enterprising and daring, like the Omegans, found themselves with a regular supply as a reward for a little elbow grease and an occasional theft. Findlay knew that, besides the Omegans, the Railen would be in a race for that as well; and the Railen had a slightly more strategic attitude about their search, which made them much more attractive to Findlay when it came time for making a deal.

Findlay's efforts at creating Brescar weren't successful for very long, and it was only through the grace of Zakmar's allowances that he was allowed to continue. The primary demand of Omegana on Findlay lay in the development of armaments and weaponry, which he complied with the most Machiavellian of attitudes.

Findlay fed Zakmar scraps of his brilliance in Findlay's hope that he would one day be able to satisfy his own appetite for rewards in the future.

For a brief moment, Findlay thought he'd actually done it and found his way into Omegan legend in the process. Time and the stubborn attitude he'd prided himself on since his youth eventually rewarded him. Brescar proved a viable fuel source, letting the Omegan fleet venture even further than the standard fuel elements in Ling Galaxy had allowed. However, Brescar's birth was not without complications, and instabilities in the fuel source showed up before long.

The problems with Brescar began, when several ships and groups of Omegans vanished from Ling Galaxy without a trace. The best calculations run by Findlay's team indicated the volatility of Brescar sent their ships through a hole in spacetime. After that, Zakmar ordered Brescar to be removed from ship fuel sources, returning to the standard fuel cell system used throughout Ling Galaxy. The rationale by Zakmar was that their eventual conquest of Ling Galaxy would bring with it all the fuel they needed, making Brescar, in the eyes of Zakmar and those who valued his word, ancillary at best.

Per Zakmar, Findlay's development was quickly buried in the Omegan arsenal. Outwardly, Findlay knew better than to flash indignation at his leader's contempt of Findlay's prized creation. Charista knew how her father felt about the shunning, even though Findlay never spoke much about it. Findlay had been denied the glory of his single most important contribution to Ling Galaxy at large. It was only then he seriously entertained the notion that his ultimate goals would've only been reached with the help of those from outside his own race. His chance encounter with Joanna further amplified his thoughts on this and it soon determined his chosen path.

It wasn't until Findlay's contact with Joanna Yamak that Findlay saw a possible use for his prized creation after all, and Brescar went from the bottom of the Omegan trash heap, aka research archives, to the forefront of the future for Findlay and his family.

Even though Brescar was abandoned, there remained, on hand, a healthy enough supply, enough for collateral for Findlay's plan. The Railen were an eager bidder, needing a quick source of energy for their own aims, and Findlay realized how much his ultimate creation was worth, once and for all.

Findlay stood on an observation platform and watched his creation. Zakmar decided the remnants of Brescar would be used only as an alternative to the standard fuel cells in Ling Galaxy. The instability was too big a concern, and Zakmar wasn't interested in any more missteps.

Findlay rested his head on his clasped hands on the observation platform railing as he admired his creation. "You're my life's work. You'll make me the greatest inventor in the history of Ling Galaxy. Ander Pimm thinks he can work me and take what he wants, but he'll see. One day, they'll all see. I'll be the one they all come to, once they see the true capabilities of Brescar."

Findlay beamed in the knowledge as his plans synthesized like the most complex of scientific theories. However, the certainty of things coming together as much as they appeared to worried him that much more.

Zakmar has the Galaxy in his grasp, but he's short sighted. He's worried about conquest and power and not as much about what comes afterward. People vanquished but still hungry are dangerous. Want leads to discord and, if unchecked, grows into rebellion. He won't keep every discontented race in Ling Galaxy under his boot. Before long, he'll have other upstarts trying to topple what he's built for himself.

Findlay noticed a nearby stack of loading crates and felt his pulse quicken. These were another in the line of his bargain with the Railen. These shipments were his ticket, for him and Charista, the paper on which he was signing the deal for their future. He'd worried about the Railen, but all things considered, he felt not much better about what he had with the Omegans. At least the Railen had shown interest in his plans and what their end result could be.

FIVE

TO FINDLAY, COMMANDER PATRACH was a distant second behind Emperor Zakmar in getting Findlay in his most tense and defensive state. When Findlay was summoned to Omegan Military Command by Patrach himself, his mind became a muddle of thoughts. He reviewed his mantra in his mind, repeated it as much as he could when the fears over what lay ahead for him weren't too great for him to focus.

While Findlay had known Patrach from their youth, the two were never close. Omegans were divided from early cycles once their best abilities were determined, and their socialization and training were held in a social quarantine apart from those with different designations. The soldiers only grew and were nurtured in an environment that fostered the best in warrior skills and training. The scientifically minded were fostered in a realm where their intellectual grasp knew no boundaries, nor were they forced to wait for the lesser minded to grasp their complex diet of information.

Findlay was greeted by two sentries at the entrance of Omegan Military Command. The large imposing figures stood a width apart. Each were covered with Omegan battle armor and shouldered a heavy pulse rifle. The Omegan military industrial complex was, no doubt, the dominant force in Omegan culture; and the fact their own command center had this level of security was a statement, for sure.

Once Findlay awkwardly explained his summons, the two soldiers wordlessly escorted him through the complex. One guard walked before Findlay, the other behind. After several minutes of this, Findlay found himself in the communications center, where he faced Commander Patrach.

"It's been a while, hasn't it?" Patrach's face showed the slightest hint of warmth.

"A while, general?"

"Since our cycles of training." Patrach's eyes narrowed.

Findlay felt a knot in his throat as he nodded. "Of course, yes. I didn't know if you'd remember me."

"How could I not? You were top of your class in the sciences. I think most Omegans in our class remember that. It's not as exciting as the military track, granted, but you have to admire anyone who achieves the best in their chosen field."

Findlay had almost felt like he could relax when Patrach's gaze got cold. "Director Mantisword, I'm troubled."

Commander Patrach's statement was enough to get Findlay's pulse running again. He lived on a jagged edge, in the knowledge that at any moment, any misstep he may have made could've led the Omegans back to him, including the discovery that the slipup at the encampment on Bertold was his fault, not Yul's. Now another death was added to the fallout of Findlay's gambit.

"I see. What's the matter?" Findlay asked.

Patrach motioned Findlay to a bank of screens, operated by an Omegan soldier. Patrach motioned to a screen to the top. "As you know, we regularly monitor activity in Ling Galaxy, broadcasts on Network and such. But we also keep an eye on our own transmissions, and I've been seeing some activity from your scientific wing that is a little out of the ordinary."

Out of the ordinary? Findlay thought. His agitated mind tried working out all possibilities for what Patrach had seen, but before too long, Joanna came up foremost in his mind.

That was my secure channel. I thought they'd stopped monitoring me like they did around Winola's sentencing.

The glum realization settled in: If Findlay had done anything at all, even something totally different, to raise suspicion, the door would've been opened to all of his activities. He feared that his privacy was already a casualty in his cause before he even realized it.

Findlay's body stiffened. He quickly reminded himself that his ruse, his performance, wasn't one that involved an intermission. "I see. I know we've been running some research on weapon development; maybe some of those projects reached outward into Network and beyond?"

Patrach eyed Findlay for several moments, waiting for Findlay's resolve, studying for any cracks that could be exploited to see the inner truth behind the fractures. Findlay did his best at steeling himself, but inwardly he shrank like a witness under brutal cross examination. Outwardly, Findlay kept his moderate cool, enough that Patrach wondered if his tension was the average reaction of the non-military warrior facing a direct examination from one of Omegana's most notorious fighters.

Findlay shifted on his feet. He'd watched Winola over their time together; she was a practiced warrior and had kept her cool in situations way worse than Findlay faced. Findlay was thankful Charista took after her mother in that respect. For Findlay, the endless pursuit of development and discovery left little time for things like strategic maneuvering, and he only got somewhere strategic with his special development of Brescar.

Patrach studied the bank of communications in silence for a few moments. "Director Mantisword, have you made any more developments on Brescar?" His eyes quickly returned to Findlay's.

"Of course not."

"I'm very glad to hear that, and I do hope it's the truth. I will remind you, Emperor Zakmar is grateful for your contributions, but he insists all your efforts are directed to our military enterprises for the foreseeable future. I trust your current station and the welfare of your daughter is enough for your compliance?"

"Of course, it is." Findlay had almost gotten used to saying the lies. Thinking about protecting Charista in the process helped him.

"Director Mantisword, we'll be monitoring your transmissions closely as a precaution. You say you're involved in research, and I will hold you to that, but know that we are watching you. Anything further that raises suspicion will be brought to the attention of Emperor Zakmar and will be treated with the utmost concern. I advise you to remember Colonel Yul and his current state."

Findlay's lips drew in tight, and he managed a quick sigh as he steadied himself as best as possible. "Message received. Hail Omegana."

Once he was returned to the entrance, Findlay hurried back to his dwelling. The net had been cast, and time for him was running short. He hoped the plans he'd set in mind were more than just hopes. A very uneasy tightness swept over him at the realization the time for giving his beloved daughter the truth about his role in her mother's death was upon him. Since his move could've meant the end of him, he knew that more than anything he owed Charista the truth.

SIX

"WE'RE RUNNING OUT OF TIME."

Findlay writhed his hands together as his train of thought once again went on a wild ride. All his plans, his hopes, the future he had in mind for him and Charista hung in the balance as Commander Patrach closed in on him quickly.

When he looked back at Charista, his body shook. "They've stepped up their monitoring on me, Charista, and now with the attack on Zakmar's fleet, it's getting harder to keep my cover. It's possible I've already been made, in fact."

Findlay clasped his arms and sat down, rocking back and forth in tension. Charista sat next to her father. "What do you think they know?"

"Patrach has monitored me; I don't think they know anything, but then again, they'd want me to think they don't know so they can find out as much as they can find out about me."

"There has to be something we can do."

"I've considered everything. The Railen are so far holding true on their agreement, but the moment it comes out about my betrayal, I'll be executed rather brutally, most likely on a feed to all Omegan citizens as an example. There's no tolerance for this kind of slight." Findlay buried his face in his hands as he sunk in to the chair.

Charista, moved at the sight of her father's anguish, snaked her arm around him. She felt as helpless as she'd ever been and rested her face against his trembling frame. "I hate them. Their promises are all empty. They want conquest, but they don't care about their own who suffer. Zakmar is so blinded by his quest for power that he neglects his best and brightest no matter what they do for him."

Findlay felt safe in the embrace of his daughter, enough that his worries flooded out of him. His voice trembled when he spoke again. "I refuse to let something happen to you. If they find out about me, they'll instantly assume you were involved, and you'll be likely imprisoned at the very best or killed along with me as a further example. Zakmar has no issue with enforcing the maximum penalty so everyone knows exactly what it means to cross him."

Findlay knew the moment was upon him. He ran from much, but the truth had gained too much ground on him. He realized if his end was near, he owed it to Charista to set the record straight about her mother. Charista eyed him with concern that mirrored Findlay's feverish expression.

"What?" Charista asked.

"I have to tell you something about your mother."

Charista blinked. "Uh huh?"

"I've told you about her, all these stories about how wonderful she was, because I wanted you to know them, to know her, the kind of Omegan she was. And that is all true, but I wasn't truthful about how she died."

Charista's mouth hung agape. She leaned backward in her seat. "What are you talking about?"

"We saw where Zakmar was going. His violent coup, the people he slaughtered, and we felt that he'd led us closer to destruction than conquering. Your mother and I agreed that Zakmar was stretching Omegan numbers too thin while our people at home were neglected. Still, Zakmar attacked UA installations while Omegana floundered. So, your mother struck back. She was out to kill Zakmar himself at the time when she was double crossed."

Charista asked, "Did Zakmar kill her?"

"Not exactly." Findlay took a shaky breath. "She was returned and questioned. It wasn't much of a fair hearing; they had enough evidence stacked up against her. She was branded a traitor, and Zakmar demanded a severe punishment for her so everyone knew what happened to those who challenged him."

"I studied torture in the Omegan Academy, the methods used to extract information or just to cause pain when that's the goal," Charista said. "What did they do, injections?"

The word shot through Findlay like a knife. Charista felt her insides go cold as she searched the eyes of her father. Findlay's answer to Charista wasn't spoken, but she'd already heard it loud and clear through Findlay's agonized gaze.

"Y-you? You killed her?"

"They forced me to. If I didn't do it, it would've been someone else. Dear, you must understand how much it has ripped me apart ever since."

Charista looked away. She felt her pulse as it throbbed in her throat. "What did you give her?"

"Charista, it doesn't—"

"What did you give her?" Charista's eyes bored into Findlay's.

"Veculus."

Charista narrowed her eyes at Findlay.

Findlay shrugged. "We had a culture of it, since we'd been working on vaccines. Zakmar wanted an example to show that not even his greatest general was immune from punishment for crossing him."

Findlay looked off, terrified at seeing his daughter's face again. He felt her hand slowly slip from his and saw Charista stand over him.

Her voice shuddered when she spoke again. "You killed my mother? How could you have let that happen? What were you thinking? Aren't you supposed to be the greatest scientific mind in Omegana?"

Charista headed for the door.

"Charista, there's more; you have to listen!"

But Charista had heard enough. She left the room and their dwelling, and sank into a sea of despair.

SEVEN

CHARISTA RAN OUTSIDE, CRYING bitterly. The cool evening air would've been pleasant, if it wasn't for the dreadful truth she was given. A thousand emotions battled for control over Charista. The torment soon gave way to a burst of energy, and Charista Mantisword took off in a full running sprint to nowhere in particular.

After a while, she felt burning in her limbs, strengthened through military training, but pushed to their limits through her sadness and rage over her father's confession. Still, she edged herself further.

She ran past Omegan buildings and the government complex in the city of Gajanan. She held in her mind her mother's face, and wondered: *How could Dad do that to me?* She was lost in a sea of emotions and questions with no hope for flotation.

Finally, her lungs had enough and she fell to the ground. Between her sobs, she punched the ground repeatedly. "Why? Why did you do this?" she cried out to no one. A question she knew in her every fiber was unanswerable for the rest of her days.

Findlay saw and heard nothing of his daughter for a week. Not even a glimpse of her around their home the day of graduation; she remained invisible, throwing herself into physical training at the Omegan Military facility. For Charista, it was the best possible solution until she figured out what her next move was.

The Omegan Military facility included housing for troops and trainees, and Charista was allowed access as a recent graduate. It was the only place she felt close to her mother or what her mother had been. She gladly took one of the bunks reserved for the training classes as the next round weren't set to start for another month.

She strained her mind for memories of her mother and knew there was nothing she could've come up with. But while her mother wasn't a memory she could dredge, Charista realized she had access to someone besides Findlay who may have known more about what happened.

Charista activated the comm. She'd seen Findlay's settings when he reached out to Joanna. As much as it drew unwanted attention on her, she needed to know all she could about what happened and just what had possessed Findlay.

Charista's transmission wasn't answered on the first several tries. She soon realized Joanna was probably careful and not accepted any contact from a pure Omegan signal.

Time to improvise, she thought. She didn't have access to Findlay's private signal, but she had something that was worth a chance.

Charista scrawled the message that she'd heard Findlay say to Joanna on their conversations when Charista was conveniently eavesdropping while denying she'd heard anything from her father.

"Our futures aren't set, but with faith will become reality."

She held the scrap up to the screen and tried the call again. The signal wasn't terminated, but the video on the receiving end remained blank. After a few moments, a nervous whisper broke the silence.

"What're you doing? This isn't a secure channel!"

"It's Charista, Joanna."

Joanna's worried face appeared on-screen. "What's going on? Has something happened to Findlay?"

"Something's happened alright."

Joanna's brow creased. "I don't understand. Charista, where is your father?"

"I need to know," Charista began, her voice with a deep tremble, "what made him kill my mother."

Joanna's face twisted in sorrow. Tears streamed down as she lowered her head. "He finally told you."

Charista's own tears blurred her vision. She blinked them away as the tightness in her stomach locked her in position. "I don't understand how he could've done such a thing."

Joanna sighed. "Sweetheart—"

"Don't call me that. You're not my mother." Charista flexed her gut, but she knew the quaver in her voice still showed through. Charista took several hurried breaths as she watched Joanna's pained expression.

Joanna nodded slowly and said, "I never intended to be. Findlay, your father loved your mother. You must realize he wasn't given a choice in what happened to her. Your mother tried to stop Zakmar, to keep him from risking more Omegan lives, but he was too powerful."

Charista swiped her eyes. "But why would Findlay agree to do that?"

"Because Emperor Zakmar threatened to kill you if he didn't."

Charista froze.

"Your parents always wanted the best for you, and when it came down to Winola's life or yours, it wasn't even a choice for either of them." Joanna winced, a compassionate smile on her lips. "Your father has been tormented by this every day since it happened. I know you're hurt and don't want to believe this could've happened. But it has. You must know how broken up he's been. Where are you now?"

"The Omegan Military facility."

Joanna's eyes widened. "You've got to be more careful! This call is probably monitored. We should disconnect. Please don't hold this over your father; he's more broken up about this than you can possibly imagine. Take care of yourself. I'll contact you in time, when I feel it's safe."

Charista nodded and terminated the call. She bowed her head and cried once again. Even though she knew more about the situation, it hadn't healed the pain of her mother's death or what her father did. At least she had more perspective on the situation: that both her parents had acted with her safety and future in mind. She made a silent promise to herself, on the realm of a military oath of service, that Zakmar one day knew her retribution in full.

EIGHT

AFTER HER CONVERSATION WITH JOANNA, Charista returned the following day to her family dwelling. It was soon to be her former home, but it already felt alien to her. Findlay was at the table where she had left him, hunched over and asleep. She took a seat across from him. As she sat, he awoke and, after a few moments of bewildered glancing, he focused on her.

"I ran as hard as I've ever run. I cried as hard as I've ever cried. I tried to figure out why this happened, but I know there's no answer and never will be. But I know also, that Mom wanted the best for me."

Findlay watched his daughter with sad eyes, reddened with emotion. He still searched for words.

Charista continued, "I can't understand what possessed you. But you were protecting me. You and mom were protecting me. I don't know if I can forgive you for this. But I also know even more what is driving all this. And I can make you pay, but if I get Zakmar, that brings all this to a resolution. A balance of retribution, anyway."

Findlay nodded as the tears cascaded from his face.

Charista went on. "Our place here was the doing of Zakmar. He put us in this position. I'm going to get myself in power one day, and the Omegans will know us; they'll know what it means to cast aside the Mantiswords. I'll do whatever I need to avenge my mother and you."

Findlay sighed. "I've tried to think of anything to help our situation, but I don't see any way out of this. Zakmar is ruthless. I saw him slaughter a decorated Omegan officer just for what happened at the Omegan outpost on Bertold system. If he learns what I've been doing with Joanna, he'll likely kill you and me. Everything we've built toward would be lost."

In Charista's abundance of fear and emotions, an idea presented itself to her. "What if I turned you in, Dad?"

Findlay blinked for a few moments.

Charista, the idea taking more root in her mind, straightened herself up. "You said it yourself, we're likely both dead. But you've planted seeds with Joanna, and if she carries on what you've started away from watchful eyes, we still have a chance."

Charista noted the wistful, pained look on Findlay's face. While all his cycles of thorough planning and calculations hadn't prepared himself for this moment, the love for his daughter and the chance for her survival made her plan seem not only plausible, but even necessary.

"If that's what it will take for you to survive, then let's do it." Findlay's body sank lower into his seat once he'd said the words.

Findlay reached for Charista, but she felt an odd distance at that point. She smiled but felt herself reserved from her usual return of affection. "There will be a time when we'll be avenged."

NINE

FINDLAY AND CHARISTA'S PLAN agreed upon, the next several days passed in quick fashion. Findlay reached out to the Railen, and after a lengthy conversation with Ander Pimm and the continued threat of disruption in supply, Ander agreed to let Charista be the broker of their arrangement. The supplies of Brescar to the Railen would continue under the guise of disposal of Omegana refuse in Ling Galaxy, a regular process.

Findlay and Charista knew, while their next move was painful, was a necessary step in their ultimate plan. Charista contacted Omegana security and Commander Patrach, and announced the defection of her father. The news was taken with outward shock. Patrach's anger at the infraction was so serious that he initially incarcerated both Charista and Findlay, holding them separately to determine the depth of the transgressions.

They endured a series of tortures, the deepest and most severe that Omegana had developed. The scientific minds offered something in the way of these devices, but the military honed and brought these horrible treatments to a very brutal application.

After nearly a month of isolation and treatments, the Omegans were satisfied that Charista hadn't the ability to have partaken in the transgressions. Charista credited her surviving the torture to her extensive training and Winola's strength in her genes.

Charista knew, as much as she'd physically survived, her mental losses were unrecoverable. The betrayal of her father was a scar on her being, never to be healed, or even covered over by how many cycles passed. She knew her only path was forward, working herself as much as she could into the Omegan military machine until, one day, she was able to exact the revenge she fully knew Omegana deserved.

Commander Patrach visited Charista as she was in a medical facility, recovering from the last rounds of her interrogation, aka torture. She lay in a bed, connected to several tubes that supplied her body with fluids. Once she caught sight of Patrach, her mouth formed a line. She attempted a salute until the soreness in her body made her stop.

"Rest easy," Patrach said. "You're acquitted of the charges. Your father will be sent for execution in short time. The fact you turned him in is your saving grace in this matter."

Charista managed a nod in reply.

"I know the treatment makes talking difficult, so I'll forget the customary respect given to Omegan military leaders. You have a hard road ahead, Charista Mantisword. You must earn my trust. After all, your parents did to ruin my good thoughts of the Mantisword name. Rest assured, I'll be watching you closer than any other graduate."

Charista tensed. She nodded again while her insides screamed for her to lunge for Patrach's throat.

Patrach continued. "Now then, you'll be assigned to a menial detail at first; pardon me if my trust is a little harder to earn. I pride myself on military loyalty. Don't worry. Do your time in your first assignment, keep your mouth shut and follow orders, and you'll find your way moving to more challenging posts when you've proven yourself in my eyes."

Charista nodded. She knew the game was Patrach's and Zakmar's for the time being, but with her getting on board, the situation would one day be hers to control.

Findlay's execution was broadcast as he'd predicted. Seated facing the screen, he wasn't given any chance at speaking a final penance. Zakmar had already ordered a close watch on Charista while her initial assignment would be ensconced heavily around a group of avowed Omegan loyalists. Zakmar demanded regular reports on Charista's activities from Patrach. Her treatment wasn't an official probation, but it may as well have been.

Charista stood in a room with fellow Omegan military as they watched Findlay receive the toxic inoculations that would swiftly take his life. There would come a time for Patrach and Zakmar; they'd all suffer dearly.

The injections took a few minutes to take hold. Charista glanced away from her spot at the far end of the room. She dabbed the moisture from her eyes as she watched the life of this Omegan who loved her more than anything slip from her. She felt the death she watched on-screen filter to her, as part of her very essence atrophied and died. Charista mourned for three people in that moment: her mother, who'd she'd just slightly known, and her father, who'd raised her from a scared youth without a mother. Finally, Charista mourned who she once was and would never be again: a bright and youthful Omegan female, full of hope with a promising future.

But as a scar formed over all wounds, Charista's hatred and promise of payback grew in place of the final departure of her father.

TEN

THE OMEGAN CAMPAIGN CONTINUED on, and their reach began to bleed into other quadrants of the Galaxy. The UA policy of sanctions hadn't slowed Zakmar down, and as a response, the UA decided to ramp their restrictions up to a new level.

Once the Omegan reach extended past their quadrant into the more central and higher populated portions of Ling Galaxy, the UA realized their diplomatic measures were pointless and the Omegans were only going to respond to stiff penalties, if anything at all.

The UA made their last attempt at negotiations as Zakmar gathered his leaders for another meeting. Zakmar was reviewing the effectiveness of new weaponry when the comm channel hailed with a message from the UA. Zakmar frowned a bit at the interruption, but decided to entertain the UA. He figured having roused their attention enough for a call was itself a victory for him.

Zakmar sneered at the image of Nic Sava on his screen.

"Yes, Mr. President?"

"Emperor Zakmar, the moves of Omegana are in violation of your treaty with the Universal Alliance. You never had authorization for your activities on the world of Kantit. The mining you've begun there is illegal, and this is your first and only warning to desist these activities immediately."

Zakmar glanced at his group about him. Silencing the audio on the channel back to Nic Sava, he muttered, "Note the phony bureaucrats, how they tremble when they see their feeble hold on order slip away. I think it's time we show these wretched the true power of our race and just what we're willing to do to make our rule over Ling Galaxy a reality."

Zakmar turned back to the screen smugly. "My dear President Sava, I'm sure I don't share your concern over the issues you speak of on the Kantit system. My people are proceeding on their course with no other concern. I advise you to not disrupt them or you'll be answering to my military posthaste."

"This is not a discussion and definitely not a trial, Zakmar. Ellene Ballo and the Nara are in full agreement with the UA on this. Your aggression threatens the very existence of peaceful life in Ling Galaxy; and as such, we are enforcing the most stringent sanctions in UA History on Omegana. Trade to and from your world is suspended. And travel will be most carefully monitored and recorded. Any suspicious activity taking place off world by the hands of Omegans will be treated as an act of war."

"President Sava, you can bottle us up, but what are you thinking about our exploits on the Tausian system?" With that, Zakmar activated a display visible to those in the room with Zakmar and to Sava himself. Tausian, a metropolitan city, was displayed. Shimmering tall buildings hosted an array of beings working while a slew of small craft wound around the buildings in a continual stream of commerce on the system. Suddenly, a group of Omegan craft burst onto the scene, firing on various targets, causing chaos and destruction as billows of smoke burst forth from several locations.

Sava froze, his scowl deepening. "You'll pay for this, Zakmar! As sure as I breathe, you'll regret this."

"I'm sure I will." Zakmar deactivated the screen and turned back to his group. Their tense faces weren't as affirmative as he'd liked, so he added, "We're Omegans; never forget. We've survived centuries of servitude, of being ordered, of worker status, but now we are ready for our rise.

"We are not a treaty!" Zakmar slammed his fist on the table, which made others in the room, especially the Science team members, flinch. Even Commander Chun jerked back slightly in surprise. "We'll never succumb to the law of the Universal Alliance. We are meant for more, deserve more, and one day we will have more. No one, not the Railen, not the Xeno, or any living beings in Ling Galaxy, not even the Nara, will have their say over what we do or who we are!"

The discussion was stopped immediately when a super-brilliant burst of light flashed in the center of the room along with a tremendously loud popping noise. Once their eyes adjusted, they noticed on the table stood a female. She was dressed in ceremonial robes including a hood that covered her face. But her scaly black skin and glowing yellow eyes weren't hidden, and she uttered a series of hisses.

In reflex, Patrach and Chun drew their weapons while members of the Omegana Science Wing edged themselves further under the table.

Zakmar was more curious than concerned and stood. "How the hell did you get in here? This is a private council. State your business before we terminate you."

The hooded figure said nothing, but strode about the narrow platform for a few moments. They then uttered more guttural noises—part gurgles, part hisses. Zakmar eyed Patrach and Chun, their weapons trained on their mysterious guest, waiting for the nod from their emperor to shower the stranger with a lethal barrage.

Zakmar was just about to order their fire when their guest spoke. "I bring a message from Malone Stanton, heir apparent to the throne of Ling Galaxy."

"Ling isn't a kingdom, but since you bring it up, the only ones who'll get that seat are Omegan blood. Consider that my message to Malone."

The hooded figure snapped to, her eyes in line with Zakmar. "Tyrants will tremble, rulers will relent, the strong will suffer. Service to Malone is your alternative to death."

Zakmar's next glance to Patrach and Chun was enough of a word. The air was sliced with the sound of weapon fire, but as Zakmar focused on their target, he felt a sharp pain in his chest. He grabbed for the area and pulled his hand back to see it covered with greyish Omegan blood.

The figure vanished from the room as quickly as it had entered. Seconds later, the sounds of groaning from the rest in the room filled the silence.

"Multiple wounded!" Patrach called into the comm from the room. "Send medical. Emperor Zakmar among the victims."

ELEVEN

THE STRANGE VISITOR WAS MORE interested with shock and awe, and a few minor injuries, including some lacerations to Zakmar himself. Once the confusion was resolved and the wounded including Zakmar were treated, Zakmar ordered a meeting with the Omegan Science team, as well as leaders from his Military Wing. He wanted a reasoned approach before more brute force. There was certainly time for bludgeoning, but Zakmar decided for the moment on a more practiced approach.

Chun spoke first. "The Looker transported to our place. We've been aware of their capabilities for some time now. The Nara had issued warnings on them and, in particular, Malone Stanton. He's ruthless and out for control of Ling. Some way or another, our path will bring us up against him, and it appears to have just happened."

Zakmar scoffed at Chun's take. "Of course, I know this. Tell me what can we do to protect ourselves from this kind of attack again."

"Not much, I'm afraid," Patrach replied. "His Lookers make runs as they want. They travel dimensionally; we don't yet have a way of stopping them. As an alternative, I advise we look a different way, in incorporating that design."

Zakmar froze. "Are you suggesting we join with them?"

"Only if it serves our interests." Patrach cautioned.

Chun grunted his agreement, adding, "Malone has apparently figured out a way to harness Essence. I don't think he's merged with it yet; we would've heard about that. Still and all, the dimension shifting abilities and threat that poses worries me. We don't want to face Malone if he does successfully merge with Essence. Let's divert some strength to that issue. We need to get on top of this problem before something like this last attack happens again. We can't have anyone standing in our way."

Patrach and others in the Omegan military offered support for Chun's suggestion, but Zakmar paused with the practiced air of someone who'd made his way to power as he had done.

Zakmar said, "Malone is a bastard, plain and simple. However, we must remember to be resourceful. I have no doubt of our strength, and when the time comes in a straight-out fight, there's none in Ling Galaxy who can match us. But we sometimes must work smarter too. Malone has a decided advantage with Essence and, for now, I'd rather work with him and help our position in Ling Galaxy get stronger."

"But why would Malone even consider working with us?" asked Patrach. "He doesn't seem to think he needs help from anyone."

Zakmar said, "We need to reason with Malone, let him see that his goals of domination can be met faster with us."

"But what then? We subject ourselves to another life of slavery, serving another master?" Patrach countered.

Zakmar said, "It will have to appear as such, for a while. Our move will be to strengthen our position and eventually overcome him." He turned to the Omegan Science team members, their group still reorganizing in the wake of Findlay's loss. "I'm counting on you to get in with his people, study their ways, figure out what we need to do to replicate their abilities. When the time comes, we'll dispatch Malone."

Zakmar's assembled group remained silent. They shared concern about his reaches, but they had to admit his ability at getting the attention and agitation of the UA was unlike any leader they had ever had. Their course forward would include more battles, but with their military strength they carried the Omegan attitude that their cause had only two options: victory or death.

TWELVE

THE UA WASN'T AS EASY TO BRUSH aside as Zakmar had assumed. Within a few days, the UA fleet sealed off several transit routes to and from Omegana, choking the resources of the Omegans. Their fuel cell reserves were enough to hold them for a bit, but the upper authorities knew it was just a matter of time before their supply of fuel would be a big concern.

The Omegan move to conquer Ling had temporarily taken a back seat to runs to keep their own people from starving. Food supplies were restricted, and the UA did all they could to squeeze the Omegans into compliance as much as possible.

Zakmar decided Malone was at least a necessity for the time being, until he at least had the upper hand on the UA.

However, contacting the Omegans brought one extra nuance with it. Frey, a former Omegan upstart, had fled Omegan society for reasons unknown. His path had taken him on a collection of illicit jobs around Ling Galaxy before he found himself on the arm of Malone Stanton.

Zakmar had known about Frey's new employment. He wasn't

aware, however, about Frey's liaison designation until the comm between Omegana and Malone's stronghold was established and Zakmar gazed into the smug expression of one of his former officers.

"Frey, what a surprise."

Frey chuckled for a moment. "That's one word for it, Emperor Zakmar."

Zakmar realized the already rough task of appeasing Malone Stanton was going to be even more painful than he'd thought. "I'm not in the mood for games here and I have nothing to say to a deserter. Connect me to Malone Stanton at once."

Frey's brow creased a bit in response and he offered a slight smile to Zakmar's demand. "I'm afraid you're not speaking with Malone until we discuss your intentions first."

Zakmar's annoyance blossomed into anger quickly. Who the hell was Malone to put up some mealy turncoat as a buffer, anyway? "I don't have time to sift through whatever you've done that got you where you are now, Frey. I want to get a message to Malone Stanton about an opportunity he'll be interested in."

Frey had handled contacts from others around Ling Galaxy that mentioned similar arrangements. Malone's swiftly growing reputation made his unaffiliated status in Ling Galaxy almost as attractive as his potential power over Essence. Unfortunately for Zakmar, Frey had developed quite a shrewd approach to bargaining, and had given Malone enough loyalty to make Frey a definite gatekeeper for access to Malone.

"I'm sure you think that, Zakmar," Frey said. "Before we go further, you'll have to give specifics on what Omegana promises for this arrangement."

"Frey, I'm offering you the services of my numbers, my military."

Frey nodded. "And just what are you expecting in return?"

"Why, the opportunity to serve the great Malone Stanton, of course."

Frey shook his head slowly. "Don't insult my intelligence like that. Tell me, what are you looking for?"

"We want access to Essence as well. We want to learn your ways. There's no reason we can't both benefit from Malone's power."

"Knowing the ways of Essence is more than just physical purity. It's a continual search for the truth at the heart of existence."

Zakmar nodded. "We've got the strength, Frey. You know we do."

Zakmar's discussions continued with Frey, part of the necessary dance for entre into partnership with Malone. Zakmar flexed every bit of his diplomatic muscle in the negotiations that followed, while keeping one eye on the coup of Malone he knew would one day come.

THIRTEEN

CHARISTA'S ASSIGNMENT WAS HANDED down very much like a prison sentence, and the nature of the job wasn't too far off from one. Given her father's offense, her assignment was changed accordingly. From her former post with the Omegan infantry in the Horde, she was moved to the most rear of echelons possible. The refabrication service of Omegana hadn't so much as claimed the honor of least glamourous Omegan assignment. Rather, the depot was assigned that title due to lack of any other occupation claiming a worse status among the hierarchy of Omegana.

The outpost wasn't even on Omegana proper. On a distant moon of the Omegana system, the refabrication plant sat in the middle of acres of scrap: crashed starcraft, mangled weaponry, both personal size and extra-large in-ground fixed varieties. All pieces in this chaotic collection shared one common trait—they'd seen their life in service of Omegana or her enemies and had been rendered useless or broken by one way or another.

Charista realized her placement wasn't just because of how remote it was. She too, like her parents before her, was deemed broken, unfit for regular Omegan service. But she knew there wasn't anything further from the truth, and the day would come that she'd prove that assessment wrong and take her place ruling Omegana from Zakmar himself.

Charista eyed the work area before her, covered with damaged pieces of Omegan weaponry and craft. Over the tables hovered a series of tools and equipment for repair. Her initial assignment involved the maintenance of Omegan hardware damaged in battle for its return. It was a far cry from the glorified battlefronts the Omegans fought on, but it was a necessary and minor department of their military complex. Not to mention, it was a suitable punishment for someone who hadn't quite yet earned her way back into the fold of the trustworthy.

Renfrid Speck, Charista's supervisor, wasn't humorous by Omegan standards, which was quite a statement. His burly frame was made all the more menacing by the posture he held—shoulders hunched forward and a slight lean toward the front. He'd stepped back from a long career training Omegan military from their initial phase, where Renfrid had the reputation of being as fierce as Zakmar among his top military and scientific leads.

"I'm well aware of your history, probie. And don't think for one Omegan minute I want you here any more than I want my head cut off. Your no-good piece of trash father is worthless space filth, and I'd just as soon see you offed like they did him."

Charista focused on her breathing until it slowed. She repeated her thought to herself. She started this not long after Findlay was first sentenced.

I am alive. I am OK. I'll make them pay.

Those words were the steps she took. Whenever times were tough, whenever it felt too hopeless for her, whenever the doubt came on and was too big to deny, she repeated those words over and over again.

She knew though that a vow of silence wasn't the way. Her path to revenge was going to take her through the ugliest parts of herself.

"I'm not proud of what happened. I can only pledge my loyalty to Omegana."

Renfrid, sensing Charista's discomfort, grinned in enjoyment. "As long as we're on the same page here. I never wanted you at this post, and for some reason I'm sure I'll never understand, Zakmar didn't want you killed in kind with your low life papa. So, do what I tell you, run these rebuilds like I say, don't give me any lip, don't make any mistakes, and I'll see about getting your sorry face out of my facility as soon as I can."

"Fair enough." Charista tensed again; she knew this path before her was her only one. But she had her mantra; she repeated it to herself so much she heard it repeat in her mind like a continual echo.

In her free time, Charista studied the monitor in the main console area. The large screen was their connection to the rest of Ling Galaxy, to Network and, for Charista, her future. She switched the view on screen to show the off-world perspective, into their immediate quadrant of Ling Galaxy. She watched the collections of stars, systems, and starcraft that passed through the area steadily. *One day*, she thought, *this Galaxy will know me. And I'll be the most powerful one in it. I control my own destiny.*

Charista found her way through the main system and the project files until one caught her attention. An alteration process. The Omegans were interested in assimilating into other cultures, including the ability to alter their physical appearances to match those of another race.

Her thoughts were jarred with a sharp slap on her hand and she glanced up into Renfrid's agitated face. "Ay, what are you doing in there? That's got nothing to do with your job." He angrily closed out the screen, and she faced him.

"I'm sorry, I was curious what was going on."

"You aren't here to be curious; you aren't paid to learn. You're here to do whatever I tell you. Remember, this may as well be a dead end for you, far as I care. Don't give me any reason to worry. That's all you gotta think about, got it?"

Charista offered a quick nod. She wondered what would happen to her if she attacked Renfrid. He was big but slow. She could've at least gotten a few good swings on him, maybe even made a run away from the place. But insubordination was bad enough; striking a superior would've been a quick end to her already troubled career.

How many things had changed for her. She thought back to Findlay's words, about making her way up the ladder of Omegan military to be able to make their big coup one day. So much had gone apart from that dream. She felt herself in a constant scramble, with only the hope of coming back to some semblance of revenge by the time everything was over.

FOURTEEN

ZAKMAR CALLED AN ASSEMBLY TO THE main hall of the Omegans. These announcements were usually reserved for big moments, so the general excitement in the room beforehand was pretty noticeable. Already relegated to a level in Omegan society a shade above discarded trash, Charista was allowed to view the event from a screen in the refabrication plant. Renfrid joined her for the viewing. Charista noticed Renfrid seemed more animated than usual. She figured, even for him, this had to be a nice distraction from their typical work grind.

The crowd hushed and Zakmar began. "My people, we stand on the edge of greatness. Our Horde is feared throughout the Galaxy. There aren't any races who dare to stand up to us. We will conquer and defeat all who stand in our way. And now, we have another tool in our collection. We have a deal in place that will guarantee our future to rule Ling Galaxy. We've reached out to Malone Stanton and will form an alliance with him."

The audience hesitated in silence at first, but then rumbling took place of the quiet, a low roar built steadily into a large sound of jeers.

Zakmar raised his arms in an attempt to steady the crowd, but it was useless at first. Finally, he leaned into the mike and bellowed: "Omegana is supreme. Have I ever given you reason to doubt me? Do I not bleed as you? Think like you, feel for you, and am one of your native blood? We emanate from the same wellspring, of Mother Omegana, and we are not different. I'd not cut my hand off, not sever my leg or my head. Then why would you ever think I'd make some agreement that would visit harm upon my blood brothers and sisters?

"Malone Stanton will lead us to our goal. We will join with him, not because we believe in him, but we believe in what he will bring to us. We fully intend on conquest of Ling, and we will handle Malone in our way and in our time. Trust me, my faithful. We must take this step to get to our ultimate goal. Believe in me, believe in yourselves, and believe in the future of Omegana!"

Charista noticed Renfrid's enthusiastic gaze gave way to one of shock. Shouts came from the crowd assembled before Zakmar. "He's a maniac! He'll betray us!"

Zakmar steadied the crowd. "We hold the upper hand. We've got our legions, our Horde. We have the weapons, the arsenal. All Malone has is a collection of devotees and some dogma. True, he does have the skills of the Lookers, which is why I want to use him. We can go without, but we would have to come up against him; and I'd rather know where my enemies are, instead of being constantly surprised by them."

Charista clenched her fists as a strong desire to kill Zakmar flooded her body. He was so smug and sure of himself and spoke without any care at all, it seemed. His people loved him for it. Omegana always celebrated the bold and the brash, but the thoughtful and resourceful were somehow left behind. Charista knew that's why Findlay never had a chance with them; he even sacrificed Winola in the hopes it would've meant something to his people, but nothing came from it. Other than a break in their family and a loss Charista knew defined every moment of the rest of her life.

She thought about her plan and hadn't any idea of when it would begin, but she knew that it was happening one day or another. She had to wait her time, though. Like her parents before her, she had a part to play, in being a good soldier and daughter of Omegana. She'd show her race proud and, when the time came, she'd make them all pay. Her vengeance would be three-fold: herself, Findlay, and Winola's.

Charista kept silent. She knew she couldn't contradict or shun anything from Zakmar, or Omegana in general, and, even with Renfrid, the rule for her at present was to bide her time. Hers was a dance, a delicate one that looked to be far reaching. Her time was coming, but not for a while. And until then, it was on her to show the most supportive version of herself she knew how.

Malone's booming voice echoed through the hall, silencing the Omegan crowd instantly. His ghastly face appeared, shimmering in holographic bluish brilliance toward the front of the room. Zakmar turned to Malone.

"Thank you, Malone, for standing with us. I think we will show Ling Galaxy just what true order for all will look like."

Malone nodded and added a smirk. "I'm sure we will, Emperor. Omegans, like you, I've been cast away from the Nara, told I was no good. But unlike the Railen, who, like heartbroken children, are scratching back to the door that was closed behind them, I'm looking forward. Ling Galaxy is our home and together we will make it the place it should be. Not with the Nara's help, but through our own efforts. We will make tomorrow the now it should always be."

Zakmar hoped his disgust for Malone wasn't too clear on his face. He had enough to deal with from the hard line Omegans who had plenty of issues with Zakmar's moves in courting Malone. While the Omegans hadn't any avowed policy against Malone, the fact that Malone was largely an unknown, his allegiance being fairly unclear to anyone except himself was part of the problem. Zakmar always looked at problems pragmatically though and, while Malone's brazen threats seemed to work a purpose with his fellow heads of state, Zakmar knew that even the brashest of megalomaniacs needed backing from a nation. The Omegans weren't the only ones with a military who could serve their might on Malone's side. Zakmar knew the sooner they reached out to Malone, the less time another race had to make their own deal with Malone to the Omegans' disadvantage.

Zakmar continued speaking over the crowd that hadn't fully settled back down. "I'm pleased to introduce the part of our arrangement with Malone Stanton. We pledge our military to be at his disposal in his moves to get the Essence he craves. We'll be given our own share of this substance, and as well he'll offer the services of some of his Lookers in the meanwhile.

"Our efforts will be on the offensive. We must keep our pressure up on the Railen. We've hit them hard, and where they live, but don't count them out for one moment. Ander Pimm is a cunning warrior. But we'll use our strengths too: Omegan might, Omegan technology, and the gift of the Lookers."

The air shuddered for a moment, and then a Looker appeared beside Zakmar. The crowd gasped at first, then offered shouts and jeers customary to an Omegan not used to anyone else sharing their spotlight or glory. Zakmar quieted the crowd down and stepped closer to the hooded figure.

"Remember, my Omegans, we are allies with the Lookers; this is our agreement with Malone Stanton. And I'm giving this Looker the explicit mission: bring me the head of Ander Pimm!"

The crowd roared in response. Zakmar bathed in their adulation. He wanted more than anything to see Ander Pimm's head. He knew it would be the start of a great collection, slain heads of his enemies. Before long he planned to add Ellene Ballo and Malone Stanton to that number.

The Looker pulled back their hood, revealing a female face. Pale skin was marked with a series of black lines in different patterns. Many Lookers decided on their own facial appearances, tattoos, in respect to their abilities. Their ability to slip across dimensions made them worshiped and feared by some, even considered demonic by those of certain faiths in Ling Galaxy.

"Marelene Webber is one of Malone Stanton's Lookers. We've

seen what they can do, and now we'll be using their power as we join forces with Malone Stanton. He wants an army; we want conquest. Together, we will succeed!"

Marelene padded about the platform before she stepped into the crowd. The Omegans nearest her formed a narrow wake as she made her way through the crowd. Zakmar watched from the back in mild amusement. It wasn't important to him that the Omegans and the Looker, or even Malone Stanton, were overly friendly as long as the understanding was in place. The end goal was Zakmar's priority.

Marelene found a challenger in the crowd. An Omegan soldier, in part spurred on by his friends, squared his shoulders off and approached Marelene as the crowd opened up a ring around the two in an impromptu contest. Zakmar made his way into the crowd as the two neared each other. They circled each other, Marelene's eyes glowing, her mouth curled in a hungry snarl. Zakmar worried the fragile detente he'd managed with Malone wasn't going to last very long with this situation, and he had to reclaim the order in the room.

Zakmar grabbed his blade and clanged it loudly against his armor. The particular steel of his blade made a very distinctive ring when struck in this way and the resulting vibration stopped everyone in the room, even Marelene. After a few moments, everyone realized the source of the loud ringing and focused on their leader. Marelene stepped towards him.

"We will work together with the Lookers from Malone. I won't tolerate any dissension. Remember, any Omegan who fails to follow suit with my orders here will be subject to the same treatment as an Omegan deserter."

The Omegans quieted down, and Marelene was more relaxed as a result. She faced the audience. "We start with attacking the Railen fleet and their hidden cache of starcraft not destroyed on the Delfina system. The biggest enemy of the Omegans is our biggest enemy. Together we will hit the UA hard and destroy the remnants of their control over Ling Galaxy. They'll learn they cannot be greater than Omegans. The Lookers and Malone Stanton are with you!"

After a few moments, the screen returned to the Omegana crest. As Charista mulled over what she'd seen, Renfrid slapped his thighs. "OK, then. Back to work, for the glory of Omegana."

Charista held a hand over her mouth when she scoffed out of reflex. *Omegana's dreams and visions aren't the same as mine. But they will be, one day,* she thought. *I'll show them who really runs Omegana, and they'll finally all pay for what they did to me and my family.*

REVENGE NEXUS

ONE

ZOE COULDN'T HAVE CARED ANY LESS what time or day it was. There were too many other thoughts in her mind for useless things like getting up, living a life, and being productive. After all, the living already had it one up on the deceased. Wasn't that enough?

The air in her room was warm, with a touch of dampness. Planet Cerulia had one continuous season of varying heat levels, and this day was no exception to that rule. Zoe swiped her brow and gazed about her abode as she roused herself from her night's sleep, such as it had been.

Zoe's flat was as unremarkable as the rest of the Cerulak accommodations. Zoe had shared this place with Zaratha, two sisters who'd grown up too fast after the death of their parents.

The flickering light of Zoe's wrist comm caught her attention. The message indicated an incoming batch of tech. At least she had work. As part of the Retooling industry in Cerulia, Zoe worked on fixing the spent and partially destroyed tech that Cerulak Harvester crews retrieved from around Ling Galaxy. It was steady work for her and, for the Cerulia civilization, a decent shot at long-term survival.

The old building her quarters took up space in had been fixed, repaired, and cinched far beyond its useful life. The Cerulaks owed their survival to the craftiness and stubborn attitude that, whatever was on hand, could be made functional.

Alongside the wall of Zoe's bedroom stood the beds formerly used by Zoe's parents. They stood upright as if they were wall supports. Cerulia sent items for Retooling once they were ready for discarding. The repurposed items were either sent to Cerulak Zamas military or sold off-world to several interested parties. For Zoe, the discarded beds had more worth for the time being, as they were where both of her parents had taken their final breaths. However, as much as Zoe knew she had to remove her parents' old furniture, she hadn't found it in herself to get rid of it just yet.

A ray of sunlight caught the token on a table towards the doorway to her bedroom. Zoe breathed an uneasy sigh. Just as the beds were for her parents, the emblem was the last memento she had of her sister, Zaratha. Zoe had only heard the news of Zaratha's death two weeks earlier, and the chaos that was her waking life was still unfolding.

Finally, Zoe's hunger motivated her to get out of bed. She paused for a brief stretch. Cerulaks all boasted green complexions of varying shades, with thick hair usually kept in tight braids. Zoe's build was a bit muscular from all her time working in Retooling.

After Zoe worked out the kinks in her body, she started towards the dining console. Still, she paused at her favorite relaxing place: the reclining chair. Zoe used the comfortable seat whenever she needed space and time for thoughts about whatever situation she faced. She kneaded the soft fabric with both hands and leaned over the chair, murmuring unintelligible words, much like a medium trying to exorcise demons. But the words were for herself, and the peace she desperately needed but was always out of reach.

Zoe's wrist comm signaled several beeps, indicating an incoming message. *Probably a status about the Retooling,* Zoe thought. Pon never missed the chance to update her people or, more to the point, be seen on video updating her people. The comm device was a common issue for all Cerulaks. It served various purposes, like identification for all Cerulia citizens and alerts about government announcements and general work schedules.

Zoe activated the Network Console near her favorite chair and watched a report of a space battle on her viewscreen. Swarms of Universal Alliance craft showered the display. It wasn't a shock to see the UA out in force. They certainly had their hands full, with word of the Omegans on the war advance and the Railen stirring up enough trouble on their own. Zoe hadn't pieced together the mechanics of the conflict even before Zaratha's death. She watched the careening Omegan starcraft on screen, engaging UA craft in a deft series of maneuvers and attacks. The sequence of explosions was pretty intense. While Zoe's Cerulak mind had begun a silent inventory of the potential haul from the aftermath, she also found herself more than a little curious about the exact cause of the fight. That was something Network broadcasts never addressed in any meaningful way.

Malone Stanton's alliance with the Omegans had them feeling as invincible as they ever had felt.

The UA had barely contained the Omegan surge so far, other than to shore up Yassel, the central planet of Ling and home to the UA headquarters. *Of course, they're taking care of their own,* Zoe scoffed. *Shame they'd never turn that kind and benevolent eye our way.*

The video from Network switched to an oversized starcraft unloading pallets of building fragments and what looked like engine parts. Of course, not all hauls brought into Cerulia were the same, and certainly not all had weaponry. But, the Cerulaks found ways of getting value in even the most diverse scrap pieces.

In the past, the Cerulaks carried more weight with the UA and Ling Galaxy. As a former key replication center, Cerulia and her Cerulak residents were once a bustling center that hosted the production of items from the basest of essentials to the more complex starcraft for intergalactic use. Zoe only knew about this period from stories, though. Cerulia's period of prosperity, like much of Ling Galaxy, came to a halt once disease and famines throughout the galaxy worsened. The increase in want was more than the Universal Alliance could address, and fighting emerged. The Omegans, Railen, and the various Syndicates were to blame for stirring up most of the trouble from there.

Once Ling Galaxy fell under problems such as famines and diseases like Veculus, the thriving Replication markets slowed and eventually shut down. The UA consolidated Replication facilities elsewhere, claiming a cost-saving measure, further lowering Cerulia and her people into what became known as the Dark Times.

Zoe found a place for herself in the Dark Times of Cerulia. Motivated by her parents, she threw herself into the new Retooling trade. She showed enough aptitude to rise through the ranks and eventually managed one of Cerulia's more prominent centers. However, while Zoe and Zaratha's parents were part of the beginning of the Retooling industry in Cerulia, the business of recovering the lost and spent tech of the galaxy brought a very imminent threat of the bacteria and pathogens sometimes linked with the discarded. The Veculus virus found its way to Zoe's parents, infecting them and making the remainder of their lives a series of bedridden days, in and out of coherence, with only their daughters and a grateful nation watching over them. With her sister Zaratha, Zoe comforted her parents in their final days.

Besides her gratitude that her parents had an end more peaceful than starving to death, Zoe was thankful they weren't there for the loss of Zaratha. One of several victims caught by Malone Stanton while he looked for a Railen Tracker, Zaratha was made a public example, with Pon Ebnora as a witness to the travesty committed on Zaratha and all at the advanced encampment for Cerulia.

Zoe eyed the tray of food, neatly packaged and ready for her breakfast in her food store, and decided against it. With her thoughts of her lost sister also came a pretty disagreeable digestive system. So instead, she opted for a walk to the Cerulak Dispensary for some hot rations; maybe her gastric distress would've eased enough by then.

A choked sob rattled its way up Zoe's throat and out her mouth. She walked on, doing her best to wipe the tears from her eyes and moisture from her nose.

Zoe credited her survival to a few things: love for her sister and an overriding belief in Cerulia. As much as things had soured, she clung to the belief that her parents' work wasn't a waste, nor had Zaratha's. To have said otherwise would've cheapened the lives of her loved ones.

Zoe's continued belief in Cerulia came out most in her work for the Retooling Service. Even the most hardened Cerulak Zamas military couldn't have denied the value of Retooling for Cerulia. Many compared Zamas to a heart; the Retooling Service was the blood. For Zoe, retooling work was simple, the results clear, and the benefits obvious. It was enough that it sustained Zoe through her dark days. Zoe figured her success in Retooling earned her some leeway concerning what she was thinking of asking Pon.

Zoe's town on Cerulia, Rufio, was one of many homes to the scores of scrap Cerulaks retrieved on their various runs. Much of the debris wound up in one of several warehouse structures, formerly replication plants that had long been stripped in the so-called good name of the Universal Alliance, as their efforts were considered more important by the acquiescing Cerulak leadership of the time.

The grey and purple of Zoe's uniform starkly contrasted with the dark and smudged piles of discarded tech and even the service vehicles gliding past the street. Zoe was glad her parents had, at least, gotten to see her promotion to supervisor before they died; showing them her uniform had meant a lot to Zoe.

Zoe's breaths quickened, and she felt her pulse pound in her throat. *It's happening again,* she thought. The feelings started coming the moment she heard about Zaratha. It was a mixture of pain at the thought of her beloved sister dying so brutally and the agony of feeling constrained in her place.

-HELP ME!-

The sound of a voice stopped her in her tracks. It was a male's, but one she'd never heard before. She looked around and saw no one nearby. Zoe shook her head, dismissed it as grief mixed with hunger, and walked on. Her thoughts came at her so randomly those days. It could've been anything.

Zoe smiled a little as she caught a glimpse of Warehouse #13. The towering structure loomed large like all Retooling Warehouses. The number 13 was embossed at the top corners of the structure with bright white paint on a dark gray background.

The air on Rufio, like the rest of Cerulia, was filled with a constant haze. Zoe adjusted the air filter on her mask, a requirement for anyone who worked as extensively with Retooling as she did.

She walked toward the street Warehouse #13 was on and quickly skipped over to the side as another transport hover glided past.

Shouts and giggles broke Zoe's train of thought, and she saw a group of five Cerulak youth who played off to the side of the street. They tossed something between themselves. It looked like a balled-up piece of metal. Their toy was probably a piece of outer armoring for starcraft, Zoe presumed. The faces of the youths clouded with worry for a moment - spent tech was reserved for handling by the Retooling group, but there'd been such an influx lately there was more than enough to catch up on. Zoe welcomed the distraction as a chance to discipline some youth who needed a little straightening out.

"Get that into the receptacle." Zoe folded her arms to compliment her glare. The youth froze for a moment before the one with the metallic piece sheepishly headed to the nearby container.

One of the other youths stepped toward Zoe. "We're between sessions in school. We were just looking for some fun."

"Then I suggest you try the Cove. The tides should be coming in this time of year."

After a few frozen moments, the group regrouped into a game of chase. Zoe eyed them for a moment more before she headed off.

Despite the necessary reminder of discipline and rule-following, Zoe found herself smiling warmly at the thought of how, not that long ago, she and Zaratha would've been right there doing the same thing.

Zoe's thoughts had drifted toward the happier times she had had with Zaratha when the pain hit her. It started as a dull headache but quickly became a piercing agony, so strong she dropped to her knees. She still heard the shouts of the youth off to her side, but they must not have noticed or heard her.

She dropped to her haunches and clasped her head as it began to throb. *What was this?* Had the pains she felt about Zaratha manifested themselves physically? Zoe jammed her eyes shut, and then a dull roar built. She briefly opened her eyes, but nothing changed. Then, a voice came through the din. It was the same voice as before, a male's.

-ZOE, I NEED YOU-

Zoe checked her wrist comm, even though she knew the voice hadn't come from there. Her pulse thumped in her throat. She had no family besides her parents and Zaratha. Her service to Cerulia had been her primary devotion, but this voice scared her.

Who's doing this? After a few moments, she picked herself up, and that's when she felt the soreness in her legs. Apparently, she'd fallen harder than she had realized. With a slightly wobbly walk, she continued. Her grief journey had been anything but pleasant, and now it seemed there were hallucinations to go with the sadness. Could that have been it - her pain of loss manifesting as voices, maybe even Zaratha's, from the beyond?

Zoe trudged on, hopeful that the voice wasn't the breakdown she feared was in her future.

TWO

THE DISPENSARY IN RUFIO TOWN offered Cerulaks the basest of nourishment. With no agricultural industry, their cuisine and consumption were made possible through their scrap business and more or less effective trading attempts. A continuing alliance with the Tillian race made more food available to Cerulaks. Beyond that and the token offerings from the UA, good old Cerulak shrewdness filled the remaining gaps that kept Cerulia above the starvation line.

A steady stream of Cerulaks headed into and out of the Dispensary building. Some were Harvesters sent out with orders for new runs in Ling Galaxy. Others were Retooling workers, going to their morning shifts, or coming in for their meal like Zoe.

Hayaat Munillo, a Harvester team lead, met Zoe as she neared the Dispensary entrance. He was tough to miss, wearing the trademark visor scrap harvesters used for the quick field assessment of tech items.

Hayaat beamed when his eyes met Zoe's. "Hey, there she is."

Zoe offered a polite smile in response. It was her best effort when her most common urge those days was to lie down and scream. "Yep, here I am."

"How are you doing?"

Zoe recognized the tone in Hayaat's voice. It was the same others used for that question to her: drenched with a definite amount of pity and hope the answer that came back wasn't too long. She planted her feet firmly and took as steady a breath as she could. She knew there was one response that satisfied the question without further probes into her lonely, sadness-enveloped hours. "Hanging in there. Got a shift. That tech won't reassemble itself."

"It sure won't. Don't worry; we'll keep you in good supply so you'll never be bored." Hayaat said.

Given the move away from revelations of her usual lachrymose moments, Zoe switched gears on the conversation to more mundane distractions. "What's the food offering today?"

"Tausian cutlets and something they're passing off as soup. It reminds me a little of this waste dump I was in not long ago."

They shared a laugh that was more Hayaat's than Zoe's. Through the brief moment of levity, Zoe noticed the concern in Hayaat's eyes. It wasn't a surprise. Hayaat knew Zaratha more than a little from the runs he had made, with people like Zaratha in support.

"You look more like your sister every day."

Zoe's breath hitched, and she quickly glanced downward and cleared her throat, hoping her emotions weren't too noticeable. "Just so happens I'm still related to her and all."

Hayaat's smile faded a bit. "You know, I could've been with her when she... It's a tough life we've got. Each of these losses stings."

Zoe had received lots of condolences, and while she appreciated the kind words, the most stinging ones involved talk of her sister like she was a stat. It reduced Zaratha's and the other deaths to the order of scrap Cerulaks hauled back. How would Hayaat or the others have felt if one of their deceased family was treated with the simplicity of a piece of molded metallic housing?

Zoe nodded. "Yeah, it stings. I just wish it hurt for Pon."

"I'm sure it does. Things have been moving, with Retooling getting Zamas up to full strength. But, despite that and general welfare improvement, Pon has a way of not spending too much time on any one thing. I don't know how she does it. I sure couldn't be a leader like that."

"My sister and the other Cerulak deaths didn't seem to bother her at all. Besides, I think we haven't been told everything about that raid by Malone."

"What do you mean?" Hayaat's friendly gaze gave way to one of disbelief.

Zoe shrugged. "It just seems pretty convenient. There was a small contingent of Zamas, but not enough for a defensive position. That said, why make a risky move like going for a Railen Tracker?"

Among the usual scrap the Cerulaks hunted, Railen Trackers were a desirable but elusive target. While Zoe and the other Cerulaks hadn't figured out the purpose of the trackers, all appreciated their value. To any race that clawed for survival like the Cerulaks, the payday for a Railen Tracker was tremendous. However, the average Cerulak's interest in the trackers stopped short of their street value. Instead, their sights were on restoring the independence of Cerulia, even from the UA, which had mainly functioned as a figurehead of late, offering sporadic military protection from the ever-growing chaos around Ling Galaxy.

Zoe continued, "Could Pon be holding back information? Maybe we've got more military available to us than she's letting on."

"Pon wouldn't have risked a Harvester crew if she didn't feel like there was ample protection."

"But did my sister's Zamas group have enough available support? She was a ground troop. What about starcraft?"

"Zoe, they had starcraft with them. I'm sure the updates Pon gives would've shared information like that. Why would she lie when every bit of positive news only improves the morale of Cerulia on the whole?"

Zoe watched a group of Retooling workers head out of the

Dispensary. They worked at a different warehouse but wore the same grey and purple uniform, only with a 45 stitched on their shoulders, indicating their home facility. She glanced back at Hayaat, his eyes full of concern.

"Zoe, if you want more answers about it, talk with Pon. As for Zaratha and her group, what I heard is they had just sent back details on where to find some Railen Tracker that Malone was after all along. Other harvester crews have picked up the hunt since using coordinates Zaratha herself sent back. This situation evolves quickly - you must remember, we're not the only people in Ling Galaxy out to grab any spent pieces of tech we can find."

"Hayaat, I really should eat before my shift. I'm allowed to meet with Pon anyway. I'm supposed to collect Zaratha's personal effects, and I've been neglecting that."

Hayaat nodded. "Of course. Hang in there, and please let me know if I can ever do anything."

Zoe gave her best smile and said goodbye to Hayaat as she entered the Dispensary.

ZOE MADE her way through the food lines in the Dispensary Complex dining area. The Tausian cutlets Hayaat mentioned looked a little dark for her liking, but her hunger pangs convinced her to try them. She grabbed enough for a meal. She headed towards the common area with a full decanter of Aquand, a common beverage throughout Ling Galaxy that mostly resembled water. The lines of tables in the large hall provided ample seating, and a healthy general roar of the crowd as the assembled ate and made conversation with their table mates.

Zoe found a spot without anyone sitting too close – hopefully enough for her whole time there to be left alone. Instead of making for any chats, Zoe focused on eating. She tried to ignore the image on the video screens along the far wall as best she could. It was Pon

Ebnora with her regular update to Cerulia on the growing conflict around Ling Galaxy and the state of the Cerulak resurgence. Zoe always hated speeches. They didn't happen daily, but they were a part of Cerulak life. Government figures, mostly Pon, talked about plans for the future, and military leaders shared information on threats and how they handled them; these talks came up more often than she liked.

"Got room for another?"

The gruff male voice startled Zoe at first, but she recognized it immediately. As much as she would've liked the solitude, the truth was a few people in Cerulia were always welcome company for her. She smiled for having an even better reason to ignore Pon's video update. "Hi, Quintus."

Genetics gave Quintus Bala a broad and well-developed frame, but his service with the Cerulak military as a heavy weapons specialist hadn't done much harm. He sat the tray next to Zoe's and eased himself onto a spot next to her.

Zoe felt a slight bit of gloom lift around Quintus. He was a regular part of her childhood when she and Zaratha were playmates with Quintus - most likely in the place of those youths Zoe had seen on her way over, playing with pieces of scrap and solving all the problems of Cerulia and Ling Galaxy in the span of a play session.

Zoe took a thoughtful sip of Aquand before she eyed Quintus again. "I don't know what I'd do without you and the Retooling service to keep me focused."

"Always nice to have something to focus on." Quintus' arms flexed almost as if they'd been listening separately from the rest of him.

Zoe arched a brow. "So, got some big maneuvers ahead?"

"Something like that."

Zoe stabbed the cutlet on her plate in thought. "Busy busy. Me too. I got an early notice we'll be handling a huge starcraft this morning. Lots of life support and weapons systems to reconfigure."

"Long as we get the first crack at them. Keep those grubby Syndicate hands away," Quintus nudged Zoe.

Zoe laughed in response. "Yeah, for sure, Cerulia first, right?"

"Yep. Of course, the Tillians are a close second."

"True." The Tillians had suffered during the Dark Times like the rest of Ling. But, unlike most other races, the Tillians had forged a bond with the Cerulaks. Their shared industrial backgrounds made them easy partners, with similar minds for prioritizing in a time when even the simplest supplies were far from easy to obtain. As a result, the two nations' alliance held fast when even the UA's promises often rung hollow.

"Yeah, we wouldn't have had our warehouse setups were it not for Tillian crews helping with refitting our machinery." Zoe sighed before she took a deep swallow of her drink.

She looked back at Quintus, whose eyes had shown more of that glint of concern a little too familiar to Zoe. "So... how're you holding up otherwise?"

Zoe looked away. "I dunno. It still feels weird, her being gone. We fought before she left, you know."

"Oh boy."

The scene had played in Zoe's mind a lot in the last few days. She and Zaratha had taken a few days and gone to the Cove for some relaxation before Zaratha shipped out. It, sadly, wasn't peaceful for long once their conversation drifted towards Zaratha's mission. "Zaratha said we needed to stick ourselves out there more, not let the Omegans get too big or cocky. I told her she was just paranoid."

Quintus' voice lowered a bit. "Was that your last talk?"

"Mmhmm."

Quintus slid his arm around Zoe's shoulder. She winced, not from the touch but from the memory of her last exchange with her sister. Like Zoe, Zaratha also threw herself into her work with Zamas, but their respective efforts at pushing past the grief caused a divide between the sisters. Zoe clung to the belief of carrying on her parents' work, that Cerulia's success depended on rebuilding their economy.

Zaratha saw the only path to peace through the end of Malone and an aggressive stance toward him at all costs.

"Sorry dear, that's awful."

"Yep." Zoe dabbed an eye. "I promised myself I wouldn't cry in the dining hall anymore."

Quintus pulled Zoe closer into a half embrace. She leaned her head on his shoulder in response.

"It's OK. I miss her, too. I still remember when we trained together. She always had more of a mind than just for the grunt trooper stuff. It makes sense she'd have gone with a Harvester group as advanced security."

"But, Quintus, they should never have been that far out without more support than they had. As threatening as the Omegans have gotten, I would've figured they'd have had way more starcraft and garrison for defense."

Quintus gazed at his food in thought. "Can't say I'm all in the know, but the units I'm with are mostly supplied up."

"But, our military isn't half as strong as it was at its height, and even that wasn't saying much," Zoe sighed.

Zoe saw a flash of Zamas pride in her friend's eyes at the challenge to the Cerulia military might. "Hey, we're tougher than you think. And, don't forget, they faced Malone himself. He's not exactly an amateur."

"Quintus, we've known each other since we were kids, and you and Zaratha trained together. Unfortunately, Malone is going to keep doing things like this to people. Until someone stops him, we're just going to be in some big pool, hoping we're not the next to get caught in his sights. It's just wrong."

"Zoe, he isn't going to get away with it."

"He has so far," Zoe looked at Quintus through tear-moistened eyes. "He just slips away, nothing doing." Zoe knew Quintus couldn't argue that. She spent lots of her free time watching Network reports; lately, Malone was all over the data stream. He had made a huge splash when he singlehandedly rejuvenated planet Agmon from dormancy into being as lush and vibrant as any place in Ling Galaxy. A cult of followers had emerged for him, too. Zoe never figured out why when Malone had been known as a Nara fugitive and cast out of their race.

"Oh, this is no good. I'm sinking again. Talk to me about something else."

"Like what?"

"I don't care. Anything. Even gear specs."

"Gear specs?"

"Yeah, sure! Never know when I'll have to remember something for a retooling job." Zoe prided herself on her memory of parts and specs over various categories. As the Retooling Service never had the slightest idea of what the next batch of tech they'd receive would be, it was not only helpful but essential they had as thorough an understanding of the variety of tech in Ling Galaxy as possible. While the high-functioning Macro Processor systems had complete knowledge, Zoe had more familiarity with tech than the average Cerulak, including several of her superiors in the Retooling group.

"Thought you'd find this interesting. Remember those two I talked about, Brynn Mak and Zakk Goulden?"

"Oh yeah, real hardnoses. What about them?"

"Well, they were talking at the hanger the other day. Some jabber they heard on Network about the far reach planet of Zormad and the trackers. It seems the Railen and Omegans stirred things up over there. Brynn's got a nose for these things, so they're getting a squadron of ships headed that way. It should be something interesting."

"All I know about those Trackers so far is they cost my sister her life. So, what are they even for, and why are so many people crazy about getting one?" Zoe asked.

Quintus shrugged. "They're part of that hunt for Essence that's going on. Malone, of course, is one of the high-profile types looking for Essence, but others are in that game too."

"So, they're trying to hijack Essence and make the rest of the galaxy depend on them for it?"

"Pretty much. As bad as things are in Ling Galaxy, anyone who controls Essence can demand anything they want."

"Well, why doesn't Pon just go for that? Why are we worried about rebuilding our tech through Retooling?"

"Small steps first. Pon doesn't want to face the Omegans or the Railen until we've more legs to stand on."

Zoe nodded. She always dealt in piles of tech; all of it had some sort of value or another. But Railen Trackers were hoarded so much they were never part of the hauls of any Scrap Retrieval. Only the forward groups in Ling Galaxy had a shot at the trackers.

Zoe managed a weak smile in response. "So, where you off to next?" She hoped Quintus took the hint she dropped in her question, namely, *any chance you can accidentally stow me away so I can help maybe find Malone, which is a little better than being cooped up here?*

Quintus shrugged. "They're sending a unit to the planet Delfina to some abandoned facility. They want to see what they can grab there."

"Oh, the Railen outpost?"

"Former, anyway. Omegans lit it up pretty good."

"Think there'll be any Trackers there?"

"Like we'd get that lucky. No, I'm sure the Railen took those out before their newborn. You never know, though. We could get a few reactor cores if they had to ditch the planet quickly. Those aren't exactly light and portable."

Zoe laughed at the image of even the largest Railen trying to haul a one-ton reactor core on their backs. "Um, no, not really. I've gotten pieces from Omegan assault victims already. They sure don't like to leave a lot that isn't burned to a crisp."

"True," Quintus shrugged. "Not exactly where I'd go on my first hunch. But, gotta realize mining planets like Delfina are notorious for having caverns or underground structures. So, it's at least worth a look."

Zoe nodded and clasped his hand. "Just be careful. I don't want to lose you too."

Quintus placed his hand gently on Zoe's. "I'll watch my six. Just keep the home fires burning here. We'll keep you in good scrap so you won't be bored."

"Good," said Zoe.

Zoe had digested Hayaat's words from earlier a bit, and she felt like throwing the idea out to her friend, at least to get his take on it. The answer was in her mind. What she had to do was clear, but her doubts fuzzed the certainty, so she needed a trusted friend's take.

"I'm gonna ask Pon for a transfer."

Quintus' eyes widened, and his chewing slowed. "Yeah?"

"Yep. I'm already due to collect Zaratha's things. So, it'll be a perfect chance. I'm going after Malone, one way or another. I figure it'll be easier if I get her to transfer me to the military."

Zoe had hoped for a little more support from Quintus, but the look on his face wasn't encouraging. "Zoe, what about your duty to Cerulia and your parents? They worked hard setting up Retooling, and you've already risen pretty high up in the ranks there. Are you ready to throw all that away?"

"I know, it's not easy for me, but I feel like to honor and, more than that, avenge Zaratha, this is what I've got to do. The Zamas must be ready for action like that, right?"

"I dunno, we're really not in the position for forward engagements like that yet. We're getting back on our feet, and, with the retooled items, it's been easier, but that kind of action is still a little out of our reach."

"Well, if I'm out there, who knows? I may just run into him."

Quintus' mouth curved in a half smile. "OK, and what would you do then? You know what he did to an outpost staffed with a squad of trained Zamas."

Zoe shrugged. "I dunno. I just want her to move me to at least one of the scout units. I'm going after him, and I'm not taking no for an answer."

They continued eating in silence for a bit longer. Zoe felt driven, with a specific target in mind, and the more someone suggested an alternative, the more it only irritated her.

"Just remember, we've got to keep our defenses up. I'd love to pulverize the maniac myself for what he did to Zaratha, but we don't have the numbers for a full-scale assault. You know he's in league with the Omegans."

Zoe had even more to chew on, thanks to Hayaat and Quintus. The burning she felt about venturing out remained, though. She just had to figure out a way to get it across to the one person on Cerulia with the power to grant her the right to get the justice her sister and their family deserved.

THREE

A FEW DAYS LATER, ZOE HEADED to the Cerulak Command Center for her meeting with Pon before her evening shift.

Zoe figured her best shot at getting her request granted was to put on an air of respect and deference and do everything short of deep groveling for her assignment change.

The Cerulak Command Center on Rufio town had more than a few scars. The Cerulak history of robust production, interrupted by chaos and many sieges, left not even their central government facility without several lesions. Damage from pulse weapon blasts scored the once proud pillars of the structure, and small piles of rubble stood as jagged memories of the Cerulak fall when their former bustling economy was pillaged and plundered.

The holo image Zoe showed of her sister and the mourning sigil, tradition for any Cerulak who had recently lost a loved one, was enough to gain her entry into the inner sanctum and Pon's area of the facility.

The layout of chairs in Pon's chambers was sparse but still elegant. A series of long tapestries lined the walls in equally spaced locations throughout the room. In the center stood two chairs, one for Pon and an empty one that was evidently for Zoe. She approached Pon and, after the customary greeting, took her seat. The cool air in the room felt different to Zoe. She'd been accustomed to the mild warm air of her abode and the warehouse where she worked.

As much as Zoe craved and even imagined how this meeting and her request would go, her nerves flared when she found herself in the actual moment. Maybe it was the noticeable drop in temperature compared to the other buildings she usually frequented. Whatever the cause, she felt the anxiety work its way through her.

"Thank you for seeing me like this, highness."

Pon offered a warm smile in response. Then, she called in an aide to bring the box of items to Zoe. She would've otherwise dismissed the collection that looked back at her as trash needing simple disposal. But, Zaratha's last effects weren't regular items; at least, not to Zoe.

The assault on the encampment must've been much worse than Zoe had heard. Not many items in the case weren't partially or mostly singed. Black char marks were a common motif in the collection. Still, there were fragments which Zoe's glance drifted towards: a carving of their family crest, Zaratha's uniform insignia, and a twin of the metallic token Zoe made with Zaratha as a sisterly bonding gesture. Zoe gripped the box firmly and gave a deep sigh. What remained of Zaratha was in Zoe's hands, and she knew she'd cherish the items in whatever state they were in for the rest of her days.

As Zoe gazed at the container on her lap, Pon spoke again. "I still remember all the work your parents did, setting up our retooling units and facilities. The Tillians did their share, of course. I know how much Cerulak blood, muscle, and effort were involved. It was a long process, but it's how we'll get our strength back in the galaxy."

Zoe lowered her head. A few moments later, she felt Pon's hands on her shoulders and Pon's warm breath as she spoke softly, close to Zoe's ear. "You've had a rough turn. Don't think I haven't seen that. I wish we could be over this plight like anything, but the simple truth is: without Retooling, we'll never return to a life close to what we once knew."

Zoe's heart clenched at the phrase 'life close to what we once knew' since that was a sad and cruel joke for her. Without her family there, the only way she could return to that life was by dying herself, and even then, she wasn't sure what would happen. There wasn't much for Zoe to cling to except the cause, and even that grip had slipped recently.

Pon returned to her seat. "I hope you know how awful I feel about what happened to your sister. I intend to make Malone Stanton pay for what he did to her and our people."

Zoe felt slightly better hearing about Zaratha through Pon's words, but she knew the retribution she craved required much more than thoughtful rhetoric. She gently moved the box to the floor near her feet and gazed at Pon.

Zoe shifted in her seat as she felt her gut tighten further. As many times as she'd rehearsed this moment, the words were still stuck inside her, so she forced others out. "I've been working hard, the retooling efforts continue, and I'll have another shipment of weaponry ready for our shock troops in several days."

Zoe sent all her possible positive thoughts out in the vain hope that, through some osmosis, Pon heard Zoe's overriding wishes and immediately granted her transfer, even gave her a weapon for her speedy mission to eliminate Malone.

"Highness, with all due respect, I enjoy the Retooling Service, and I appreciate your confidence in me through my promotion, even ahead of some with more seniority. But, I see my sister all the time: when I'm awake, when I'm asleep; the image of her death haunts me. I'm distracted in my work, and I feel I'd be best suited in a forward Zamas unit pursuing the bastard, Malone Stanton."

Pon's eyes flickered, and her lips pressed together before she replied, "Malone is too powerful for us. We must strengthen our position first, and we still need Retooling more than soldiers. With our current troop strength, our best bet is for a solid defense. We must build further to be able to handle forward engagements. I don't want to lose any more like Zaratha and her group. Vengeance is a powerful motivator, but not if it's blind. Zoe, I know how much you want to exact your revenge. I'm negotiating deals with not only the Syndicates but the UA. Their goodwill efforts towards us have been small, but their investment in our supply chain gives us hope that we can finally become the independent nation we once were. The Retooling Service is the only thing that will guarantee our future and, as a valued retooling asset, I can't see fit to grant your request. I'm sorry."

The rejection hit Zoe harder than she thought it might. In all her mental run-throughs of the conversation with Pon, she figured there was at least some possibility of getting a no, but hearing it most definitely was a slam more than she'd expected.

Zoe sighed and thrust herself back into her seat as Pon continued, "I've heard stories like yours from many of our people. Their lives were ruined by what we've suffered during these Dark Times. But, all you have to do is think of the Railen. They languished for twenty cycles on Delfina. Then they followed the words of that maniac, Ander Pimm, and lashed out at the Omegans. Now, they're a race of Nomads, floating free in Ling Galaxy and, most likely, will one day be incinerated in the crossfire between the UA and Omegans."

Part of Zoe, the youth who grew up under the Cerulak banner and believed in the strength of her people, heard what Pon said and knew it was the truth. The Railen had been dealt their own hard blow as exiles from the Nara. And the Railen went the way of seeking vengeance by any means necessary, and it ended up costing them their world. The Cerulak youth had slowly increased in numbers, and while Zamas also grew slowly, it would be more formidable in future cycles.

But, the other part of Zoe, the one who mourned her sister's loss and wanted revenge on a scale not even the Railen were capable of, knew the only way she would ever feel peace again was once she stood over the cold dead body of Malone Stanton, killed by her hand. So, Zoe tried again, her voice more emotionally shaken than previously. "Highness, again, I request to be reassigned to the Zamas units for hunting down Malone and bringing him to justice."

Pon's eyes widened. "Zoe, I appreciate your determination and energy. But, you must remain where you are for now. Don't worry. Malone isn't going anywhere, and I suspect there'll be good chances for you to see him before this is all over."

Pon's word was final, but only on the reach of the Cerulak world. But, Zoe wondered, *what else can I do? I've never been off-world enough even to know where I'd go. Traveling through Ling isn't going to be easy.*

The realization settled on Zoe that her play was a bust for the current round. She picked up the box of Zaratha's items and left for home. She had time before her next shift that evening, but not enough to digest her latest blow of Pon's rejection and where it left Zoe.

BACK IN HER ABODE, Zoe wondered if Quintus could've helped her. Quintus had his own back to worry about, though. She wasn't sure if ditching their heritage and Cerulia for a wild goose chase that could end up killing them was an idea Quintus would ever consider.

Against her better judgment, Zoe activated the screen that connected to Network. After a few moments, some updates collected and presented themselves in front of her.

"Show me Malone Stanton," Zoe called out. She smiled as the screen shimmered slightly. Typically, the sift would've prevented reports coming through that hadn't been specifically about Cerulia. But, Zoe had become practiced in altering this, so her searches on Network were less restricted.

The screen became a blur, a jumble of pictures, text fragments, maps, and several national flags. Then, Malone made a speech on planet Agmon, where he restored the desolation to a place with food and even a future.

Zoe browsed the reports beyond Malone, but they became a jumble of scenes that only confirmed for her what she already believed. While other planets seemed to be at the ready call of the UA, she'd never seen any of them set foot on Cerulia. She wondered if the UA even knew they still existed. Clearly, the UA and Ling Galaxy didn't care for her, much less Cerulia.

Zoe settled into her makeshift bed as soft sobs overtook her. She felt adrift, a ship without a course. Her pain had become a companion for her. She wished she knew of a way to get around it, but in an odd sense, it was also comforting. All that lay ahead for her was her work. Pon's rejection stung, but she'd started getting used to these downturns.

Zoe found herself trying to cling to that love of country she'd known all her life, but it felt like it was slipping. *I have to do something, but what?* she thought.

She knew, as much as she wanted to dismiss Pon's sincerity toward her, that Pon had the best in mind. Zoe hated how stuck she felt, but she was. She had to focus on making it through to the next day, the only thing that gave her any direction for the time. Maybe one day it will be different.

Zoe grabbed the token from its resting place on a shelf near her bed and pulled its more tarnished twin from Zaratha's box. Zoe clasped the curved metal pieces in one hand. They caught the light in the room, and the etchings on both still showed up after all the time had passed. The Cerulak words for sister and eternal bond brought more tears to Zoe's eyes. *I can remember her even if she's not here,* Zoe thought.

I'm all that's left of the Enix family. I'll see a way through this. If I have to work my way up to being a Cerulak leader one day, so be it. But we'll rise out of this place. Things will be better; there will be more to this life than what is here already.

A dull boom jarred Zoe out of her thoughts. Her mind switched gears from wallowing to the moment. Retooling was a messy business; sometimes, a ruptured reactor core made it back to their warehouses. But, something in Zoe's gut had her thinking otherwise. *It could be a weapons test,* she thought. The Cerulak military did them from time to time. Sometimes, even the best retooling job needed a little bit of verification.

Her mind still dissatisfied, Zoe tapped the comm device on her wrist. The small bracelet displayed a feed of the security video systems at her warehouse. There'd been a report of some activity, but the scans done by personnel on site only returned reports of possible energy discharge from some fuel cells. It wasn't unheard of, as retrieved starcraft parts often included fuel cells. Zoe was about to settle back down when another pain, like the one from earlier, hit her. However, this one was much more intense. The voice she had heard before was back, but it was far more detailed this time.

-ZOE, COME TO WAREHOUSE 13 NOW-

Zoe felt her neck go cold, and she froze with fear. She had it with theories; it was time for solid facts. Her shift wasn't due to start for another two hours, but that was too long to wait for answers. So, she grabbed her suit, a handful of rations, and a pulse pistol for good measure before she set out into the late afternoon air of Rufio.

FOUR

THE STREETS AROUND ZOE'S NEIGHBORHOOD were empty. The skies were clear, and the blaze of their orange sun was enough to warm the air around her. The burnt stench of transport exhaust fumes hung in the air. The only sound that would've filled the air during the day was the occasional transport and a few of the youth on their Skipper vehicles, light and nimble hovers that traversed the grounds away from the streets and pathways.

Zoe arrived at Warehouse 13, checked in, and headed for the shift supervisor's console. Sasika Pettet sat at the desk connected to the bank of computers. She had shown promise from back when she was a rising cadet in training, but Zoe had noticed, since her assignment to Warehouse 13, that Sasika also suffered from strict attention to procedure. In most cases, that would've been a big plus, but it only annoyed Zoe at the moment.

A series of holographic images danced in the air as Sasika worked controls on the board. Zoe made it to the desk without the slightest reaction from Sasika. However, Zoe startled her out of her work-related trance when she spoke.

"Situational awareness is a good thing, Sergeant Pettet."

"Aye, Lieutenant Enix." Sasika's breaths were still hurried as her initial shock wore off.

Zoe looked at the console, where a video scan of the facility was underway. "We've got security measures in place, but there's no way of knowing when someone might circumvent them."

Saskia removed her control visor. "Of course, Lieutenant."

Zoe glanced over from Saskia's worried eyes back to the console. "What's the building status? I got an alert and headed right over."

Saskia wiped her mouth and shrugged. "Looks like an unstable core in the starcraft wing. I've ordered it sealed as a precaution until we get the source mitigated."

Zoe knew the next move would be for a drone review of the area to identify the exact source and determine the best course for containment. But, Zoe had other ideas in mind.

"I'll check it out. Stand down on the drone probe. Keep your comm open, and I'll call back with a status."

"But, Lt. Enix. The standard procedure?"

"The procedure, Saskia, is to have these ships ready in time. Need I remind you we're expecting our Zamas Military here in a few days to collect another batch of repurposed starcraft? I won't leave anything that important in the hands of a drone. There are too many variables at play here. It takes less time for me to sort it out. So again, stand down and keep your comms open. I'll contact you again if there's any trouble."

"Aye, Lieutenant Enix."

Zoe strode off from the console and down the wide corridor. The admin section was at the warehouse's outer layer, consisting of several shells of protective walls. Retooling work brought several hazards, which required extra levels of protection. The Tillian architecture provided the Cerulak facilities a measure of safety, but their protocols fulfilled the rest of the equation.

Zoe first passed a collection of armored pieces lined up neatly on a series of racks. They were once parts of starcraft outer casings, fabricated building parts, and spent reactor cores. Any tech in the outer area was deactivated from any powered charge and considered harmless, ready for perusal. The inner section of the warehouse was reserved for tech still somewhat functional and, therefore, at higher risk for accidental energy discharge.

Once Zoe arrived at the portal to the inner section, she looked behind her to the shift console and Saskia - both had become pretty small in the distance. The console was the management point of the warehouse and the main point where Zoe and her team handled all receipts of tech and their subsequent release. It was the common resting place during a shift and where Zoe would be soon enough. But not before she solved the mystery her mind wouldn't let her forget.

After several more minutes, she arrived in the starcraft wing. The graceful vessels stood in a row, their respective fuselages decorated with varying levels of charred burns. The first few crafts Zoe passed were on the rehabilitated side. While many still showed superficial scoring marks, these starcraft were internally repaired and vetted. Cerulia wasn't out for cosmetic beauty in her starcraft, as long as structural integrity was guaranteed. The ships were also fitted with the crest of Cerulia and would see service very soon, with Zamas troops heading in for the latest shipment. But Zoe's gut told her this wasn't where she was supposed to look, so she continued on her walk.

Past the refurbished craft, through another series of reinforced doors, lay a batch of the newly received. Each of these ships had various amounts of damage, from minor breaks in their outer shells to near-total mechanical dismemberment. These starcraft's outer casings were unique collections of mechanical carnage, each with a series of fractures, blast charring, and breaks and tears through the outer hulls that rendered the craft in some way or another useless. That is, useless until their harvesting by the Cerulak crews for Retooling. The air in the inner room was danker. Shift workers would be around at some point, lighting the area and filling the musky air with the sounds and smells of Retooling work.

The noise of ruffled fabric jolted Zoe to a quick stop. She extended her light, but she only saw the dull armoring of starcraft around her.

"Who's there?" Zoe hoped her voice had more authority behind it than she felt. It could've been an errant worker, caught up in their day before they realized the time. *They should've known better than to play games like this.*

Zoe continued slowly through the pathways between the ships. If this was someone from the Retooling team, they were on their way to disciplinary action.

A small collection of tubing cascaded to the floor behind Zoe in a loud crash. Fear tightened her chest as she spun around, her hand firmly around the handle of her weapon. She neared the sprawled tubing and took a few short breaths. "Last chance, I'll fire on you if I have to. Show yourself now."

Zoe unholstered her pulse pistol and stepped around the nose section of a cruiser when a pair of piercing blue, glowing eyes stopped her short. She flung her light around, but the beam only lit up the darkened hood and cape of the figure as they stood only a few feet away.

"Who are you; what do you want?" Zoe shouted. A million thoughts raced through her mind. A far-fetched part of her mind would've admitted that she considered for a moment that it was somehow Malone. *I'd heard he's got telepathy. Maybe he tracked me here after he killed Zaratha.*

But the figure said nothing. Instead, it just plodded forward. Zoe took a measured step back. "Don't come any closer. I'll shoot." She aimed her weapon at the center mass of the dark figure and waited.

The figure stopped. Finally, in an echoed voice, it said, "I'm not here to harm you."

"I'll decide that for myself. Let's start with what the hell you're doing here?"

The figure shifted its hood and gave a series of heaving coughs before it replied. "I was hoping you'd tell me."

The deflection annoyed Zoe. "Were you a prisoner on board a craft? All the ships in here were taken from -"

"- space and their field of use, yes. I'm aware of the Cerulak way. I suppose that's the answer we're both looking for."

Zoe nodded. "Typically, a craft is cleared of all life forms before it's returned."

The figure responded with a chuckle that quickly devolved into more coughs. "Well, that's just it. I'm not a typical life form. And, I suppose, my appearance is a bit troublesome."

"More than a bit." Zoe took another step forward.

"I should tell you, whatever stroke it was that landed me here, I know there's a reason for it. And I'm betting it's you, Zoe."

Zoe felt a deep pain in her gut at the sound of her name spoken by a stranger.

"So that was you I heard asking me to help you?"

A slight bow of the head was all she got in reply.

"I dunno how you did that, but it really hurt. Don't do that again, alright?"

"Of course – I'm sorry about the pain, I was a bit desperate to reach you, and I felt it best to contact you using my telepathy. I forget it can sometimes cause discomfort."

Zoe cocked her head. The answers she'd gotten hadn't done much for her ease of mind yet. "How do you know my name, anyway? I don't know who you are. Why do you even care about me? Do you think I'm stupid or something? I'm responsible for thousands of pieces here. I've every reason to stun you and bring you in for disposal, just as soon as I'd bother listening to a word you say."

The figure regarded her with sad eyes. Zoe couldn't read its face under the dark hood, but the slumping of its shoulders made her wonder just what its intention was. Then, suddenly, the figure heaved, and a series of wet coughs echoed around them. "I'm aware of your loss. The Cerulaks, anyway. Your people were ambushed by Malone Stanton not long ago, yes?"

"Yeah, just like anyone who bothered to check on Network would've known. So, what's it to you?"

"It so happens that I'm looking for Malone. I'm actually very interested in him."

"Did he send you here to finish us off or something?"

The figure shook his head. "No, child. Nothing like that. It's true, however, that he... Malone and I were friends in the far past. You see, I was once a Nara, like Malone. We knew each other and grew up together. But, we were both cast out by the Nara forever."

The more the figure talked, the more Zoe forgot about it being a problem for her.

"Please, I'm not well." The figure showed one hand, where a trail of bright green blood oozed out until a few drops hit the floor.

Zoe marveled as the realization set in that the figure was a Nara. "I've never seen a Nara up close before."

"Former Nara." The figure swiped at the greenish liquid that lingered on its lips. "But, if you'd like a more proper name for me, you may call me Pietro."

"Fair enough - Pietro."

"Don't worry. In my present state, I couldn't hurt you even if I wanted to."

Zoe found Pietro's choice of words just a shade less than a mild threat. At least for the moment, Pietro hadn't appeared to be summoning any electrical fields or unsheathing any weapons. Her continued curiosity took care of the rest of her doubt for the time being.

"Let's get back to you telling me why you're in this warehouse, so maybe I'll feel a little better about you being here."

"The best I can recall, I was traveling through space in what I thought was an unassuming craft."

"What craft and where from?" Zoe asked.

Pietro paused for a heaving bout. "I was left in Ling Galaxy to fend for myself. Surely you wouldn't begrudge a beggar scraping by, by whatever means they could get to sustain themselves. My time after exile from Grondia has been a chaotic series of moves. I'm guessing the craft found was near the Far Reach planets. Good enough?"

Zoe nodded, and Pietro continued. "I've got no allegiance to the Omegans, and certainly not to the UA, but I'd hardly be seen as a threat. Or, at least, so I thought. But evidently, my craft was suspicious enough for the UA to haul me in. And, not being one for incarcerations of any length, I decided to try my luck. The result was a heavy barrage of fire directed my way. Through some miracle, my ship was spared, but from the attack and my general state, I was a little too weak and, I suppose, I collapsed - for how long, I don't know. Next thing I knew, my craft and I were brought here; I assume the haul from one of your crews."

Zoe imagined being stranded in space with no one at all. Furthermore, being wounded to the point of being helpless. She admitted that, at least, despite her terrible series of losses, she had a home front that offered her support. People like Quintus and Hayaat and even Pon. Pietro was indeed a lone survivor. She pitied him for it.

"Ok, so you're a Nara. Go on. Why did you leave Grondia? I thought it was a paradise."

"Not leave by choice, child. Disconnection. It's a most involuntary and cruel process. That's mostly to blame for the way I look. The Nara aren't just content to punish those who violate their laws. In Disconnection, a Nara's body is physically altered to prevent return to the home world of Grondia. The planet exists on the other side of a dimensional barrier, through which only Nara and their specially designed craft can cross."

"And yes, other than their draconian penalties, Grondia is otherwise a paradise. Center of Ling Galaxy, where the life of all in Ling Galaxy emanates. I had many responsibilities there once. I was part of the team who oversaw processing Essence until it was made into the Orbs that are delivered to Ling Galaxy to sustain the galaxy itself."

As intense as it must've been for him, Pietro's story still wasn't adding up for Zoe. "Why were you removed from Grondia? Did you kill someone or something?"

"No, in fact, for a good while, I was quite the model citizen. I had the eyes and ears of the Nara machine. I rose through the ranks, blazed through my training, and was ready to ascend to even higher responsibilities. I learned all about Essence and knew as much as my instructors or even more before long. As a result, I was placed in my profession for several years before most of my peers even graduated."

"Malone, on the other hand, was branded a troublemaker early," explained Pietro. "He always had a problem with following even the most basic Nara instruction. His parents were part of a romantic movement among Nara who believed Essence wasn't for us to give away, but for Nara to use for their betterment and ascendence into a new order of consciousness. While I was never about their philosophy, I did see the potential for Essence beyond what the ordained Nara mission was. So, Malone and I eventually came together. His insatiable desire for action, paired with my ability to analyze the facts presented to us. We eventually devoured all the profuse lines of Nara writings about Essence, and all it had to offer via their texts. In those writings, I finally found a truth our teachers had denied us. Malone used my years of ongoing research and formed it into the basest of hypotheses."

"Anyway, I showed Malone my project with Essence. Left alone, it's the source of life in the galaxy. But why would anyone ever leave something that great alone? Surely there are more applications. If this substance can sustain life, surely it has potential for creating it as well. The Nara had in their grasp the potential for ultimate power. Who knew the galaxies that lay beyond Ling? With Essence fueling our weaponry, we'd be a force in the Universe. So why settle for the confines of a single galaxy?"

Pietro's words stunned Zoe. For all her life, her world consisted of Rufio town, her family, and her work. She knew just enough about Ling Galaxy that was filtered to her through the Cerulak sift from Network. However, her worldview had enlarged by epic proportions in just a brief conversation with Pietro. His story filled her mind with other ideas. Revenge was still utmost to her, but perhaps there was more. No one she'd talked with had even mentioned anything like what she'd heard from Pietro.

Zoe asked, "How did Malone turn on you? What happened?"

"Well, once I showed Malone my work, it hadn't taken him long to push me out one day. Finally, he said he had something to show me. So, we met near the Essence plant on Grondia. The huge structure enclosed all the important work with Essence. I remember so much about that day."

Zoe noticed Pietro's voice wavering with the memory. She thought, at first, it was another coughing spasm, but this seemed to be more on the emotional level.

"I asked Malone, 'What exactly are we doing here?' He smiled at me and said, 'I want to thank you, friend, for what you've shown me. It's time we focus our work on realizing the true potential of Essence.'"

Pietro swept aside the folds of his robe and displayed the series of scars covering his body. Zoe gasped in shock at the lacerations and scarred skin that abraded most of Pietro's frame.

"How did he do all of this?"

Pietro winced. "Essence, child. He used what I showed him against me. Before I was ready, he sent a surge through me, enough to disfigure me like this and incapacitate me for long enough for Malone to call our Nara Security force and report me. It's a wonder I wasn't killed by what Malone did. I have to think that was his goal - to leave me alive. Maybe he thought by only maiming me, he'd let me see all he would do from the ideas I fed him. Because I thought he was my friend. It later made sense why we'd been so close to the Essence plant. Malone reported me for Essence manipulation, a most serious crime in Nara law. I was Disconnected and left in Ling Galaxy."

Zoe winced at the wounds and watched the sadness in Pietro's eyes as he adjusted his robe back into place. Malone's trail of deception and murder wound way further through Ling Galaxy and time than she could've ever guessed. Zoe couldn't have imagined that level of brutality. She was hell-bent on getting Malone, but she couldn't have sold out anyone like her friend, Quintus, or even Hayaat for that goal.

"I was cast out of Nara like the Railen and several others. Those who'd committed crimes against the Nara. I was a bastard, thrust into this galaxy and forced to scrape by on my own. Since my exile, I'd heard reports of Malone. He'd been sent to prison because he not only violated Nara rule but was in active plots to overthrow the Nara system. It figures he'd have found his way out of incarceration somehow. Probably convinced his guards to join his cause."

Besides the unbelievable depravity of Malone's ambition, Zoe's mind was stunned by the depth of Pietro's injuries. "How did you survive with those wounds?"

"Oddly enough, the Nara had the smallest amount of sympathy for me. My wounds were treated to the point of sparing my life. But my body was modified, and I was forbidden to return to Grondia from that point on. Since then, I've survived on a moderate level, doing my best to channel Essence in Ling Galaxy however I can. So much of what Malone has in his abilities now, I've been able to do for myself. He is several steps up on me with his Essence orb. And, I'm just not the politician he is, so I don't have the legion of followers he does. But, maybe now my cause will gain momentum, with individuals like you behind me."

Zoe smiled a bit. "I'm a Cerulak. I've sworn an oath to Pon Ebnora and our kind. It doesn't mean I can't support the enemy of my enemy, I guess."

Pietro smiled. "I suppose I can live with that. But, anyhow, there you have it. I've come to regret what I've done, and I know, whatever happens, I must stop Malone. Not for the Nara's sake. They don't care about me any more than they do for their other cast-outs. No, I want to stop Malone because he betrayed me. He stole what I'd developed. He took my plans and used them for his own. And I want your help."

"Show me your face," Zoe said. Her skin bristled at the thought of finally seeing him. Pietro eyed her for a long moment. "How will that help you believe me more than you already do?"

"It'll show you trust me. If you want my help, I must know that you have faith in me. I can't follow someone who won't even show me their face, and the fact you hide yours won't work with me. It's a starting point and something I'm going to insist on."

Pietro chuckled a bit in response. "If I must."

Pietro's hands grasped the edges of his hood, and in one swift motion, he uncovered his head. Zoe gasped out of reflex. Pietro's skin was dark brown, with a series of ridges that looked like scars from a succession of burns. The glow of his eyes hadn't dimmed, even without his hood on. A low amount of stringy grayish hair topped Pietro's head in a random pattern. He managed an awkward smile at Zoe's reaction.

"I don't think I'll ever forget your face," Zoe muttered.

Pietro replied with a combination of heaving and chortling. "I don't suspect you will."

Zoe let Pietro's appearance settle on her for a few seconds longer before her mind snapped back to the task at hand. They quickly needed a hiding place in the warehouse for Pietro if she was to be his accomplice. "Look, there are crews that come by for gear or to drop off another haul all the time. I have to keep this place working. You can stay if you want. I'll find you a spot, but you've got to be quiet and keep a low profile."

"We've got to hide you in the meanwhile. I'll tell the team there's been a reactor leak, and I'm personally investigating it. I'm a group leader here, and the output of this place is on me, so they'll give me a little time to check out something as serious as a reactor problem."

"That shouldn't be a problem. But, I would have an easier time if you had any medical assistance available."

Zoe thought about the supplies at the front office. They kept the most basic of items. Food wasn't exactly a luxury. "I can grab you some med supplies. If you're hungry, that'll take a little doing. We're under tight rations here, but I'll see if I can slip you something."

"Why are you doing this, helping me? Why aren't you reporting me to your superiors?"

Zoe felt her emotions pushing in multiple directions. She knew people like Quintus would've expected her to cut Pietro off, stun him and bring him back. But her vengeful side was an edge stronger. "Because, one day, you're going to help me. I want to kill Malone. I have to find a way off-world, but I've never flown a ship into space."

"How do you think I got around in Ling?" Pietro coughed. "Wasn't easy, but I've seen my way around a few consoles, enough to make me a pilot who won't crash a starcraft anyway."

"Fair enough. So, let's get you well enough for travel again, and then we talk about what you're willing to do to help me get Malone Stanton."

For the first time since she could remember, Zoe saw an opportunity. It wasn't clear-cut and required more than a bit of trust in Pietro. The Cerulaks made it clear they wouldn't be spending time or resources on Malone. While Zoe couldn't have denied this was a dangerous thing in and of itself, she knew there was no way she'd ever rest until it happened.

FIVE

Z OE'S WORLD HAD BEEN JOLTED AGAIN with the presence of Pietro. Of the many feelings she had over his company, she felt a solid but odd kinship with him: alone, with no family, and in pain. While his maladies included more physical issues than Zoe's, she admitted it felt like she'd looked in a mirror.

They agreed it would be best for Pietro to hide around the wing with the finished starcraft. Fewer crews lingered in that section than in the area with the craft waiting for rework and Retooling, which would, at least, give them more time to figure out a plan while Pietro was nursed back to health through Zoe's regular delivery of spare rations.

Zoe found enough extra provisions at the Cerulak center to get a small but steady stream of supplies to Pietro. Sometimes it was just an extra bread roll. On other occasions, she managed to grab an extra ration or even some med packs without attracting too much notice. The Cerulaks were in such a hurry to get the latest batch of Retooling done; it gave Zoe the excuse of an occasional late-night shift and an alibi on the extra supplies. The inconsistent documentation of their food was her saving grace.

A few contacts came in via Zoe's comm channel from Quintus. He checked on her periodically, but she resisted replying. She wasn't sure how to explain to Quintus what had been happening with Pietro anyway. Zoe didn't know if she was more afraid of Quintus knowing or telling her something she couldn't have dealt with, like her continued harboring of a mysterious entity would've likely been considered treason.

Nightly, Zoe and Pietro began a ritual. She arrived and headed towards the cargo bay at the far end of the warehouse. The bay had been cleared of radiation by Zoe not long before. Even though she'd warned Pietro of the physical danger, he seemed unconcerned. Zoe assumed he'd been through enough so-called treatment from the Nara and whoever else, that a little radiation was the least of Pietro's concerns.

Pietro accepted the food happily. Most nights, it was a simple nod, and Zoe was off, trying not to linger too long for fear that particular area may have been monitored. The cargo bay walls, reinforced to prevent radiation leaks, gave them an extra advantage as it was easier to trick a scan should any curious Cerulak decide to check for life forms. Zoe wondered if and how Pietro's body would've shown up on a scan. Given what he'd been through, she wondered if he'd still be classified as among the living anyway.

On one visit, Zoe felt it was time for a more in-depth report from Pietro. "How're your wounds?"

Pietro glanced at his arms as he slowly chewed. "I guess they're improving. I sure miss when I was a Nara. We healed pretty quickly from injuries, sometimes within hours. It was the common belief that our proximity to Essence accelerated our healing, even slowed the aging process."

"What was it like, being around Essence like that?" Zoe asked.

Pietro's face lit up with a glow of fond remembrance. "Essence is the true source. The UA Mystics talk about life, but as a Nara, I was very close to the origin of that life itself. It's one thing to have blind faith, but I had visceral proof. I truly long for that again, somehow. But, for now, I'll accept the justice of ending Malone."

"What do we do then? How do we get him?" Zoe felt her face flush with excitement. All the hours spent imagining her revenge, the idea of it happening very soon was almost too much for her to bear.

"Child, if it was that easy, do you think I would've ended up half maimed and on your planet? There're any number of bounty hunters in Ling. The Syndicate alone would've stopped Malone if he wasn't so good for their business. But, you must understand, it takes a lot of finesse to get a target like Malone. This will be a time-consuming effort."

For the first time in a while, Zoe felt a smile come over her face. Her days had changed a bit and hadn't been as filled with sadness, regret, and sorrow. Instead, a tinge of hope blended into the mix, a quite overdue ingredient. Pietro hadn't completely earned her trust, but he had offered her the one thing none of her kind had yet: the chance for revenge.

SIX

ZOE WASN'T SURE IF SHE FULLY BELIEVED Pietro or was just too twisted up about Zaratha's death, but he'd successfully convinced her about the ship caper as a good idea. After all, Pon hadn't offered anything more than some so-called condolences by way of speeches, and assurances that the revenge on Malone would happen, in time. *She's as bad as the UA,* Zoe thought. *Feeding us with enough hope to keep us from starving, but it's never anything other than empty promises.*

While deep down Zoe knew Pietro wasn't a sure thing, he was more driven for action than anyone in Cerulia, except for Zoe herself. She figured he was keen enough to realize Zoe's access to the armory was an asset. Zoe just had to make sure Pietro was on the level about giving Zoe what she wanted in the end. Pietro tried his best to keep in the shadows, which was easy for him.

It hadn't taken Zoe long to rule out Pietro's former ship. Besides being in a condition that landed it in the Cerulak Retooling service, the craft needed a good round of work by the Cerulak crews, which meant a far longer time hiding and covering for Pietro than Zoe was interested in.

Instead, Zoe took Pietro for a look at the retooled starcraft. Each was ready for another excursion into the stars, their hulls gleaming with a redemptive shine.

"Any of these look good to you?" Zoe asked.

Pietro strode back and forth in silence down the rows between the ships. His hands pressed together at his chin. "They're all junk compared to Nara starcraft, but our situation doesn't allow for pickiness."

"If we're gonna do this, it's gonna be on one of these ships, so you better choose."

Pietro nodded and glanced back to the room's far end, where his gaze froze. He signaled Zoe to follow, and he approached the craft. It was dark in color, with some strange markings on its tail. The dim light reflected on the name embossed on the side of the fuselage: *Outspan*.

Pietro folded his arms, a triumphant gleam in his eyes. "Zion class cruiser, pre-Transient Warp era. Even without the latest engine, these ships had enough strength to get around the galaxy quickly. Basic light speed on these would be very advisable. This *Outspan* craft should serve our needs nicely."

Zoe shrugged. To her, all the craft and tech she saw in her place were tough to distinguish between. They were all, in her mind, pieces that would one day be useful again. She felt a little similar to them in that respect. Her life was in a queue, waiting for something to rearrange the broken pieces back together until something fit, something took, and she felt like herself again - or, at least, a close facsimile.

Zoe ran her hands over one of the former blast points on the *Outspan's* structure. "I've heard it said that the repurposed starcraft in Ling are much better - they've proven their durability by taking fire head-on."

Zoe's nerves ramped up a gear. While it felt like she had a great opportunity to get Malone with Pietro, she worried about how stealing the *Outspan* would go down. What if Pietro wasn't able to handle the security? Surely Zamas would've swarmed the place as they left in any starcraft without authorization. Pietro had gotten stronger recently, but she still hadn't seen much in the way of him being a physical threat. If he had any control or abilities through Essence, she hoped he would show them fast.

Zoe's gaze lingered on the *Outspan* when Pietro's voice jumped her out of her semi-trance.

"Are you alright?" Pietro's eyes showed concern. "I'm sensing you're having doubts about this."

"You're saying we can tear across Ling Galaxy, and just the two of us will bring down someone whose rallied thousands of people to support him on nothing more than a promise. I just don't know how much we'll be able to make a difference."

"Even one individual, with enough determination, can make a mark. You have to decide for yourself. Change requires action."

Zoe heard Pietro's words and glanced back at the *Outspan*. In the thriving era of Ling Galaxy, Zion Class cruisers like *Outspan* often made supply runs to all ends of the galaxy. Their versatility made them handy tools for the nefarious, and Zoe mused their little enterprise fit neatly into that column.

"Where exactly are we heading, anyway? Having a course would sure help."

Pietro frowned a bit, his arms folded. He strolled around under their craft. "Malone's been hopping around Ling Galaxy pretty quickly. I say we start with some of the Far Reach planets and work our way in. The fighting between the Omegans and the UA should divert their attention from the Far Reach."

It sounded good enough to Zoe. But, she wished she could've talked with Quintus before they left. Maybe he would've told her it wasn't such a bad idea, doing what she was going to. Or, he would've said she was as nuts as she thought, trusting a strange outcast she'd met days earlier. But, her grief and hunger for revenge obscured the other voices that she'd listened to until the path ahead seemed clear, even if it may not have been.

"Well, let's go with the *Outspan* then," Zoe said. "We can, at least, make a go of it that way."

Pietro nodded. "Load up, let's get star-"

The whine of the large entrance door broke up their conversation. Pietro hissed. Zoe felt her throat tighten as a group of Zamas soldiers walked in. Her frayed nerves worsened when she saw Tarmun with them. She noticed his eyes focus on the already powered-up craft.

"They've come for the batch of weapons," Zoe whispered to Pietro. "Hide yourself. I'll take care of this."

While Pietro crouched down with a series of grumbles, Zoe stepped out from the rows of craft onto the main concourse and headed toward the arriving troop delegation. Tarmun caught sight of her and waved her over. She walked up with a cautious gait, with the hope her story held, and they had no reason to check the ship that had just happened to be in standby mode.

Zoe gave a salute to Tarmun, who returned it after a moment. "Ready for the delivery?"

Tarmun's face twisted in a slight scowl. "It's the regular delivery time, so we're ready."

Zoe nodded hastily. "I've got your supplies ready in the back." She motioned down the hallway, but Tarmun paused.

"What were you doing with that starcraft over there?"

Zoe swallowed the knot in her throat. "This craft failed one of our final verification checks. It could be nothing, but I didn't want to release it until I make another pass, ensuring it's flight and combat ready."

Zoe prayed that bone was enough for Tarmun to be satisfied, but instead, he took a step toward the craft. "Looks in good shape to me. You know, we're gunning up for a run. I'm hearing about potential trackers in the far reach, and we could always use a fast ship to get us there."

"You don't want to trust that heap before we vet it, Captain." Zoe's tone had drifted into begging. She hoped Pietro hadn't set his sights on Tarmun and his group, which had all tabled Zoe's delivery for the moment and focused on the craft, its engines now in a partial burn, casting a glow in the far end of the cavernous room.

Tarmun's eyes narrowed into a glare; his voice sharpened to a bark. "Lt. Enix, I order you to transfer that starcraft to us now."

Zoe searched for reasons, excuses, and even unveiled threats that may have redirected Tarmun's attention away from the ship, but she realized it was hopeless, especially once Tarmun muttered, "Someone's aboard that ship right now."

Pietro was done hiding. Tarmun eyed Zoe with disbelief. "What the world is going on here?"

As Tarmun stepped past Zoe toward the craft, she felt panic take hold. The other Zamas troops nearby unshouldered their rifles.

"Wait!" Zoe shouted. Tarmun turned back to her. Zoe's mind raced for any kind of explanation that would've been remotely acceptable, but her extended pause was the worst possible non-answer she could've provided.

Tarmun pointed at Zoe. "What are you pulling here?" He slowly trained his rifle on her chest. "Whoever's on that ship, make them stand down now, or you'll be charred remains."

Zoe froze. It seemed that Pietro had gotten what he wanted and was ready to thrust her to her fate. She closed her eyes and hoped for warm thoughts of her sister as she begged a million times for mercy in her head. Several loud blasts came next. Zoe's body shook with the thundering reports, but she slowly realized she remained among the living. Soon after, she noticed the grunts and groans and opened her eyes to Tarmun and his group, laid out on the ground.

"Give me your hand!"

Pietro's voice howled above the engines as the craft was now overhead. Pietro himself was on the entrance ramp to the ship, extended downward a few feet from Zoe. Pietro reached for her with as much of a smile as Zoe had seen on his face since their first meeting.

She glanced back at her past and decided her future, however uncertain, had the best shot at revenge with Pietro and reached for his hand as their stolen starcraft made a hasty exit from Warehouse 13 and all of Cerulia.

SEVEN

SINCE THEIR ABRUPT DEPARTURE from Cerulia, Zoe remained in the navigator seat as Pietro skillfully guided the *Outspan* at a blistering speed into deep space. Zoe eyed the rear view of the craft on the ship console, where Cerulia rapidly grew smaller in the distance. Zoe was filled with many thoughts - regret certainly one of them. While she knew, in her heart, she needed to go after Malone, the other losses already adding up weren't anything she wanted. *What if one of those in the warehouse had been Quintus?* Just the thought drove a deep chill through Zoe. As a distraction, she eyed the flight controls of the *Outspan*.

Through her Retooling work, Zoe had become familiar enough with the general layout panels of starcraft, but it was quite different now that she was aboard one out in space. After a few moments of watching the various scopes and indicators, she turned back to Pietro. "It's so busy."

Pietro smiled. "Never seen a craft in actual flight before, I take it?"

"No. Back in the warehouse, I've fired up and tested components, but one at a time. Seeing the ship in full service, it's-"

Zoe still found herself unable to complete a thought, but she was mesmerized. The concert of alert tones and fluid energy the ship took on its own as it glided through space was a sight for her.

Pietro seemed at home at the ship's console and directed the *Outspan* on a steady arc toward the Far Reach area of Ling Galaxy.

"We must vanish for a bit to work out our plan," Pietro said. He glanced at Zoe with triumphant eyes over their successful impromptu heist. "That was fun, wasn't it?"

For the moment, Zoe had accepted her status as rescued from a close call. She shifted in her seat. "Not my idea, but I'll take being alive over what they had in mind." She lowered her head.

Pietro watched her with compassion. "It's ok. Yes, you're now an outcast. I've been one for a while now. I get what that's like. It hurts and can certainly be scary: being an unknown, all by yourself. This galaxy doesn't care for those who can't contribute."

" I had a place and a life back there, and I just threw it away. You were cast out. There's a difference." Zoe retorted.

Pietro set the *Outspan* on autopilot and leaned back with a deep inhale. Zoe had seen the look before. Pon had shown a similar expression. It usually happened before Pon launched into a speech about some greater good garbage like the rest of the politicians on Network did about any number of things. Those who died in famines, succumbed to Veculus, or converted to following Malone, were all part of some master plan to those in power, acceptable casualties in a process that most leaders claimed or at least acted like they were in control of while, in reality, none of them knew the next move. Their only play was recovering from the current predicament and keeping their core base happy come re-election time.

Pietro moved near Zoe. She glanced away, but he pulled her back to his eyes with his hand.

"Zoe, listen. The situation you're in, this whole galaxy is in, is because a few people decided it best they be in control. They don't care about your sister; they don't care about your people. Your government accepted this. I give them credit for that. But they've, in turn, forced their people into making things right. I believe all races have to have some stake in their future, but to declare your own race slaves until that happens is not only foolish, it's very destructive. How many of you are living for anything other than the next haul? There's no spirituality, no family, no growth. What do you have to offer Ling Galaxy in the end except for production? Believe me, the UA would enlist you all tomorrow, but you'd be no better. You can't live a life based on providence. There has to be more. That's what I'm doing. That's what I want to get out of this. If you'd stop and think, I'm the best hope for Ling Galaxy to thrive as it was always meant to."

Pietro made his way into the common forward area adjacent to the bridge. Several feet back, the corridor opened into a more flowing space with a table for plotting courses and other general work. After a few moments, Pietro called Zoe to join him.

"I'm going to try contacting Malone. I don't know if this will work, but it's worth a try. I want to see where his head is now."

"Is it a good idea to let him know you're around? Shouldn't we be more secretive?"

Pietro smiled. "Child, I won't be speaking with him. I'm only connecting with his being, seeing where he's located. We can track him on Network, and I have, but what I'm going to try here should give us his location, to the planet and even relative to his exact position. So, if we're going to get him, this is how."

While Pietro focused his body, Zoe did her best to hide a chuckle, figuring that was the last thing Pietro wanted to hear. But it was funny to her: the sight of Pietro's gyrations on the floor. She'd never been one for UA Mysticism. Zoe had lost enough family that it made the idea of some benevolent force watching over, guiding and, even more so, providing for them seem pretty ridiculous.

Zoe waited for Pietro's confirmation, but instead something caught his eye. For a second, Zoe wondered if she'd entered incorrect coordinates. "What is it? What's wrong?"

Zoe followed Pietro to the bridge console, where he pointed to a nearby quadrant on the navigation display. "It can't be."

Zoe looked at the mini display window Pietro had opened. Aside from a few nearby asteroids and some random space debris, she saw an inconspicuous cargo ship escorted by a collection of UA fighters.

"Some kind of cargo transport; maybe a prisoner ship. I've seen a couple, partially dismantled, anyway. So, what's got you worried about it?"

Pietro clasped his chin, gazing at the convoy as if it were an ancient artifact he'd studied his entire life. Then, he jabbed a finger toward one of the other ships escorting the transport. "That ship is Nara class."

"Nara? I didn't think they traveled in Ling like that."

"They don't." Pietro finally glanced back at Zoe. "Not only is it Nara class, but that's the ship of the Hierarch. Ellenc Ballo is in Ling."

"Who?"

"Leader of the Nara, child. It looks like our friend, Malone, has drawn Ellene Ballo into the fray."

The lift in Pietro's voice had Zoe wondering. Nara were typically unseen. She'd never even seen any until Pietro. The Nara's place in Ling were as deliverers of Essence. And, the ones who came to Ling weren't anything like leaders. But now, there were three: Pietro, Malone, and Ellene. Was the hunt for Essence that big of a threat they sent the Nara Hierarch into the mix?

Zoe was puzzled by Pietro's sudden shift about Ellene and why Pietro was distracted by her.

Zoe asked, "Can't we use Ellene to get Malone?"

Pietro shrugged. "She's certainly a game piece. I'm not interested in hitting Ellene right now, however. But, she could be useful to us."

The Nara starcraft shimmered much more brightly than the other ships around it. Its brilliant color shone as vividly as a jewel against the blackness around it.

"What's Ellene like?"

Pietro mulled the question over with a few muffled chuckles. Then, as he checked some of the shipboard monitors, he replied,

"Very particular. I'm surprised she's shown her face in Ling like this. It shows how desperate she is."

A series of loud explosions jolted Zoe out of her seat. The *Outspan* buffeted wildly, and several alarm notifications blared on the console.

"What was that?" Zoe asked as she climbed back into her chair.

"Oh, it's them," Pietro replied glumly. He tapped a control on the console and displayed the rearview, where two fighters were close and fixed on their ship.

"Who?" Zoe asked.

"Railen. It's fair to say they don't know who's on this ship. They just want it. They too were former Nara, cast out for their crimes. They spent years in Ling Galaxy surviving and now are out for recompense. Revenge against all. Retribution is their only creed. They don't care who and how. They just want to see everything burn."

Zoe grabbed the *Outspan's* controls and swung in an evasive move. "There's got to be something we can do here."

Pietro pounded his fist against the wall. "Nothing I'd like to."

Another series of blasts resounded, but these found their mark. The ship shuddered violently, and the console panel blinked off for a few moments, then back on, only to display several alerts.

"They've damaged our shields. We're not going to last much longer like this."

Zoe glanced at the proximity scan for any local systems they could duck down into. If they could at least remove themselves from the *Outspan*, they could survive, hoping the Railen just wanted to take fresh scrap.

When things seemed at their worst, and Zoe had yet again prepared herself for a reunion with her sister, another series of blasts sounded, but these were different. A new grouping of starcraft entered the scene. Zoe and Pietro watched as the new craft lit into their attackers until the Railen ships were obliterated in brilliant showers of light and debris.

Their ship comm crackled to life with a voice speaking a language Zoe didn't recognize. Thankfully, Pietro did.

"That's Omegan. Hit the translator, quick."

The jabber turned to intelligible speech. The voice through the Outspan comm was scratchy but deep. "Starcraft, identify yourself."

Pietro cleared his throat. "We are charges of Malone Stanton. We were on a mission to retrieve vital tech for his eminence when we were overrun."

Zoe noticed the mirthful look in Pietro's eye. For some reason, despite their attempted ruse and the prevailing fact the Omegans may not have even believed it, she felt a strange calm over their uncertain outcome. The comm was silent for a while, but then an answer came. "Carry on. Watch for stray Railen and UA ships. We may not be so close next time to assist."

"Understood, thank you. Hail Omegana."

"Hail Omegana," came the reply.

The Omegan craft zoomed away from the scene.

ZOE HAD KNOWN ENOUGH about the Omegans and their attitude towards anyone who wasn't. Some of the smashed and burned tech the Cerulaks recovered included Omegan parts, but those weren't as plentiful as the others. Omegans were known for their ruthlessness and also their fighting skill. It wasn't many a fight they lost, and even fewer they walked away from willingly.

"How did you do that?"

Pietro still looked out the front of the *Outspan* with a satisfied grin. "I guess I still have some abilities after all." He slowly turned and faced Zoe. "In addition to work I've done with Essence, I was a quick study in the field of mental grasp. It's an ancient technique only a few Nara have ever been able to learn. It's only taught to a select few in Nara Instruction, those determined to have the highest aptitudes."

"So, you fed them the idea of leaving us alone, and they went with it like that?"

"Yes. Exactly like that."

Zoe was amazed that Pietro openly admitted to commanding the minds of other beings with the cavalier approach of someone hauling containers of space scrap. Suddenly, she was afraid about who else Pietro may have tested or used his abilities on.

"So, is mind control how you got me to cooperate and get you this ship?"

Pietro's mouth formed a line, taking in a slow breath. Then, he stood and approached Zoe, his hands outward and his arms at his sides. "I can understand why you'd suspect that. The truth is, I've been adrift in this galaxy for some time, and it's been quite lonely. I know there's more to this life than just accomplishing something. I need to have people around me that I care about. That's exactly what Malone has done for himself. I can tell those people who are massing in his honor truly believe in what they've seen, even though you and I both know his real agenda is more sinister than his devoted acolytes care to admit."

Klaxon alerts sounded on the bridge, and several warnings flashed on the forward screen. Zoe ran some checks until her worst fear stared back at her from the console. "Pietro, the Regulator's been hit. We're not going to get far at all without fixing that. We've got to find a port or something. There's too much damage on these console indicators to ignore."

Pietro nodded. He then activated a map scan of the area and flicked his hand about, moving the display among the various moons and planets nearby. "Ahh, planet Bertold. It's got a port, and it's still under UA control, for some reason. So, let's head there, see if we can get some help."

Zoe toggled through the controls, and with Pietro's guidance, they angled the dinged, slightly smoking *Outspan* toward Bertold and a hopeful respite for repairs.

EIGHT

"**I**T'S SO BLUE!"

Zoe's eyes were fixed on the landscape as it cascaded past the forward viewport of their cruiser. Deep bluish oceans that looked to stretch to the horizon gave a stark backdrop to a series of islands that appeared occasionally. She caught Pietro's chuckle and glanced over at him.

"Pretty remarkable, isn't it? Bertold has been called the Well of Ling Galaxy for a good reason. There's plenty of industry here harvesting aquand for other planets which aren't as saturated," Pietro said.

A large collection of islands quickly passed below their ship. A collection of giant starcraft were positioned near one island, and she noticed large receptacles that scooped massive amounts of the bluish liquid into them.

"So that's where they get our Aquand."

"Good chance of that. But we're not here for a drink break."

Zoe's eyes met Pietro's. "Of course. The Regulator. This place looks pretty sparse on tech for repairs. Think we'll have any luck?"

Pietro shrugged. "Oh, I think we'll find something. Bertold has a few ports of record. We just have to find one with a decent market."

Pietro's confidence eased Zoe's concerns a bit. She figured Cerulia couldn't have been the only planet in Ling destitute enough from the Dark Times to have been in the scrapping field. So, Pietro guided the *Outspan* closer to an island cluster until their mostly aquatic foreground became a large plateau of dry land.

"Here we are. Kandam City."

Kandam City boasted a spaceport, trading market, and a series of smaller settlements. Pietro guided the *Outspan* to an open area near one of the markets, touching down for a mostly uneventful landing. As Zoe got up from her seat, she wondered what they would offer in trade for a new Regulator.

"Please tell me you've got a Wenzo crystal or two under those robes."

Pietro offered a mild glare in return. "No. But, for the resourceful, credit is unlimited."

Pietro headed toward the rear of the Outspan, his robes billowing behind him. After a moment of watching him exit and shaking her head at his flippant attitude, Zoe searched the *Outspan* for anything that could've helped them make a trade. Pietro was pretty confident, but even Zoe knew that in the real world of Ling, besides hard currency, items of value were the only true transaction method with any chance of success. *Outspan* had been readied for Cerulak Zamas use, so a series of troop arms were aboard. Zoe pulled out two long-range pulse rifles from storage compartments. The guns wouldn't have equaled to a Regulator, but it was a start. Next, she added a series of charge explosives and some rations to her haul. The pickings were slim, but Zoe felt better about having more to barter with than Pietro's attitude.

Zoe met Pietro outside as he surveyed the area and the trading market nearby. Feeling the weight of everything, Zoe plopped the case of rations and gently laid the charges down when she noticed Pietro looking at her.

"What is all that?"

"Currency. I don't know if you've ever done any trading. I haven't exactly, but I know the value of items. We're not going to get a Regulator for free. We have to give something in return."

"And you think you've got sufficient value in that pile?" Pietro added with a smirk.

"Maybe not, but it's a start. You have a better idea?"

"Child, I chose our landing spot because the trading markets are less patrolled by local security forces. Don't you think we could've just headed over to that spaceport and done some quick thievery, taking a Regulator off one of those ships and then making a break for it?"

Zoe eyed the port, where several cruisers stood, being fueled. "We wouldn't have gotten far. As sparse as the port is, I bet it's tightly monitored. Harvesting Aquand is a key industry in Ling, so they've probably got that locked up tight."

"You're astute and correct." Pietro strode about Zoe as she eyed him. "No, I've not come all this way to be picked up for simple tech theft. These trading markets give hope to so many in Ling Galaxy. We just have to wait for someone as needy as us to get here and grab what we need from them."

"And this stash?" Zoe nudged the rations container with her boot.

Pietro eyed the pile with mild pity. "Save the rations. Trade the weapons if you want to get more nourishment. But leave the explosives on board. Never know when those could come in handy."

Annoyed at Pietro's sparse sharing of information, Zoe yanked the ration packs into her arms and grabbed the explosives as gingerly as her annoyance would allow.

As she reached a free hand for a rifle, Pietro said, "Leave the weapons. I may have use for them after all."

Zoe looked into Pietro's eyes, wondering for a moment if he was joking. But, after he stayed silent, she replied, "This stuff isn't as light as it looks, by the way." She went back up the catwalk and wondered just what kind of situation she was in with Pietro. She felt more like an indentured servant than a partner in a revenge plot. Once she got back to the *Outspan* cargo hold, she tossed the ration pack onto a counter and laid the explosives behind one of the seats to the rear of the bridge. After a moment of pounding the counter near the rear cargo hold to bleed off excess aggravation, she returned outside and saw Pietro talking with an elderly Mardak. The short hairs on their body all had a bit of greyish tint. Zoe approached, and after a few moments, she caught Pietro's gaze. He extended a hand and beckoned her closer.

As Zoe neared, a noticeable stench invaded her nostrils. While she glanced around to see if a waste vehicle had come close by, she realized it was the Mardak.

Pietro smiled warmly at her. "Ah, glad you came back so quickly. Zoe Enix, I'd like you to meet Rezin Salko. Rezin is a retired member of the Aquand harvest teams on Bertold."

Rezin, amid a series of groans, straightened himself up. "Hello, Ms. Enix. I was telling your partner here I came into the markets to get some odds and ends for my return trip to Zormad. He asked me about the Aquand industry here on Bertold and that you two were looking for an investment?"

Zoe, unsure of Pietro's ruse, played along out of curiosity. "Yes, that's correct. We've been location scouting, and I've seen several harvesters around. Are there open areas not subject to claim?"

"Well, I can't say I'm the best versed in those matters, but I think you can check with the council on Bertold Island. It's roughly a two-hour flight from here, give or take the abilities of your craft."

Pietro laughed and patted Rezin's back. "Yes, of course. Thanks to the trading market, we'll hopefully get a few things for the rest of our stay here. Tell me, Rezin, would you care to have some dinner with us this evening?"

Rezin's face twisted with concern. "Oh, I don't know. I've been on Bertold longer than I expected. I really should be shoving off."

Pietro said, "Please, I insist! I can certainly make it worth your while somehow. I've got skill with these trading markets. I bet I can get you more items for your return home. Seeing the family, I take it?"

Rezin shuffled in place. Zoe still hadn't grasped Pietro's use of Rezin in their repair calamity, but she felt a little sorry for the elderly Mardak.

"Oh, I suppose the missus wouldn't mind another day's wait for my return. Provided you can get me some Bertolian fragrance or something?"

Pietro chuckled. "I can't imagine we couldn't find something along those lines. Zoe, I'm going to take Rezin to the market for some shopping. Why don't you join us?"

Zoe followed Pietro as he worked his way through the market with Rezin. It amazed Zoe how Pietro moved Rezin from cautious prey to willing participant in such a short time. After some beverages and a bit of trading, Pietro had managed to get a fairly impressive haul for Rezin and themselves. None of the items included a Regulator, however. By this stage, though, Zoe figured Pietro knew what he was doing. She only hoped whatever it was wasn't too rough on Rezin. He seemed pretty nice, if not a little out of sorts.

They found themselves behind Rezin's craft in the evening. Nights on Bertold proved to be of the chillier variety. Zoe wrapped her arms around her frame and edged closer to the torch pit. While primarily intended for meal preparations, the heat it generated came in handy on cold nights. Of course, staying warm wasn't exactly its intended purpose, but Zoe wasn't in the place or mood to complain about it, given how far she was from everything she knew.

Pietro had parlayed the gold trim on his robe for some Grondian Ale and had shared it with Rezin. The old Mardak had relaxed a bit, but Zoe was still on guard about the situation, despite Pietro not showing any malice.

Pietro held his cup high. "To the glory of Ling Galaxy. May she one day remember all the poor lost souls under her care and give them the treatment they all deserve."

"Snallack!" Rezin exclaimed as he lifted his cup in kind. Zoe eyed Pietro quizzically, and Pietro shrugged. Then, after a moment, Rezin let loose with a belch and wiped his mouth. "Forgive me; sometimes I forget where I am and lapse into my native tongue."

"Not a problem, friend. Drink up!" Pietro guided the bottle to Rezin's cup for a refill.

"What are you doing?" Zoe hissed, but Pietro gave her a stern glare in response.

"You know, Rezin, if I'm not mistaken, your craft is of an older line in Ling Galaxy."

"That's correct, before the days of that Transient Warp business. Back when starcraft were tough, and they had what it took both for intergalactic travel and for a brawl now and then."

Zoe hadn't recognized the likes of Rezin's ship, which surprised her a bit. The tech she'd seen in Warehouse 13 seemed to be only so many years old, which made her wonder about the exact age of the strange ship.

Pietro, still engaging with Rezin, said, "Magnificent vessel. If I'm not mistaken, that had one of the earlier uses of the Hayes Targeting systems?"

"Oh, I'm not much of an old soldier. But Mardaks were always ready for a fight. We're not given a lot in Ling Galaxy we don't scrap for ourselves, you know."

Pietro nodded. "Your kind has been mistreated for a long while. There'll come a time for you. You'll get what you deserve, believe me."

Rezin leaned back in his seat, seemingly content. Zoe marveled at Pietro's way, and seeing Rezin's change over a brief period, from unsure to downright friendly with Pietro, had her wondering just how much of her change towards Pietro had been about the same thing. Zoe, like Rezin, wasn't exactly in a place of fulfillment, and she wanted so badly what Pietro seemed to magically fill or, at least, gave the strongest impression he could.

After another long swig of his drink, Pietro wiped his mouth and nodded toward Rezin's craft. "That's it. I can't take it anymore. I'm not going to get any peace until I look at that console of yours."

Rezin chuckled a bit. "You're pretty curious, aren't you? Ok, I suppose it's the least I can do after the company you've given me and the fragrance." After a few unsteady attempts, Rezin got to his feet and stumbled toward the craft. Pietro set his cup down and stepped back quickly to Zoe.

"Get ready for my signal - you'll need to pull that Regulator out once I'm done."

"Done with what?" Zoe hissed.

Pietro responded with a look that told Zoe so many things she feared. Unfortunately, her concerns about Rezin weren't unfounded, and her heart sank as she realized she was an accomplice to whatever Pietro had in store next.

Zoe followed them from behind and lingered inside the aft section of the craft as Pietro guided Rezin up slowly. The ale had worked a number on Rezin, so much so that Pietro needed to almost carry him through the corridors to the front of the ship.

Zoe looked around the hold section. It was stowed with a few unremarkable items. A store of rations for a return trip. Old and spent harvesting equipment that had a layer of grime on it, probably from some kind of land mining. She figured Rezin would've sold any aquatic mining equipment upon his retirement.

The dull hum of the onboard ship systems was the only sound Zoe heard for a while. Zoe wondered what the signal was when a klaxon buzz sounded over the comm, scaring her. The shrill alarm buzz came with Pietro's voice over the speakers.

"Zoe, harvest the Regulator. I'll be right down."

It took Zoe a few minutes to locate the access panel. It was different from other craft she'd worked on in the past, but the design of the engines, particularly the Regulator access, wasn't that much of a different layout. Without tools at her disposal, she was left to hand-loosen the connectors. Her hands were soon covered with a bit of grease, but she held a Regulator after some wrangling of latches.

Finally, she slid out of the maintenance hatch to see Pietro, his robe decorated with grayish blood.

Zoe froze for a moment before speech found her. "What did you-"

"I did what was necessary for someone on a mission like ours. As did you."

Pietro grabbed the Regulator from Zoe's hands and walked past her. "Come now. It's time we get back to our mission. The sooner we get Malone, the better."

Zoe weakly followed in silence. The sooner the better was right, but the rising body count on this quest had become harder and harder for her to stomach.

AS THEY RETURNED TO SPACE, Zoe was anything but settled in her seat. The thought of Rezin and whatever Pietro had done to him was a tough visual to shake. Even though she hadn't seen whatever Pietro did, the idea of that kindly old Mardak being killed just for their mission weighed on her. She did her best to push the feelings down and thought back to why she was going along with this in the first place.

"Pietro, you didn't have to kill Rezin, did you? So why did you bother giving him the ale, making friends with him, the whole lead on?"

Grief tore at Zoe. She hadn't even known of Rezin's existence hours earlier, but the feeling of his death partly from her cooperation with Pietro stung her deeply. "I don't understand why you couldn't have just stolen it from another craft or even stolen it from his."

"It's simple, child. I had to show you what commitment is. You've been committed to a life on your former world. What has that given you? Safety, security, a purpose, a value. You're someone because you believed in that cause. But now you've got another desire in your heart. Your service to your beloved country isn't enough anymore.

You want to kill, but you're not a rabid animal in the street. You're an intelligent being, capable of things, but maybe not yet of murder. But now, you see what it takes. You've committed yourself to a cause without thinking of the depth of what your desire is. Murdering one of the most notorious beings in Ling Galaxy isn't the fodder for a child's playtime. The level of depravity needed to kill Malone Stanton means you must also be relentless. You must stop at nothing, including stealing from a kindly old soul like poor Rezin. Just think of how sad his family will be to find out about his murder at the hands of a mysterious assailant. We were removed from the municipality of Kandam City and their UA delegation. The trading markets are where the real economy of Ling Galaxy resides. And that economy allows for the appropriation of resources to the quick and the determined. That's what we are, and for the greater good of relieving Ling Galaxy of its greatest enemy, a few poor souls killed as collateral damage are more than acceptable. So, ask yourself, Zoe Enix, just how far are you committed to your goal?"

"Where are we headed now?" Zoe asked, her eyes looking out the front canopy into deep space.

Pietro returned to the navigation console and tapped out several calculations. "We need a play. We're alone and not very formidable. I can't match Malone by myself. He's got too much on his side. So, I'm going to develop a play against his weakness, and when the time comes, we'll use that very soft spot to crush him. We'll be hiring someone for our plan," Pietro muttered. "Someone with skill. A smuggler should work fine."

"Why do you need someone else? I thought you had skills enough to go after Malone."

Pietro smiled at her. "Glad you've recognized that. But, truthfully, the hire isn't for direct attack. This is part of my plan; truthfully, there's one smuggler I need to get the job done. However, luring that party in will take some work. I've tracked him around Ling Galaxy. Our party has a few ties to planet Wenzo. So, it's a safe wager he'll be back there at some point."

"Mmhmm." Zoe leaned back into her seat. She'd been on the go so much she hadn't realized how exhausted she was but was quickly reminded, and felt her eyelids go heavy. Finally, she drifted off to sleep with the sound of Pietro's voice mentioning a planet called Wenzo.

AS PIETRO BROUGHT the *Outspan* into the skies over Wenzo, Zoe eyed the swiftly approaching port and clutched the pulse pistol. After landing, they headed for the town of Marwen. Zoe observed the area's inhabitants, as much as the scattered rabble of shabbily dressed individuals would've counted as the citizenry of any organized nation.

Zoe followed Pietro until they were across from the Dark Passage bar. The exterior was a mangled mixture of girders, likely former building pieces, twisted into an industrial-themed marquee that screamed a lot of things about the bar, none of which were overly friendly. The bar's title was emblazoned in shiny gray letters amid the blackish woven metal pattern. It would've been pretty acceptable as a prison entrance were there not bar grub and libations for sale.

"Are you really going in there?" asked Zoe.

"Of course."

"What exactly in there helps us to get Malone Stanton?"

"Because, my dear, now that you've had a lesson in commitment, you must learn approach. We can't run a search for Malone in a straight line. He's far too cunning not to see that coming. So, we'll do the next best thing - the trackers that can locate him. I'm going to look for soldiers for hire here. These bars are good for a few things, like a night's pleasure and a reliable mercenary."

That was enough for Zoe. She could've used more time, preferably with some strong drink, to further drown the image of Rezin's blood on Pietro's cloak. Once Pietro headed towards the bar, Zoe lost herself for a few moments in the scene inside. She hadn't been in any places like this, even on Cerulia, in her life. Cerulaks weren't much for frivolity past a young age and usually immersed themselves in work. Places like the Dark Passage weren't usual topics of discussion for them.

A group of bulky-looking beasts squeezed past Zoe and Pietro into the bar. They wore medium-grade armor and looked to be warriors of some kind. Pietro nodded in their direction. "Soldiers for hire. See, we're in the right place. I won't waste my time dealing with them one-on-one, though."

The hulking creatures looked like they could've mangled just about anyone they wanted to with their bare hands. "Why not grab one of them, give them a talk, and we get moving?" Zoe asked.

Pietro shook his head while his eyes darted around. "Places like these usually have a broker. I'm starting at the top. I suggest you stay close and don't make eye contact. Stand near but not too close to me. As I said earlier, the reasons for coming to this place are pretty simple: looking for work, looking for a fight, or looking for physical gratification."

Zoe narrowed her eyes and glanced back around the dimly lit room. A long bar divided the area pretty evenly with a few empty spots. She headed for a seat along the bar and saw Pietro follow suit.

After they sat for a few moments, a blonde female bartender came by. She had the world-weary look of someone who'd spent too many hours working in a place like the Dark Passage and was every bit aware of that fact. However, the sight of Pietro melted the barkeep's calm facade a bit into one of blunt surprise. "Um, hi?"

Pietro nodded. "Greetings. I won't waste your time with idle chatter, and I can already tell my appearance has you wondering just who or what I am. Believe me when I say that's none of your concern, and you shouldn't worry about finding out. Understand?"

The barkeep nodded.

"What's your name?" Pietro asked coolly.

The bartender blinked as she attempted to regain her composure. "Dian."

"Wonderful. Dian, I understand this is a great place to hire individuals for work, for various trades."

"It can be." Dian glanced downward, pretending to wipe the bar.

Pietro nodded. "Relax. Keep up your charade. It's best for you anyway. What I'm offering in payment is probably higher than most of your average clients would even consider."

Dian's eyes darted about behind Pietro. "Mmhmm."

"I'm looking for Railen trackers." Pietro had lowered his voice a tad, as even he knew the seriousness of that kind of request.

That brought Dian's eyes slowly back to his. "Railen-"

"-Trackers, that's correct. Now listen. I've got two million in Wenzo Crystals for whoever can deliver one to me."

Dian's eyes widened a bit. She glanced around before she leaned in closer to Pietro, lowering her voice. "We've got a lot of smuggler play in here. I can't rightly say who the best is. I mean, that kinda thing is more about personal preference, who's less of a dick, who's messier about the jobs, things like that."

"I'm sure you have your ways of doling out the work. I'm not going to leave the usual coordination to you, though. This is too serious a run for me to do that, but I'm fine with you passing the word around. I trust you know what I'm talking about and how serious it is."

Dian nodded. "Yep. But you know, I'd feel a lot better about asking around if I knew there was some take in it for me."

Pietro seized up a bit. Zoe noticed Pietro's back heaved more with several sharp breaths.

Finally, Pietro responded. "I can give you five hundred UA credits for your trouble."

Dian nodded. "I'll see who I can rustle up."

Pietro nodded. "Good enough. Give me something to leave a contact channel. Do me a favor and give this out only to someone who is up to the task. Remember, I found this place and you. Don't think I can't return just as easily and be a serious problem for you."

Dian slid a bar register and marker to Pietro while she continued her spree of pretend cleaning. Pietro grabbed the implements, and after a moment's pause, he wrote while a devious grin formed on his face.

Pietro slid the finished note back to Dian and patted the bar gently. Dian seemed relieved. "Are you having a drink or anything?"

Pietro stood. "No, that will be quite enough."

Dian quickly nodded as she pulled off the page with Pietro's note and slid it into her pants pocket. "Ok, then I guess that's all."

Zoe and Pietro headed out of the Dark Passage. She'd thought the visit would've cleared things up about Pietro's search, but they'd only added more questions and mysteries. *Why was Pietro willing to hire someone to find the Trackers? Why had he risked exposing himself in a public place like that?*

"Stop right there," Zoe commanded Pietro as he prepared to move them back to their ship.

Pietro lingered in his stance and eyed Zoe for a few moments before he relaxed and stood upright. "What?"

Zoe flung her arms upwards. "What? Oh, I don't know. Suppose you tell me more about what you're doing here. I helped you get that ship because you told me - no, you promised me - that you'd bring me to Malone. But so far, all we've done is kill some of my people, a Mardak, and go to a tavern attempting to hire someone to find Trackers. We're nowhere nearer to Malone than before we began, and I wonder if I haven't made a mistake coming all this way with you."

At first, Pietro looked at Zoe with annoyance, but then a smidgen of compassion blended in. "I sometimes forget what it was like to be the betrayed one, the one with the ideas that someone else took over when I hadn't the control I thought I did. Let me explain. I want to get Malone to corner himself, and this is the best way to do that."

"Well, what will hiring some random soldier get us?"

"We're not hiring a random soldier - we're aiming to get Malone's son to find a Railen Tracker, so we can kidnap him and use him to draw Malone to us."

NINE

BACK IN HER SEAT, ZOE'S MIND wandered again. Plenty had happened in just over a day, and she wasn't sure about any of it. Her path had become as jagged and uncertain as it ever was.

Pietro's take on the Trackers at least made more sense than their previous capers. She accepted they needed the Regulator for a workable craft, but the death of Rezin was a breach. Didn't others deserve their piece of happiness too? And, what was happiness for Zoe if it meant someone else died for it?

A proximity alert sounded on the console. Zoe adjusted the scan and zoomed in on a convoy passing. She recognized the Nara craft from earlier. *Their ships look so pristine,* Zoe thought. *I wonder what one of those would fetch on a trading market?*

She showed the convoy to Pietro. After a few moments of studying it, he waved his hand. "She'll be in our sights soon enough. We must remain focused on the true prize."

Zoe tapped Network and accessed several feeds of updates from the planets across Ling. Multiple stories cascaded down the holographic display. She grabbed several that showed groups wearing some sort of ceremonial robes.

"Is that some kind of religion, like UA Mysticism?" Zoe asked.

Pietro eyed her with a grim look. "Oh, it's Mysticism, but more like the church of Malone. Those robes are a nod to ceremonial Nara garb, but they've been bastardized with Malone's mark. He's setting himself up as a prophet. If he keeps this up, he won't have to fire a shot. His people will take over Ling Galaxy for him."

The growing admiration for Malone worried Zoe regarding her plans. The blossoming support for Malone surely meant more people were willing to stand in the way of anyone who came after him, and she appreciated more and more Pietro's idea of a subtle approach to take Malone out of the picture.

Zoe expanded the report on Network, and she and Pietro watched the briefing together. The story explained Malone's doings on Agmon. Because he'd had so much success there, he decided to carry it on and head to planet Tausian, where Malone not only provided relief to a starving community but he took up residence with them. His move wasn't just to win over people and leave them to succeed or starve on their own. Instead, he remained for a time in a place, and his residence at Tausian had seen a legion of followers spring up, who erected shrines and temples to him.

"The Tillians have been starving for a while, like the Cerulaks. Can't imagine how bad off they are if they even considered following Malone." Zoe muttered.

She glanced at Pietro, who studied the report on screen intently. "We're not going to get too close to him unless we draw him out."

Zoe looked at the video of followers and wondered just how much Malone had a hand in Network and dictating the course of what was shown to the galaxy.

"They must've seen the slaughters, the murders he's committed, right?" Zoe turned to Pietro. "How can they deify him when he's a murdering bastard?"

Pietro shrugged. "It doesn't matter what the truth is if you can create a reality that sufficient people believe in." Then, with a mild chuckle, Pietro added, "I sense the snare we set on Wenzo is about to be sprung."

"Now then," Pietro paced, his arms folded behind his back. "I need to have the comm unit on this ship ready for when our prey from Wenzo takes the bait. Angle the ship in line with the nearest large star cluster. I want to make sure the reception is perfect."

Zoe worked with the controls for several minutes until the ship's pitch and yaw thrusters responded. Adjustments still took her some time. Pietro soon joined her and verified the *Outspan's* position was suitable for his comm contact.

"Keep an eye on that signal monitor. You'll see it adjusting, for better or worse, depending on your alignment." Pietro glanced out of one of the side views while Zoe kept working her controls.

Zoe jumped a bit when Pietro grabbed her shoulder.

"There, that's it!"

Zoe looked toward the end of Pietro's gnarled extended finger to a ring of stars arranged in an oval.

"Point the ship there."

Several more angling attempts passed, but then their craft was aligned.

"How are we supposed to know he'll be calling?"

"Remember, child; I can search minds. This individual wants a great deal, and the bait we left for him is too good to pass up."

Once the *Outspan* was proximally aligned for comm contact, Zoe set the ship to auto mode. She eased herself out of her seat and pulled into a full-body stretch. Her time spent working in the retooling factory hadn't left her much chance for lounging around, and the excessive amount of sitting she'd done in just a short while on the *Outspan* had taken a toll with a series of sharp pains along her back and legs.

She strode back to where Pietro sat near the Comm portal and launched into a routine of standing stretches. She gasped in mild discomfort as she felt her limbs slowly work their way back into being fully stretched. She later noticed Pietro watching her, a curious glint in his eyes.

"Something on your mind?"

Pietro quickly blinked and shuddered. "Hmm? Oh, no, I was just thinking about how we'll intercept Malone when the time comes."

"I still don't understand why we didn't go after Ellene Ballo. If she's who you say she is, I can't think of a better target to have Malone gun for."

"The problem with Ellene," Pietro countered, "is she'll likely have more than a few defenses with her that we won't be able to beat. All she'd have to do is have some Essence handy, and she could reduce this craft and everything in it, especially the two of us, to a lovely bit of space vapor."

"Well, doesn't Malone have the same ability?"

"Maybe. But Ellene having Essence is a certainty, especially if she's ventured into Ling. I'm not sure of how many Essence powers Malone has yet. Based on his stunt on Agmon, he's got the growth potential of Essence harnessed."

"Have you ever held Essence the way Malone has?"

The question startled Pietro. He glanced sideways, a pained look on his face. Zoe wondered just what had happened to him. The fact that he'd first realized the concept of harnessing Essence made her wonder just how he knew it was possible.

"I have been able to, but since they altered me like this, I don't know if it is possible anymore."

"Well, Malone did it, and wasn't he altered?"

"Yes, but he also had something I didn't: charisma. He developed an industry around himself, finding hope for the lost and discarded in Ling. I imagine he assembled a team, probably including other disconnected Nara, and worked out at least a few of our post-exile physical kinks. People talk about the Syndicate, but Malone's Network is far more dangerous. Their members aren't out for the quick pay and making a living, however devious it is. No. Malone's crew is in it for belief. And belief in a cause, especially a very destructive one, is one of the most powerful forces out there."

Zoe felt a very uneasy feeling throughout her body at Pietro's words, coupled with the wild look in his eyes. For the first time since she had learned about Zaratha's demise, Zoe wondered if the journey of retribution she'd been on was one she had the stomach for after all.

After a long moment at the comm with no incoming transmissions, Pietro rose and headed away for more meditation. While Pietro continued his chants, Zoe retreated to the rear of the Outspan. The comm station called to her. She'd been gone from Cerulia long enough. Maybe she was too far off from ever returning home. But the loneliness she'd felt, briefly absent while with Pietro, was back again. While she knew being back in Cerulia was probably a very doubtful option, she at least needed to grasp for a piece of home, something and preferably someone with whom she could talk. She tapped in the access code to contact Quintus. The comm cycled through the connection routine for a few moments, and then she heard a voice twisted in disbelief.

"Is that really you?"

Quintus appeared on the screen. His face was ashen. Aside from the dirt marks, his eyes said most of what Zoe had been feeling. "Zoe, what's going on? Are you ok?"

Zoe bit her lip and touched the screen. Her throat clenched, but she was too happy to keep quiet, no matter how shaky the words came out. "Hi, yes, I'm fine."

"There's been a major lockdown at Warehouse 13. I heard about a craft theft, and you'd been reported missing."

Zoe strained herself. She wanted to tell Quintus everything so much - that it wasn't her fault, that Pietro had overpowered her. But, the truth was, she'd been so focused on her path that she hadn't realized all that it may have cost her.

"Quintus, I've made an ally. Someone who can help me with what I've been wanting."

For a moment, Zoe thought the connection was broken, but no, it was Quintus frozen at the idea that Zoe's disappearance wasn't out of her control. Zoe saw in Quintus' eyes, the piecing together of precisely what may have happened at the Warehouse on Cerulia.

"Zoe, did you kill those Zamas soldiers?"

Her sides went taut. Quintus eyed her with widened eyes in silence. His question hung in the air between them.

"Not exactly."

Quintus' eyes winced; his mouth was agape. "Not... exactly."

The hope in Quintus' eyes slowly faded, and Zoe's happiness at seeing her old friend quickly jumped to desperation. She realized, at that moment, the friendship between them was at the very least tarnished, if not fractured beyond repair. Zoe's belief that a conversation with Quintus was the cure for all she'd missed was tossed out. Still, she was anxious for him to understand her. Quintus had to have known. He knew what she'd been through, what she'd been going through.

"You have to understand, Quintus. There was no other way."

Quintus bowed his head. "You're one of my oldest friends, Zoe. This is bad. Whatever you...you shouldn't have done this."

The truth in Quintus' words stung Zoe deeply. She knew he was right, but equally as much, she felt trapped in her current course - a path chosen for her that diverged from the rest of her former world.

"Are you going to tell anyone?"

"How could I not? Isn't that what you would've done? What happened to you? What happened to my friend?"

Quintus said no more. Zoe's body shook as she cried out, "I had to. There was no other way."

But the screen went black. Zoe's last tie to her people was gone. So, what was left for her? Blind vengeance?

SOON AFTER ZOE'S last call to Quintus, Pietro's mark took the bait. As Pietro assessed, Malone had been drawn out of hiding. Zoe had drifted into a fitful sleep after her painful conversation with Quintus, desperate to find the way back to her old self that her trip so far had destroyed.

"It's him!"

Pietro's explosive statement jolted Zoe awake. He was at the fore of the *Outspan*, his body bathed in the amber light of the map display, and one planet in particular was zoomed in so much it took up most of the screen.

After a few moments, Zoe stood and approached Pietro as she wiped her eyes. "Planet Tausian?"

"Yes, of course!" Pietro glanced at Zoe before he looked back at the map display. "How could I have missed it? Tausian was always a center of production in Ling, even before the Dark Times. Their distribution of Essence was always a shade higher than the other planets. The level of Replication they are capable of couldn't have been centralized, as it was deemed too volatile. As much as he needs control over Ling Galaxy, he has to have a hand on Replication. With the other planets like your home world being rendered useless, that makes Tausian an absolute gem of a target for him. See here; the UA has been staging craft nearby. This has to be it!"

WHILE TAUSIAN HAD ONCE BOASTED a replication center, the native population of the planet hadn't appeared to have embraced or even benefited from the massive production environment. Zoe wondered if she'd made a mistake on the scans of the planet's population of Tillians, but it seemed that about twenty-five percent were organized in highly industrialized areas. She recognized the Replication layout, as many of the ruins on Cerulia dealt with abandoned Replication facilities. But, aside from the very metropolitan locations, there was a much more significant portion of the planet that consisted of a series of tented cities and what looked to be farming areas. Still, every one she viewed seemed overgrown, even covered over with sand, partially or entirely. She'd only heard about how the Tillians lived before then, but somehow she always imagined it to be different.

"Replication is the key to Malone's future," Pietro explained. "I know your world hosted a Replication industry for a while, so I won't bother with the details. But Essence, now that he's able to wield it, he'll have to reproduce it to become the supplier the Nara used to be and eventually turn his aim to eliminating Grondia. The well-intentioned but clueless lot the UA has been amassing their forces. A working Replication center is far easier to start with than the derelict remnants on your home world and the rest of the Far Reach planets. Malone will eventually head there, I'm sure of it. We just have to be near when the time comes and hope the snare we've set with his son takes effect and draws Malone out of his protective area."

Zoe looked back at the screen, and a deep ache hit her gut at something in the view of the area. She zoomed in closely on an object. It stood out from the drab background around it. The more she zoomed in, the faster her pulse beat in her throat until she recognized the person. The helmet and cape had been all over Network. The outfit of not just a warrior or a conqueror, but someone who claimed themselves to be the savior of Ling Galaxy himself.

"It's Malone. Pietro, look!"

TEN

ONCE ZOE OVERCAME THE SHOCK of seeing Malone in person for the first time, other emotions quickly took hold. She'd wanted this, dreamed of this, needed this for so long. She'd often wondered if it was even possible. Then, finally, Pietro made it happen for her. Pon Ebnora, with all her influence and power, couldn't even make this happen.

Zoe stared at the readouts of the *Outspan's* area scan in disbelief. "I thought Tausian was an advanced, developed planet. The Tillians who live here, they helped us rebuild Cerulia. They're technically gifted. Why are they living like this?"

Pietro glanced at the readouts and shrugged. "Prosperity isn't very contagious. Tillians clung to their simpler ways and chose a life away from the chains of technology and progress. It gave them a simpler life but also made some struggles of theirs tougher than others. There was a largely rural population of Tausian, as in many areas of Ling Galaxy. They supported their side of the world with crop production and fed the industrialized portion. But the famines hit them, like many others. Coupled with Veculus, it drove the once proud community into survival mode, much like your home planet."

Tears formed in Zoe's eyes as she watched the groupings of Tillians and heard Pietro's ongoing assessment of them. He talked about their deaths from starvation with the ease of someone reading assembly instructions. What hurt Zoe most was how much these poor, needy creatures gave their knowledge so freely to Cerulia when they themselves had next to nothing.

"What could Malone possibly want with them? They're no threat at all!"

"Spectacle, child. He wants spectacle. At this point, Malone can travel into a black hole, and he wouldn't be alone. Network would follow him. He's too well known to be ignored. He's caused enough of a stir in Ling Galaxy that any deed he does is captured. His Lookers, remember, disrupt whatever Malone doesn't want the galaxy to see, so the image of Malone to the masses remains a benevolent providing figure. He's winning this war through diplomacy, which is the best weapon available."

Zoe guided the *Outspan* on a mildly wobbling arc toward the settlement while she strained her eyes for a closer look. She hadn't made readouts of any substantial tech in the area, but there were plenty of life forms. Her Cerulak blood, long cooled from her endless mantra of revenge, suddenly found a new chill point as she realized what she was looking at.

"These are refugees at best, Pietro." Among the many casualties of the conflict in Ling Galaxy, the group before them was from another place, or maybe several. They were hunkered down and braced the best they could for something that may hit them or not. Uncertainty was just one of several unpleasant rules by which they lived. And Malone, the noble and decent one, had seen fit to take shelter among them.

"He's hiding in plain sight, using those Tillians as shields for himself. It's the basest of acts I could've ever expected from someone as ruthless as he is. See? He doesn't care about life; we've got to end his."

Zoe stared, motionless and silent. She heard Pietro's assessment, and whether he admitted it or not, Pietro had a philosophy that wasn't that far removed from Malone's. And suddenly, Zoe felt physically out of her body and watching the scene from somewhere else, from someone else's mind, from the sense of a sister watching her flesh and blood killed by Malone. *They're both in this,* she thought. *The less I do about this, the more I'm involved. It's not right to have anyone suffer.*

Zoe realized that what she wanted, what she needed, that she believed more than anything would've brought her peace, would, in this case, only further the cycle, creating more suffering in those left behind. *I can't stop them, but I can stop him.*

Zoe grabbed for Pietro's arm, and after a moment, he turned. But the look in his eye had changed. It wasn't the kindly supporting glance she'd seen. This had a far different glint.

"We're going to kill everyone down there."

"What?"

"Those are Malone's people. We must take them out. There's no telling how much he's infected them already."

"Pietro, these are Tillians. They aren't serving Malone. I know this for a fact. If anything, they are being held hostage."

Pietro replied with a silent glare.

"They are one of the few friends Cerulia has. I can't do it!"

Zoe shook at the realization that Pietro's vision wasn't so much for ending Malone but for becoming something similar himself. It was bad enough thinking of the deaths of her fellow Cerulaks in Warehouse 13 and kindly old Rezin. The murder of the Tillians, a race that had only offered Cerulaks comradeship, something her parents supported, was too much. Even her sister, Zaratha, couldn't have supported that. Zoe knew, no matter what, while she wanted Malone dead, furthering the trail of blood Pietro began only moved her down a path of becoming like Pietro, or worse yet, Malone.

I let Quintus down. I let Pon down. If I don't stop Pietro now, I'll let my parents and Zaratha down. And that I won't do.

"That's an unarmed settlement, Pietro." Still, Zoe tried to reason with Pietro over how killing even more innocents wasn't the right way to get Malone. Zoe glanced into Pietro's cold eyes, and a chill hit her body at the lack of remorse she found in them.

"N-no, we can't take out those Tillians."

"I'm not concerned with saving a few pathetic life forms. Don't you realize who that is? We'll lose our chance if we don't attack him now."

Zoe held onto her desire for revenge against Malone for so long, but she hadn't thought about what that revenge would've looked like. *What are we really doing here?* She wondered. *Any one of them down there could've been Zaratha. Am I any better for being part of their deaths than Malone was for killing Zaratha?*

The question asked, the answer was in front of her too, but she had ignored it. But now, it slapped her like a deluge of ice-cold water. The vengeance that had infected her soul, her entire being, had been revealed to be toxic. This wasn't her. This wasn't the sister Zaratha remembered, and it sure wasn't who Zaratha would've wanted alive, carrying on her memory.

Pietro shouted. "The weapons on this ship will easily lay waste to those people. Malone won't have time to fight back. What's the matter? From the moment I knew about you, I've known the desire that burns in your heart. I've given you what you've been wanting, haven't I? Now, do as I say and finish this!"

Pietro's eyes glowed a brilliant deep blue, and Zoe felt the anger that coursed out of his body. It wasn't hard to notice. He frightened her on their first meeting, but here he'd become scarier than she could've imagined. *Will that be me?* She wondered. *Will this rage consume me to that point one day? It can't. Zaratha wouldn't have wanted that.*

Zoe watched the Tillians surrounding Malone. Young males and females. Families. Babies. She squeezed the control yoke until her hands burned like fire. Her insides tensed until she shook.

Then, Zoe jerked her body to the left. The *Outspan* rolled

sharply in response until they were aimed at one of the nearest mountains.

Zoe looked into Pietro's wild eyes.

"I'm not helping you kill any more innocents."

"Not even innocents surrounding Malone Stanton?"

Zoe shook her head. "When we first met, and I told you about Malone Stanton, you said we'd only kill him. I'm not killing anyone that doesn't deserve it. My sister didn't deserve it, and neither do they."

Pietro frowned deeply. "This is our cause. Malone will kill far more than the few you see there, child. Don't think you're saving the galaxy by just protecting a few."

Zoe's path of revenge had taken her through the depths of her anguish and had driven a wedge between her and her people, even friends like Quintus, forever. It cost her so much, but with her life, she knew the enemy she was after had been hidden from her. It wasn't Malone but those who believed as he did. Pietro, as noble as he portrayed himself to be, was nothing more than another Malone, and while Zoe couldn't have killed Malone, she had in her reach the ability to at least stop someone who looked to be just as evil. Had she let Pietro kill Malone, what would Pietro have become? Another tyrant to one day decide another Zaratha was out of line enough to deserve being killed?

Zoe quickly hit the controls for a quick path out of the area, but Pietro slammed his fist on the console. She jumped and yelped in fright.

"Don't even think of that. We're finishing this, and you're going to help me. Don't you want this? This man killed your blood. It's time for revenge."

Pietro had so many gifts and abilities, but Zoe realized he was missing one thing that she still had. Connection to a family. She missed them, and it was too late to go back. But, she still had a play... one chance where what she did could've at least honored what her parents believed. So, with a steady hand, Zoe swung the *Outspan* around. Pietro stumbled about the bridge and clutched the walls for support.

"What are you doing?" Pietro's eyes glowed with a near neon tint.

"I can't stop you from doing what you want, but I can stop myself from helping you."

Alarms rang on the Outspan's onboard system as it veered on a beeline course for the nearest mountain ridge. Pietro, pinned down by the shift in g force, growled at Zoe, his voice twisted into a vibrating screech. "Stop now!"

But Zoe didn't. She felt more like herself and Zaratha's sister than she had since her fateful meeting in the Warehouse. She wasn't sure if this was the end, but she was ready for it if it was. Finally, her thoughts and conscience were clear.

400 METERS TO IMPACT.

Thoughts of Malone dimmed. *Malone won't get what's coming to him from me, but he'll get something someday.*

Someone will show him, to keep him under control, make him know what he stood for was nothing that Ling Galaxy wanted or ever needed.

250 METERS TO IMPACT

Zoe grasped the controls so tightly her hands burned. She felt a hand on her shoulder and leaned forward, but Pietro's hands began to snake down her arms in an attempt to free them from the controls.

100 METERS TO IMPACT

He won't get me.

He won't reach me.

He's failed.

This is for you, Zaratha.

I love you.

In her final moments, Zoe felt a euphoric rush as years of pain over her losses and the pure hatred she felt over Malone whispered out of her system like an expelled infection. She cried tears of relief and joy as her surroundings were engulfed in white light and fierce heat.

The *Outspan* met the unremarkable mountain on Tausian in a spectacular explosion. The fuselage of the Outspan was smashed in an instant into a small cube. Pietro had held onto a lever for the release hatch on the top, which broke free on impact, ejecting Pietro along with it.

PIETRO WOKE IN A DAZE. His vision blurred; he rubbed his eyes for an instant until the searing pain in his hand was too much, and he bellowed in agony. He raised himself slowly to a seated position. The ground beneath him was brittle, coarse, and dry. Through his clouded sight, he still made out the column of black smoke that wafted from where the *Outspan* had impacted and exploded into a million fragments, taking with it the only individual in Ling Galaxy who'd helped him at all.

His mind stirred at the sight and the thought of Zoe gone, and he was filled with confusion and anger. *How could she have done that?* He wondered. *I could've helped her. Unfortunately, she was too selfish to see it.*

Pietro staggered to his feet. His cloak and clothing were in tatters, and from the look of the ever-growing cloud of smoke from the crash site, he was stranded on the planet indefinitely. Finally, after a few hours' walk, he reached the settlement of Tillians he'd spotted previously. Although the collection of tented abodes was anything but advanced or even tech-heavy, Pietro knew, in time and some personal investment, opportunities were possible, even from the most unlikely of places.

Once the Tillians nearby caught sight of Pietro, they huddled and gave loud whoops. The cries were intent on scaring Pietro, but he strolled, his hands in the air.

"I come in peace," he spoke slowly. "I was a prisoner who escaped. My captors crashed that ship on your planet. I offer you my sorrow and hope to make reparations."

Pietro stood a good two to three feet taller than the Tillians. Their small builds were nonetheless stocky. As Pietro moved, they edged closer to him in curiosity.

One of the Tillians, the tallest one of the group, approached Pietro. The cloaks that covered them were adorned with a ceremonial-looking hat. After a slight bow, they started. "We are a simple people. We don't tolerate aggression. If that's your cause, leave us in peace."

Pietro offered a slight bow in response. "I assure you, that's not my intent." He glanced around but saw no one around who hadn't appeared Tillian. "Tell me. I was looking for a Malone Stanton. Do any of you know where I might find him?"

The cloaked Tillian cleared his throat. "He transported off this planet. Said he had preparations to make."

Pietro gnashed his jaw. *Interesting move there, old friend. This chase of mine will continue later.* Then, nodding, he said to the Tillian chief, "Would you be so kind as to shelter me until I can arrange a way to get back to my people."

Pietro's offer was cautiously accepted. He was thankful the charm he'd developed during his exile from Grondia had taken hold, at least somewhat. He had to figure his way off-world from this place, however. The nearest craft available wasn't too close, and the meager abilities of the Tillians to communicate with the outside world were a significant problem for him. Still, he realized the isolation he once again found himself in was a little like his initial exile from Grondia. And, while that was a long road to pass, he had made it through that and had confidence he'd find his way back again somehow. However, Malone was still in his sights and wasn't ready to let that go.

Pietro crouched in the tent as the viewscreen blinked to life, and the picture changed to Pon Ebnora as she addressed her people on Cerulia. They'd reached another benchmark, and their forces had become strong enough for a more forward push into Ling Galaxy. No longer were they going to be the punching bag of the galaxy and cast aside by the more deliberate and powerful Omegans or even the resurgent Railen. The Cerulaks were ready to stake their claim in the galaxy.

"Good," Pietro thought. "More recruitment opportunities."

He believed to his core it was not only possible for him to continue, but his ordained destiny. He pulled the bowl of soup close and inhaled the fragrance of the spices for a moment before he hungrily devoured the warm liquid. It wasn't great, but like so much he'd done to get to where he was, it was enough.

STRATAGEM AWAKENING

ONE

"CAREFUL WITH THOSE measurements."

Charista Mantisword nodded at the order from Bezar Hornell, her shift commander. Charista had checked the calculations on the navigation console several times. There was more going on than just a review from an ornery supervisor, though, and Charista knew it. She tapped controls with way more effort than necessary, and the display cycled through several very familiar views, but Charista knew the scrutiny was just part of the routine that was her life.

The navigation screen blinked, showing the plotted course of Omegan frigate *Trussel* in green, indicating a successful chart. Charista glanced up into Bezar's scowl and replied. "Course plot successful." *Do we have to go through this every single time?*

Bezar glanced past Charista at the display before he walked off with a series of grunts.

That's the nicest response I've gotten from most superior officers on this mission.

In reality, things could've been much worse for Charista, given her history and, more so, her family's history. Her father Findlay was executed for sharing troop moves with the enemy Railen. Findlay's action at the time was intended to be strategic, but it backfired in the worst way. After a challenging assignment in Omegan Retooling, where she reworked spent tech into being reusable, Charista was given her job on the *Trussel*.

Charista edged up from her seat and peeked up and down the hallway. She figured she at least had a few minutes, based on how often someone came by to second guess whatever she'd been doing. Her navigation duties handled for the moment, Charista took to her favorite hobby. In addition to course-plotting and comms, her console gave her access to Network.

Network's galaxy-wide collection of transmissions from comms, news reports, and recorded conversations was a mess. Without the benefit of good curation, the UA implemented the system in an attempt to spread information throughout Ling Galaxy. The growing efforts at maintaining distribution networks throughout Ling made it a challenge, so Network grew organically, about as orderly as the average mold spore colony.

The screech of static burst over the comm speakers until Charista adjusted the frequency enough. Still, the data stream, like a typical one from Network, was a long line of audio chatter and video clips. Finding helpful information on Network wasn't entirely impossible, but it was time-consuming without the benefit of a Sift Routine.

Once the Omegana Sift Routine appeared on Charista's screen, she disabled it. She entered her bypass codes she'd developed, which triggered a few warning messages. Omegana wasn't concerned about most of the information on Network, just the bits that dealt with troop moves and the UA. Charista wanted a deeper dive, so she'd created her own private Sift Routine. Charista flexed her fingers. Her father taught her ways around even the most stringent Omegan technological defenses, and those were thankfully still breakable with some effort. Omegana valued the power of a gun or blade far more than that of tech; a soft underbelly Charista was glad to exploit.

A clip about the Railen appeared and stopped Charista from her casual skim. The Railen race were already divided, but thanks to a well-organized Omegan assault, most of the Railen race were nomads. No word was given or even clear on where the Railen would end up, but a video of their motley collection of craft headed for an unknown destination looked sad to Charista.

Charista glanced into the hallway again. So far, she hadn't been spotted scanning Network with a non-Omegan Sift, which was forbidden since it was beyond her assigned duties.

Footsteps sounded down the corridor. Charista hid the Sift Scan and returned her console to the Navigation view. The footsteps got louder.

Charista craned her neck for a view and saw Isaac Pyatt nursing his handheld device as he walked. In the Omegana military, kiss-ups weren't discouraged, but bravery was what gave an Omegan soldier the awards and status they all craved. Isaac had mastered the kiss-up part for sure. However, he hadn't quite established himself in the bravery in battle category, which explained his assignment to *Trussel*. Isaac had only been out of the Omegan Academy a year before Charista, which was enough for him to outrank her.

She'd returned to her console, watching the indicator of the scan, a pulsating icon. She watched the screen for a few minutes until she heard Isaac immediately behind her.

"Status on our course?"

Charista stiffened and spun in her chair until she met Isaac's devious grin. "Calculated, with alternate intercepts factored in. I anticipated we'll run comms checks to planet Agmon before landing, so I brought our trajectory near the more populated side for an easier test."

Isaac nodded and tapped notes into his device, held close against his uniform's pressed gray fabric. *How can gray fabric have a shine?* The few ribbons on Isaac's chest area also seemed to glimmer mockingly. *Isaac must have little to do besides memorizing regulations into rote memory and how universally crucial those were to anything worthwhile. I bet his primary mission was finding the failings of those other than himself.* "Very good, I'll pass that along to the captain and -" His eyes focused past Charista toward the console.

Please let him not have seen anything. I hid the search, didn't I?

Isaac pointed toward Charista's screen. "What's that?"

Charista swallowed hard and turned slowly. *Of course - the Sift Routine had signaled completion; the flashing indicator on the screen was as subtle as a punch to the face.*

Charista's neck tightened as she scrambled for any halfway decent alibi. "Environmental analysis-"

"-Are you running a Sift?" asked Isaac.

Charista clenched her fists. Isaac had been a busybody to not just her but several others on the ship. Charista watched him previously breaking down crew over uniform code violations and even improper maintenance processes.

I bet the suck-up would make someone check the Trussel exterior mid-flight if he could've gotten away with it.

Once the initial wave of apprehension settled on Charista, it was replaced with one of her many mantras, calming focused thoughts she used in the months and years since her father's execution.

My path is forward, my cause is right, and no one will stop me.

Charista's mind, honed and developed through her early years of watching her father work, and her mother's warrior cunning intellect gave her faculties a sharp focus. But, that said, Charista also knew that while Isaac was an idiot, she had a role to play for the time, one of the dutiful officers who begged more than anything to remain in the good graces.

Once Charista relaxed, she replied to Isaac, who was still fixated on her screen. "You're pretty good at knowing regulations. Did you forget the one about scans of a planet without a confirmed Omegan presence before arrival? T85-13?"

Isaac's face simmered with resentment. Even a stickler like himself had to admit the rule of regulation was as gospel as any religion could've ever professed. Charista savored the change in his expression from triumphant whistleblower to off-put sycophant.

Isaac only replied, "Just report any required course deviations as soon as they are identified."

"Don't I always?"

Isaac's eyes narrowed. "Carry on." He thrust himself down the corridor.

Once Isaac turned the corner at the far end, Charista gave a shuddered sigh. It was a good play for her, and she wondered how many more she needed before getting to a position of power where she was the one to whom everyone else answered.

A series of aches bloomed along Charista's upper and lower back. The pains reminded her of how long she'd sat in her cubby. Her shift ran several hours, and the seat made that time feel way longer. She was in the middle of a half-hearted attempt at a stretch when several low-pitched creaks distracted

Charista's attention. Two crew members dashed down the hallway past her cubby entrance a few moments later. She glanced out into the hall in their direction for a moment before she shook her head. The *Trussel* had such a reputation for malfunction it earned the far from desirable nickname, the "*Trashel.*"

Charista caught a few words from the crew as they worked on the issue. Evidently, some stabilizers had malfunctioned and were being patched per the order of the day. *Trussel's* fate once they returned to Omegana wasn't filled with a lot of bright hope, but as long as they returned in one piece, that was enough for Charista.

The sound of boots clanking on metal drew Charista's attention up the hall. This time it was Kindra Montes. When their eyes met, Kindra smiled slightly as she walked up close.

"Are we done with this voyage yet?" Kindra asked.

Charista smiled a bit. Her tension eased at the sight of a friendly face for a change. Kindra came up with Charista in the Omegan academy, but the two knew each other from childhood. While news of Findlay's crime and sentencing drove most Omegans away from

Charista, it hadn't lost her Kindra as a friend. Charista was grateful for Kindra's seeing through the perceived disloyalty of her father.

Charista sighed. "If only we were back at home port. But, I guess we have this mission to Agmon first, right?"

Kindra nodded. "Off to the lovely planet of Agmon, now that Malone Stanton has worked his magic on it. Of course, we don't get much play time, just a simple housing set up for an Omegan garrison."

"Yeah. Tell you something else; I'm done with Isaac Pyatt." Charista sighed.

Kindra shook her head violently at Charista's assessment. "It's bad enough being on this scrap heap of a frigate, but dealing with his issues too? What's his problem? Jerk gets good marks in training, so he sticks it to everyone else?"

"He got you too?" Charista asked.

"Yeah, on my analysis reports. We're supposed to run these scans of Agmon, right? Ensure we've got the best spots for the Omegan installation. He decides to review my report and contacts Captain Risberg about it. That little bastard got me my second reprimand inside of two weeks."

"Oh, that's right, your second... you little uniform code violator."

Charista shook her head as Kindra swiped at her arm. The only good thing about Kindra's news was it confirmed Isaac's diligent attention to all things procedural wasn't saved just for Charista. Instead, Isaac had the distinction of being an equal opportunity annoyer. "At least your father wasn't branded an enemy of the state. I'm lucky I wasn't permanently placed in a sanitation detail some-where." Charista's pained chuckle betrayed the truth behind her words.

Kindra patted her friend's arm. "It hasn't been easy for you, has it?"

Charista shook her head glumly.

"Guess I'll have to team up with Adarsha to cheer you up, as long as we can break her away from her post with Security." Adarsha, another classmate of Charista and Kindra's, shared space on the *Trussel* with them. The two were Charista's only saving grace on a ship where the rest of the crew saw Charista as some kind of infection to be cleared up as soon as possible.

Kindra glanced back up the hallway, then back to Charista. "Look at it this way. We're on this stretch for another four weeks, give or take. Once we're back on Omegana, we'll have a little break before our next deployment, especially if they get smart and finally ditch the *Trashel* - I mean, *Trussel*."

That got a chuckle from Charista, and Kindra smiled at her friend's brief lift in spirit.

Charista stretched again, working on the endless knots in her back. "Guess I should get back to work. Wouldn't want to give Isaac another reason for a write-up."

"Right?" Kindra nodded. "OK. Let's meet in the galley next time our shifts line up."

Charista nodded with a smile, and Kindra took off down the hallway.

After a few more useless attempts at easing her back pains, Charista settled back into the hum drum of her work, eyeing the onboard systems of *Trussel* and checking the ship's progress on its designated course. Her almost serene focus was jolted when the comm squawked to life with several voices. The Omegan Horde, deployed sections of the Omegan army, proceeded throughout Ling Galaxy on various missions. The underlying directive ordered there were never less than two Horde units in proximity of each other, ready to consolidate if any team needed extra firepower, while keeping their overall objective of canvassing as much of Ling Galaxy as possible.

The view on Charista's console, showing a holographic chart of Ling Galaxy, flickered several times. Charista tapped the display panel, correcting the issue. The stars and systems of Ling floated about the room. A blue line indicated the *Trussel's* position and course all the way to its end destination. Charista switched her view to the rest of the nearby planets. Together with Malone Stanton, the Omegan goal was to canvas Ling Galaxy and lay claim to it, one piece at a time. Yassel was the ultimate prize, but the more footholds they established first, the more the UA control of Ling slipped away.

Since Isaac made his regular round by Charista, she figured she at least had a little time to contact Joanna. Charista knew she still had to be careful - communicating with the Railen, sworn enemies of the Omegans, was a fast track to imprisonment at the very least. Despite the risk, Charista craved the moments with Joanna. It was her last link to her father's memory, someone who knew him as Joanna did.

Charista hoped she timed her next round of supervisor checks as she closed the portal to her cubby and activated the comm to Joanna. Charista immediately noticed Joanna's former Railen uniform, or what was left of it. The garb Joanna still wore from her Railen outfit was reduced to a single patch, but she kept it along with a heavy cloak, with her uniform remnants as a sash around her neck.

"You're hell-bent on keeping that, aren't you?" Charista asked.

Joanna's eyes closed with a knowing grin. "I'm a Railen, Charista. Vengeance is in our DNA."

"Not unlike Omegans," Charista replied. They shared a laugh over their respective heritage of betrayal and abandonment. Joanna's contributions helped her fellow Railen from their start as bastard Nara outcasts to a technologically capable race. She gave them the tools that went with the raging lust for power and revenge that was homegrown.

"How are you doing since the flight?"

Joanna shrugged. "It was hard and still is. We've settled on a moon around planet Cerulia. We had a few vehicles tucked away, so we'll be regrouping in little time."

"I guess we'll run into each other out here at some point," Charista's throat tightened in worry about the idea of her and Joanna on two opposite sides in the same conflict. The average Omegan had no use for the Railen and weren't at all beyond obliterating the Railen, and the feeling was mutual. The attack of the Omegans on the former Railen stronghold at Delfina was just another in a series of pushes each side made against the other.

The warmth in Joanna's face faded. "Listen, dear. I know you've got plenty to worry about already, but I have to tell you something."

Charista leaned in closer to the screen. The fragile system she'd set up with Joanna depended on many things, and a possible change in any of that worried her.

"The Brescar shipments were halted." While Essence remained the primary source of life and energy in Ling Galaxy, many attempted to replicate a usable substitute. Brescar was Findlay's attempt, and while well worth the effort, the volatility associated with the substance was too much for Omegana to use. The excess quantities of Brescar were kept with the plans by Omegana of disposing the stuff one day, once the Omegan conquest was less of a priority. Findlay, and Charista after his death, arranged for Brescar to be sent secretly to Joanna, who carried on the work to make Brescar a viable energy source in Ling Galaxy one day.

"Halted?" Charista said the word with a mix of surprise and annoyance.

Joanna nodded.

"I'll check with Edin when I get back to Omegana. That's all I can do." Charista took a shuddered breath as she felt her pulse rattle in her throat. "Will this ever get easier?" She knew Joanna had no answer for that, but still asking the question made her feel like she was doing...something.

Charista rubbed the back of her aching neck. She was in a race for several things but only felt like she slipped further behind with each day. *Things have to work out at some point. Joanna's smart like Dad; she'll get Brescar usable somehow. Besides ruling Omegana, energy dominance is the only other true power in Ling Galaxy.*

Joanna gave a pained smile in response. "It's OK, dear. We've just got to keep pushing."

The determination in Joanna's voice made Charista realize since the Railen kept up their crusade after all the horrible situations they faced, there was no reason Charista couldn't have persevered either.

"I'm closing this comm for now, so I don't test my luck any further," Charista smiled and added a wave.

Joanna grinned in kind as their transmission ended.

CHARISTA RETURNED to glances at Network and the other part of her job, checking the comm transmissions for anything that affected the *Trussel's* mission. While most of the comm was standard Horde transmissions, giving unit numbers, locations, and status, one message broke over the rest and caught Charista's attention, just by the name it mentioned.

"Stanton has been sighted near far reach planet Tausian. Requesting assistance."

Oh, the god needs help from Mother Omegana now?

Charista scoffed. The Omegans had entered into a pact with Malone Stanton, thanks to their Emperor Zakmar. Zakmar was most interested in Omegan domination of Ling Galaxy, but was shrewd enough not to butt heads with Malone, at least for a time. Instead, Zakmar saw in Malone a chance for them to side with a huge threat and take Malone's attention off Omegana, so Zakmar could one day have a structure in place to handle Malone and keep him in control.

A quick scan of the sector of Ling for Tausian showed a few Horde units in proximity, so Charista repointed the message to those groups, notifying them of the issue.

Malone has everyone eating out of his hand. He'll be at my feet one day, just like everyone else.

An alert klaxon blared on the comm and activated the video screen on the unit. Charista was startled by the image of

Commander Chun on screen. After a moment, she snapped a salute.

"Connect me to Risberg immediately."

"T-the captain, sir?" Charista asked.

Chun's brow creased. "Are you deaf, ensign? Transfer, now!"

Charista forwarded the communication to Captain Risberg. She wondered what was so urgent about their mission. The *Trussel's* trek was light years from conquest for the action hungry who wanted only a long and violent spar with the enemy. The *Trussel's* primary foe was boredom. Her threat, sagging crew morale over being relegated to one of the more meaningless assignments in the eyes of Omegans like the Horde.

A series of chimes echoed through the halls, indicating the current shift's end. Charista leaned back in her seat in relief. *It seemed like it would never get here.* As she collected her things, she thought about all the pieces in play... Malone, Joanna, the Railen, the Omegans, even pitiful little Isaac. *So many options, just what to do with them all?*

It was a question for another time.

———

ONCE THE *TRUSSEL* reached a distance of three standard days from Agmon, Captain Risberg called a crew briefing to review deployment procedures and confirm all crew assignments.

Charista was headed to the meeting when a hand grabbed her arm and stopped her short, and her eyes met those of Commander Pit Darin, or simply "Pit." Pit was larger than the average Omegan, with a resting scowl and broad frame that gave most Omegans second thoughts about grappling with him. He began his Omegana military career during the last few years of Nara Service. The scars that adorned his face and arms hinted at plenty of stories, and Charista knew she wasn't interested in hearing any of them.

"Where you going, traitor?"

Charista's face flushed hot. "Heading to the briefing as ordered, sir."

Pit gnashed his jaw. His face had the usual greenish scales of the average Omegan, with an extra assortment of scars. Charista forced back a gag reflex at the odor of Pit's breath, which reeked with a rancid rotted meat smell and some strange hint of something burnt. For any junior officer, joining a new crew came with at least a few moments of harassment by one or more senior Omegan officers, and Pit had bucked for the position of high priest of the Omegan Church of War for a long time.

"Just because you're on this ship don't mean I got to like it. You're on my watch, so keep your mouth shut and follow orders. I'll jettison you outta here if you get on my bad side, understand?"

"Affirmative." Charista's voice was low, her eyes locked into Pit's. After a moment, Pit grunted and sauntered off.

The briefing was short and sweet. Omegans were coming to establish their own Garrison on Agmon to extend the reach of the Horde, and *Trussel* was delivering supplies needed for their forward base. The crew was instructed to keep scans out for the UA craft since the movement of supplies to Agmon was sure to arouse UA attention. While *Trussel* had armaments, it was short on the kind of weaponry for a full-out battle if the UA moved to overpower and confiscate their craft for any number of trumped-up UA violations.

Pit Darin assigned the crew tasks on Agmon to deploy the Omegan base structure. While Kindra and Adarsha were given set up and configuration tasks, Charista's assignment kept her onboard, running the analysis for the return trip. She'd have liked a slight bit of on-planet time. Long voyages locked on starcraft weren't great for the psyche, but Charista figured with Pit in charge of her welfare, she wasn't getting comfort anytime soon. *I'm sure Isaac has his little hand-picked list of ground crew, and I'm a few light years away from being included there.*

ONCE THE TROOPS aboard *Trussel* and those already on site organized their operations, *Trussel* left Agmon, returning to

Omegana. As productive as the primary mission had been, Charista's ultimate goal needed more simmering before it was ready. Her biggest fear at that point was not knowing what happened to Edin and the Brescar deliveries. *Either he was killed or arrested.* Neither was good, but an arrest would've brought more trouble than her reputation already invited.

TWO

ON HER NEXT SHIFT DURING the voyage home, Charista returned to her Network Sift when a wave of emotion hit her and instantly stopped her thoughts. It happened like that, from time to time. She'd been fine, focused on her work, plans, and sadness struck her without warning. She knew what it was when it happened, though. She was an adult orphan, trying to figure things out. There wasn't even the shell of Omegana's camaraderie to comfort her. While the average Omegan had plenty of news and stories about the Horde wreaking havoc in Ling to stir their pride and bolster their spirits, the nation and its goals diverted from Charista's awhile back. She was along for the ride but wasn't in for any benefits.

Charista's latest Network Sift run brought back more information, but she wasn't sure how much was helpful. She flipped through reports from the UA on just how well they thought Ling Galaxy held on during the tough times, chatter from the Railen, dealing with their recent exile, and various fragments of transmissions from Syndicates around Ling Galaxy: soldiers for hire and those who managed a profit even when so many faced starvation.

Your parents are gone.

Charista blinked the tears away and waited for the feeling to pass. It did; it just sometimes took a bit. But she was ready; she'd wait until she felt better. This time it held a bit more, so she shut her eyes and reached for the controls on her screen. She'd done the task enough, first in training in the Academy and then later in prep for her assignment. The job wasn't overly complex and easy enough that the routine diverted attention from the pain she felt. It would get easier one day, she promised herself. She just didn't know when.

After so many hours of searching through the endless geyser of information, the data and video streams became a blur to her. She'd looked away for a moment, feeling another bout coming over her emotions, when she glanced back and saw something unexpected on the screen.

This could be something... a report on a movement of Xeno from planet Zormad to Yassel and UA headquarters. The UA is engaging with the Omegans and others all over Ling; why risk sending a transport through all the fray? That's pretty boneheaded, even for the UA. Still, Charista's curiosity was yanked quite firmly toward the story, so she dug further.

The reports were few, but it was unusual enough that she found them fascinating. The Xeno had made an unremarkable entrance into Ling as a fledgling race on a feeble ark ship. No one knew what brought Xeno to Ling Galaxy, but they seemed mostly harmless from all appearances.

The Xeno were an interesting case to those who took a little time and studied their story a little deeper. The debate in Ling Galaxy over many things washed over the Xeno, while some barely considered them a footnote. It wasn't until rumors spread about the Nara taking an interest in the Xeno that Charista thought there might be some value in the derelict race. After all, they'd not only been enduring the rough, unfamiliar conditions of Ling Galaxy itself, but the Xeno had made a dangerous, even crazy trek over numerous sectors from a distant galaxy to Ling. As powerless as they may have been, they showed they had more than enough stamina for who knew what else.

Charista adjusted the scan from *Trussel's* course toward the UA transport ship headed to Yassel and thoroughly checked the contents. Detailed charts appeared, listing counts of lifeforms aboard, ages, and other vital information. She stored the output of the personnel tallies on a Data Tag and stuffed it in one of the inner folds of her uniform.

In any case, Charista believed the Xeno weren't as mewling as what most of Ling had written them off as. The Railen had a few runs with the Xeno, but it was a mess for the Railen, at least at first. The Xeno fought back and killed several Railen in the process, and when the Railen returned to finish the job on the Xeno, even that mission wasn't a complete success.

The Xeno are as much a bastard race as the Railen, but they're tough. Maybe they'd be interested in some kind of alliance. They probably just want to survive. They could be handy if the rumors I've heard about them and Essence are true.

She gathered her notes and headed for the captain's quarters. Kai Risberg, captain of the *Trussel*, had seen his share of fights in his youth, a time that had passed him by a bit. But, in his middle-aged Omegan years, he managed a commanding authority over the crew of the *Trussel* and ran the ship without insubordination.

Charista snapped a salute at the entrance to Risberg's quarters. "Sir, thank you for agreeing to see me. I wanted you to know soon as I found out." Charista activated her display tablet and held it out for Risberg. He eyed the device for a moment as if it was a questionable piece of meat. "What exactly am I looking at?"

"Sir, it's the Xeno. I know they're not a serious threat to our mission, but I think we're overlooking something valuable there. The UA has just sent a mission through the lines to planet Zormad to bring the Xeno to Yassel."

Risberg steepled his fingers and leaned back in thought. For a moment, Charista beamed in anticipation of his praise for her insight. Just because the *Trussel* was on the low order of service in the

Omegan fleet, it hadn't meant the ship or its crew had nothing valuable to offer.

However, with an annoyed grunt, Risberg arched his brow and stared blankly at Charista. "So what?"

"Sir, we have enough Horde deployed throughout Ling. The UA convoy is fairly light. It wouldn't take much Omegan craft to overtake it and grab that asset. If the Xeno are that important to the UA, that makes them important to us, so we should intercept that convoy. Anything that hurts the UA has to be good for us, right?"

Risberg leaned back in his seat as his eyes narrowed. Charista had been in the captain's service long enough to know what came next wasn't anything on the order of a glorious citation of her enterprising discovery. "Ensign Mantisword..." Risberg said Charista's rank with the emphasis like her even having that rank was a slam against the Omegan military. "You've been assigned to this ship because you've distinguished yourself in the last piss hole they stuck you in. Don't for a moment think I forgot what put you there. I lost good troops in that maneuver your father leaked to the Railen. I don't want to hear any more about your searches in Ling Galaxy, which are unauthorized and unnecessary. Omegana has her sights on all of Ling Galaxy. This takes a wide-reaching effort by the Horde, Ensign. You'll learn what that means one day. The Omegans won't be avoided; we'll be around. If this convoy is en route to Yassel as you say it is, they'll be found, either en route or when we advance on UA headquarters in time. That's enough for now. Get back to your post, and don't bother me again unless it's related to your duties."

Captain Risberg pointed to the door before he returned to his viewscreen, a readout of the *Trussel's* current course and nearby planets of note on it. Charista snapped a salute so sharply that the fabric on her uniform gave a loud rustle. "Aye aye, sir." Charista spun on one heel and left.

Charista felt her face flush hot as she walked back to her post. *Why do they even bother giving me any assignment besides rooting through the junk in Retooling? They'll never listen to my ideas until they get something useful handed to them.*

Back in her station, she activated a scan for the portion of Ling Galaxy where the UA transport had likely been and ran a search for Omegan craft in the vicinity. She smiled when the battle cruiser *Praximus* came into view. *I don't care what Risberg thinks. We can't let this pass by. Intercepting an innocent convoy would be easy for the Praximus, the way Captain Ve Bartosik thought of himself as the Prince Hunter of Omegana.*

Charista smiled as she again disabled the normal processes on her panel. Her father's skills worked through her again, and she found herself able to create a very official-looking transmission.

"Attention *Praximus*: large convoy leaving planet Zormad en route to Yassel. Passengers and cargo aboard are believed to be Xeno, among other valuables for the UA. Proceed at once on an intercept course. Slaughter all that are not of Xeno origin and return craft and contents to Omegana."

Charista smirked at the message. She knew the lies in the text were more than necessary to give her people and herself a chance at finding the true path to power in their fight.

Her insides knotted up with tension at realizing what she'd just done. Spoofing a comm wasn't the best idea for anyone who wanted to keep a low profile, but the chance at grabbing the Xeno seemed worth the risk. *Malone has his spectacles; the Horde have their conquests. Omegans respond best to bargaining chips. It's about time I collect some. I just know there's something to these Xeno, and if I can help them, maybe they can return the favor.*

THREE

FINALLY, CHARISTA'S SHIFTS WITH Kindra and Adarsha lined up, and they met in the *Trussel's* Galley. The large room hosted seating for a hundred, roughly one-fourth of the crew onboard the freighter. A serving area at one end offered the best barely digestible rations the Omegan military was forced to provide. After getting their servings of glorified animal feed, Charista and her friends grabbed a table at the far end of the hallway from the entrance. Charista worked on eating while Adarsha and Kindra filled her in on their work on Agmon. They talked over the general crowd noise as others on the same shift grabbed their food and chatted with their table mates.

"Charista, you would've hated Agmon. I mean, the temperate climate, the fresh air," Adarsha rolled her eyes.

Charista threw a balled-up napkin at her friend's face. She relished the times they had like this, sporadic as they were.

"Serious, what was it like down there? I saw lush trees on the video screens." Charista eyed her friends like a lawyer waiting for a witness' response.

Kindra glanced at Adarsha, who had a mouthful of food, then

back to Charista. "It's something. I'm amazed by what Malone did there. The preliminary scan data we had on that place showed it near extinction. Even with the modest supply of Essence the planet had, it wouldn't be long for it."

"Then, how did Malone adding more of the same Essence make it suddenly so better?"

Adarsha swallowed her bite of food. She glanced at Kindra before she replied, "I dunno about that, but I know this one won't admit she's in love with Malone and already believes he can do anything. Me, I can't figure it out either."

"Shut up," Kindra elbowed Adarsha in her midsection. Adarsha recoiled back with a series of giggles.

"At least Malone is better than those filthy Railen," Adarsha added.

Kindra's face bunched up in disgust. "Please, we're trying to eat here. Don't ever bring up those scum around me. The best day for Ling is when all Railen are dead."

Charista met Kindra's eyes and saw the search for approval in her friend's glance. Charista swallowed the lump that formed at the thought of Joanna and gave a quick nod in reply. *There's no way they can know about Joanna and me. But what about what I did with the Praximus comm? Would they have thought it was a good idea?*

A warm surge shot through Charista's frame, and she glanced downward in silence regarding her food. Soon, she felt a touch on her arm and looked into Adarsha's eyes.

"What's wrong?"

Oh, I'd love to tell you. I wish I could. But that would only involve you, and I can't do that to you, my friend.

"Oh, Pit was giving me trouble before the pre-Agmon briefing."

"That old slug?" Kindra shook her head. "I've had enough of him too. He's still riding that rep from years ago when he was a chief of a Nara unit. Times have changed. He's not so tough jockeying the 'Trashel' now. Some Omegans have to tell themselves they're not the decrepit burnouts they are."

Adarsha smiled and nodded in reply. "Don't let Pit bother you, Charista."

Charista nodded. *It wasn't much of a lie, and it was as much of the truth I wanted to share. Oh, my friends... what is going to happen to us? How can I do what I need to overtake Omegana and not hurt you?*

Adarsha smiled warmly, her eyes filled with concern for her friend. "Look, let's just finish this voyage. I'll grab you for some sparring when we get home before our next posting. Get your mind off things for a while."

Charista nodded. With a shaky breath, she patted Adarsha's hand on the table. "Deal."

The threesome finished their so-called meal and headed for the exit, with Charista trailing slightly behind. Seeing her friends in person, like in old times, gave her a feeling of peace. Unfortunately, the momentary serenity was shattered by a hand firmly gripping her shoulder. She stopped short and looked over into the smug gaze of Isaac Pyatt.

"Captain Risberg wants to see you. He found out about your stunt with the *Praximus* and is pretty upset."

"Of course he is."

CHARISTA MULLED her possible responses on her walk to the Captain's quarters. *We're at war. Why wouldn't we share strategic information with fellow troops?* But Risberg, like the *Trussel*, had accepted their state in the universe as couriers, not combatants. She wondered what he did to earn the military honors on his uniform.

Risberg's expression was way different from Charista's last visit with him. Instead of the disconnected glance of someone preoccupied, he now peered at Charista with eyes that blazed like angry coals on a fire.

Charista took the hot seat with no fanfare. She clutched the arms of the chair and braced for impact. Risberg said nothing for a while.

Then, after a lengthy glare directly into Charista's eyes, he prodded about, the only other sound in the room, a series of disgruntled groans. Opening arguments by the good captain were wordless, but Charista had a fair enough idea of what her sentence would be.

"Ensign Mantisword, you and I have a problem."

Charista squeezed the arms of her seat so tightly that her hands felt like they were on fire. It hadn't stopped her racing mind, and it sure hadn't eased the heavy soreness in her midsection as she eyed Captain Risberg like a condemned prisoner awaiting execution of sentence. *Risberg believes a Captain is god of their ship, and all heretics of that religion are subject to the full wrath.* She had no idea what that involved, which only worsened her panic. Risberg was undoubtedly from the old order of Omegans, who according to stories, trained their ranks in torture camps intending to make the soldiers as resistant to pain as possible. The scars on Risberg's arms and face provided evidence that those stories were more than Omegan legend.

In an instant, Risberg clutched Charista's arms and leaned into her, his face mere inches from hers. The stale stench of his breath triggered Charista's gag reflex.

I thought the food in the Trussel galley smelled terrible.

Charista gasped and felt cold sweat bathe her entire body. She saw his gaze, even though she avoided eye contact.

"You see," Risberg began, "I worked with your father in the Science Wing. A seasoned warrior now and then gets called in for testing equipment Findlay and his team built. While all Omegans were expected to be battle ready, we accepted those with the most capable minds served Omegana better in labs than on the battlefield. So, I knew Findlay. I can't say his betrayal surprised me. On the contrary, it was almost a relief to me when I heard about it. I hated that someone with as low tolerance and resolve as Findlay Mantisword had gotten away with the accolades he did. And then, you, his daughter, were assigned to my ship. I couldn't have cared less what kind of military mind your mother was - I fought against having your traitor blood under my command at first. But then, I wondered, what if I lost you in an accident? A frigate isn't known for combat engagements, but after all, with the war we're in, who's to say we weren't overrun? I can't imagine many on this ship would've questioned something like that. But, still, my code to protect my crew held fast."

Charista swallowed a large lump in her throat. She lost the ability to speak but felt it wasn't the right time anyway.

Sure enough, Risberg continued, first grabbing Charista's chin and guiding her head until she looked deep into Risberg's eyes.

"The only reason you're not being vaporized is that the Horde confirmed the info and are on an intercept now. But, that doesn't excuse your flagrant disregard for my order. You're on very shaky ground with me, young Ensign. I'll be getting reports from you daily via Isaac. And, you better believe you and your activities will be monitored for the rest of this voyage."

"Sir, I had what I thought was good intelligence -"

"-on a cargo of puny Xeno. You ignored my direct orders and sent the notice out to Captain Ve. I'm not interested in the result. Your insubordination is unacceptable. A chain of command is first a chain. And, you broke it. If you can't follow small orders, you can't be trusted to follow large ones."

Risberg slammed his desk as punctuation to his sentence. His gaze bored deep into Charista's eyes. Her pulse rattled in her throat, and she felt a wave of heat as it flashed over her entire face.

Risberg leaned in close once again. "You're confined to research duties for the rest of this mission. You'll review fleet schematics for the rest of this voyage. That should give you time to think about the value of following orders from your commanding officer."

With a single gesture, Risberg dismissed Charista from his quarters. There was no point in any objections, and she knew it. Risberg was judge and jury on his ship, and she had no plans on testing the executioner part. Her trip back was more painful this time around. Charista's gloom lifted a little when she saw Adarsha coming toward her in the hallway.

"We saw Isaac grab you in the galley. What happened?" Adarsha's eyes were full of concern for her friend.

Charista slumped against the nearby wall. "I'm restricted to research for the rest of this trip."

"Why?"

Charista leaned against the bulkhead until it felt like it would either break off into space or absorb her into it. "I sent a comm to the *Praxiumus* against Captain's orders."

"Why?"

Charista looked up slowly at her friend. "I saw intel that the UA sent a convoy to transport Xeno back to Yassel. Risberg said to ignore it, but I alerted them anyway."

Adarsha's face twisted in pain. "That was a bad idea. He's no hero of mine, either, but he's still the Captain."

"I know, I know." Charista folded her arms and glanced up the hallway.

"Was this what was bugging you at lunch?"

Well, that and the fact I'm working with Joanna, a Railen you and pretty much every other Omegan wants to kill. "Yeah, you could say that."

"Well, it's done. If you want my advice, let things fall where they do on the Xeno. You're better not to get involved with them."

Charista met Adarsha's eyes again. "Won't be too hard for the rest of this mission; no more comm or nav for me. I guess my meals will be handed through the door."

A tear formed in Adarsha's eye. "At least you're not in the brig."

"This will make my review back at home even more interesting." Charista sighed.

"That's still going on?"

"Of course. My dad was an enemy of the state, remember? They watch me hard even when I follow the rules."

The two friends hugged while Charista cried a bit into Adarsha's shoulder. Unfortunately, Charista was again relegated to being ignored, reminded how she was a blight on Omegana that needed to be kept in a vacuum in the hope she one day withered and died. Once they released their embrace, Charista took a few steps down the hall before she looked back at Adarsha through tear-soaked eyes. Adarsha held her hand to her chest, her voice a pained whisper.

"Hang in there!"

THE *TRUSSEL* SHIP library was musty, which was quite the accomplishment for a facility that hosted a collection of digital books. The shabby room owed its rank smell to virtual non-use. The Science Wing had provided the materials in the room, but beyond that, the library served very little use to most of her crew. While ships like *Trussel* were equipped with documentation on the Omegan fleet, the average Omegan's interest in the literary, even informational prose, wasn't even slight. Weapons and fisticuffs were way higher on the list of leisure time activities than reading.

A lone robotic camera watched the table in the center of the room, which was Charista's new workstation for the rest of her trip. The smooth gray and black steel arc fixture that ended in a very ominous-looking eye lens reminded Charista that as much as she thought and felt that she was utterly alone in the room, she never was. She wondered what they'd have expected her to do in a sealed room with no access to comms other than the ship address system.

Wow, these chairs suck. Charista nestled as best she could against the firm unforgiving steel seat and chairback and pulled up schematics. Her eyes began to swim after the first few hours, and her mind drifted in and out of clearness.

Charista did that, of course, until her mind kicked back into gear. In the idleness Risberg sentenced her to, Charista's mind took more than enough opportunity to reassess her situation. While Charista visually digested diagrams, specification charts, and designs of the Omegan starcraft in use along with the experimental variants, she forced thoughts of her situation into her mind to keep herself feeling productive.

This is just a setback. Risberg will try to fry me on my review for this. I've just got to take this all one move at a time. I'll get through this review, and Joanna will get Brescar working right. We just have to get to that next step.

FOUR

THE ENGINES OF *TRUSSEL* SLOWED to a deep rumble as the craft eased its way to the port on Omegana. The vessel made contact with the landing platform with a mild jolt. Charista smirked at the other crew who'd stumbled at the sudden halt of their ship.

A series of air jets blasted outside, and the central gangway lowered slowly. Charista followed the rest onto the dock boarding area and into the processing facility. As a Frigate crew, they didn't have nearly the armaments or gear to deal with as the infantry units carried, so their trip through the facility wasn't long. Several bins were about, and Omegan supply personnel stood nearby to receive any spent med packs, charge units, and various odds and ends from their run in space.

The crew of *Trussel* arrived back on Omegana without much fanfare. The ongoing war required regular attention by Zakmar and members of the Omegan military machine, so the customaries like greeting a returning crew were gone. For the rest of Charista's shipmates, their return meant time back at home port: visiting with families and a few typical days of R&R. For Charista, it meant days of solitude. Only this time, something else went with it: her usual review board, but with the extra job of determining what her actions on *Trussel* deserved in the way of punishment.

Once their crew was dismissed, Charista wandered about the port and surrounding areas. Her pack strewn over her back, she walked a bit through the streets of her city.

The city of Gajanan, the capital of Omegana, was always busy with activity. Transport crafts carried companies of Horde troops on deployments. The large, bullet-shaped starcraft lurched gracefully into the air until they reached orbital status. Smaller craft darted about the area in lower overhead patterns, carrying passengers and supplies around. Zakmar's push for Omegans to dominate Ling Galaxy sure hadn't hurt business.

The vast hulking structures of the Omegan Military and Science wings greeted Charista silently on her walk. She pulled the straps on her bag tighter and breathed in the fresh air for the first time in a while. She was cooped up for so long, and the soreness in her lower back and legs had left them with an annoying throb, so she figured it best if she walked a bit before she returned to her housing unit.

She hoped she found out whatever happened with the Brescar shipments quickly. One Omegan would've had an explanation, provided they were still around to give it. Still, with Risberg's eyes on her, she worried about contacts out in the open. So, for the time, she settled for a stroll to work out the body cramps her confined voyage left her.

The air in Gajanan was hot. The pungent smell of spent munitions tickled Charista's nose. The latest crop of military trainees was at it, of course. She glanced toward the Omegan training facility and saw a collection of Omegan starcraft on their tarmac, surrounded by a group of recruits. Not long ago, Charista was one of them. She paused for a moment and watched the eager Omegan military hopefuls, reminiscing on how her life was so much easier not that long ago.

Omegan residences in Gajanan city were somewhat nicer than in less municipal areas. Towering structures, with designs that weren't too different than the facilities for the Omegan Military Instruction and government building. Black, smooth steel columns jut from the surface upward into collections of windowed habitats, arranged in a honeycomb fashion.

Charista still had time before Risberg could've tried anything. The Review Board took a few days to assemble, given the state of Omegana's multiple troop deployments around Ling Galaxy. Zakmar's quest bled the homeland of some of its law and order, a necessary cost for the ultimate goal of conquest.

A sudden touch on Charista's arm stopped her short. Her guts tensed up, and she slowly looked back to see Adarsha's smiling face.

"Hey! I'm going to see my folks. How about we meet tomorrow?"

Charista nodded. "Well, I don't know when they'll call me in, so if it happens, I'll let you know."

Adarsha smiled and grabbed Charista's shoulder. The two shared a look that said enough. Charista grinned at her friend as they parted.

Charista swung past one of the Omegan Supply depots next. Several Omegans walked past her on her wandering trip home. She passed a group of Omegans that wore the tell-tale patch of the prison facility. She wondered just what it was like in the Omegan penal complex. Her father's crimes were too severe for him to be there very long, and since she'd already done a stint on the Retooling service, she wasn't eager to give her superiors any ideas about shoving her in that direction. The Review she faced could've handled that anyway. She figured she'd have let that come in time if that's what it was to be.

She began to think about the evening's meal when she heard a sharp whisper to her right.

"Hey!"

The voice came from a close by a group of power replicators. The structures were scattered about Omegana. They powered the energy grid of planet Omegana. Their trademark deep hum was so familiar that the average Omegan dismissed the white noise, which allowed her to hear the whisper that was barely louder than the equipment.

Charista stepped closer and noticed the tip of a boot from around the far corner. "Edin, is that you?"

Edin Herlan had known Charista since childhood when they played games before the worries of life became too big to ignore. He hadn't the physical stamina that a dedicated Horde trooper required, and his intellect wasn't the sharpest. Still, he made up for it with a very diligent work ethic, which gave him more than enough assignments in the Omegan machine, seeing to the fitting of Omegan starcraft, moving cargoes about, and whatever else needed doing at the time. However, Findlay had taken notice of Edin's drive and had him do basic delivery work for the Science Wing.

Edin poked his head around with a slight smile. "Sorry, I wanted to talk with you."

"It's OK. I know why."

In addition to Edin's reputation in the Omegan supply chain, he helped Charista set up a delivery method for Brescar to Joanna.

Charista stepped behind the power replicator, away from the walking path and hopefully out of earshot of the passerby Omegans.

"Joanna said there was a break in her Brescar supply."

Edin shook his head. "I did everything I could, but with Zakmar stepping up operations, the demand for supplies from Military and the Supply Depot shot up too. They've pulled our standard deliveries and redirected them to the Horde."

"They must've seen you loading Brescar if they caught you by surprise."

Edin glanced downward. "Yeah, they did. I told them I was working on disposal."

Good thinking, Edin. They already think the stuff is too volatile to be around. "Was that good enough for them?"

Edin shrugged. "For now. They're more concerned with keeping the Horde stocked up." Edin's eyes were full of worry. "What will we do about the rest of the Brescar and Joanna?"

Charista smiled and clasped Edin's hand. "Don't worry. Just keep in touch. I'm going back home, and I'll think of something." She heard herself say the words and knew she honestly had no idea what she was going to do. Nevertheless, it still felt better saying she'd come up with something. She only hoped that eventually became the truth.

Edin gave an understanding nod. "I'll be waiting. You know where to find me."

Charista kissed Edin lightly on the lips, and they parted. Like anything in her plans, the contact with Edin was a risk but a calculated one.

———

CHARISTA ARRIVED BACK at her housing unit 813. It hadn't been the same since Findlay's death, and it never would be again. She flung her pack on the dining table and lept into a chair, pausing for a long stretch. The material wasn't the most plush, but it was eons better than that chair on the *Trussel*. Her uniform was dirty and needed cleaning before the Inquiry.

Laundry can wait. She sighed in the silence of the room as her worries for the moment gradually drifted away from her.

After a while, she pulled up to a seated position. Her extended walk home helped her soreness out to a point, but there were still more pains to address. With a series of stretches, she worked her muscles that went sore with the idle sitting, especially in the library. She got to her feet and strode from the front room to the study area, where a large monitor on the wall greeted her. The display rotated between Omegana updates and Network in general.

Her home comm rang; it was Kindra.

"Well, hey there," Charista beamed.

Kindra smiled in kind. "I hope you're doing OK; they didn't waste time on new assignments for me. I've been redirected to a unit supporting one of Malone's new projects."

Malone was so active; he's even affecting my few close friends. "Wow, so when are you shipping out?"

"Couple of days. Have they set your review date yet?"

"No, maybe they need time to muster, with so many leaders out in forward Horde operations," Charista added a heavy sigh to her statement.

"I was hoping we three could have another day to relax together. If you can get Adarsha, you two should do something. I'll be thinking about you, my friend!"

Charista touched the screen, wishing the contact could've been directly on Kindra's face. "Me too. You be good, and we'll see each other soon."

Charista ended the comm and let her thoughts drift back to the Xeno. Stories about them had spread around Ling Galaxy like a virus. Some believed they had the potential to not only locate Essence but manipulate it. But the unknown was always an excellent place for rumors and speculation.

She thought about people who may have had an idea of the Xeno's worth. She wished she'd have been with the Science Wing on Omegana for a change. They had the first crack at the Xeno and what potential they had. But she'd been forbidden, and her father Findlay's record ensured that Charista and the Mantiswords were never allowed in again.

But she remembered someone who could've had an idea about the Xeno. She sure knew enough about the Omegans already.

Charista pulled her modified comm from its hiding place. She'd learned more than a little from her father over the years and had developed a comm untraceable by Omegans for contacting Joanna.

Joanna smiled at Charista's face when their session began.

"Hello dear, I still can't get over you as an officer now." Joanna beamed.

Charista shrugged. She appreciated the attention Joanna gave her and the interest she took. The void Charista felt over having no family on Omegana for sharing good news was slightly lessened by Joanna and her kindness. "They've done everything they can to keep me at the lowest level of responsibility. And my latest bout may keep me there for good."

"What happened?"

"Oh, I spotted a UA transport and asked my commander about it. I thought it was strange, the UA doing that through a war zone. But Captain Risberg hadn't any thought about following it. Instead, he thought it was a waste of time and ordered me to focus on my duties. But still, I sent the info to an Omegan cruiser, and it led to the capture of the Xeno."

Joanna nodded. "Strange thing to get punished for."

"Well, Captain Risberg specifically ordered me not to."

"And you did it anyway." Joanna's eyes drifted downward.

"It was risky, careless, even stupid given my family history... I know that. It could've been a cargo of food or something minor. It wouldn't have been the first time Network was wrong."

"Are you OK?" Joanna asked.

"My review board will rehash what I did and find new ways to make me miserable. Other than that, I'm just lovely."

Joanna nodded. "That was a bad idea, Charista. Still, it sounds like it paid off, more than they'd let you know, I bet. As for the Xeno, they've got some strange properties. I've studied them a bit, and we've sure had a rough time with them. I think they may be useful with Essence, maybe even Brescar too."

"Why can't Brescar just replace Essence? Wasn't that the whole idea?"

Joanna nodded. "Of course it was. However, Brescar still has a lot of volatility. I'm working on that, and your supply helps my experiments and modifications."

"About that supply," Charista said, "I have to figure out a new delivery chain for you. Edin was caught up in the expanded deliveries to Horde units, and we don't have access to the craft like before."

Joanna's lips formed a line. "I understand. I hope I can get replication working at some point, so I can duplicate the Brescar you've already sent. Until that happens, I'll be praying you restore delivery somehow."

Charista said, "I'll let you know. Alright, enough about me, how are things with you? What have you been cooking up over there?"

"Well, I've been working with the Brescar and got some of it weaponized."

Charista was stunned. She'd heard Findlay talk about energy properties of Brescar, and at the very most outside of that, a chance it gave a tremendous amount of speed to ships, maybe even rivaling the Transient Warp drives that remained fastest in Ling Galaxy for the moment. "How does that even work with the instability issues?"

Joanna smirked. "I've been tuning Brescar over time. It's been slow but promising. Our leader Ander and the rest know you have given us this. So, they'll remember that, which isn't bad for you or me."

Charista savored the compassion in Joanna's eyes. Joanna placed her hand on the screen as she said, "Dear, I promise you, I loved your father and made him a pledge that I'd watch out for you always, and that's what I'm going to do."

FIVE

CHARISTA'S SUMMONS ARRIVED two days after she returned. Her spirit sank when she saw the red digital document at the top of her incoming messages. It was there just when she'd thought she had a few days to not think about it. Breaking rank and sending the kind of comm Charista did would've earned any member of an Omegan flight crew time in port, admin leave without pay, a stint in Retooling, or worse. But, as Charista was already subject to reviews from her father's past, her latest deviance only added a healthy amount of fuel to that already blazing fire.

I just wish they'd give me a chance to breathe. How am I supposed to ever prove myself again if they're holding dad's past over me each waking moment?

As Charista fumbled with the manual controls that adjusted the light in the main room lower, a chime tone sounded on the viewscreen on her wall. Charista looked over to a report of the incoming haul of Xeno prisoners. *Maybe this will help my case. Of course, I'm sure By-the-Book Risberg will have his way with me on the insubordination charge.*

She flopped down into a chair. *Time to get ready for yet another grilling.*

AFTER A FITFUL SLEEP, Charista woke up earlier than usual. She sprung out of bed, her mind chock full of ideas. This time, her schemes focused on her review. Charista imagined how her mother Winola prepared to lead troops into a skirmish. She also thought about her father, developing Brescar, steeped in the knowledge that any wrong step or move would've meant the end for him, probably planet Omegana and maybe even Ling Galaxy. Charista wasn't leading a skirmish, though, nor was she making complex calculations on an energy-producing matter that could've had drastic consequences.

Her battle was of the will. Her fighting arena was the Inquiry Hall. Her weapons: words. Those alone had enough power behind them, and she knew she had to be careful.

The Omegan Military escorts arrived promptly to pick her up. Once they put Charista in wrist restraints, they helped her into the transport for their ride to the center of town. The trip was mostly silent; the only noise in the cabin was the occasional chatter over the vehicle comm. Charista watched the Omegan buildings as they drifted past on their drive. Gajanan had many facilities for production and retooling, but the military was undoubtedly the most prominent presence there. The Science Wing had their collection of structures, too. Charista smiled as their vehicle passed the building where Findlay worked up until he was removed from his post. Despite Findlay's achievements in Omegan weapon power supplies and building structures like the one the *Trussel* crew installed on Agmon, his legacy, besides in the memories of Charista and Joanna, was betrayal.

The transport jolted to a stop. Charista glanced out the side window at the entrance to the Inquiry hall. Her two escorts exited first and helped Charista to the sidewalk at the bottom of the vast set of stairs leading into the hall. Several Omegans walked either up toward or down from the entrance. Amid the crowd, up ahead of them, Charista noticed one Omegan female in a military uniform covered with regal robes, facing Charista with a curious look on her face. As they climbed the steps, Charista caught more than a few glances from Omegans passing by in either direction. Omegans usually had no use for anyone in restraints. The common belief was that an Omegan in shackles was already guilty, especially given Charista being near the Inquiry hall.

As she got closer to the lone figure in the lavish uniform, Charista was relieved when she recognized their face.

Aunt Ardy.

Ardene Onopco was a high-ranking member of the Omegan Military. Furthermore, she served with Charista's mother and had been a close family friend for years. Growing up, Charista knew her as "Aunt Ardy."

When Charista and the guards were close enough, Ardene took a step closer. "Aside from the circumstances, it's great to see you."

Charista savored the relief of an unexpected familiar face. "Same here."

Ardene's face hardened to a steely military demeanor as she regarded Charista's escorts. "I'll take it from here. You two are dismissed."

The guards glanced at each other for a moment, then one grabbed Charista and pulled her to Ardene's step. Ardene clutched Charista as the two guards snapped a salute and exited.

Charista's arm throbbed from the guard's final grip on her, and she threw a glare back toward her former escorts, already on their way down to their vehicle.

"Omegan sentries are on the lower order of intelligence at the academy. They reserve the flight and advance combat assignments to those with more aptitude," Ardene said softly.

Charista took another look at Ardene's outfit. It wasn't field issue for Omegan Horde troops; instead, it was more ornate, with golden trim along the dark black tunic material. A formal outfit, used for ceremonies...

...and sometimes inquiry boards.

"Are you - on my review?" Charista asked.

Ardene leaned closer as they walked. "I am. Once I heard about you coming in, and what happened with you on the *Trussel*, I wanted to help."

I didn't realize insubordination would get around the Omegan military so quickly. I guess Aunt Ardy was keeping a closer eye on me. While the odds against her were still four to one at best, she felt better having someone with Ardene's chops in her corner.

Charista turned back to Ardene's warm grin. "Just so happens, the Xeno have become a hot topic over here since that stunt you pulled."

"I knew they were useful."

"Don't get ahead of yourself. Not much has changed on Omegans wanting to rule all of Ling since you've been away. But, there are cracks in the armor, and I understand several on your review board are interested in the Xeno. Some feel the Xeno could be weaponized, and it would be better to have them as an option than leaning too much on Malone for our goals. So, I'm bringing up the Xeno's value to Omegana in your review. Maybe we can deflect the discussion onto the value of what you did. Don't misunderstand; even if we can sell the Xeno's worth, you're still in for an awful assignment. But, if we keep you out of prison, I'll call that a win."

Charista's mind raced through possible arguments, but nothing stuck out to her. "I'm in a bad place, aren't I?"

"Afraid so. I've arranged to escort you to chambers while we wait for your hearing."

"How did you pull all this? I figured you'd be attacking UA head-quarters on planet Yassel by now."

Ardene shrugged; a slight smirk found her face. "Zakmar owes me. He and Malone are deep into their love affair, working on the conquest of Ling. I just had to get away from those two for a bit. Besides, I didn't want my favorite niece facing the dogs without a little protection." Ardene chuckled softly as they headed inside the hall.

CHARISTA ATTEMPTED a comfortable position in her seat but knew it was useless. Her chair faced a raised dais adorned with the Omegan crest, where five chairs held the board members reviewing her case. At an Omegan Review, the board didn't even remotely consider comfort for the one under examination. The Omegans wanted every discomfort possible in the hope the unease led to more chance revelations and damning bits of testimony that anyone in that much pain would've offered for some relief.

Once the proceedings began and after the list of charges was read to the assembled, Kai Risberg wasted no time going for the throat.

"She's a disgrace to the Omegana Crest! Insubordination from someone with the Mantisword's history of defiance deserves the maximum penalty!"

Risberg's assessment of Charista rang out in the ceremonial chamber. She winced at the sharp rebuke but noticed by their expressions that the Omegans present weren't as eager to support Kai's statement. Like many of the elder Omegans, Kai had become prone to a few slips of judgment himself, and the idea was brewing that Kai's time in active service, at least on a command level, was past the point where it made sense.

Nabarun Sule, presiding over the ceremonies, extended his hand toward Risberg in a silencing gesture. "The accused's crimes are noted, Captain Risberg. I agree her permissions with Tech need to be removed for an extended period. As to her ultimate penalty, this board will determine that in a short time." Sule was the Commandant at the Omegan Military Institute. Charista read the enjoyment on his face and wondered if that included a dismal outcome for her.

She figured anyone steeped in training procedure also enjoyed the procedural side of the Omegan Machine.

After the opening barrage, Ardene strode about in the gap between Charista's table and the dais. "The accused is in review because of her father's history. There's no denying the severity of Ensign Mantisword's act of sending a comm transmission against orders, but let's consider for a moment what her actions gave Omegana: the Xeno. Our fight to overtake Ling Galaxy hasn't been without trouble. We've already lost several Horde units to UA forces. We don't have a clear path to victory. Our alliance with Malone has given us more teeth in the fight, but others are still biting us. We need to claw back. Remember our legacy, fellow Omegans... we are physically formidable, but might without strategy eventually falls flat. The truth is, we are at war, and in war, sometimes advantages make the difference between prevailing or not. There's plenty of debate over the value of the Xeno. Why don't we look at that for a moment, since this insubordination by Ensign Mantisword gave us an incoming asset?"

Risberg groaned in response. Charista figured Ardene could've named the exact color of the dais table, and Risberg would've objected. "General Onopco has chosen to deflect our discussions to the Xeno, using the topical subject of our recent acquisition. Let me make my feelings clear on this matter. I ordered Mantisword not to alert the Omegans about the Xeno convoy because I didn't want to waste time from Omegan operations. And, just because the incident we're discussing netted us a group of Xeno, it's no reason we should hold a collection of bastard outcasts from a distant galaxy as some great hope. Even if what we've heard is all true, and Xeno can wield Essence, that only makes them a threat in my eyes. We can exterminate them once they are housed on Omegana, for all I care. Xeno are simply a blight on what we are. Our scientific minds will realize that once they've had their time to poke and prod."

Synne Aren on the dais was another salty variety of Omegan old soldiers similar to Risberg. "What could a puny Xeno offer the likes of us? We are the supreme race in Ling Galaxy, are we not? We stand at a threshold of being the controlling force in Ling once we handle our ally Malone Stanton, that is."

Ardene glanced at Synne. "Malone has given Omegans a decent chance, but we shouldn't rule out the thought of Malone Stanton being removed one day. Omegans have had one master already with the Nara; the last thing we need is another with Stanton."

Nabaran smashed his gavel on the table, sending an echoed thud into the room. His voice boomed in the large hallway. "Malone Stanton isn't for debate here. We're all aware of the transgressions on the Mantisword name, and we've given extra attention to Ensign Mantisword's activities since. She's handled her duties with resolve, even the tiniest scrap repurpose detail, and we should consider that."

Kai retorted, "Oh, should we? What if we're under attack and need coordinates for assisting craft? Do we count on her to provide that information, or maybe she'll continue on this path? Who knows, maybe she's got some other connections."

"The truth, Captain Risberg," Nabarun offered, "Is while Ensign Mantisword was flagrant, her actions provided Omegana with the capture of the Xeno. Moreover, their apparent value to the UA makes them, at the very least, a bargaining chip for us. While their final worth is still up for debate, I appreciate the strategic nature of her insights."

"Well, that is only worthwhile if we can deem the Xeno have some use." Kai quipped.

Nabarun's eyes narrowed. His voice was steady and low when he spoke again. "I'm ordering the Science Wing to evaluate the Xeno, mentally and physically. We should at least rule out their abilities with Essence. As for the accused, she will be escorted back to chambers. Then, this board will decide the disposition of Charista Mantisword's case."

THE BOARD DELIBERATED Charista's case for three hours. She paced back and forth in the small room that felt like a step above a prison cell. A lone seat stood in one corner, and on one wall was a monitor that flashed the Omegana crest.

I wish I could talk with Kindra or Adarsha. Just hugging them would be nice. It sounded like Aunt Ardy made some sense to the board. Who knows. Oh, when is this going to stop?

After what felt like a month for Charista, Ardene appeared. Charista searched her Aunt's face for any hints of how it went. Aunt Ardy was a seasoned warrior, though, and her demeanor held.

"Please tell me I'm not getting execution," Charista muttered.

"Not at all. It's a victory... of sorts. You're of course done with any starcraft assignments for a while. Risberg also wants nothing further to do with you. No surprise there."

"So, where am I going?"

"Supply service."

The words came like a slap across Charista's face. One of the minor assignments in Omegan society, the Supply Service dealt with lower order things like rations and part deliveries. It was an excellent place for someone who wanted to be forgotten, so Charista realized it was the prime choice for her sentence.

Charista felt Ardene's arm around her shoulder, and her voice was soft.

"Supply Service is better than Retooling, Charista."

"I think it's worse, Aunt Ardy. At least Retooling let me stretch my mind a little. Supply service means I'm a bonafide drone."

"And you've lost rank; you're back to officer candidate."

Charista shook her head. *Was there ever any end to all this?*

Charista leaned into Ardene's embrace, looking into her concerned eyes.

"Charista, listen. You're free. You're alive. That was my main goal. Just do what you're told. Omegana values loyalty, and yours will be much harder to prove for a while. It isn't impossible, but it's going to take time."

"What are the Omegans going to do with the Xeno?"

"I don't know. Omegana's attention to the scientific hasn't been the same since Findlay's death. Zakmar wants weapons, not innovation."

"But this is intelligence!" Charista felt like she was still in the inquiry and felt the pain as she looked into Ardene's eyes.

"Charista, pay your dues now; things will improve in time."

Charista sunk further into her seat. She knew Aunt Ardy was right. But, she also felt helpless, like any step she made forward was quickly erased with two to three steps back.

SIX

THE OMEGAN DEPOT WAS A SHORT but wide building from which the Supply service delivered all the necessities throughout Omegana. Of course, those assigned to the service weren't envied for their jobs by members of the Omegan military or any other citizen. Still, the simple truth was that supply was the lifeblood of Omegana.

Charista's days in the Omegan Supply service became a blur, leaving her housing unit early to catch a transport to the Depot for her day's assignments, then running pieces of repurposed equipment from Retooling over to the Omegan Military wing.

Charista wasn't alone in her sentence, either. Isaac Pyatt, technically innocent of any involvement in Charista's Xeno comm transmission, but still complicit by the manner of being a supervisor over her, was given a temporary reassignment to the Omegan Supply Service. Charista figured it was collateral damage from her infraction.

Each day, Charista gathered in the large Depot main hallway to receive assignments for the day. The giant warehouse structure had a musty smell. Occasional dust wafts and the stale odor of smoke and random chemicals gave the place a very industrial feel. A fleet of transport vehicles lined one side of the large room. These were loaded for deliveries by several crews on hand. Charista fell in with the groups running deliveries, while the more experienced staff were relegated to sorting and organizing inventory for distribution.

Before the tasks began, there was often a group meeting where Griffen Nys, Captain of the Omegan Supply service, briefed the entire crew on the current demands of the Supply service. Griffen was the most detailed officer Charista had seen yet. His uniform was so impeccable, it made Isaac's look sloppy. Griffen strode back and forth, looking at his digital pad while Charista, Isaac, and the other assignees waited for his word.

"Omegana will rule Ling Galaxy one day. No true Omegan will dare debate that. But, we won't get there any quicker unless our nation is prepared. Our military has the strength, but it's up to us to keep the supply lines going, and that's what I expect of each of you. Now, the rules. No back talk. Several of you are here because you washed out somewhere else. If you thought this would be an easy assignment to work your way back, think again. Supply runs deliveries at all hours to Omegana. You'll work 15-hour shifts and like it, understood?"

"Yes sir!" Came the response from the assembled group.

One of the Supply Sergeants weaved through the crowd as the assembled workers pressed closer. Charista edged closer, but it wasn't much use. This was part of the daily routine. She wondered if the more aggressive in this surge of Omegan bodies got the more choice assignments.

The Supply Sergeant's eyes narrowed slightly when his gaze met Charista's. He flicked her orders over. Charista grabbed for the document as it smacked into her chest.

Charista grabbed the ticket and squirmed out of the pile to read the details.

Homestead. Great, I'm delivering rations or something.

Charista also noticed an additional assignee on her run. None other than Isaac. She glanced about until she saw him several yards away, eyeing a similar document. Without making visual contact with Isaac, she glanced back to the transports and matched the vehicle number with her orders. *Maybe if I leave fast enough, I can ditch him.*

Unfortunately, Isaac met Charista when she was almost to the vehicle.

"Don't think for a Tausian minute I've forgotten what happened. You better believe I will do everything possible to make your life a living hell until I get out of here."

Charista narrowed her eyes. "Suck it up, Isaac. I'm sure you'll weasel out of this in no time."

CHARISTA AND ISAAC'S run took most of the day to complete. Afterward, they returned to the Depot. The warehouse, filled with vehicles and Omegans in the early part of the day, stood half empty, like a mother animal waiting for her young's return. Charista parked their vehicle alongside the few others back in the hall and headed toward the rear of the depot, where crews of more senior Supply workers handled the incoming materials for future deliveries.

After a few minutes, Charista caught sight of Edin and motioned him toward the rows of parked transports.

"So," Edin began, "What's your plan for Brescar?"

Charista swiped at her brow. The temperature in the depot was always much warmer than the outside. The continual traffic of large transport vehicles in and out spewed enough rancid exhaust to keep the place pretty stuffy and warm.

"The Horde shipments are leveling off. I think you'll be able to grab one of those freighters soon. Just put a small amount in for now. We don't need any more attention than we already have."

Edin nodded.

"Tell me again, how much Brescar is left?"

"My last count came to 30 cases, each with approximately two tons of Brescar."

Charista marveled. Joanna was probably going to get Replication figured out anyway, but having that large a supply still around was nice. Her main concern was how long Edin's story of disposal to hide his shipments of Brescar to Joanna held up with the Omegan authorities.

At the end of one day, Charista noticed a group of Supply workers watching a large video screen in the Warehouse. The Xeno were brought in and received by Zakmar himself.

I guess they want to study the Xeno before mutilating them after all. At least getting busted for pointing out their convoy wasn't for nothing.

After the initial reception, the Xeno were brought to the Omegan prison with as much fanfare as the delivery of fabricated building components. She eyed her display tablet that showed a rough count of the individuals in the group. There wasn't time for more detailed information, but she was ready to find that out herself.

SEVEN

CHARISTA'S ROUTINE IN SUPPLY SERVICE gave way to drudgery. The days ran to weeks, and while she thought about her plans, they seemed to drift into a daydream. She even got better at tuning out Isaac's bickering. Nevertheless, her tasks continued to be as menial as she could've imagined, running food rations and checking on the supply relays for power converters.

One day, the mundane stopped abruptly. It began with the sound of weapons fire as Charista and Isaac were on one of their regular runs. At first, she thought it was a weapons test. But as it continued, given its location, she knew it wasn't a drill. The noise came from the Prison area, and the sight of UA ships further confirmed what she thought.

Then, a mysterious comm entry over their vehicle's speakers.

"Requesting assistance from Omegana security, Prison under attack, repeat, prison under attack."

Charista met Isaac's gaze, his eyes filled with bewilderment.

"Could that be a drill?" Charista asked.

Isaac frowned a bit and eyed the comm speaker. "I can't imagine why they'd do that at the prison."

Charista grabbed the comm and replied. "Omegana Prison, please repeat; sounded like you said you're under attack?"

"Affirmative. It looks like an attempted prison break."

Charista accessed the video feed of the detention building on their vehicle's console. Sure enough, a collection of UA ships and troops battered the area. She slammed her fist on her thigh, angry about Omegan carelessness over home defense, especially regarding a valuable asset.

While Isaac wrung his hands, Charista felt the gears in her strategic mind slip back into place. *Of course, the UA saw enough in the Xeno to grab them first; why wouldn't they have risked a mission to the Omegan stronghold?*

Charista smashed her hands together. "Isaac, we have to help them."

"With what? We've got a load of medical supplies."

"There's weapons at the prison. Our fellow Omegans are in trouble. What about the Omegan credo about 'No Omegan forsakes another'?"

"That's fine talk from a Mantisword." Isaac eyed Charista with a deep snarl.

"A Mantisword who's trying to do the right thing and save other Omegans right now. Are you helping, or should I report you ignored Omegans under siege?"

Isaac gnashed his teeth, his eyes glaring at the unfolding scene on the monitor. "Damn it, OK."

Charista flung the vehicle in gear and headed toward the prison building. She craved a battle for several reasons. First, it was ingrained in Omegans, given their desire for absolute rule. Bloodlust was bred and fostered in their kind for centuries. Second, the chance at action after weeks of a painfully dull routine felt like the best medicine she could've gotten.

Once Charista and Isaac arrived at the Prison, they met a small force of Omegans that scurried around with pulse rifles toward defensive positions for the oncoming attack. After a few minutes, Charista found Jamon, the warden. He was a burly hulk of an Omegan. He looked about at the rush of troops with an agitated gaze, but once his eyes met Charista's, a sneer found his face.

"Well, if it isn't the Traitor."

Aaand they know me here too. Figures.

Isaac spoke next. "Captain, we heard your distress call. Unfortunately, we don't have much in arms, but we're here to assist however we can."

Jamon glanced over to Isaac and nodded. "We could always throw this one toward the ships."

Really? They're about to be blown up, and they still don't want my help?

The ground rocked with a series of blasts. Charista steadied herself against a nearby wall. Jamon's voice lifted to a decibel level of an Omegan training instructor. "Troops to the outside embankments and put fire on the craft. Those on interior security fortify the holding levels. Keep those prisoners safe. We lose so much as one; You'll all pay for it!"

Charista and Isaac joined the remaining officers in getting weapons. Charista grabbed a helmet and proceeded outside toward the forward defensive positions. The evening air was dry, with a slight warm breeze coming. A series of UA small fighters swarmed the skies above.

Jamon strode about as Charista and the others crouched behind the elevated embankment, their pulse rifles trained on the approaching ships. "We know what's here; I want to know what's coming and how big our threat is."

An officer with a head visor tapped the controls and gazed directly at the inbound craft. "Another cluster en route. Large Transport or two, with several small fighters."

"They're not an attack unit," Jamon muttered. "There'd be at least a few cruisers in there. They were hoping for a snatch and grab."

"The Xeno," Charista offered.

"Brilliant deduction," Jamon countered. "Well, they're ours, and they're staying here, understood?"

Shouts of confirmation and the telltale whir sound of rifles powered up answered Jamon's call like an eager congregation.

The collective group of Omegans on hand numbered fifty, with no starcraft support. Whatever was about to happen was sure to include a slaughter of Omegans. Charista knew what she would've done if she had a say, but remembered how acting quick in the past wasn't her best move.

"Sir, maybe Omegana can send support?" Charista asked.

Jamon glared in response. "I've already called them, Officer Candidate. What do you think that comm was for? Omegan military is scrambling what they can to give us reinforcements."

Several blasts from the approaching starcraft peppered the ground nearby. Jamon took an angry swipe of his brow. "I'm heading to the command tower. It's not much, but it's got the best vantage point and a few guns. At least we can throw more fire on the UA from there."

Isaac edged up onto his feet. "Sir, I have experience with anti-ship weaponry. I can assist."

Jamon's mouth curled. "Can't hurt at this point, come on."

Charista shook her head as Isaac trotted off behind Jamon like a loyal pet. *You do have a way of weaseling up to whatever CO is nearby, don't you?*

Her attention returned to the fray, Charista steadied her weapon. Her fellow officers were also there to her right and left, ready. They waited quietly, but she noticed the look in her fellow troop's eyes: heightened readiness.

Blasts from the smaller craft lanced the ground. Charista wobbled in her position while dust rained from the overhead canopy. *They'll send the small ships in for us. The transport won't have a lot of weapons; they're more worried about loading up the prisoners there. If we keep a low profile, we can hit them when they start to leave.*

Three of the small starcraft shot in an arch formation on a direct course for the platform where Charista and her group waited. A barrage of pulse fire shot up the embankment. The structure shook violently on the impact.

Charista winced as the metal around them heated up. The craft flew past and seemed to disappear, but Charista knew better. "They're coming back around. This unit won't stand much more than that. We've gotta move!"

The firing on their position stopped. Charista glanced up and saw why. The craft swiveled their course into a path toward the command tower. The guns from the building were small, but they peppered the starcraft for all they were worth. But it wasn't enough, and the three craft launched a volley of missiles that slammed into the tall structure with a cacophony of explosions. Charista and her fellow trench mates were knocked to the ground. When she looked up again, the former tower lay on its side, a mixture of mangled structural pieces and fires.

After the first wave of panic hit Charista, she felt her nerves calm, and the warrior spirit of her mother took over. "Take cover!"

She barked the words with such authority; the rest around her followed without question.

Charista stood up quickly. Her visor filled with dirt, but she was at least out of the hulking target of a defensive position she'd been in moments earlier. She noticed in the darkness a few others had taken her up on her move. She held her rifle up and pointed to an outcropping in the near distance.

An Omegan to Charista's right shouted, "Over there! Service connection. We can get behind it until reinforcements get here!"

It wasn't the best circumstances, but even in that brawl, she saw something. It wasn't her fellow soldiers huddled for cover. Instead, it was a hand terminal clipped to the waist of a fallen Omegan that lay face down in the debris. Charista grabbed the device, flipped through screens until the display showed controls of the facility, and pulled up the security recording. The system was designed to report any breaks or at least attempted breaks, but the video would've captured the assault and, more so, what was done by the Omegans who defended the place.

As other Omegans around fired on the UA craft that swarmed about, Charista weaved and stumbled over the pieces of the destroyed tower. While the structure lay on its side, she thought maybe the top portion was still there. If nothing else, the auto-destruct for the base should've been easier to find if she had started from the central tower.

A wall of flames lapped at her legs, and she scooted back, her feet rolling on a busted pipe that protruded from the ground. She went through a broken window and found herself inside the command center. A few bodies were scattered over the floor. She smirked at the sight of Isaac's body, unconscious. Jamon was nearby. His frame was covered with multiple cuts, and trails of darkish gray blood oozed from several places on his body, including his mouth. Still, he had a comm in his hand.

"Where's that damned backup?"

Charista saw the expression on Jamon's face, and instantly, she felt something. It wasn't compassion but a bit of recognition. Jamon was in a panic, and Charista savored the helplessness. *See, that's what it's like when you're in a tough spot. You've all kept me in one for a while now. Now it's your turn.*

As the chaos continued, Charista's thoughts rose above the conflict as a plan shot into her mind. It was more than a comm sent against orders; it was even more than her father or mother's attempts to improve their situation. Charista had a role in this attack, and it was that of a savior. But it was a story she had to write, and she had details to arrange.

Charista's hand squeezed the handle of her pulse rifle tight, and she held the weapon across her shoulders, behind her back as she stood.

Jamon's voice was a rasp, mixed with the blood that now gurgled in his throat. "Get down. Are you crazy? They can still obliterate this place and all of us, including you!"

While Jamon had focused on the next move at hand, Charista had already looked ahead in the game - her game. And, a play materialized. It was a bold one, but completely smart. It was even necessary given where she wanted to be.

So, Charista ignored Jamon's warning. She was still very much aware of the fight but suddenly realized she had an option. One maybe she'd had earlier and hadn't taken, but this time, she knew what she had to do.

Charista flung her rifle to a ready position in a single motion and fired several volleys into Jamon's chest. His body jerked violently as it broke into warm pieces of flesh as blood cascaded around it. She waited for a few moments until Jamon's gurgling heaves stopped. She then edged herself closer to Isaac. He hadn't budged since she entered the busted tower. *No sense in leaving anything to chance; I'll never get this good an opportunity again with the fight outside masking anything in here.*

As the pulse shots sliced Isaac's body into an unrecognizable pile of flesh, a surge of power went through Charista. Some of it was payback, some was power, but most of all, she felt more justification than she could've ever imagined.

When it was over, Isaac and Jamon's bodies lay in a heaped pile. Then, after what seemed like several hours passed, Jamon's comm crackled to life.

"Omegan Air Support Unit with visual on bandits, contacting ground crew, anyone there?"

Charista yanked the comm from Jamon's dead hand. "Charista Mantisword - they slaughtered our CO, but there's a few of us left, get some fire on those ships ASAP!"

CHARISTA MADE it outside in time to see Omegan starcraft mopping up the remains of the failed UA rescue attempt. She saw one UA fighter burst into a brilliant explosion. The Transport had pulled away, and the other UA Craft engaged the Omegan ships as they beat their retreat.

Charista met with a group of Omegan support troops, who eyed her with concern. She noticed the lieutenant insignia on the one to the front and observed the name embossed on their uniform breast pocket: Garton Hammon. The annoyed glare on his face told her the best move was for short answers and a wide berth.

"Where's Jamon?" Hammon's question came out like an order.

"Dead. I helped him contact Omegana military, and that's all he was able to do."

"We have to check for survivors. There could be more in that rubble." Hammon eyed the crumbled structure.

Charista nodded. "Understood, sir. We still have a substantial asset below: the Xeno. I recommend we load them out ASAP before the UA doubles back with more ships."

EIGHT

WITH THE HELP OF THE OMEGANA MILITARY, Charista and the surviving detail soldiers were pulled out, and the Xeno prisoners were relocated into the Science Wing facilities. The incident was relayed back to Omegan command, and Charista was heralded a hero for her actions. She bristled with the praise while wondering if she'd covered her tracks as well as she thought she had. Charista had taken a significant step forward, though, and that was good enough for now.

With help from her old friend Edin, they grabbed one of the damaged UA starcraft, and Edin worked out a deal to repurpose the ship for another delivery of Brescar. It was a short-term fix, but Charista was grateful for the extra time to figure out how to get the supply chain to Joanna restored for good.

Charista had made her move the right way and was assigned to a combat unit. She knew she had the best chance to be seen for her skill and eventually begin the rise up the ranks required for her eventual coup.

Entering the Science Wing felt odd for Charista since her father's death. In his former workplace, she felt good, being near to at least his spirit, but the betrayal that went with the Science Wing was the other side of that picture. Once she got to the holding area for the Xeno, she was met with a small but decently armed group of Omegan soldiers. A simple flash of her credentials was all it took, and she was escorted inside.

That's right; I'm Officer Candidate Mantisword no more.

Charista met Sergeant Hussey Ganesh at the observation desk. After a moment, the sergeant's face showed recognition of Charista, and his mouth formed a line.

"Ensign Mantisword, how can I help you?"

Charista glanced past the desk down the hallway, where two Omegan guards strode toward the far end. "I'm here to evaluate the Xeno prisoners. I understand their processing hasn't started yet, so I'd like to do some of my own checking."

Ganesh glanced up the hallway, then back. His eyes widened a bit. Clearly, there were no plans for the Xeno, but again, the Omegan priorities left the collection of prisoners to more or less rot away for the time being. "I suppose you can have a pass through, but don't take too much-"

"-thank you, Sergeant. I'll mention this to your shift commander when I'm done."

Charista pulled a hand terminal from the rack to the side of the desk while Ganesh opened access for her to the inner holding area.

PRIVATE WOSLEY PRIOR led Charista down into the holding area. The Omegan battle armor heavily accented his medium build. He strode with his rifle to his side, a mildly disinterested glint in his eye. After a few twists and turns down the corridors, Charista found herself walking along a row of cells.

"I can't figure out why we keep these nasty Xeno here. They're an infection if ya ask me. They probably started Veculus, ya know."

Charista nodded. *Grunt, I don't need your amateur analysis.*

The Xeno faces were a mosaic of moods, ranging from desperate and sad to irritated and angry. The hall was thick with the pungent odor of bodies that hadn't been cleaned in some time. The yellowish overhead lights added a slight burning scent to the air.

"Are any of these military?" Charista asked Wosley while she scanned her terminal for any information. The data appeared to be pretty straightforward, a headcount, not much more. Nevertheless, she hoped the guard had picked up some good old-fashioned intel.

Wosley frowned and offered a mild chuckle. "I dunno. They were all on that transport, mixed together. A few of 'em tried making trouble, but we shut that down right quick. They probably had warriors in the lot; not sure how many survived, though."

Charista stopped at one of the cells, where an adult female gazed blankly at her. Charista's eyes met the Xeno's, their long black hair was tousled, but their piercing stare was striking. Charista glanced back to Wosley. "I think I'm good here. I'll check a few of them out and call you when I'm done."

"Fine with me." Wosley already started back up the hallway, only slowing to add, "There's no bounty on these, and I'm getting tired of wading through their scummy mess. You wanna do a few of them in; I won't notice."

After a few moments, the heavy door at the end of the hallway clanged shut, and the rattle reverberated through the hallways. Then, Charista was back studying the Xeno. She recognized a UA symbol on her uniform and figured her initial instinct was right. Charista eyed the profiles of the Xeno until she matched the face with a file in her records.

"Selina... Ravencraft?"

Selina said nothing but glanced back at her accommodations. The rest of the Xeno looked more or less docile. Many hadn't worn any outfits that screamed military or even aggressors. But, in Omegana's eyes, they were all subjects, and the more she got from them, the better for her own sake.

"Listen, Selina. You probably think you shouldn't help me at all, but if you give me a chance, I think you'll find I can help you."

Selina's eyes slowly worked back to Charista's. Charista smiled a little, feeling like she'd at least made a crack in the facade.

"According to my records here, you were one of the leaders of this group."

Selina kept quiet but eyed Charista through a pair of eyes stained with annoyance and anger. "Guess that's the rumor."

Charista nodded. "I know you've been through a lot, and I know you're probably not sure why you're even with us."

Selina stared at Charista. "I'm guessing all that commotion when we were moved here wasn't exactly the plan?"

"Your friends at the UA tried to rescue you, but in their usual way, they underestimated the situation before they jumped into it."

"Mmhmm."

"I can help you, but I need to know you'd be interested in helping me."

Selina arched a brow. "Does it involve us going free?"

"It could."

"Are we supposed to join you or something?"

"It's not quite that simple." Charista took a slow breath and offered a smile. "The truth is, I'm fascinated by your kind.

You don't want to be here. My people don't even really want you here, other than it gets you out of their way. But I'm interested. Ellene Ballo seems to think you can control Essence. So, maybe we can help each other."

"Why don't you ask her then?"

"That's just it; she's vanished. We're unsure where to find her."

"Yeah? Guess we can't help you out there... too bad."

Charista shrugged. "Selina, you can be upset about your situation, but until you realize the galaxy doesn't owe you unless you contribute to it first, you'll never rise above the mealy state your kind has perpetually been in."

Selina slammed the walls of her cell. The electropulse responded with a loud twang noise and sent a shock into Selina's hand. She yelped and pulled her hand back from the wall, which glowed bright red at the spot she'd hit.

"Selina, don't do that again. These can hold much bigger things than your kind."

Selina only offered an annoyed glare in response.

Charista realized convincing Selina involved more than just some well-aimed words. "How about we take a walk? I'll show you a few things we're trying here, and you can decide just how important it is you work with us or not?"

Charista saw the Xeno as a chance that hadn't been wasted. She'd made it to the next step despite all she'd faced, overzealous superior officers, reviews, and orders to avoid the Xeno at all costs. What came afterward was unclear, but she had found her footing again, and her next step wasn't too far away.

COLLATERAL CRISIS

ONE

S ELINA RAVENCRAFT WAS BACK at NewEarth for two
days and already knew the colony was ancient history. No
clairvoyance was required for that assessment; the community of humans on planet Zormad had seen far better times. Selina
stood on top of the former ark ship *Intrepid* and watched the chaos
that was, until recently, the colony of NewEarth, her home. At least
the *Intrepid* was already broken down. The rest of NewEarth was
recently ravaged by a unit of marauding Railen, just one of the collateral effects of an intergalactic conflict spreading further into Ling
Galaxy.

"Hey Selina, where y'at?"

Warrah Malek's voice over the comm gave Selina a welcome
pause from the lurid landscape. "I'm on the *Intrepid* wreckage,
checking the scene. What's up?"

"Oh, just pinging you. Thought you might have been with the
Nara on their ship."

Selina gazed over at the *Dionysus*. It wasn't quite the size of the
Intrepid but bigger than a cruiser. The blue steel starcraft was as

much a mystery as a standout, a pristine oblong sphere amid a sea of chaos and devastation.

"Yeah, no. Like they'd let a dirty Xeno on there with the Hierarch."

Warrah chuckled. "Well, I've heard Zed wants you to meet with Ellene."

"Oh yeah, and just where'd you hear that from, Ms. Malek?"

After a few moments of silence, Warrah giggled.

"What, does Ramsey talk in his sleep?"

Ramsey Nock was one of the most notorious trainers in the Regulation. While many found him imposing, Warrah was drawn to his outward strength, and the two became an item not long after Selina and Warrah became active troops in the Regulation.

Warrah finally found her composure. "Hey, Zed keeps his cadre up to speed, and that's not just you, Ms. Ravencraft."

"All I know is Zed wants me to shadow Ellene, and in a million years, I'll never understand why."

"Whatever the reason, don't forget us little people when you're big and famous."

Selina laughed out loud, a guffaw that she desperately needed. Warrah was one of Selina's oldest friends from the Regulation. The bond they forged in training was a tonic for Selina, especially in chaotic times.

"Well, don't take too long up there."

Selina sighed deeply. "I won't. See you in a few."

Plumes of black smoke dotted the scene, from housing areas to the NewEarth Council building, and even Ward's Commissary. The once popular gathering place for NewEarth residents was sliced nearly in two by Railen armaments during the skirmish.

While the reason for the Railen attack remained a mystery to many, Selina knew why they came. She clutched the Disruptor device, a small cylinder, against her thigh in its hiding place as she walked down into NewEarth. Had it not been for Selina's last-minute abduction during the Railen attack, she may have lost the device, and her life like several Regulation troopers did.

The air was filled with a thick sour smell. While the attack happened two days prior, the fires had only begun to die out. A group of Regulation troops passed Selina, carrying another litter of bodies from a former residence on NewEarth. Each new sight of remains gave Selina a grim feeling.

A flash of light hit Selina's eye. Once the momentary glare passed, she looked in the direction where it came. There was the *Crimson Lance,* her one-time ride. The freighter coughed steam from various ports while Ket Durban worked on some access panels with help from W915, or "Dub," his robot assistant.

Instead of being in the thick of the Railen attack, Selina was yanked off-world and onto Ket's ship. At the time, it was because of a Railen Tracker she had on herself. Ket was out for the tracker only, but the situation parlayed into an arrangement: Selina's return to Zormad for getting the tracker to settle a bounty he'd accepted.

Ket made good on his promise, returning Selina to Zormad. Selina also stuck to her guns, namely the Tracker Ket drooled over, and kept it on herself until she'd set foot back on Zormad. Since their return, Ket quickly fixated on his next move, which had absolutely nothing to do with the salvage of NewEarth. Selina knew the smuggler had his payday in mind, and the cargo he carried did no good for him as long as he stayed on Zormad. *You would think the creep would look around and stay a while to help, but whatever.*

Selina arched her back in a pointless attempt at getting the knots out but gave up after a few tries. Unfortunately, the soreness and throbbing were there to stay. The discomfort was collateral damage on her body for the swift moves she and the Regulation had taken with everything that happened in a short time.

A collection of Regulation troops met Selina as she got to the beginning of the former housing areas of NewEarth. Citizens milled around, many working on clearing their housing units out, so there were plenty of jobs to which Selina could direct soldiers. The feeling of troops following Selina around, several of which were older than her, was odd, but she pushed beyond that to do what was necessary.

Her father Erick, one of the first humans to ever set foot on Zormad, did so much to get NewEarth started that Selina felt pain at the colony's current state. She imagined her father nearby, giving comfort in his presence.

Selina's status on NewEarth quickly went from up-and-coming graduate to kidnapped to a leadership role within the Regulation. Jared, Selina's supervisor, was one of many casualties of the Railen attack, along with other Regulation commanders. Zed survived and moved quickly to pull up those best qualified. Given the situation, "alive and breathing" was an essential prerequisite.

A rancid smell hit Selina's nose, and she realized she'd gotten close to the pile of human bodies, recovered from the attack. The remains were brought toward the outskirts of NewEarth, where several left tokens, small notes, and mementos of their lost loved ones. The makeshift memorial site was a grim reminder of what the survivors truly lost in the attack.

A burst of warm planet Zormad air kissed Selina's face as she wiped the thin layer of sweat from her brow. In addition to Selina and Zed, the council of NewEarth survived to a degree.

It regrouped fast, quickly brokering a deal for migration into the nearby city of Tas Ralong, in hope the reduced visibility within the Mardak city lessened or even dropped the target on NewEarth's back. The Mardaks, residents of Zormad for centuries before humans arrived, built a relationship with the NewEarth group over time. The Railen attack helped to cement the bond further.

Among the scenes of disaster mitigation, a long and snaking line of humanity had begun forming toward Tas Ralong. Landcrawlers, large trucklike vehicles of NewEarth, helped to a point. But, the refugees desperate to get to safety gave way to a hasty migration in any way possible, mostly on foot.

A few shouts caught Selina's attention, and she saw Warrah stooping over a pile of debris with several other Regulation officers.

Selina froze and debated looking away. Unfortunately, sights like that often meant another corpse found in the rubble, but thankfully, it was a few crates of food stores.

Warrah's group was moving their find onto a landcrawler when Selina walked up.

"How goes it?" Selina asked.

Warrah shrugged. "We found a few days of food, which is at least something."

"Yep."

Once the ration box was loaded, Warrah joined Selina for a quick walk around the scene. What remained of the housing units was quickly being broken into piles of valuable items among a sea of charred and mangled trash. Whenever Selina thought she had adjusted to the sight of so much debris, she got another shock of a once familiar location from NewEarth reduced to a pile of rubble beyond recognition.

Selina managed a nervous cough and looked about, but she soon felt Warrah's hand on her arm.

"Hey... you OK?"

Selina wanted to blame the smoke for the tears in her eyes. Warrah slid her arm across Selina's shoulders. "I know. We're all in this together, don't worry about a thing."

"Oh, I've got plenty to worry about."

"Well, you're an officer now."

Selina sighed. "I'm an officer because I didn't get wasted like the rest were." Selina knew, at least in part, there was nothing she could've done. She had no say in being nabbed from the Railen attack by Ket. But the whirlwind of being back on Zormad in the middle of the demolished NewEarth and her elevated role left her mind spinning for answers.

"I gotta check on Ward. Gonna be a lot of mouths to feed still, so Ward's got to be up and running soon to handle that."

Warrah nodded. "I'll keep on with the clean-up. Don't worry. We'll be back to schooling these Regulation guys in no time."

The two friends shared a small chuckle and tight embrace before they parted. Selina next headed toward the Commissary, where Ward Dixon watched a group from NewEarth dismantling his building. The large sign that once hung over the main entrance was among the destroyed parts. The colored and lighted marker was a familiar and comforting symbol not just of NewEarth, but the restaurant signage of the Earth humans left behind decades earlier.

Ward's eyes were heavy as he watched his place like a worried parent. Selina stood next to him for a while before he spoke.

"They were after us for something, weren't they?"

Ward's face was still fixed, his eyes tarnished with fear. Selina slid her arm across his back. "Yeah."

"I don't understand - why kill us? What the hell made us deserve this? I don't get it."

Several yards away, a Regulation trooper appeared from the command center. The structure, like most around NewEarth, had seen better days, but the Regulation kept its use up until the move to Tas Ralong was complete.

As Selina watched the Regulation officer make their way over to the housing unit, Selina's mind returned to Ward. *I should tell Ward about the Disruptor. It was dad's, but I'm the one who had it when the Railen returned for it. That's why they attacked. But, if I tell him, he'll know who has the Disruptor too, making him more vulnerable if they return.*

"Ward, the Railen are just out to make trouble. I've heard on Network they do this all over Ling."

Network, otherwise known as the consolidated collection of comm transmissions throughout Ling Galaxy, was a mash-up in many unhelpful ways. However, it was also the best way to glean any helpful information about movements in Ling Galaxy, provided you took the time to filter out the sprawling array of transmission threads.

Ward nodded. "I forget you listen to that Network jumble."

They stood in silence again. Selina knew, as important as places like the Commissary were to talk, laugh, and share in good times, the support NewEarth citizens showed each other in bad patches made NewEarth a lasting community.

More wafts of smoke made Selina's nose itch, and before long, she busted into a coughing fit. Then it was Ward's turn to soothe her.

"You don't have to wait with me, Selina. You better check on the ones who got it worse."

Selina nodded, glancing back at the burning pile of corpses. "We'll all be in Tas Ralong soon."

"You say that like you don't think it's a good idea."

"There's no other option right now. That doesn't make Tas Ralong the right move. What's so different over there, besides bigger buildings? The Railen know we're around, and we're an easy target. It won't take much for them to come back."

Selina's vision suddenly clouded with tears, but she knew it wasn't the smoke this time. Selina's mother Laurina was one of the casualties of the attack. The sting had only begun to set in, and she found herself ravaged by waves of grief randomly in between bouts of frantic work to help with the salvage and relocation efforts.

She felt a nudge and looked up into Ward's compassionate eyes.

"She was a good woman, Selina. She won't be forgotten."

Selina nodded wordlessly, tears flicking from her face as Ward pulled her into a tight embrace. No words would've better filled the silence. Selina needed a moment, and Ward was happy to allow her that.

Ward spoke gently into their embrace. "We'll get through this."

Selina only managed an emotional "Mmmhmm."

FEELING SLIGHTLY MORE COMPOSED, Selina said her goodbyes to Ward as she watched the movements of troops gathering pieces of NewEarth for the move. She'd waited long enough. Ket and Dub's work on the *Crimson Lance* had finished. While the idea of him sticking around was ridiculous to her, the more stubborn part of Selina figured it was worth one more attempt.

She neared Ket as he closed an exterior access panel underneath the *Crimson Lance* fuselage.

"So, you're really leaving?"

Ket's eyes lit for a moment at the sound of Selina's voice, and then a world-weary smirk took over his expression. "I gotta make good on this payday. If I don't come through, I've some pretty nasty threats against me."

"Ket, come on. You've seen what's going on here. We're short on help right now and could use a good pilot like you. You gonna chase paydays the rest of your life?"

Ket whistled, and Selina heard the whirrs of Dub's propulsion system behind her. "You just need to dig in deeper, and it looks like you're doing that. What do you need a flyer for?"

Selina noticed a lot about Ket in her short time with him beyond a stark portrait of his bravado. He was brash and bold and had a way of working through problems, especially the lethal kind. However, Selina caught glimpses of someone else beneath that tough and some-times arrogant exterior: someone warm and caring. Selina was uncon-scious when Ket took her aboard the *Crimson Lance*, and he could've easily killed her. But Ket didn't. As they returned to Zormad, Selina realized she felt something toward the smuggler. Still, it remained unsaid between them. Selina hadn't felt an attraction to anyone since adulthood. She'd mainly worried about living in and moving out of the shadow of her father's legacy. The idea of sharing anything besides a Regulation assignment with someone hadn't come up on her radar until Ket.

Selina stifled a gasp when Ket clasped her shoulders. His greenish eyes peered deeply into hers, and Selina froze. "Look, you've got my contact token. You can call whenever you want."

"You'll be on the far side of the galaxy in a few days anyway." Selina glanced offward, unconcerned about the wounded tone in her voice.

Ket leaned in, and his voice softened. "Selina, I gotta do this. It's what I am."

She nodded and backed up from his grasp, noticing Dub to her side. "Take care of this maniac for me, will ya?"

Dub glanced to Ket and back to Selina. "Don't I always?"

Selina managed a polite yet fake smile and turned from the two. Almost as quickly as their paths crossed, they diverged. Selina felt a sting of the separation, but the loss was just one more for her, and she had to brace herself to continue the important job of saving the rest of her people who survived and were determined to stay.

TWO

SELINA HAD BARELY LEFT the *Crimson Lance* when she heard a voice to her right.

"Selina, a word?"

Ellene Ballo, Hierarch of the Nara, came to Zormad a day after Selina's return. The Mardaks verified Ellene as who she claimed to be, but even a confirmation like that wasn't enough for Selina. Ellene was a two-part mystery. The first was why the leader of the Nara, a prominent race in Ling Galaxy, was suddenly so interested in humans. The second was why Selina was suddenly ordained caretaker of Ellene during her visit to NewEarth.

While Zed and the rest of the leadership focused on the migration to Tas Ralong, Zed had Selina talk with Ellene. The assignment bugged her, and at the moment with Ellene trailing her, her irritation percolated.

Selina strode down the rows of housing units while Ellene walked beside her.

I'm not a diplomat. That was my dad's thing, Zed. "I'm not sure what I'm supposed to say to you, Ms. Ballo."

"Please, call me Ellene. Look, Selina. I know you and your people are in a world of pain right now."

"What clued you in, the pile of bodies?"

"I'm here to tell you I can help your people survive and regain your stature, even ascend to a greater one."

NewEarth never had polished and perfect residential districts, even in its best state. But for Selina, until a few days ago, it was home. Seeing so many buildings destroyed, with many more on fire or in severe disrepair, shook Selina to her core and had her in full-on fight mode.

Selina strained to keep the tremble out of her voice while holding onto that air of command she figured everyone expected from her. "Ellene, a third of our population is dead, including my mom. Most of our buildings are ruined, or at the very least, need serious repair. I've got a lot to keep track of, so I'm a little busy now."

A quick burst of warm air swept past, fluttering Ellene's flowing hair. The Nara were stewards of Essence, the life-giving substance to Ling Galaxy, but that was all Selina knew about them. All the suffering that hit NewEarth in just minutes made Selina wonder what Essence was worth since it hadn't prevented the colony's destruction.

"Selina, I'm truly sorry about your mother. And, the rest of your dead - what the Railen did is horrible. But, they want to rule this galaxy and don't care who or what they destroy to do it."

Selina bit her lip to stifle a cry. She didn't know why at the time, but something in her mind said to hold firm because showing Ellene any more emotion than she already had would've weakened her in Ellene's eyes. Selina's eyes closed as she spoke slowly, her voice straining to contain her emotions. "Why attack defenseless people? We weren't strong enough to face the Railen when we did. It's only blind luck that kept them from killing everyone here."

Selina felt Ellene's hand on her shoulder.

"Selina, the Railen and Omegans only succeed when fear thrives. The more they scare everyone, the better for them. It's not necessarily about what you have. You want safety for your people; it's what anyone reasonable would want. What if I offered you and your people accommodation in the safest place in Ling Galaxy?"

Selina looked into Ellene's thoughtful eyes. "Where exactly is a 'safe place'?"

"Planet Yassel, headquarters of the UA. They've got good defenses and always have a garrison on hand. You'll be near the seat of the UA government and president Nic Sava. It's the best place you could be right now."

Planet Yassel, central in Ling Galaxy, seemed almost mythical in the descriptions Selina heard of it. She imagined shimmering cities of colossal towers, where the population led the good life. The mental pictures were equally glamorous and frustrating, given how far life on Zormad was from that ideal.

Selina turned toward a crew clearing one of the housing units. The three covered bodies near the front of the property said plenty about the outlook there. Selina swung her boot at the ground, sending a spray of crumbled soil toward Ellene. "Where were you when we were under attack? We could've used you then."

"I know, and I'm sorry." Ellene's eyes met Selina's with a sad look. "This conflict has stretched our abilities far more than ever. I hope you realize that while we failed in helping some of your people, I'm here now to prevent this from happening again to more of you."

"Ellene, as tempting leaving Zormad sounds right now, our council makes decisions like this. If they decide you're for real, they'll still have to bring this to a vote among our people. That's how we make decisions, and Ellene, we're short on trust right now. Mardaks are our most reliable option."

Ellene nodded. "The Mardaks are certainly rugged. Their survival in these conditions with little outside assistance is a fine testament. Be that as it may, your presence here has roused the attention of more than just the Railen. I'm afraid more trouble is headed this way soon. If I'm right, even your partnership with the Mardaks won't stop further bloodshed."

A series of shouts interrupted their conversation. A crew of Regulation troops and regular citizens was in the middle of bringing down a partially demolished building, and its structural pieces had shifted dangerously. "Ellene, we have to get to shelter before more trouble comes. Immediate safety is top priority; for now, that's Tas Ralong."

Ellene's smile widened. "Then I offer my assistance in that regard. I can shuttle people on the *Dionysus*, at least thirty at a time."

Finally, she's being helpful. "You'd do that for us?"

"I'm ready to show beyond words what I want to do for your people."

"Alright then."

Selina pulled over a few Regulation officers who set up a transfer with Ellene and the ready-to-move NewEarth refugee population. Soon, a group of residents trudged over toward Ellene's craft. Selina grabbed a few cases of clothing and food to help with the rest of the migration when she caught up with Zed again.

"How's it going?" Zed asked.

"It goes. Although, if anyone asks me when this is gonna end, I may punch 'em."

They shared a laugh. The chronic stress of disruption had washed over the entire NewEarth population. While several of the older generations remembered the first migration to Zormad, the twenty passing cycles mellowed the agitation of uncertainty for those generations and made them more adaptable. However, the severe damage to NewEarth, a civilization that had only begun to expand with new births, was a difficult hurdle for many.

Zed offered the half grin Selina knew meant many things. At that moment, she suspected it was due to her unofficial designation as Ellene's chaperone.

"So, how are you and Ellene getting on?"

"Oh, wonderful. She's the perfect mix of inquisitive and annoying I've needed in my life, so thanks for that."

Zed chuckled amid a wince. "Oh, she's not that bad. I guess she mentioned the migration to Yassel."

"Yep."

Zed shrugged with a slight laugh. "Can't say it's the worst idea I've heard. But this quick show of support by the UA after nothing for twenty years has me suspicious."

"Same. So, Zed... you ever gonna tell me why you have me, a Regulation officer for less than a week, spending so much time with her?"

"Simple, she asked for you by name. I was kinda hoping you'd tell me why. Whatever she has in mind for us, you're a big part of it."

THREE

ONCE ELLENE WAS WELL INVOLVED with helping the migration, Selina turned her attention to the breakdown and relocation of the greenhouse facilities and structures. She wasn't as bothered about the physical move as she was about who she had to deal with because of it.

Ryan Rinaldi, lead of the agricultural efforts, was only five years older than Selina. Still, he spoke to her and everyone else as if the entire migration to NewEarth was his idea.

Selina quickly got familiar with Ryan at the NewEarth council meeting right before the Tas Ralong migration started. However, Selina never realized how much anyone in NewEarth hated the Regulation until she heard Ryan's 10-minute barrage of complaints. His detailed and eloquent series of gripes left Selina wondering how Ryan had any time to grow and maintain the crops for NewEarth's food supply.

While Ryan's level of bickering coming from an average citizen would've gotten them dressed down quick, his abilities to produce as many crops as he had gave him a high reputation among NewEarth citizens. A fed dog is loyal to its master, after all, and Ryan's influence over the mood of NewEarth rose commensurate with how well he kept the population fed.

Selina made another pass by the remnants of Ward's Commissary, which by then had dwindled to a shell, with a few more units left to move from it. Ward traded waves with Selina as she walked. Nearby Ward's broken-down site, Selina came across a young couple working on a food development fixture. The man was stooped over the device, holding a section of a food processing unit. He was stocky, with a long mane of curly brownish hair.

"I'll help," Selina said as she trotted over. The agricultural types, known as "Agros," were all devotees to Ryan's groupthink, and this couple was no exception. It was pretty clear to Selina in the deep glare she got from both of them.

Selina grabbed one side of the food device, and the load righted itself as she and the other two walked carefully toward the path to Tas Ralong. After a few moments, Selina said, "We should get this unit onto a landcrawler or the *Dionysus*. It's a long walk to Tas Ralong, ya know."

The man glared. "Sorry, we don't trust the Regulation's landcrawlers with our delicate gear. Ryan wants to supervise all moves once we get to our staging area."

Selina nodded. "Ah. What're your names?"

"Everet." The man answered with the finesse of a boxer's jab.

The woman eyed Selina briefly before saying her name as if it was an alibi. "Claire."

"Well, Everet, Claire... with everyone from NewEarth moving at once, a lot is going on right now. Ryan's probably busy. How about I help you?"

Claire squared her shoulders, taking a step towards Selina with narrowed eyes. Selina bowed her frame in response, inching closer to Claire.

Ward's booming voice interrupted the moment. "What y'all doing, trying to break your backs?"

Ward showed his usual lopsided grin with a curious look in his eyes. Everet cleared his throat. "Nothing you need to worry about."

"Yeah, until I have to cook it up. Why're you walking it? That don't make sense." Ward shook his head, adding a nod to Selina.

Everet took a steady breath and spoke slow and deliberate, with annoyance in his voice. "The system is delicate; I'm worried the jostling might jar something loose."

"And walking it is safer?" Ward shook his head with a chuckle. Selina knew it was up to her. As much as Ryan may have fed his people about not listening to a non-Agro, in the move to Tas Ralong, the Regulation had the rule of law.

"Look, we've moved complex weaponry on these transports. It's not a baby's cradle, but it'll be fine, alright? So again, let's get this loaded. You wouldn't want to be here when the Railen return, right?"

Everet and Claire traded looks, and after a few moments, Everet said, "I'm calling Ryan."

Ward motioned Selina over while Everet and Claire contacted Ryan for a pass by. Selina gazed sharply at Everet, daring him to look up from his comm unit until she felt a nudge from Ward and caught his amused expression.

"Don't be thinking what I think you're thinking over there."

Selina stared at Ward for a second, but his papa-like face melted her resolve, and she chuckled. "Oh, I'd love to teach those two a lesson and good."

Ward snuck his arm around Selina's shoulder. "I know. You've your daddy's temper, no doubt. But since he's not around, I'll have to set you straight."

Selina scoffed. "All they're worried about is their crops and not the odds of being gunned down again out here. Their idealist leader has them believing we can share and be all kumbaya with the rest of Ling Galaxy, but you and I know that ain't so. Like the Railen would be nice if we just fed them, sure."

"I know, Selina. But the truth is we can't survive without Ryan either. No matter what, we've a supply chain, and right now we need Ryan for that."

Selina stared at Ward for a long moment. Survival was a multi-tiered construct. But, the threat to life still hung larger in the balance for her, and the Agros stalling made her nuts.

Selina went ahead and called for a landcrawler vehicle. Several minutes later, with as much pomp as he could've mustered, Ryan showed up. He wore the trademark goggles the Agros used for soil analysis. Ryan first made a big show of looking over the supplies with Everet and Claire without acknowledging the presence of Selina and Ward, who were well within caustic staring distance.

Selina and Ward watched the threesome as they went from reviewing the items on the scene to a pretty spirited talk, with more than a few glances thrown at Selina.

Ward nudged Selina. "Hey, they want me to look at some heavy food prep units. You gonna be okay if I leave you here?"

"I'm fine." She saw the concern with a tinge of doubt in Ward's eyes. "Really, Ward, I'm a big girl."

"No doubt. Still, don't clock anybody. Remember, you're supposed to be keeping the peace."

Selina hugged Ward tightly before he left. The landcrawler arrived a few minutes later. Selina gave the driver the heads up to stand by, and then she headed toward Ryan and the others. Ryan's back was to Selina, but Everet's eyes met hers and he motioned to Ryan, who faced Selina with a look that carried every bit of the smugness Selina expected.

"Ryan, as I told Everet and Claire, we've got the residential side moving. Now, the Agros need to catch up, so we don't disrupt our supply chain more than it already is."

Ryan's mouth formed a line, and he nodded dismissively. "Selina, our equipment is delicate, and that stampede you've got going to Tas Ralong right now doesn't have me too confident in moving our gear just yet."

Selina bristled at Ryan's attitude. In regular times, Selina was ready to cut off someone who wasn't falling in line, but with Ryan, she was far too close to taking a swing at him, but she mustered up one last amount of Regulation reserve for the jerkwad.

"Ryan, I'm sure you saw or heard about that attack by the Railen - you know, the whole reason we're moving in the first place? The Railen aren't gonna care if you've got a few more seedlings to baby or something. If they return and smoke us all, that's gonna be the end of everything, even your little plantings."

Ryan stared at Selina a long moment before he said, "You know, Everet... you and Claire can help me with something back at the greenhouse. So why don't you head over there? I'll finish up here and deal with Selina."

Everet and Claire nodded and walked past, giving Selina another stink eye before leaving the area.

Selina flexed her arms and felt her gut tighten as if she were about to throw a punch. While part of Selina realized Ryan was most likely pushing her buttons, the side of Selina mixed between grieving her mother and stress over protecting those left behind had sapped her patience.

"Ya know, Ryan, all this moving will get people more worked up for food. Ward's operation isn't up yet, so how about we at least get these food crates moving."

Ryan gazed off at the containers. His eyes slid back to Selina, and a smirk found his face. "We'll see. Sure could use a few extra hands with dismantling if you can spare the time, officer."

Selina had ingested a nasty cocktail of equal parts indignation from Ryan and overall fatigue from the NewEarth situation. Having her fill of Ryan for the moment, she said nothing else but instead walked toward the nearby food crates.

Selina grabbed the first container when she felt Ryan's fist slam down hard on her shoulder. "Did I say you could touch *that*?"

Wrong move, guy.

Selina maneuvered Ryan into an armbar and rotated her torso until his body flung over and knocked into another crate. Ryan yelped and gasped as Selina eyed him. "Did I say you could touch *me*? Now then, maybe I didn't make myself clear. I'm taking your food supply to our people. You know, the ones you've been feeding all along? See, they've been moving for a couple of days. A lot haven't eaten much, some not at all. The elderly need extra attention, in case you forgot. Your food production facility is moving in another day. I suggest you make that happen ASAP and don't make me or my team come back here and move it for you because we will, and you won't like how we do it."

"Selina, stop!"

Ward's voice interrupted Selina's thoughts, and she looked at Ward's fearful expression. Then, realizing her overstep, she let Ryan up slowly. Ryan's eyes darted between Ward and Selina, grinning like a lawyer winning a court case. Then, maneuvering his arm around, Ryan said, "Well, let's just see what Zed has to say about this."

FOUR

SELINA AND RYAN'S LITTLE DANCE made the news around NewEarth fast. Even in a mass migration, scrapes between a Regulation officer and the leader of the Agricultural wing were the last thing anyone needed.

Selina regretted losing her cool more than anything she did to Ryan. The jerk had it coming for a while. However, she wasn't looking forward to the collateral damage her tussle did with her standing in Zed's eyes.

Zed and Ryan were already seated in the Regulation temp command center's planning room when Selina arrived. Like the rest of the building, the room was stocked with various supplies.

As bad and annoying as she found it being around Ryan, having Zed mediating made it ten times worse. Selina bristled under Ryan's gaze and contemplated how much popping him good would be worth the extra disciplinary action.

Selina had previously seen Zed agitated during the move, but his anger was directed toward her this time.

"Damn it; we don't have time for this. I'm the lead of NewEarth now, and you both know that. You two will cease whatever's going on here, and you'll do it now, understood?"

Selina swallowed a lump in her throat. "Chief, I was only trying to help them out."

Ryan's eyes avoided Selina's as he leaned forward. "Zed, I appreciate what you've done to keep the peace during this move, but you and your officer here need to know the Agros have the best interests of NewEarth at heart. Given all we've faced, I have to run my program as I've been doing. That includes moving our hardware and crops as I see fit."

Zed stood, and paced around in thought. Selina searched his expression for any hint of what was coming, but came up with nothing. *There's no way he's gonna give Ryan a free pass, is there?*

"Ryan, as far as running your stuff, you're right. But, you have to move faster. Our supplies are stretched along with our people. The more we get to Tas Ralong, the more we'll need the Agros to keep everyone fed. The Regulation will continue to look out for everyone, and you will observe our directions. Even Selina's."

Ryan's lips drew taut, and his eyes darted between Zed and Selina before Ryan offered a slight nod in response.

Zed steepled his fingers. After a few moments, he gave both Selina and Ryan a pointed stare. "OK, we'll get the Agros' food and gear moving quicker, and you two will keep the peace, even if it means being as far the hell away from each other as possible."

An uneasy quiet filled the room after Zed finished. After a few moments, Ryan stood and headed back outside. Selina was about to follow when Zed grabbed her arm.

"Sit down."

A deep ache hit Selina's gut as she slowly pawed for a chair. Zed clasped his hands together in thought.

Oh great, I'm getting a crappy detail as punishment.

"Selina, watch your temper. You're a lot like your old man. He got hot sometimes too."

"Ryan's been pushing me for a while. You know that, right?"

"Ryan's a prick, OK? I get it. But he's done a lot for NewEarth, and plenty of people pay attention to what he says. You and I know Ellene's Yassel offer is the best idea. But, the more we're seen lashing out, and the less we keep the peace, the fewer people will listen to whatever we suggest, OK?"

Selina nodded.

"Look, you've been handed a lot real fast. From our first moment in Ling Galaxy, we've never had it easy on NewEarth. Me and your dad Erick used to get in all kinds of problems, fighting off the random raids, bickering with the Mardaks when we were still not on their good side yet. Whenever things got terrible, and I felt like we were a day or two from just being wiped out for good, Erick would look me in the eye and say, 'You never end the fight.' That was him. That kind of determination kept me going then and will keep NewEarth going now."

Hearing stories about her dad that she hadn't heard before was a special kind of salve for Selina. Ever since she lost her father, she pieced together in her mind a quilt work of memories of him. Some were her own recollections, and the rest were stories from Zed.

Zed added, "You're handling a lot pretty damned good, in case you haven't heard that from anyone."

An unexpected burst of emotion hit Selina, and she managed a combination cough and low chuckle at the sudden kudos from her leader. A smile found Selina's lips for the first time in a while. Zed's words and hearing another piece of Erick's history were a welcome boost.

Selina took in a relieved breath and stood. "OK. I'll head back outside, see where else I can help."

Zed smiled back. "By the way, comm just came back about 20 minutes ago. Ellene's finished moving the rest of our group to Tas Ralong. She's coming in and wants to talk more with you."

AS GOOD AS Selina felt about standing up to Ryan, she knew Zed was right. Selina hated losing her temper quickly, but nothing had been the same since she returned to Zormad. All the suffering she saw all day long cut her deeply. *The Regulation is supposed to preserve order. But will we ever get back to that order with all that's happened now?*

The *Dionysus* touched down near the makeshift command center with a graceful flourish. After a few minutes, Ellene emerged. Once her eyes met Selina's, Ellene headed over, a smile on her face.

The road ahead for humans had a pretty definite fork in it. On one side stood Tas Ralong, the safe bet. Close by, NewEarth's survivors would be guests of the Mardaks, who at least were marginally interested in having humans around and did not want to blast and pillage them to oblivion. On the other side lay Ellene Ballo and the great unknown of planet Yassel.

Either move was risky, and the time to pick was close.

Selina was about to say hello to Ellene when her comm unit signaled with an alert:

"Omegan unit of starcraft spotted approaching planet Zormad. Alert and activate all available defenses."

FIVE

THE SKYLINE TOLD SELINA all she needed. A squadron of Omegan craft flew directly toward the remnants of NewEarth, wings abreast. It was probably another random raid, but any disarrayed group like NewEarth at that point was easy picking for anyone like the Omegans.

As klaxon alarms blared, several Regulation soldiers dashed out of the command center as Ellene looked about.

Ellene's eyes met Selina's, with a glum look. "So, we've got company."

Selina moved her pulse rifle to ready position. "Mmmhmm. I hope the Mardaks are ready for a fight."

The screech of a landcrawler's brakes rang out to Selina's left. Warrah jumped out and ran up close, her curly locks billowed behind her. "What's the plan?"

"Dunno. Zed's getting details and calling for Mardak help in the command center."

Soon, other Regulation landcrawler vehicles arrived at their location. The Mardak militia had maintained a modest force, given all their struggles in Ling overall. Their armory included several light fighters and two medium cruisers. The fleet wasn't tailored for intergalactic conquest, and even a last-stand defense of Zormad was a bit of a stretch. Still, the Mardaks were used to being one of the forgotten races of Ling and had tempered that neglect with a certain stubbornness that kept their race alive.

Ellene grabbed Selina's arm. "I can help."

"Ellene, I'm glad for what you've done so far. But *Dionysus* doesn't look well-armed. I've seen transport ships with more fire-power, frankly."

Ellene laughed. "Oh, Selina, there's more to strength than star-craft weaponry."

Once Zed appeared outside the command center, he was met with a rush of Regulation troops. Selina and Warrah jogged over, arriving as Zed started his briefing. He knelt in the center of the group, glancing about as he spoke.

"The Mardaks will provide help. They're the next biggest target beyond us, and it won't take much for the Omegans to include Tas Ralong in this hit. The problem is they'll need a few minutes, and from the look of those Omegan starcraft, we have a few seconds before we're in the heat."

Warrah scoffed. "We have to hold a spread-out position with maybe two-thirds the force we had before?"

Zed said, "That's right, Warrah. We're 25 strong, but we've gotta fight like 200. So, dig in. The cavalry's coming, but we've got to put as much fire as we can on the Omegans until then. Drivers and gunners, take the landcrawlers, use the pulse cannon. Set up the best perimeter possible. For the rest, find the best fighting positions you can. We'll give them all we got and make them pay for every foot they get closer to us."

The idea of a last stand hadn't occurred to Selina, but the feeling was palpable, and the weary yet resigned glances of her fellow Regulation troops told her that this may be it, and it was time for her to step up with her comrades. Of all NewEarth citizens, the Regulation believed in defense of their lives with force.

Their job wasn't determining the political nuances of the topsy turvy world of Zormad or Ling Galaxy. They just knew a job was there to be done, and that job at times involved force. It was in their hearts to protect what was left of NewEarth to the last person, weapon, and round.

The troops gave a rousing shout before heading to the fight. Selina's heart thumped in her throat, realizing their odds against the Omegans couldn't have been worse if they all lay flat on the sand, their arms raised in surrender. Still, she pushed forward, heading toward the landcrawler with Warrah, when she felt a hand on her shoulder and turned to Ellene.

As several Regulation troops nearby began digging in, Selina suddenly realized she was stuck in place. Her feet felt like they were tied to the Zormad surface, and her attempts to move only hurt her legs.

What is this? Am I panicking?

Warrah yelled for Selina to take cover, but Selina remained stationary. Then, Ellene's gaze finally told Selina her body wasn't frozen from panic but something Ellene had done herself.

"Ellene, we've got this." Selina's tone had every bit of the emphasis of an order behind it, even though she was still frozen in place.

Ellene's warm eyes darkened suddenly, so much it made Selina nervous. When Ellene spoke again, her vocal pattern twisted with an ethereal sound. "Selina, you don't want to do this."

Something in either the change in Ellene's eyes or maybe her vocal inflection jarred Selina. She held her weapon up and slightly pointed away from Ellene. "Excuse me?"

Ellene smirked amid narrowed eyes. Her glance darted toward an Omegan craft that darted past them. "I said you don't want to do this."

Selina felt fear in her gut as Warrah took off in the landcrawler. "Ellene, what's going on?"

"Selina, I'm sorry. I haven't told you everything yet. I wanted you to make your own decision about what you and your people do, but to do that, I first need to show you just why I'm so interested in you."

Selina knew fairy tales. Those stories were one of the carryovers from Earth that remained with their new civilization on Zormad. But, for most of her adult life to that point, she assumed stories about wizards and brave warriors on journeys fighting evil creatures and mythical spirits were an invention of desperate parents attempting to give their children something to cling to, something to focus on, but mostly to get them to sleep.

But what Ellene did next was like nothing Selina had ever heard about in any story or real account.

Ellene strode toward the Omegan craft, which swooped down and fired indiscriminately at the rubble of NewEarth, the ground, and in some cases, running individuals. The sky had darkened with smoke, and the bevy of Omegan starcraft circled overhead like a pack of hungry predators savoring the scent of the kills, both the fresh ones and the ones about to happen.

Explosions from rocket fire punched the air. The foul stench of burning pieces of fabricated building components itched Selina's nose.

Ellene walked through the fray with studied calm. Selina yelled for Ellene to take cover, but Ellene never acknowledged Selina. Ellene instead climbed on a pile of rubble, formerly a piece of housing, and flung off her cape. The overhead craft slowed their pace as a deep rumbling sound built.

Ellene stood and glanced about. Her long mane of blonde hair wisped about like sprigs of wheat in a gentle breeze. Her light bluish skin stood out sharply against the gray background.

Ellene's slender body arched into a fighting stance, and a screech pierced the air. Selina grabbed her ears and noticed several others nearby did the same; their faces strained with the overwhelming noise. Selina looked about for the noise source but realized it was Ellene, whose flowing golden locks of hair had burst into flames.

Selina caught a glimpse of Ellene's face when she looked back, and Selina gasped at the sight.

Ellene's eyes became two glowing orbs which cast bright yellow light as intense as a sun. Suddenly, a sizeable Omegan starcraft bore down on her. Ellene thrust her arms up toward the approaching ship, and a series of energy bolts burst from her hands toward the craft, shattering it into a spectacular explosion. Barrage after barrage of pulse cannon fire from other Omegan ships hammered the ground around Ellene, but she stayed in place, casting out more energy bolts that sliced any craft that flew too close to them. The sky lit up with explosions.

Then, Ellene flung herself up into the air and flew on an attack through the rest of the pursuing Omegan barrage until finally, the remaining ships turned in retreat.

Once the threat was gone, Ellene lowered herself back to the ground. The air was filled with the stench of smoke. Wails from the injured drifted over the air along with the wafts of smog. Selina, realizing she was still holding her ears, slowly lowered her hands and walked toward Ellene.

Ellene picked up her cape and adjusted her hair as if she hadn't just self-levitated and vaporized a group of Omegan starcraft with beams from her own body.

Ellene hadn't acknowledged Selina, instead she glanced around, her eyes showing sadness when she saw the hurt Mardaks and humans.

Selina remembered all the fights she and the Regulation had been in, especially the last showdown with the Railen. *Ellene could've headed off all of those attacks by herself.* Selina saw Zed, and he had a look on his face that Selina imagined matched hers.

"What the hell was that, Ellene?"

Ellene simply gazed coolly back at Selina, then Zed for a moment. Her expression then warmed a bit, and she managed a polite smile. "Essence, Selina. That's why I need your help so badly."

Selina blinked. "*My* help?"

Ellene smiled. "We'll talk about that very soon."

Moving to Yassel was still a risk and a long shot for safety. But, having Ellene's power as security would've made the trip much safer. Selina only wondered about her part in Ellene's strange powers.

Zed cleared his throat. "Well, that was... great and scary at the same time. Do you mind telling us why you didn't bust that out sooner?"

Ellene's smile was a mix of triumph and concern. Ellene approached Selina and Zed as the landcrawler vehicles nearby came in closer to their spot. "I don't like to direct through fear. That's Malone Stanton's way. However, powers like mine are terrifying to the uninitiated, and I intend to use reason to convince you to come to planet Yassel. I would greatly appreciate if you let me explain this to everyone."

Zed replied, "OK, Ellene. It's still everyone's choice whether they stay or go, of course."

Whether or not they went to Yassel, Ellene's performance wasn't going to be secret very long around NewEarth. Selina only wondered if it was enough to convince those who rooted themselves in the idea of gathering and hunkering like Ryan and his posse of Agros.

SIX

THE TAS RALONG WAREHOUSE THAT became NewEarth's new location was a vast structure. A collection of several medium-sized buildings connected via corridors and featuring a large common area, the once cold and stark facility took on new life as a hasty collection of living areas. A makeshift platform stage was built toward the front entrance using a series of emptied storage crates.

Once a bulk of NewEarth residents gathered in the common area, they were ready for Ellene's presentation. Selina stood at the side of the stage with Zed and Ellene at center. Dirty faces in the crowd were a standard dress. Selina imagined she looked pretty messed up herself, given all the moving and dragging of equipment she did in the dry Zormad heat and dust.

Another common trait in their group was fatigue. The fear of being killed by the Railen was terrible enough, but a forced evacuation of everything they owned in days with little to no sleep had everyone looking wearier than they had ever been.

The warehouse's interior boomed with the crowd's sound, but

Zed quieted them down after a few moments. "OK, everyone, we've all been through a lot, and despite that, I'm glad to see we've gotten this move done pretty well. Ellene Ballo of Grondia wants to talk with us. She recently helped turned back an Omegan raid on our group, so for me that earns her a few minutes of our time to hear what she's got to say."

Selina searched faces in the crowd. Many looked at least curious about Ellene. She also saw the Agros, Ryan smack in their middle, the lot of them toward the crowd's right.

"Citizens of NewEarth, my name is Ellene Ballo of the Nara. Your time in Ling Galaxy has been fraught with danger, struggle at best. I'm here today to offer you a chance to rise above that. You may have heard of our race. First, let me say we've been stewards of Ling Galaxy and Essence for millennia.

"I want you to know we're aware of your history in this galaxy so far. You've been mistreated, and while we haven't been able to help you in the past, we've taken steps. Unfortunately, Ling Galaxy has plummeted into war. Malone Stanton and the Omegans are making their play for control of Ling and the Nara. That means things will only get worse for everyone, including you here. But I want you to know there are many fighting for peace. The Universal Alliance stands as a beacon for order, and as a full supporter of the UA, I'm here to say you've got an option beyond your current agreement."

Shouts from the crowd interrupted Ellene. Not a surprise, the other Agros nearby had adopted Ryan's outrage.

Ellene continued in her speech. "The truth is, you are not safe here. It would be best if you came with me to planet Yassel, the seat of the UA. I understand the risks are considerable. But I ask you to think of the risk of doing nothing. You've already lost your temporary home, and that was to a smaller group of Railen. The Omegans have also shown themselves very recently, and Malone Stanton remains a huge threat. How long do you think you'll last hunkered down on a Far Reach planet before another attack? Spirits preserve you if the Railen or Omegans determine this entire planet as a strategic target."

Ryan's shouts got much clearer. "We've survived for over twenty years now. If any are to blame for our problems, it's the Regulation, agitating outsiders like the Railen. I say these attacks are their fault."

Shouts came in response to Ryan, mainly from his fellow Agros propping up their fearless leader. Worse, Selina saw others in the crowd who weren't Argos but still clapped in approval of Ryan's theory.

Ellene's eyes met Selina's. Wordlessly, Selina saw something in Ellene's gaze that said *no one believes that. Trust me, what this man says will only harm your people if he convinces others. Stick with me, and we'll sway them.*

Selina took a sharp breath in and held it. She balled her hands into fists so tight they burned.

Turning back to the crowd, Ryan in particular, Ellene continued, "I know much of what you've suffered hasn't been anything in your control."

Ryan sneered. "Maybe Malone isn't so bad after all. From what I've heard on Network, it sounds like Malone's got the right idea of caring for everyone. For that matter, maybe Essence itself is where we should focus. I heard it revitalized a whole planet. So why shouldn't we look for Malone's help, and not yours?"

Ellene's face changed immediately with Ryan's challenge. She walked off the stage and into the crowd, until she stood face to face with Ryan. Selina looked at Zed, who shrugged.

Ellene stretched her arms out so her robe billowed and straightened over her frame. Her tone became gentler than Selina would've expected. "I understand your distrust, Xeno. However, you must realize Ling Galaxy is filled with many races of beings, and most had suffered long before you arrived. My kind has fueled this galaxy, but with that comes a delicate balance to maintain. Don't you think we would've used our control over Essence to destroy Malone and the rest if we had the ability? We need all races working together to handle the needs of the many. Safety and security only happen through cooperation. Essence doesn't offer perfection; it only offers life."

Ellene glanced about before facing Ryan again, her eyes staring like a medium deeply into Ryan's nonplussed expression. "You and everyone else must hear my next words and remember them well, or it could mean the end for all of us. Malone Stanton is not your savior. He's not the one to bring anything to Ling Galaxy other than his special variety of chaos."

Ellene pointed a finger toward Ryan. "This one might tell you about Malone Stanton's miracle on the Agmon planet. Agmon, a near lifeless body not unlike Zormad, was returned to a lush paradise teeming with life and sustenance thanks to Malone's wielding of Essence. But, be warned, those manipulations have caused imbalances in Essence that have already begun to degrade life elsewhere in Ling Galaxy.

"Malone is quite clever and has gotten a special order of followers in short time. He promises things like saving worlds and letting all Essence flow freely. But, Essence was never meant to be molded by any living being, served to do the will of one. Malone wants everyone to believe he can provide life to all and hold everyone hostage to his plans, but his desires only lead to destruction. Essence flows from Grondia, and that creation lets Ling Galaxy exist. That creation exists through a careful balance of energy, which the Nara oversee. If Essence is overused, it could destroy the galaxy. That's a very inconvenient fact for the likes of Malone to mention, but one you should all be very concerned about."

Selina saw the crowd flare up into a series of conversations and heated arguments. She edged closer to Zed and nudged him. "What do you think of all this?"

Zed folded his arms as they both studied the crowd below. "Ellene wouldn't have bothered with us if we weren't useful to her somehow. In any case, there won't be any quality of life on Zormad for us. Of course, people like the easy path, which for now is staying.

Maybe this convinces enough of them about going to Yassel. That may be the best thing we've done in Ling Galaxy yet."

Selina agreed on the move, but her role regarding Essence left her wondering just what this migration to Yassel would cost her in the end.

SEVEN

ELLENE'S OFFER TO NEWEARTH went as well as Selina could've predicted. Out of 3000 people, 1700 agreed to the trip to Yassel. What remained after the vote was the dividing of essentials and preparing for departure.

The NewEarth council gathered in the admin room of the warehouse to review the next step in the transport to planet Yassel. The growing pomp of their body was quickly reduced to partially slipshod chairs huddled around a rusted-out table.

Zed began, "The transport the UA is sending, *Evangeline,* has enough space if anyone changes their minds about coming along. I know this is sudden; believe me, I wish there was more time to investigate alternatives."

Selina caught Ryan's cocky grin. In the division among those leaving and staying, Ryan was elevated to leader of NewEarth. Selina couldn't have been leaving the colony soon enough after that.

"Something on your mind there, Ryan?" Asked Zed.

Ryan cast an annoyed look at Zed and Selina as he stood. "A few things. We've busted our asses developing sustenance for NewEarth, not to mention getting on the good graces of - I don't know - the only group of aliens in this galaxy so far who haven't minded us breathing their air. Now, we're being penalized into giving up crops because some of us naively think the UA will save us?"

Selina grasped the handle of her pulse pistol and squeezed it tight.

Ryan continued his sermon. "Sorry, I don't see why we should jump on board with the UA just because they claim their location is more secure. Besides, isn't planet Yassel under attack by the Omegans now? I know that's true, even with the spotty connection to Network that we have."

Selina said, "Safer is better than nothing. Excuse me if I don't trust this building that was probably here way before we set foot on this planet. You wanna stay, bone up on your Mardak and blend into Tas Ralong? That's on you. But you've got a week to make up your mind."

Ryan narrowed his eyes. "I'll have you all know I'm telling anyone that'll listen why they should stay too, including those who voted for a ride on your little transport. So have fun with your new captors."

Ryan slid his chair back, making a loud screech. Zed reached for him as he left, but it was useless. "Selina, get a head count of people and let's start organizing. I don't want to hold this over any more than we have to. It's a helluva long way to Yassel."

EIGHT

EVANGELINE LANDED ON ZORMAD a few days past the estimated arrival date. After a lengthy approach sequence, the transport eased to a gentle touchdown a hundred yards from the outskirts of Tas Ralong. The craft, a large oblong sphere, was decorated with an array of lights cascading in sequence about the fuselage. A progressive chain of living quarters and common areas adorned the ship from aft to fore. A massive bank of engines at the rear gave off an intense hum as they cycled during the ship's landing phase.

Selina worked with the Regulation and ran shuttles to and from the craft loading food stores and other supplies. Like the earlier migration, a new procession formed of those loading themselves and spare items aboard for the trip to planet Yassel.

While helping with the loading process, Selina noticed a change in the general expressions of her fellow humans from earlier. Where the looks of fatigue and worry were familiar after the Railen assault, and even in the temporary warehouse, now there were many more looks of hope. Those who committed to the Yassel move showed the relief pretty clearly on their faces without needing any verbal response.

Ellene stood next to Selina, a hopeful smile on her face. "Well, what do you think?"

Selina felt herself smile as she answered. "I have to say, I'm impressed. We're not used to others helping us except for the Mardaks."

Ellene nodded. "I hope you realize now I hold you and your kind's safety as a priority."

"Mmmhmm."

"I understand some refused to join us?"

Selina glanced offward and nodded quickly. "Some still don't trust the UA."

"And you do?" Ellene pawed Selina's shoulder

Selina's face flushed hot. She freed herself of Ellene's grasp. "I trust you to deliver, and you've done that so far."

Three UA fighters stood alongside the *Evangeline*. The sleek black starcraft consisted of a slender central tube with a pair of swept backward wings, each featuring a barrage of missiles and pulse cannon. Toward the rear, two tail fins angled upward and out. *Well, their fighters look tough enough. I just hope their flyers they got for this have the chops for handling trouble.*

The UA fighter pilots' all-black suits gave off a surprising gleam in the muted sunshine of the overcast and windblown air on Zormad.

"Shouldn't we have more of an escort?" Selina asked Ellene.

Ellene shrugged. "I've seen fighter compliments of three before. Don't forget, *Dionysus* will be along too. It's not as agile as those fighters, but we'll have some protection on our journey."

Selina went to leave, but Ellene held her close. "I promised we'd talk about Essence and what I have in mind for you, so let's do that on our voyage."

THE SCENE of the NewEarth residents boarding *Evangeline* was a tapestry of emotion. The crowd of departing citizens and remaining residents milled about outside the ark ship. Between teary goodbyes between the departing and those staying behind and frantic arguments over what possessions were necessary, the story of NewEarth's life had taken an unexpected turn toward a marked division.

Selina wondered if she'd ever see those staying behind on Zormad again. Despite all the problems of Zormad, it gave humans a home in Ling Galaxy. Selina hoped the opportunities were greater in the world of Yassel, with more of a thriving metropolis.

With the loading of *Evangeline* almost complete, and the boarding of her passengers underway, Selina strolled through the crowds and back into Tas Ralong for one last bit of unfinished business.

Zed was clear in his order, but Selina wasn't ready to let things go with Ryan. *If I can get the creep to go to Yassel, we'll save more people along the way when his devotees see their big guy isn't so against the move after all.*

Selina found Ryan working on the last group of crops to be delivered to *Evangeline*. Ryan handled the delicate vegetation as if it were a newborn child. For all purposes, it may well have been. Crops weren't limitless, and Ryan's food was sure going to be a significant part of their survival until their place on Yassel was established.

Ryan spoke without glancing up at Selina.

"Are you here to help me move these seedlings?"

Selina walked about while Ryan continued working on the garden trough with a gleeful smile. He had secured a lot of food for sure. Several crates stood by, ready for relocation.

"Ryan, I don't wanna hear you bitching about how I'm doing it wrong. So, how's about that?"

"Then what *are* you here for, Selina?"

"Giving you one last chance to see if you'd change your mind, come along to Yassel and keep our people together."

Ryan's eyes met Selina's. After a defiant laugh, he shook his head. "Oh, you just can't take it, can you?"

"Take what?"

"The possibility someone else has a better idea than your trip to Yassel. I hope you have some protection - some pulse weapons at least. You're about to be outnumbered, and I hope you didn't just sign yourselves up to be some experiment for the UA."

While Selina's muscles ached, she held herself in check. *The fool isn't worth it.* "We're almost completely loaded; make sure your supplies get on board."

"Will do," Ryan muttered.

"Good luck in the wild," Selina said, her arms folded.

Ryan's eyes narrowed and a smirk found his lips. "That's more than I'd expect from you or anyone else from the Regulation."

"That's all you're gonna get. You really doing this, huh?"

For the first time, Selina caught a sincere glimmer behind Ryan's eyes as he studied her for a moment. "I know you don't understand my choice. I don't trust well-meaners like Ellene. I've listened to Network, just like you. You think you're getting some lavish life up there on Yassel? I'll be surprised if you even get there without being picked off by a squadron of Omegans in a few days."

Selina knew Ryan's bleak outlook wasn't totally out of the possibilities for them. But she'd been into the Tas Ralong scene, and what she'd heard of the rest of Zormad hadn't offered any more promise.

"Ya know, Ryan, you've been a big pain in the ass for a while now. Just because the Regulation has some presence and can defend our people, it doesn't mean we brought those attacks on ourselves."

Ryan chuckled again, then strode around his greenery, his pride and joy, as if the vegetation was an expanded audience on his side that cast jeers and insults Selina's way. He finally flung his arms over-head. "Life is about more than taking aim, Selina. What we give back to people matters more. Maybe one day you'll learn that. I'm sorry you lost your father and now your mother, I am. My folks made it a few years after I was born; they're both gone now too. Fact is, we're in

Ling Galaxy now, and the best thing we can do is keep out of the way of this fight Ellene mentioned. Yeah, I saw what she did against the Omegans. We're ants to them, Selina. I'd rather settle for a quiet place out of the fray. That's my way. You do yours."

Selina knew she just got as much closure as she would ever have from Ryan. There was no winning him over, and she was OK with that, but the lingering contempt for the protection NewEarth had been under was a bitter taste she knew she wouldn't wash out of her mouth anytime soon. "You better reach out to the Mardaks. They're your best shot for support now if things get rough again."

Ryan nodded, not looking up.

"Goodbye, Ryan. Take care of what's left of NewEarth for us." Selina started walking away until Ryan's voice stopped her.

"Wait."

Unlike before, Selina noticed that Ryan's shields of arrogance and self-righteousness weren't there, and his tone sounded more like a concerned family member.

"Take care of yourself too, Selina."

NINE

EVANGELINE SHUDDERED AS ITS thrusters built strength to lift the mammoth starcraft off the ground. Soon it eased through the air, slow and gently. Joined by the UA fighters and the *Dionysus*, the convoy quickly shot to the skies, leaving Zormad behind.

While the interior of *Evangeline* was cleaner than the filthy Zormad warehouse, the temperature aboard was much more relaxed than the radiant heat to which humans had acclimated on Zormad. The corridors of the *Evangeline* were bright, with blue and white luminescent accents woven into a pattern on the walls. Selina was impressed with the UA's attention to detail on an Ark ship. While she'd only seen remnants of *Intrepid*, the craft used in the initial trek to NewEarth, that ship was far less elaborate than *Evangeline*.

One primary access corridor ran through the center of *Evangeline*, like a spinal column. Connecting side pathways several hundred feet from each other lead to the individual sleeping quarters. Selina strolled around the hallways as the craft shuddered and rumbled on its way. She spent a few minutes walking around, checking how the

NewEarthers were settling in for the trip. Soon, Selina came across Warrah, reviewing a hand terminal.

"Look at you, embracing the UA tech early."

Warrah glanced up, her long curly hair wisped to one side. "I'm not letting anyone get one up on us. The more we know about Yassel and these people before we get there, the better off we'll be."

"So, what are you learning then?"

"So far, I'm pulling details about *Evangeline*. The ship can do basic but not transient warp."

"Anything else good, like rooms bigger than ten feet square?" Selina chuckled.

"Nothing worth mentioning so far."

Selina ran a finger along the terminal, which displayed a wireframe model of the ark ship. She flung her finger about, and the display updated to show the locations of the residents on board.

Warrah shrugged. "We have enough rations to hold us for a month. Since they sent *Evangeline* to us, I'm hoping they'll help if we need something, but we'll see, right?"

Selina smiled at her friend. "I'm glad you're here. This would've sucked without you."

"By the way, Ket's a jerk, OK?"

A lock of hair fell across one of Warrah's eyes, but her supportive smile wasn't covered by anything. The pangs Selina felt since she parted with Ket remained. "I know. I'll be fine; I will."

"I mean, if you ask me - and you still haven't but should've, I think you should've clocked the dude. He sees NewEarth on fire, people running for cover, and he doesn't offer to help?"

"He's a fortune chaser, Warrah. At least we didn't have him along to see him bail when things got rough."

"True that." Warrah gave Selina a side hug. "Besides, you still got me - I can't leave my training sister behind, now can I?"

Selina leaned forward until their heads touched. "Well, sister, I gotta head back to my room. I'm due for a little chat with Ellene on things."

SELINA HAD many worries about what close exposure to Essence could mean for her. She'd heard stories about people physically harmed or even obliterated through the power of Essence. The display Ellene put on during the NewEarth attack was a pretty clear example of how destructive the stuff could be.

Selina activated the comm portal in her room, and Ellene's face appeared on screen after a few moments.

"How are your new accommodations?"

Selina looked at her spartan quarters. If it weren't for the somewhat adequate bedding, hygiene station, and comm setup, she'd have easily compared it with a holding cell at the Regulation precinct. "OK, I guess. We won't be here forever, so that makes it tolerable."

"I know. So, to start, let me take you back to the early times of Ling Galaxy."

Ellene's eyes darted about; her mouth drew into a line. The existence of the galaxy through Essence was probably not going to be handled in a single conversation. "Ling Galaxy came to be through a series of cosmic shifts over hundreds of millennia ago, where the earliest forms of Essence generated an entire galaxy around itself. Planets, moons, stars, and everything else came into being over many cycles, what your kind knows as years. Among these celestial bodies, Grondia was formed near the center of Ling, as the wellspring from which Essence emanates."

"So, Essence... is it an energy source?"

"In Essence's most common state, it provides for life and sustenance on an entire planet. The Nara were the first life forms in Ling Galaxy, and we were taught about Essence."

"Taught by who?" Selina asked.

"They are known to us as the Gazer. An ethereal form that gave existence to all life in Ling Galaxy and created Essence, which flows from Grondia. The Nara were charged with being stewards of the Essence in service of the Gazer.

"From there, life began in Ling Galaxy and grew over thousands of cycles. Other planets were formed and populated. Civilizations developed, and the Nara kept their word as first in Ling to bring Essence out to all worlds, sustaining them and life in the galaxy.

"With that life came freedom for all, which eventually caused other things to happen. But, as you know, life doesn't always follow a straight path. Eventually, imbalances appeared. At first, it was greed for more resources. Then, others wanted more control, selfish thinking infected the minds of many, and fighting ensued. Finally, the Nara themselves were challenged to maintain their mission. So, the Scions were created."

"The Scions?"

"Imbued with the very Essence itself and given abilities, like what I did back on Zormad. A Scion's task was to maintain order, and keep the balance in Ling."

"What do you mean by balance?"

"The life Essence creates and makes possible only happens when the flow of Essence guided by the Nara is properly maintained. We simply call this the balance. But, even with Essence in its normal state, suffering still remained. Those ills come from the freedom of choice all in Ling Galaxy have. Some choose greed, corruption, and actions like those lead to wars like the one we are currently experiencing. "

"But, you had Scions. Why didn't you set up every Nara as a Scion up to keep control?"

"We tried that, with several volunteers. That painful process taught us of the strong temptation with Essence. It can tempt even the noblest Nara, and pull at the tiniest of the mind's imperfections. A mind not as focused and pure can be swayed, and the power Essence offers can become a tool for the wrong individual. Even the Nara, raised in isolation from the galaxy, aren't immune to that lure of power. Malone Stanton is a prime example. He was once every bit the Nara citizen I am. Had we given him this power, Ling Galaxy may not have lasted until now."

Selina shuddered. "Well, I don't know where you got the idea about us, but we're not near perfect either."

"I know, Selina. It's an enormous risk that could have serious consequences for you. That said, the war upon this galaxy makes some risks worth considering. Your kind has shown enough resilience through the long trip you made here. That shows you've got a rugged spirit."

"But is that enough?"

"I'm willing to bet it is, Selina. Ling Galaxy has always had freedom, but safety is a challenge. Having justice will keep us safe, and I think the Scions are what we need for that to happen."

Selina's thoughts went to Kreela, the kindly old Mardak woman who latched onto Selina so abruptly when the two met at the trading market on Zormad.

"Ellene, not long ago, I met a Mardak female named Kreela who was very interested in me. She kept talking about how I had something going on, something I wasn't aware of yet. Is that why you're so fascinated by me? Are you seeing something in me like this Kreela did?"

Ellene nodded slowly. "There is a prophecy from ancient Nara times called the One from Without. It talks about a period of terrible tribulation in Ling Galaxy, where the very fabric of existence will be nearly torn by someone called the Great Usurper. Through the power of diplomacy, this Usurper rallies a large army to their side and wages war against the very heart of Ling Galaxy. Many die as a result of this, but in time, the One from Without rises up to destroy the Usurper and restores peace to Ling Galaxy."

An empty feeling welled in the pit of Selina's stomach. Ellene's original request quickly went from simple to gargantuan. "Ellene, what exactly are you seeing in me? I'd like to know. Frankly, I'm not feeling like much of a hero at all right now. I couldn't save my people from getting killed by the Railen or Omegans, and I've been stumbling to figure things out ever since."

Selina buried her face in her hands as her body shook with sobs.

The emotions poured out of her; at least she was alone, not around the UA or other Regulation officers.

Ellene's voice softened. "Selina, look at me."

Through a veil of tears, Selina gazed into Ellene's warm face.

"I'm going to be there with you, and I won't lead you astray. Remember, everyone has a place, and you matter."

Selina climbed onto her bed, wishing she could've asked her mother for her thoughts on her predicament, at the very least to have a hug.

WITH SEVERAL WEEKS remaining before their arrival on Yassel, Selina's routine for the voyage slowly took shape. Talks with Ellene about the Scions and Essence, regular rounds of the ship, and the occasional pissing contest with the UA troops aboard who were more than determined to assert their control.

Selina was on one of her regular strolls when rhythmic footsteps sounded behind her. Two UA Sentries approached from up the hall. It was the humans' ride, but it was still the UA's craft. The duo of officers stopped when they neared Selina and gave a polite nod.

The two guards were humanoid in appearance, but they gave Selina the same vibe she'd gotten since humans set foot on the craft. This voyage wasn't a benevolent rescue. It was more like the UA was checking off a list.

The stockier sentry spoke first. "Something wrong, Xeno?" Their uniform showed UA Officer insignia on the collar.

"I'm checking on our people. Habit from being a peacekeeper on Zormad."

Officer Stocky's vocal patterns loudened into a bark. "That's unnecessary. Security is covered. Better get back to your room. Never know when we'll hit a rough spot on this trip."

"Rough spot?"

The other UA sentry spoke with a nasal tone. "Asteroids, debris?"

The tone of the duo's answers was way more coddling than Selina wanted, needed, or was up for tolerating. "You know, we have our peacekeeping force, which is UA affiliated. Maybe you haven't heard of the Regulation, but we kept the peace on a Far Reach planet for over twenty years before you all showed up."

Stocky's mouth drew into a line. "That's fine, but we've orders to keep this voyage on track, and we don't want disruptions."

So, we're a disruption now? "Mmmhmm." Selina's jaw twitched. Clearly, they weren't interested, but Selina figured she'd find the group's commanding officer and see if maybe the UA goodwill hadn't flowed down from the top yet.

"OK then. If you boys need any assistance yourselves, let me know."

The two eyed each other for a moment. Then, finally, the stocky one glanced back at Selina slightly amusedly. "We'll be fine."

Without any other acknowledgment, the sentries continued down the hall. Selina felt a slight sting at the brush aside but kept on her original path. She'd been through enough, and even a UA Sentry wasn't going to brush her aside that easy.

Selina wandered up to the *Evangeline* fore section and found Captain Farlane studying charts of the remainder of the journey to Yassel. Farlane eyed Selina with an annoying glare, his mouth in a firm line.

Still ticked at her run in with the UA sentries, Selina scoffed and leaned back against the wall, her arms folded, giving Farlane her best burning scowl.

Several chirping alerts from a nearby console distracted Farlane. Once he tapped a few controls, he looked back at Selina. "What's wrong?"

"First of all, you should've told your crew this babysitting they're doing isn't necessary. We're not terrorists. We're scared people trying to get to safety. Second, how about telling us more about what's ahead for us on Yassel? All we know so far is Ellene Ballo wants us there.

I'm not getting a warm and fuzzy that anyone else on this ship cares, including you, Captain."

Farlane closed up the charts and held them across his chest. Selina noticed a bit of recognition on his face as he stood, his head downward in thought. After a minute, their eyes met again. "I don't know the plans for your people because no one has told me anything. We were ordered to bring you to planet Yassel, and this was given top priority. But, since you're pretty observant, I'll add that several parties don't think this operation was in the best interests of the UA in general."

Selina narrowed her eyes.

Farlane continued, "Ellene Ballo has enough influence to override many objections, making this trip possible."

"Then what do you think, Captain?" Selina added weight to the last word, spoken like it was more accusation than recognition. "I have to say the UA guard patrols give me a strong prison vibe. According to Ellene Ballo, we're a little treasure. Whatever we end up being worth, for all we've been through, we deserve more dignity than this."

Farlane wrinkled his nose. "You think you're the only ones who've had it bad in Ling Galaxy? Let me tell you something; we had problems long before your kind showed up. Malone, the Omegans, and Railen are the latest troublemakers around here. The UA's been cleaning up messes since before you were born, and things aren't settling anytime soon. So, sit back, and be grateful someone decided to give a damn about you. There's plenty who'd kill for what you've been given."

Selina leaned back against the bulkhead, the confusion in her deepening. *If this was the welcome wagon, what's waiting for us at Yassel? Maybe this trip was a mistake?*

Farlane continued, "I'm no diplomat, and I disagree on sending a large transport with minimal starcraft escort into open UA space in the middle of a war." Farlane's lips drew taut. "When you're in a position like mine, you get used to giving and dealing with the hard truth, and that's what it is."

"Uh-huh. Well, sorry to spoil whatever you had planned, but there's almost two thousand people on this craft with no say in what's happened to them since we've been in Ling Galaxy. I know there's a war on, but how about some damn respect for Ellene Ballo and what she sees in us that you haven't considered?"

Farlane's gaze held on Selina. She folded her arms, her breaths came quick and short, but she stayed still. They both remained like that until more warnings sounded on the console. "Ugh, proximity indicators again. Look, I don't have to like my orders to follow them, OK? Now excuse me, navigating through rogue asteroid belts isn't exactly an autopilot procedure."

After Selina left the bridge, she made one more pass through the halls, with an extra effort to walk close to the passing UA guards, before returning to her room. She almost entered when she saw Warrah approaching slowly.

"You OK, Selina? I heard your chat with Farlane."

"Oh yeah, how?"

"I was at a console seeing what info on Yassel I could pull on a scan."

"Uh huh. I'm fine. I just..." Selina thrust herself back against the bulkhead near her door. As she looked into Warrah's concerned eyes, thoughts raced in Selina's mind: about what she'd seen since being on board, Ellene's words to her, and how important she and the rest were supposed to be. It was a mismatch, and Selina was ready for the truth to come out, whatever that was.

TEN

BLARING KLAXON ALARMS GOT the next word in between Selina and Warrah. After a few moments, a group of six UA soldiers with pulse weapons jogged past, grim looks on their faces.

"Wonder what that's about?" Warrah asked.

"Whatever it is, I don't think it's a drill."

A series of loud blasts sounded in the distance, and the floor beneath them shook.

"Are we... under attack?" Selina asked.

"OK, I'm gonna find Zed. Meet me in the supply room."

After Warrah took off down the hall, Selina had another thought. She slipped back into her room, and opened the comm back to Ellene. The video screen remained blank at first, but then Ellene appeared. The fear on her face was unmistakable.

"Ellene, what's going on? We hear blasts outside the ship-"

"-the Omegans have engaged us. Selina, I don't have time to tell you more; just please listen. If the Omegans capture you, just follow along."

"Follow along?!? I thought we were fighting them!"

"There's more to it. Look, we'll send someone, I pro-"

The line went blank.

Panic hit Selina like a slap to her face. *Was Ellene killed? No, that couldn't have happened. Why does she want us to follow along if the Omegans capture us?*

A series of shouts came from the hall outside her door, along with quick footsteps in both directions. Whatever was happening, she had a job to do. That preceded any grand plans Ellene had and any One from Without junk.

The Regulation and whatever UA Unit is here will defend this place to the last. Maybe there's hope for the calvary yet? Selina grabbed her contact token for the *Crimson Lance*. Ket was probably too far away to make it in time for anything. Even if he did, what could he do against the Omegan squadron out there? Still, it was worth a shot.

Selina placed the token in her comm portal and sent a simple message to Ket.

KET, WE'RE IN TROUBLE. ARK SHIP *EVANGELINE* UNDER ATTACK FROM OMEGANS EN ROUTE TO PLANET YASSEL!

ELEVEN

SELINA TROTTED UP TOWARD THE FRONT of the ship. Farlane wasn't around, so she grabbed another of the crew.

"What's going on?"

The officer's face twisted in agitation. "What are you doing here?"

Selina's face flushed hot. "Stop treating us like cargo and tell me what the hell's out there!"

The officer narrowed his eyes. "Alright, an Omegan Horde unit looking for trouble found us."

Selina knew about the Omegan Horde. The Omegans kept a significant presence throughout Ling Galaxy, and the word about their horde was even if the unit seen was small, others were likely not far away. The smart move was never threatening a horde unit because your odds could quickly turn sour. This threat, even when only perceived, gave the Omegans more confidence to agitate and lash out at will around Ling Galaxy.

Selina saw six starcraft on a nearby monitor, one of which was a large cruiser. In addition, one of the UA fighters escorting the *Evangeline* exploded from a missile blast.

"What about the *Dionysus*?"

The officer barked several orders into the comm before he gave Selina a why-are-you-still-here look.

"The *Dionysus* took heavy fire, best we can tell, they escaped."

Escaped? Ellene handled Omegan starcraft when she was by herself, why couldn't she do more in a ship?

"You gonna call for backup?" Selina asked.

"Just stay out of the way and get back to your bunk." The officer returned to a monitor console, looking at damage indicators for *Evangeline*.

Screw this. Selina bolted back into the main hallway, past a group of UA soldiers racing toward the bridge, and headed for the storage area for NewEarth.

The interior lighting on *Evangeline* dimmed. Several people ran back and forth, and the hall was filled with shouts from several directions. Selina felt herself slipping into the chaos but reminded herself: *get a grip. You're an officer in the Regulation. Hold it together, even if you feel like you can't.*

Selina found Zed with Warrah, pulling out Regulation weapons.

"What took you so long?" Warrah asked.

"Oh, trying to get the plan from the crew. I may as well have asked the airlock for its opinion."

Zed asked, "Did you see anything on bridge monitors on how bad it is?"

"At least five Omegan starcraft. Already took out one of our fighter escorts."

"What about Ellene?"

Selina struggled with the true answer to Zed's question. "She's gone. The *Dionysus* bailed."

"What?"

"They said the *Dionysus* took a lot of fire, maybe they took off to save themselves."

"Well, that's great. Guess there's nothing we can try that isn't riskier than what they're already doing," Zed replied.

"Of course, pulse rifles versus starcraft cannon isn't a fight at all, is it?" Selina asked.

"No, but the *Evangeline* has a few exploratory craft on board. They don't have firepower, but they're fast as hell." Warrah said.

"Can we even get to them?" Selina asked.

"Well, seeing as the UA's distracted, we've a good chance of that," Warrah said.

"We'd be zinging around out there trying not to get hit while everyone back here is helpless. Not an option." Zed shook his head.

Evangeline shook with a blast nearby. Shouts came over the onboard comm. "Taking fire, taking fire! Everyone shelter in place, brace for impact!"

Selina hunched, her back pressed against a crate. She hated being stuck like they were, but it was out of their control. They'd made a deal with the UA and had to wait it out until it was over.

The remaining Regulation officers showed up, filling out their group to twenty. While Warrah handed out weapons, Zed briefed the squad.

"First, activate your envirosuits. If they blast a hole in our side and we get sucked into space, you'll at least have 30 minutes to get to safety."

With a sly grin, Warrah thrust a pulse rifle toward Selina, which she gladly accepted.

Zed continued. "Second, I don't want us all bunched up. Since the UA is at least acting like they want to save the *Evangeline*, I want a small unit of me, Ravencraft, Nock, and Malek covering close to the main airlock. The rest, keep comms open and fall back further onto the ship. If you see UA troops, let them get into position, but don't let them push you too far out either. Beyond that, stay low. If you have contact, give 'em hell. The UA troops are the first line of defense. If you see one fall, fill the gap. Blast anyone in your way before they blast you. Remember, we are the Regulation. We adapt, overcome and survive!"

The group gave a resounding "HUUH!" in response.

As the other troops fell back into position, Selina, Zed, Warrah, and Ramsey made their way up the hallway. Soon, the thundering of footsteps rumbled behind them. A group of four UA troops passed, each of them with an activated pulse rifle in ready carry.

Selina flung her pulse rifle up as if to say *Hey morons, we've got weapons too.* Zed held the muzzle of her rifle down. "Don't bother. They're interested in saving the *Evangeline.* That's enough for now."

"You mean they're interested in not being sucked into space," Warrah countered.

"Whatever. The main airlock is straight ahead. Get behind cover somewhere close and wait. Any shooting starts, there'll be chances to join in."

To their front, near the airlock, the group of UA soldiers increased to ten and had formed a half circle around the entrance to *Evangeline.* Zed and Selina edged up nearby until they were twenty feet from the UA troops. They crouched behind storage crates that lined both sides of the corridor.

Selina bumped Warrah's fist, and they shared a grim smile. "Ready for this?"

"As I'll ever be," came Warrah's whispered response.

The *Evangeline's* main airlock let loose with a loud hiss and a series of loud grinding noises.

"This is it. Selina, take the right side. I'll cover left." Zed said.

Ramsey edged over to the side where Selina knelt while Warrah took the left side behind Zed. *Whoever comes through won't get by without a fight. They might want us, but they're gonna pay a lot for it.*

Assorted growling roared outside the airlock.

"Any of you ever see an Omegan up close?" Zed asked the group.

Warrah shrugged. "Mostly in training simulations."

Selina nodded. "A few, in skirmishes around Tas Ralong."

Ramsey said, "Nasty suckers. Look like walking lizards. They have a vital spot in the neck if you can zero on that between all that damn armor they usually wear."

Selina's stomach fluttered as they waited in the hallway. "You never end the fight, right Zed?"

Zed looked over with a proud smile as he gave Selina a quick thumbs up.

After another long moment, the airlock burst into a series of sparks, and the lights shut off again. Selina focused on the darkness and saw the glowing red eyes of their party. The UA troops let loose the first barrage. The blasts from weapon fire slammed into walls and created a spray of grayish Omegan blood before them. Selina activated her pulse rifle. The trademark whistle and momentary hum were a little comforting, a familiar sound in the middle of a desperate fight.

The air thickened with smoke. Selina heard Zed bellowing orders in the foggy cloud of dust and debris. Then, another UA troop let out a series of yells that ended in gurgling heaves.

Seeing Ramsey jump up, Selina edged forward, firing several short bursts.

"Zed!" Selina shouted, but no response. Finally, she stood enough that she saw a huge Omegan. This one was easily seven feet tall and covered in a series of armor and a helmeted enclosure. The Omegan let out a guttural growl as it trained eyes on Selina's. She froze in place.

Before she made any move of her own, she heard a series of shouts behind her, and there stood Farlane with several of the crew, firing on the Omegan intruders. Finally, the hulking Omegan gave up on Selina and surged past her on a one-way collision course with Farlane's group. The scene was a chaotic mix of weapons fire, swung and dismembered limbs, and assorted screams of agony. Finally, after several seconds of this, the towering Omegan stood alone in a pile of limbs that had once been Farlane and his crew.

Selina turned but found herself face to face with the barrel of an Omegan pistol. Her in-suit translator removed any doubt of what was happening.

"All Xeno drop weapons and place hands on head."

TWELVE

THE OMEGANS MADE SHORT WORK of Ramsey and Warrah, leading them off onto their craft. However, Selina and Zed were brought face to face with Ve Bartosik. An imposing helmet topped off the Omegan commander's look. A dark steel set of battle armor with several char marks and etchings of an Omegan battle creed completed the ensemble. Ve's scaly, grimy face with deep red glowing eyes gave Selina more than she wanted as a focal point.

Selina watched Ve's large frame as he studied her in a visual dance with the first echelon who dared resist Omegan intrusion and capture.

"Welcome aboard Omegan starcraft *Praximus*. But, first, where's the captain of that ridiculous vessel we pulled you from?"

Selina eyed Zed for a moment. Then, finally, Zed said, "He's still aboard and unavailable. You should've talked with him before that big lug of yours ripped the whole crew into chopped meat."

Ve responded with a devious smile and snort. "They chose to resist. Besides, it shows again how well Omegans handle even the best the Universal Alliance can offer."

"You think a lot of yourself, don't you?" Selina muttered. Ve quickly moved in so close to her that Selina saw every pockmark in the nasty glare on the Omegan's face. His breath fogged her visor.

"Don't get smart, Xeno scum. You're lucky we got orders to take you alive, or you'd be limb stew like your UA friends right now." Ve looked Selina over like she was a load of rotten meat that needed disposal. "You know, some of our crew have been wondering just how fried Xeno tastes. Now then, before we stow you with the rest of our cargo, tell me... where is Ellene Ballo?"

"I don't know who you're talking about," Selina said.

Ve slammed his fist into Selina's chest. She yelped and stumbled backward onto the Omegan directly behind her. As quickly as she'd fallen, Selina was shoved back upright. A heavy soreness throbbed through Selina's core.

Ve leaned in closer to Selina. The rancid stench of Ve's breath permeated the filtration systems of her envirosuit and had her gag reflex in overdrive. "I'm not in the mood for games, Xeno. Tell me where she is before I hurt you where you don't get back up."

Zed said, "She went ahead of our convoy to scout."

Ve scowled for a moment. "We'll visit her soon enough," Ve growled a few moments longer before he swiped the air between him and Selina with a dismissive wave. "Put this filth with the rest in the hold below. I'm tired of their stench."

While they were grabbed and force marched down the hallway to the lower decks of *Praximus*, Selina's mind traveled between stabs of pain from the firm hold on her arms. Her hope of getting to planet Yassel and finally some long-term safety was gone. Ellene was pulled out of the picture along with the small team the UA sent as support.

Still, Selina clung to hope that Ket had seen her message. It was all she had, even if that was an interstellar pipe dream.

THIRTEEN

SELINA AND COMPANY SPENT THE REST of the voyage in a series of dank, dark, and smelly storage containers. Selina spent the first few hours wondering what formerly occupied their holding area that gave it such a foul effervescence.

Once the *Praximus* landed on Omegana, the captives were escorted through a series of rooms and industrial facilities. The air was musty and damp. Selina saw the Omegan crest in several places, including wall banners that stared back at Selina like an evil specter.

Their walk took them through a network of tunnels. Low lights gave slight visibility among the overall darkness. They passed alongside a mechanical area with loading docks that spewed toxic smoke into the air, dimly lit rooms with terminals and conveyors, and a chorus of metal screeching on metal. At least Selina hoped it was mechanical noise and not the screams of something in the darkness.

Soon they entered a large hall. A well-lit stage was the obvious focal point, and the stench Selina had experienced with Ve seemed to have been multiplied by a million. An ominous clamor filled the air, and she realized that there was a large crowd assembled, and clearly, she and her fellow captives were the featured item of the moment. Their escorts prodded them on their march toward the grandstand.

Several spotlights lit the darkened space just enough so a series of banners hung on either side of the main platform stood out as prominent. The two flags closest to the center had an identical crest on them, while the other two banners had some strange letters; Selina assumed some Omegan phrase on the order of "Tonight's Menu: Human."

On either side of the pathway they walked was a series of bleachers that rose forty feet above Selina and the others. The seating wrapped around and sloped upward to the ceiling, giving the design a Romanesque look. Omegan citizens filled the chairs, collectively bellowing a series of taunts, screeches, and other random snarls filled the stale air.

Selina spotted Warrah in the crowd, but too far away to talk. Selina's gut relaxed for a second until the shouts revved up again, and her belly tightened all the more.

When they arrived at the aisle's end, they were pushed up further until they were closer to the platform. The area wasn't large enough for them, but their group filled out the sides, and the rest were still back in the walkway behind Selina. A series of chimes sounded, and the assembled crowd began a chant. It was a series of clicks, hisses, insect-like noises, and whoops. The coordinated chant reverberated through the entire auditorium. Selina felt a chill go through her, wondering if the carol was a pre-slaughter signal. Her heartbeat throbbed in her neck. Zed looked to be holding his cool, but Selina noticed the beads of sweat on his forehead and face.

A booming voice echoed across the room from a series of nearby speakers. The masses responded to the booming voice with their refrain, in a sort of religious chorus.

A few sharp prods at the backs of Selina and the others, and they were walked over to the side of the stage. A group of Omegans stood at the center of the dais, wearing ceremonial cloaks.

Selina struggled against her wrist restraints, but she knew it was pointless. Ever since they'd arrived, she hadn't seen any less than double the amount of Omegans near her and her fellow captives. A cordon of troops stood before them, dressed differently than their initial escorts. The line of Omegans had more regal-looking armor, and their faces were shielded behind masks. Although Selina wondered what the point of the pomp was, she assumed their final destination included two stops: pain and suffering. Her eyes burned with sweat.

Finally, a loud tone sounded, followed by a disembodied voice. "Hail Emperor Zakmar."

All troops snapped to attention, which sent a roaring thunder of echoes through the hall. As punctuation to this, the Omegans yelped an Omegan phrase, some kind of salute, Selina assumed.

At the front of the hall, the line of Omegans split in two, each half separating to make an entrance for Emperor Zakmar. He strode in, a collection of capes swept behind him, an ornate helmet over his head, as the Omegans in the crowd continued their chorus of cheers and salutes. Selina hoped no one had noticed her eyes when they rolled.

Arriving on stage, Zakmar stood for a moment and savored the welcome before he thrust his hands up, silencing his obedient drones of an audience. "Today, we have received a gift, through the effectiveness of our Horde. You may wonder why I am so excited by the puny Xeno here. Our spies have informed us that Ellene Ballo wants to use the Xeno to build an army to attack Malone Stanton and Omegana. So, not only will we stop that from happening, but we will learn what about the Xeno makes them so valuable and use that against Ellene Ballo and the UA to destroy them both once and for all!"

Cheers abounded. Selina was struck in the back and doubled over, along with the rest of her party. Shortly after this came the bellowed cry, "Onto the stage, Xeno!"

Selina caught the Omegans behind them, blunt staves in their hands and glances that were neither welcoming nor patient. She looked at Zed, whose eyes were as narrow as she'd ever seen them. "Gonna teach these asses some manners when I get a chance."

"Shh," Selina replied.

Soon, their group was front and center, with nothing between them and Zakmar. The compliment of Omegan troops flanking their leader presented their weapons as a not-so-subtle reminder that any escape attempts were likely to be suicide.

Zakmar was dressed in regal robes. His skin was above average in scaliness by Omegan standards, and his reddish glowing eyes added a cold fury to his face. His mouth was turned into a terrifying grin.

"I understand Ellene Ballo isn't with your group." Zakmar scowled. "It's time she and the Nara learn along with the UA that Omegans control Ling Galaxy. Any movement around Ling Galaxy, including one for your people, is prohibited unless I approve it. So, welcome to Omegana. I want you all to enjoy the rest of your short lives. You can make the rest of your time easier on yourselves by doing exactly what you're told."

Selina tensed as their group was led off. She struggled against the forced march, but it was useless and only got her another rap, this time on the cheek.

A sharp jab hit Selina in the side, and she looked in the snarling face of an Omegan holding a spear toward her. "Move it, Xeno. You're headin' for our prison. You might wanna think of it as your gravesite."

FOURTEEN

SELINA AND THE NEWEARTH CAPTIVES were brought to an Omegan holding facility. The buildings were as dark and cold as they'd seen since their arrival on Omegana. Smells of decaying flesh hung in the air.

They were placed in a series of cells, each of them sized for groups of 40. Once locked in, a series of periodic feedings went on for several days. The meals, such as they were, involved little more than several containers of barely identifiable items that resembled some sort of meat and liquid with a strong metallic taste. Eventually, their excess hunger dulled the average palettes enough that accepting the dubious protein intake wasn't so crazy anymore.

Selina wasn't sure how long this routine went. With no windows to even guess the time, the length of their stay was measured mainly by periodic visits with food.

Throughout the time, Selina kept regular contact with Zed. With the only clear access point to their location the single door used by the guards, it was pretty clear their escape wouldn't happen without a lot of luck and outside help.

The increasing amount of facial hair on her fellow male inmates,

Zed especially, was one more thing that gave Selina a loose idea of time passage.

Zed pawed at his beard. "This has to be the longest I've ever grown this."

Selina smirked. "Just when I thought you were ugly enough."

Zed responded with an amused glare. "So, what do you make of Zakmar's line about making us an army?"

"Well, it's not that different than what Ellene was telling me she wanted for us. I think no matter what happens, we're worth something to both sides. As long as they don't blow us up in the crossfire, anyway."

They shared a brief chuckle at their fix, but their quick moment stopped when the lights dimmed. A collection of dull thumps shook the ground, and klaxons blared outside.

"Any chance that's about us?"

"Maybe," Zed replied. "Maybe Ellene sent a distress call."

"You don't think she got wasted?"

"Naah. Not by them, anyway. There's a reason behind it, but I can't figure that out. As for whatever's happening out there, I say anything bad for the Omegans is good for us."

Selina thought how nice it would've been if they were armed. They just had to hope that whatever happened, they could get over on a guard soon and get out of their collective mess.

The noises outside were a cacophony of engines from starcraft, blasts from cannon and small weapons fire, and an assortment of shouting. It was anyone's guess, though, how it was going and just what it all meant for their situation.

An idea jumped into Selina's mind, and she grabbed Zed for a quick chat about it, but a loud clang quickly stopped her plan at the end of the hallway. Of all the unrecognizable sounds, she could've picked out that one anywhere. It was the main hatch entrance to their holding area. Soon afterward, a line of emergency lights cast a subtle glow in the hallway, enough that Selina made out the faint outlines of Omegans who walked down, and then she heard the voice of a female Omegan.

"Attention, Xeno prisoners. My name is Charista Mantisword. In a moment, your cell doors will open. You'll then file into the corridor and form a single file line. Guards will direct you from there. Do not, I repeat, do not do anything other than follow their exact instructions, or you will be shot on sight and left to die here."

Selina managed a low sigh as she followed suit with the rest of the prisoners and was escorted out of the holding area. Their trip took a series of turns and even involved a walk along a narrow catwalk amid heavy piping stretched in either direction for miles.

Soon, they arrived at an underground rail transport and were escorted into some heavy-duty windowless cargo containers. There weren't any seats, so the order of the moment was to fit in so the Omegans could close the doors. Unfortunately, Selina had gotten mixed up in the shuffle and was separated from Zed.

Despite being in close proximity to the others, Selina felt as alone as she'd ever been, and for the first time in a while, real fear crept over her and sat with her like a most unwelcome guest.

They rode for several hours. Charista met them once their ride ended, and escorted them to another facility, and they were again brought to holding areas, though these were much nicer than before.

Charista said, "You are now resident products of the Omegan Science Wing. You'll be brought out one at a time or in groups, whatever the need calls for. Until then, relax, and know your true purpose is about to be discovered."

Selina edged closer to Zed. There were so many questions and no answers, but Selina needed at least to vent her confusion.

"Zed, were we pawns all along? Maybe Ellene and the UA needed us for something, and they don't anymore?"

Zed took a deep breath and looked ahead as their group was marched deeper into a well-lit building filled with monitor screens along the walls.

What seemed so simple just weeks earlier had become another

labyrinth of the unknown. Being a prisoner of Omegana was nothing Selina imagined when listening to Ellene's grand ideas about Essence and what it meant for her future and those of NewEarth. Whatever came from their situation, they were a piece in a larger game, and her fear for their survival chances had never been greater.

Suddenly, Selina felt Zed's arm around her shoulders. The light was dim, but not so much that she couldn't see Zed's tired but determined glance.

"You never end the fight, Selina."

THE ESSENCE WARS SERIES

All of these titles are available individually on Amazon.com

HAVE YOU READ THE VALKYRIE CHRONICLES SERIES?

Forced into a life she hates by the government of Lebabolis, the last human nation on Earth, Ana Crucinal must comply with her pre-ordained future or undergo Realignment. But when her brother falls ill, Ana joins up with the resistance in an attempt to flee Lebabolis—only to learn that the true threat lies elsewhere: an alien race known as the Omegans. All of this was foreseen. A thousand years ago a man living in New Orleans had imagined the future Ana now lives in. He wrote about the resistance, the alien menace, everything. Desperate to save themselves and the remnants of the human race, the resistance formulates a plan to do the only thing they can think of: travel back in time to save the future.

With her enemies closing in, Ana knows this is her one chance to save herself, her brother, and the resistance. Failure is death and the never-ending enslavement of humanity.

Buy the books of the Valkyrie Chronicles Series on Amazon today and find out why so many have fallen in love with Ana and her mission.

Menace Ascending (short story prequel)

Cataclysm Epoch (novel)

Settling Darkness (novel)

Valkyrie Rising (novel)

The Valkyrie Chronicles Complete Series (novel, box set)

WANT A FREE STORY?

Destination Exodus is a prequel story I wrote for the Essence Wars series you just read. This story features Erick Ravencraft, father of Selina Ravencraft, as part of the group of humans who leave Earth and the Milky Way galaxy in the hopes of survival. Can they navigate the dangers standing between them and their goal? Click this link to get Destination Exodus for FREE!

The Essence Wars Continue!
Crucible of Legacy, the first FULL LENGTH novel in the Essence Wars Series, is coming soon! Get ready to hear the story of Pierce Sava, son of the current ruler of the Universal Alliance, Nic Sava. Pierce had more than a few disagreements on how things were run, and decided it best he went his own way, in the wilds of Ling Galaxy. Employed by the Syndicates, Pierce is content with his life of running cargoes and mixing it up with his friend Ket Durban. But, when the UA and Nic Sava face a crisis, can Pierce find it within himself to return to the life and the love he left behind, to help the UA restore their crumbling order as the Essence Wars rage on?

ABOUT THE AUTHOR

Paul Heingarten spreads time between writing, being a musician, and, since 2002, a career in Information Technology. He lives in the southern United States with his wife Andrea.

OTHER TITLES BY PAUL HEINGARTEN

The Harvest (short story)

Leave from Absence (novel)

The Monitor (short story)

Natural Election (short story)

Cataclysm Epoch (novel)

Settling Darkness (novel)

Valkyrie Rising (novel)

Menace Ascending (short story)

Xeno Reckoning (novelette)

Gambit of Dares (novelette)

Quest for Dominion (novelette)

Quantum of Destiny (novelette)

Vengeance Directive (novelette)

Balance of Retribution (novelette)

Destination Exodus (short story)

Revenge Nexus (novelette)

Stratagem Awakening (novelette)

Collateral Crisis (novelette)

www.ingramcontent.com/pod-product-compliance
Lightning Source LLC
Chambersburg PA
CBHW051054030726
47504CB00006B/1622